HER DARK HALF

PAIGE TYLER

sourcebooks
casablanca

Published by Sourcebooks Casablanca, an imprint of Sourcebooks, Inc.
P.O. Box 4410, Naperville, Illinois 60567-4410
(630) 961-3900
Fax: (630) 961-2168
sourcebooks.com

Printed and bound in Canada.
MBP 10 9 8 7 6 5 4 3 2 1

With special thanks to my extremely patient and understanding husband. Without your help and support, I couldn't have pursued my dream job of becoming a writer. You're my sounding board, my idea man, my critique partner, and the absolute best research assistant any girl could ask for.

Love you!

Prologue

Adana, Turkey, 2013

"CRAP ON A STICK! WHY THE HECK DID THE WEATHER have to pick tonight to unload on us?"

Alina Bosch glanced at her watch again before turning her attention back to the industrial buildings across the street from the small fourth-floor apartment they'd turned into a tactical operations center for the mission. She and her team were in the Yüreğir district, one of the low-income sections of Adana, where streetlamps were few and far between. That, combined with the cold rain that was coming down in buckets, made it nearly impossible to see what the hell was going on over there.

But she didn't need to see much in the way of details to know it was time to move on their target. Two vehicles, one an expensive four-door sedan and the other a midsize moving van, had pulled up in front of the buildings ten minutes ago. The van had pulled straight through a roll-up door into a maintenance garage area while two men in dark clothes had left the sedan and run straight for the main door of the building. People making a delivery in the rain wouldn't be unusual, but it was two in the morning, which made it damn suspicious.

Alina and the other four agents of her CIA team were in Adana to stop members of al-Nusra Front, a jihadist faction of the growing Syrian rebel movement, from obtaining the necessary chemicals to make sarin nerve gas. Analysts within both the CIA and NSA had good intel suggesting the group was close to a deal with a local supplier in Turkey for the two most critical ingredients to produce sarin—methylphosphonyl difluoride and isopropylamine.

The really scary part was that the rebel group didn't intend to use the sarin against the Syrian government but instead planned to gas a few thousand innocent civilians—people they were supposedly trying to protect—hoping it would provoke the United States and other western powers into launching a full-scale war against the current Syrian regime.

Alina supposed that if you couldn't take your enemy out by yourself, then you needed to get someone bigger to do it for you—even if it meant your own people had to pay the price.

As she watched the garage door roll down behind the moving van, Alina got a twitchy feeling in her stomach. The deal was going down right now; she was sure of it. If she and her team didn't go in soon, they were going to miss their chance completely. If that happened, there was a good chance that a lot of people were going to die.

Unfortunately, moving on their target at exactly that moment was a problem, because her team was presently one person short.

"Jodi," she whispered softly over her shoulder to the petite, dark-haired woman leaning back against the kitchen counter, cell phone in hand. "Anything on Wade yet? He was supposed to be here thirty minutes ago."

Jodi Patterson, the youngest and newest member of the team shook her head, her curls bouncing. "I've been alternating between calling and texting him for the past twenty minutes. No luck. He's probably shacked up with some local girl, if he's not sleeping it off in a ditch somewhere. Then again, it's always possible he lost his cell phone in a damn poker game."

Alina cursed. They didn't have time for this. Next to her, Wade Sullivan was the most senior and experienced field operative on the team. Unfortunately, he was also the least reliable. Worse than that, he was the one guy on the team she flat-out didn't trust. Crap like this was exactly why.

While the senior leadership back in Langley loved the guy, to Alina, he'd never been more than a problem waiting to happen. The man drank too much, got off on winging his way through every mission, and didn't give a damn about the job he did or the people he did it with. It was a given that no one on the team trusted him to cover their backs. However, their bosses in the States seemed not to care about that since she and her team always got the job done—even if they did that in spite of Wade instead of because of him.

Alina left the window and walked over to the kitchen table to gaze at the floor plans of the industrial building spread out there. Looking at all the red marks and arrows drawn here and there, she groaned as she realized the worst part of Wade AWOL's status. He was the intel lead on this mission. He'd not only come up with the tip that had led them here and had slipped in the previous night to scout out the building and bugged the room where the Syrian rebels and the local supplier were meeting, but he'd also scoped out all the entrances and blind spots. Even though all his intel notes were sketched out, she'd still rather have Wade here to go over everything one more time. Instead, he was off somewhere getting laid—or drunk.

"What do you have on the wire?" she asked Jodi.

Jodi pressed her fingers to the wireless earpiece she wore and closed her eyes. Pressing the earbud didn't do anything, but Alina supposed it helped her focus on what the people in the room Wade had bugged were saying.

"I have four, maybe five male voices," Jodi said. "Two are speaking fluent Turkish. The others are using a combination of Turkish and Arabic. They're mostly making polite conversation right now, but they've said the words *anlaştik mi* several times. That's Turkish for *deal*. A few moments ago, one of the Arab men asked how many drums would be involved."

"We going to do this or what?" Fred Stewart's gravelly voice rumbled through Alina's earbud over the encrypted channel. "If they're already talking about deals and how many drums, there's no way this meeting is going to last more than another ten or fifteen minutes. If we don't go soon, we're going to blow our chance."

"I know," Alina told her other teammate. "But Wade is still MIA, and our original plan was based on four of us going in. It's going to be tough trying to pull this off with just you, me, and Rodney."

"Not like we have much of a choice," Rodney Miller said in his Southern drawl. "If they drive out of here with those chemicals, we're never going to find them again. And when the Syrian people get attacked by some extremists using nerve gas, we're going to know it was our fault. You ready to let that happen?"

Alina didn't answer. Pushing the image his words

had painted out of her head, she continued to scan the floor plans and maps on the table in front of her, trying to see a way three people could pull this off. But she couldn't. There were too many doors, hallways, and rooms to cover.

She'd been working with Fred and Rodney for nearly four years. They were both well trained and knew how to handle themselves in a tense tactical situation. But there were at least five people in the building across the street, maybe as many as ten. This wasn't a job that consisted of walking in and eliminating the bad guys. Her team didn't do that kind of work. They'd been brought in to confirm these people were involved with a scheme to manufacture sarin nerve gas, then take them down while capturing as many of them alive as possible.

Stopping these guys with her full team would have been difficult enough. Trying to do it one man down when they were a team that was already too small for a mission like this would be nearly suicidal.

"You know," Jodi said in a tone that suggested she knew Alina wasn't going to like the next words coming out of her mouth, "I could take Wade's place on the raid instead of sitting on my hands in here."

Alina bit back a curse. She should have known.

The biggest reason Alina had grabbed Jodi out of the pool of new agents at Langley was because the girl reminded her of herself at that age. Smart, aggressive, eager, and more than a little bit reckless. Alina was taking her training slowly so Jodi wouldn't end up making all the same stupid mistakes she had made back then. And because she and Jodi had become good friends. Maybe Alina protected Jodi more than she would have another agent in the same situation, but she wasn't going to apologize for it.

"Forget it, Jodi," she said. "You aren't ready for something like this, and you won't be for a while."

Jodi made a face. "Are you serious? Dammit, Alina. I've been on the team for months, and so far, you haven't let me do anything but watch computer monitors and listen to radios. This isn't why I did all that training back at Langley. I'm ready for this. That's why you selected me to be on your team, isn't it?"

"I selected you to be on my team because I thought you had the potential to be a good field agent—with the proper experience. And until you get that experience, your job is to watch computer monitors and listen to radios."

Jodi scowled. "How am I supposed to get any experience if you never let me do anything?"

Alina opened her mouth to answer, but Rodney interrupted her.

"Alina, I'm by the back entrance of the building near the garage. It sounds like they're loading the truck," he said softly into her earpiece. "If we're going to do this, it needs to be soon."

"Stand by," Alina said to Rodney, then looked at Jodi. "Anything from Wade?"

Jodi glanced at her phone and shook her head.

"Dammit," Alina muttered.

She and her team were here to stop this deal. That's what they were going to do—with or without Wade.

Spinning around, she headed for the door. "I'm on the way down," she said over the radio. "Rodney, you'll go in the back as planned. Fred and I will go in the front.

Once we get inside, he'll split off and help you cover the garage, while I handle the conference room."

The two men acknowledged the change in plans without comment. The adjustment would mean that Alina would be covering the largest concentration of bad guys on her own, but there wasn't anything they could do about it.

Hand on the doorknob, she turned to look at Jodi. "Stay here and monitor the wire. Let us know if you hear anything."

Jodi probably would have argued, but Alina opened the door, walked out of the apartment, and headed for the stairwell.

Outside, Alina yanked the collar of her leather jacket up as she jogged across the street, trying to keep the cold rain from slipping down the back of her neck. She was only partially successful.

"If this turns into a shoot-out, make sure you avoid those chemical drums," Alina whispered into her radio as she hopped on the curb and moved closer to the building. "They may not contain nerve agent yet, but we don't want to breathe that crap anyway."

Fred reached the front door of the building before she did. After a quick peek through the glass, he picked the lock, then swung open the door. Alina drew her pistol as she met up with him. He did the same, covering her as they both entered.

"We're in," she whispered over the radio.

"Ditto," Rodney responded.

Alina stopped for a moment, listening. She heard soft voices coming from a room down the hall on her left. She didn't hear any other sounds, not even from the garage where Rodney said he heard them loading the van. Did that mean they'd already finished the deal and were about to move?

She gave Fred a nod and pointed in the direction of the garage, indicating she wanted him to back up Rodney. Tightening her grip on her pistol, she headed for the room down the hall. She was halfway there when she realized something was wrong. It took her a moment to figure out what was causing the hair on the back of her neck to stand up, but then it hit her. The layout of the hallway and rooms off it was wrong. Or more precisely, the drawings Wade had made were off. The room the voices were coming from was on the wrong side of the hall, directly across from an adjoining corridor to her right that wasn't even supposed to be there.

She shouldn't have been surprised Wade had screwed up the details. He wasn't necessarily big on that kind of crap. But combining it with the fact that he hadn't bothered to show up made her stomach knot.

"We're in the maintenance bay," Fred said over the radio. "There are a few drums that might be chemical, but no people."

Crap.

"Something isn't right about this," Alina said.

Her instincts were telling her to bail, but they couldn't do that. Not until they apprehended the bad guys.

"We're on the way to your location now," Rodney said.

"Roger that."

Taking a deep breath, Alina took another step toward the door. Even through the heavy wood, she could clearly hear the men talking inside. She didn't have Jodi's knack for languages, so she wasn't sure what they were saying, but from the laughter, it sounded like the negotiations were going well.

She glanced over her shoulder to see Fred and Rodney hurrying down the hallway toward her. They looked as confused and worried as she was.

"Jodi, we're going in," Alina whispered over the radio before giving Rodney a nod.

Rodney stepped forward to kick in the door when Jodi's confused voice floated across the secure radio channel. "Guys, something's wrong. The men are starting to repeat themselves. I think—"

That was all she got out before Rodney's boot connected with the door, sending it flying back on its hinges. Alina and Fred followed him in, ready to deal with however many armed men they found.

The room was completely empty except for the portable CD player sitting in the middle of the table, Turkish and Arabic voices coming from the speakers.

Alina cursed. "It's a trap. Get out!"

But it was too late. Men armed with automatic rifles flooded into the hallway. Alina scrambled over the table along with Fred and Rodney just as the men started shooting.

Fred flipped the table over, and Alina knelt behind it and returned fire, putting round after round through the group of men charging through the doorway. At this distance, it was impossible to miss her targets, and several of them went down.

But the reverse was also true.

Rodney went down first, a bullet hitting him right in the forehead. Alina felt her heart break as her friend slumped to the floor, but she couldn't even spare him a glance. It was all she could do to drop the empty magazine out of her 9mm and reload so she could keep shooting.

Jodi shouted over the radio in her ear, but Alina had no more time for her than she had for Rodney. A bullet zipped past her shoulder while another whizzed past her head. Yet a third shattered the wood of the table she hid behind, showering her with splinters. Even though she knew any one of those shots could have finished her, she forced herself to ignore them, to accept that she wasn't dead yet, and to shoot back as fast as she could.

Just when Alina was sure it was over, that there was absolutely no chance she and Fred would live through this, their attackers halted as another one of them fell to the floor dead. The remaining two spun and fled for the door. Alina clipped one in the hip just as he and his buddy disappeared around the corner.

Alina quickly reloaded in the event that the men came back with reinforcements. She'd just slammed the magazine home when a flash of movement on her right caught her eye. She turned in time to catch Fred as he started to sag to the floor.

"Oh God, Fred. Not you, too," she whispered.

She got her arms around his shoulders and tried to settle him to the rough concrete as gently as she could. Still holding on to her gun with her right hand, she used her left to put pressure on the wound that was soaking the front of his jacket with blood. Those two assholes had shot him before turning tail and running.

Fred looked up at her, a mix of pain and fear in his gray gaze. He tried to talk, but no words came out. Tears in her eyes, Alina rocked him and murmured that it was going to be okay, even though she knew it wasn't. As Fred died in her arms, she wondered if the Agency would ever tell his wife and kids what had really happened to him. She doubted it. That wasn't how they worked.

She was just easing him to the floor when she realized Jodi was still shouting at her over the secure radio channel to tell her what was happening.

Alina reached up to adjust the volume on her wireless earbud, not sure what the hell she was going to tell Jodi, when she realized she wasn't even wearing her earbud anymore. It had gotten dislodged in the fight. She had no idea where it had gone.

And yet she could still hear Jodi's voice.

She looked around and saw a radio lying on the floor near one of the dead shooters. It was too big to be one of theirs, but Jodi's voice was coming out of it loud and clear.

That's when everything hit her. The prerecorded voices designed to lure them into this room, the way the well-armed attackers had known exactly when to ambush them, the low-tech rebels having access to a CIA-encrypted radio frequency, and Wade never showing for the mission. A mission he'd set up almost completely on his own.

Wade had betrayed them. He never showed because he'd set them up to die.

Heart pounding, Alina ran out into the hall and snatched the radio off the floor. This ambush might not be over.

"Jodi, get out now!" she yelled into the radio as she ran for the front entrance, her heart hammering in her chest. "The mission is compromised. Communications are compromised. Cut and run!"

There was silence on the other end of the line. Then, "What about Fred and Rodney?"

"Dammit, Jodi. Go now!"

More silence. "Understood," Jodi finally said, and it tore at Alina's heart to hear the fear in her voice. "Falling back to rally point Charlie now."

Alina almost stepped into another trap outside as the two shooters who'd disappeared earlier stepped out of the darkness and started shooting. She fired off one shot to make them duck, then darted back into the safety of the alcove.

"Negative, Jodi," she said into the radio as she peeked around the concrete corner of the entryway to make sure the men weren't coming toward her. "It's not just the operation that was compromised. It was the team. Don't use any rally points, safe houses, transportation assets, or money drops that were set up for the mission. Do you understand what I'm saying?"

There was a moment of hesitation, then, "I understand. Good luck, Alina. I hope I see you again."

"You will," Alina promised.

She heard the pounding of footsteps over the radio and knew Jodi was on the run.

Alina shoved the radio in her jacket, then stepped out to face the two men. If they still had their radios, they'd know Jodi was making a run for it. Alina would be damned if she'd let them kill Jodi, too.

She walked across the street, ignoring the downpour as she aimed slow, steady shots at the corner of the building the two men were hiding behind. That kept their heads down until she was close enough to put herself right in their sights, encouraging them to come at her.

They obliged, stepping out and lifting their Russian-made automatic weapons. She put the first man down before he got off a shot. But the second one was ballsy, standing his ground and taking time to get a bead on her. He fired first, the round of his AK-47 tearing through her jacket, skipping along the left side of her torso, ripping open the side pocket, and spilling her confiscated radio to the street.

The pain of the wound—and that of Fred's and Rodney's deaths—sharpening her focus, she put a 9mm ball round right through the center of the man's chest. He bounced back off the wall behind him, then tumbled to the wet ground.

Only after she was sure they were dead did Alina finally lower her gun. She put it away, clutching a hand to her side as she bent forward to collect the radio. She'd intended to pick up the radio and toss it in the bushes along with her weapon, but then she heard a thump and clang of a heavy metal door on the back side of the apartment building. Alina breathed a sigh of relief knowing her friend was going to get away, but then she heard another sound that was impossible to mistake for anything other than the pop of a silenced weapon going off.

Alina sprinted for the front door of the apartment building, slamming open the door and racing down the hall as fast as she could. She still had a hundred feet to go when she heard Jodi's soft voice over the radio.

"Screw you, Wade."

There were several more pops, then silence.

Alina ran as fast as she could, but it took her a few

minutes to find the door that Jodi had shoved open. It was tough, because the building was large and had at least two exits on each side of it. When she finally found her friend, Jodi was curled up in a ball beside a big trash can. Wade was nowhere in sight.

It almost looked like Jodi was sleeping, but the hand she had clenched to her stomach was all the proof Alina needed to know she wasn't.

Alina gently rolled her friend away from the trash can to find she was already dead. Two shots to the stomach and three to the chest. Since Jodi had cursed Wade before she'd died, the son of a bitch must have shot her in the stomach first just because it would hurt, then followed up with the kill shots to the chest. After he'd let her suffer a bit. He'd always been such an asshole.

Sitting on the wet ground, Alina wrapped Jodi in her arms, squeezing her tightly as she finally let the tears come. A part of her knew she should get out of there before the police showed, but she couldn't make herself move. She needed time to cry for her friends before she let them go.

Slowly, anger replaced the horrible, soul-crushing sorrow. While she was furious with Wade, she was mad at herself, too. She should have seen this betrayal coming. She'd always had some reservations about him, but instead of trusting the instincts that had been screaming at her from day one that Wade was a piece of crap, she'd gone along with the flow, assuming the Agency wouldn't have hired him if he was dirty. That assumption and lack of faith in her instincts had gotten the three most important people in her life killed.

Sirens echoed in the distance, but Alina ignored

them. The police would congregate around the industrial building first, securing the perimeter, searching for survivors, trying to make sense of the scene, and talking to witnesses from the apartment building. They wouldn't get around to searching back here for a while.

So she stayed where she was, hugging Jodi to her chest as she made a solemn promise to all of her teammates that she was going to do whatever it took to track Wade down and make him pay for what he'd done. No matter how long it took or what bridges she had to burn to make it happen, she was going to find Wade, and she was going to kill him. And no one was going to stand in her way.

Chapter 1

Quantico, Virginia, Present Day

"THE DIRECTOR WANTS YOU IN HIS OFFICE ASAP."

Trevor Maxwell glanced up from the hot dog he was eating to look at the guy standing in front of his table. Short and stocky, the man was regarding him like something to be scraped off the bottom of his shoe. Trevor resisted the urge to bare his teeth in a snarl and took another bite of his hot dog. He wasn't really hungry, but at least lunch was a pleasant break from the monotony of an otherwise miserable day. And the cafeteria served damn good hot dogs.

Unfortunately, he'd had a lot of miserable days at the Department of Covert Operations, the secret government organization where he worked. It came with being labeled a traitorous freak.

"You have a problem understanding what ASAP means?" the man asked, a buttload of attitude lacing his words.

Gaze never leaving the man, Trevor slowly finished chewing, then swallowed. "It means Dick Coleman wants me in his office *as soon as possible*. I'll go just as soon as I finish eating. Because I couldn't *possibly* leave before that."

The man looked like he wanted to say something snide in reply, but when Trevor let his eyes glow coyote yellow and his upper canines slide out far enough to extend over his lower lip, the guy quickly changed his mind.

"Whatever," the man muttered. "Your funeral."

The comment probably would have come across as more ominous if the asshat hadn't shuddered before walking away. But hey, the people who had been brought into the DCO lately didn't have a lot of experience with shifters, and seeing a man sprout claws and fangs—not to mention flashing gold eyes—was a bit much for a lot of them to deal with. Most of the other people around the cafeteria were regarding him with the same mix of hatred and revulsion. It wasn't only the muscle-headed thugs Dick—or rather Thomas Thorn, the man Dick answered to—had hired lately. The agents who'd worked alongside shifters like Trevor for years were throwing him dirty looks, too.

Trevor supposed hating shifters was sociably acceptable now that John Loughlin, the former director of the DCO and de facto champion of the organization's shifter program, had been killed when a bomb had exploded in his office.

The day John died, everything had changed. Now the covert intelligence organization the man had spent more than a decade building from the ground up was quickly falling apart from the inside out.

One look around the cafeteria proved that. It was lunchtime, yet you'd never know it from the handful of people scattered around the room shoving food in their faces as if they couldn't wait to be somewhere else. The place used to be filled with agents, analysts, and other support personnel at this time of day. While there'd always been some who were antishifter in the DCO, their numbers had been more than offset by those who realized the good that people like Trevor and his kind brought to the organization.

Somehow, John had perfected the concept of pairing shifters with highly trained covert operatives. People had said it would never work, that shifters were little more than animals and couldn't be trusted to work in a team environment, much less be given missions critical to national defense. John had proven the doubters wrong, fielding teams that had accomplished things that should have been impossible.

But John's death had led to a complete change at the top of the organization, and the new regime was blatant in their opposition to all things shifter. These days, there were probably half as many people working for the DCO as there had been a month ago. Trevor couldn't blame them. Why stay when Dick's first act had been to announce that the very shifters John had trusted had conspired to murder him? There hadn't been any proof of course, but then again, when had that bastard Dick ever let something like proof get in the way of what he wanted? Hell, he'd barely let John's seat get cold before sitting in it.

Trevor seriously doubted that anyone with an ounce of intelligence believed any of the supposedly rogue DCO agents had been involved in John's death. But when those twelve men and women who formed the backbone of John's shifter program had gone on the run within hours of his murder, people either accepted they were guilty as charged or smart enough to know they'd never be able to prove their innocence before they were eliminated.

Either way, lots of good agents had read the writing on the wall and bailed. The moment they were gone,

Dick had filled their positions with trigger pullers who spent most of their time chasing the rogue shifters or sitting on their asses.

It made Trevor wonder what the hell he was still doing there.

Trevor was still contemplating that—and whether to get another hot dog—when two men walked into the cafeteria and immediately headed for his table. Considering there was a twenty-foot-deep buffer zone of empty tables around Trevor, that might have put him on guard, but since they were among the few friends he had at the DCO, he turned his attention to the plate of french fries just begging to be eaten as Jake Basso and Jaxson West slid out a couple of chairs and joined him.

"Not a good idea for you guys to be seen with me," Trevor said between bites. "Not only could it be hazardous to your career, but it might end up getting you killed."

Jake, a former Navy SEAL and technically still a member of Trevor's counterintelligence/counterespionage team, reached over and snagged a fry off the pile with a laugh. Since Trevor's team had essentially been disbanded, Jake wasn't anything but a good friend and coworker now.

"What career?" Jake asked. He was a big guy with dark-blond hair, blue eyes, and a slightly crooked nose thanks to a fight he'd gotten into in high school. "I haven't done anything but clean weapons at the firing range since everything went to hell around here. I think I'd appreciate someone trying to kill me just to relieve the boredom."

Yeah, Trevor guessed Jake's career was already shot. Thanks to him. Something else for Trevor to feel crappy about. But Jake was damn good at his job, and his SEAL background would ensure that he'd land on his feet, even if he wasn't likely to use anyone around here as a reference on his résumé.

Jaxson West, on the other hand, was kind of screwed. As the DCO's head of security, he'd answered directly to John when it came to securing both the training facility here on the back side of Quantico as well as the main DCO offices in downtown DC. Given that his boss had been assassinated on his watch—and that Dick hated his guts—Jaxson was in serious trouble. Dick would see that the man was blackballed in the covert community just because he could. But looking at the big, dark-haired guy sitting there so relaxed, you'd be hard-pressed to know the man was counting the days to unemployment.

"You hear anything from Lucy?" Trevor asked.

Jaxson grabbed a handful of fries. "No. But then again, I never expected to. The only reason she stayed at the DCO was because of John. With him gone, there's nothing to keep her here."

Even though he tried to cover it up, Trevor knew Jaxson was hurt that Lucy had walked away from the DCO without ever saying a word to him. He'd been closer to Lucy Kwan, the feline shifter that John had found in China, than anyone. Trevor had always assumed Jaxson and Lucy would end up together.

Who knew? Maybe she'd come back someday. It wasn't like she had to worry about anyone trying to hang the traitor label on her. No one in the organization, not even Dick, would be dumb enough to accuse the petite Asian woman of anything. While she might look like the sweetest angel ever, she was the most cold-blooded, ruthless killer the DCO had ever employed. And that was saying a lot, considering the kind of people the organization had associated with over the years.

"You should have gotten more fries," Jake pointed out as he snatched up the last half dozen or so in one big hand.

Trevor chuckled. "If you'd told me you'd be joining me for lunch, I would have."

Jake shrugged. "I wasn't planning on it. Jaxson and I were heading down to the pistol range to burn off a little stress when one of Dick's new muscle-headed asshats walked past us muttering about the damn freaky shifter in the cafeteria. Since there are only three of you guys still hanging around and the others are too new to possess the ability to piss people off quite like you, we figured we'd stop in and say hi."

"That was mighty kind of you," Trevor said. "I think."

"You haven't heard from Ed since I talked to you last, have you?" Jake asked.

Trevor frowned at the name. Ed Vincent, a former Air Force Pararescue, had been the first man John had teamed up with Trevor when he'd come to work at the DCO eight years ago. Jake had joined them a little while later, and since then, the three of them had traveled the world, covering each other's backs more times than Trevor could count. When John had been murdered, Ed had up and left without saying anything to anyone, not even Trevor and Jake. Clearly, Ed hadn't been as tight with him and Jake as Trevor had thought.

"Nah, I haven't heard from him," Trevor said. "Maybe once he gets settled."

Jake nodded but looked doubtful. "Maybe. How about Tate Evers? He and his guys have been gone for weeks."

"He called about a week ago from a little town just inside the Panamanian border called Cerro Punta," Trevor said. "Dick has them down there scouring the jungles of Costa Rica and Panama, chasing down rumors about hybrids that might have survived the fighting back in November."

Jaxson shook his head. "Hunting for hybrids in the middle of the jungle without a shifter to help them track is insane. It will take months."

No kidding. Hybrids were man-made versions of shifters, and the ones the DCO had fought with down in Costa Rica had been almost rabid. That was what happened when people tried to use science to create something rare and unique.

"I think that's the idea." Trevor picked up his bottle of Gatorade and took a swig. "The real DCO teams are out chasing ghosts so they won't get in the way of the so-called investigation into John's murder."

Jake snorted. "Dick has to know those idiots he has gallivanting all over the globe earning frequent flyer miles have no chance in hell of catching a shifter."

"True that," Trevor said.

Thank God.

Not that Dick was truly the one giving Tate's team or any others their orders. The person really pulling the strings was Thomas Thorn.

Since its inception, the DCO had been run from behind the scenes by a shadowy group called the Committee, a nebulous collection of eight current and former House and Senate elites who'd held powerful positions on their respective intelligence panels. While nothing had officially changed within the Committee's structure, John's death had scared most of them so much that they'd gladly ceded most, if not all, of their authority to one of their members—Thomas Thorn. Which was a mistake, since Thorn was almost certainly the man who'd had John killed.

"You want to head down to the range and punch a few holes in some targets?" Jake asked. "You can imagine it's Dick if it helps."

Trevor chuckled. "Sounds like fun, but Dick asked me to meet him"—he glanced down at his watch—"nearly thirty minutes ago. I guess I should probably get over there before he decides to go ahead and just fire me already."

Neither of his friends laughed.

"What if he does?" Jake asked. "I mean, I don't understand why the hell you're even still working at the DCO. You could walk into the Defense Intel Agency Headquarters at Anacostia-Bolling and walk out with a great job within minutes. Why the hell would you want to hang around this joint and get treated like crap?"

Trevor had asked himself that more than a few times. Pushing back his chair, he stood and picked up his tray.

"It's complicated," was all he said.

———※———

The minute Trevor walked into the main DCO administration building and saw the memorial plaque with John's name, as well as his secretary Olivia's, on it, he remembered exactly why he stayed and put up with Dick's and Thorn's bullshit. Contrary to what he'd told Jake and Jaxson in the cafeteria, it wasn't complicated at all.

He could have bailed the moment he'd heard John was dead. He'd been up in Maine, dealing with some demented doctors who'd been trying to create hybrids of their own, and it would have been easy to jump the border into Canada and disappear.

Feline shifter Ivy Halliwell and her husband/partner, Landon Donovan, had wanted him to go into hiding with them, and he'd been tempted. He was smart enough to know what life at the DCO would be like without John there. But in the end, he'd wanted to come back and get the son of a bitch who'd killed John. He'd liked and respected John. It was the least he could do for the man.

Admittedly, coming back had been risky. Dick could easily have labeled Trevor one of the conspirators and tossed him in some supermax prison, never to be seen again. Hell, Dick could have had him executed, and no one would ever have known that, either.

Trevor only hoped that Dick wouldn't realize how closely Trevor was aligned with Ivy and Landon. Outside of one mission in Tajikistan, they'd never officially worked together, so it was possible he might not. Crazy, but possible. Ivy and Landon hadn't liked the idea of Trevor staying but said they'd help him any way they could.

"If you even think Dick or Thorn are onto you, promise you'll run, okay?" Ivy had said before she and Landon had gone off the grid.

Since then, all communications had been handled through burner phones, code words on various chat loops, and trusted messengers. It wasn't the same as being able to talk face-to-face, but it was good enough.

As he strode down the hall, Trevor marveled at how

quickly the bombed-out part of the building had been repaired. He couldn't even smell the smoke residue anymore over the scent of fresh drywall, paint, and carpeting. No one would ever know a bomb had taken out the whole middle section of the first floor and part of the second right above it.

For a man who'd sworn up and down that he wanted to catch John's killers, Dick had been damn quick when it came to destroying any evidence of the bombing. The new director had had the entire damaged section of the building demolished and removed within days of the murder. Fortunately, Trevor had slipped into the smoking ruins that first night, fresh off the flight from Maine, when the heat had still been so bad it'd melted his boots and burned his hands. But he'd found more than two dozen pieces of the bomb, so it had been worth it.

Unfortunately, he hadn't known what to do with them right away. Normally, he would have turned them over to the DCO analysts and tech people and let them do their magic. But most of the ones he trusted had left, and the ones who'd stayed freely admitted they had no skill when it came to bomb and explosive forensics.

Because Dick had so many people watching Trevor, it had taken almost a week to get a message to Ivy and Landon, letting them know what he needed. They'd given him the name of Danica's former FBI partner in Sacramento, Tony Moretti.

Trevor had never met the man, but Danica and the others trusted him, so that meant he would, too. But with people watching him, it had taken another week to get everything packaged up and sent out there. Since then, he'd been waiting to see if the FBI labs could come up with anything. He wasn't expecting much. It wasn't like Thorn was an idiot. He wasn't going to hire a bomb maker who'd be dumb enough to leave any solid clues behind. Moreover, Tony would have to get the bomb remains evaluated without tipping off anyone as to where the bombing had occurred. They simply couldn't risk word of the investigation getting back to Thorn or Dick.

While he waited, Trevor had been trying to find the bomber another way. DCO training officer Skye Durant and intel analyst Evan Lloyd were helping, but it was slow, excruciating work. He had things he could be out there doing, leads he could be checking out, but he couldn't, not when he was under constant surveillance. He would have asked Jake and Jaxson for help, but he didn't want to put any more people in danger than absolutely necessary.

Sighing, Trevor walked into the outer waiting area of the newly renovated director's office. The monstrously large desk his secretary, Phyllis, was sitting behind probably cost more than John's entire suite of furniture from the old office. There were paintings on the wall that appeared to be original pieces from the early colonial years, and the coffee machine set up along the side wall looked like something you might need an engineering degree to use.

Phyllis glanced up from her computer. Nearly sixty, she had short, curly gray hair and a thin, almost beak-like nose, on which a pair of half-moon reading glasses were perched.

He grinned at her. "I'm here to see Dick."

The woman didn't return his smile. Now that he thought about it, Trevor wasn't sure the woman knew how to smile. If so, she'd certainly never done it around him. He was pretty sure Dick's secretary didn't think much of him, though whether it was because he was a shifter or a smart-ass, he didn't know. He preferred to think it was his animal nature. He didn't mind being looked down on because he sometimes had claws and fangs. He'd been born that way and couldn't do anything about it. But his wit? That had taken him years of hard work to develop. He hated to think the effort had been wasted.

"Director Coleman is expecting you. And has been for nearly thirty minutes," she said scathingly.

"Great! So I guess that means I can just let myself right in."

The older woman didn't seem amused by that. Then again, Phyllis never seemed amused. Or angry. Or alive, for that matter. Maybe she suffered from a perpetual case of resting bitch face.

"You most certainly will not. I'll announce you," she said in a tone that suggested she considered him somehow unworthy of that honor.

He smiled even broader. "Well, how about that? I've never been announced before. I mean, sure, they announced my number all the time back in prison, but that's not the same thing, you know?"

He was hoping to at least get a disdainful glower out of her, but not even that comment could crack her bland facade.

Good sarcasm was simply wasted on some people.

Getting to her feet, Phyllis came around the desk and led the way to Dick's office. She knocked once, then stuck her head in and told her boss Trevor was there. A moment later, she opened the door and motioned him in.

"Announcing someone would be more dramatic if you had a big staff you could thump on the floor a few times," he pointed out, unable to resist poking her one more time. "You know, kind of like they do in Renaissance festivals?"

Phyllis stood there holding the door open, regarding him with absolutely no expression.

"Nothing?" Trevor shook his head. "I'm standing here working it, and you're just going to leave me hanging like that?"

Phyllis arched a brow. Damn, the woman was tough.

Giving up, Trevor walked past her into the office. He barely made it through the door before Phyllis closed it. He supposed he could consider that a small victory. He might actually get a rise out of her at some point.

Thanks to a keen sense of smell, Trevor knew there were three people in the office before he got inside—Dick, Thorn, and some woman he'd never seen before. He was interested in who the new woman was, what Dick wanted to talk to him about, and why Thorn was there, but he chose to ignore them all for the time being as he took a moment to appreciate all the changes Dick had made to the director's office.

Okay, *appreciate* was probably the wrong word. Trevor was never one to appreciate gaudy displays of excess, and that's what Dick was all about.

The first thing that struck him was that it was bigger than before. Actually, it was nearly three times the size of John's old office. Like the outer room, this part of the renovation had come with loads of pricey furniture and over-the-top artwork. Based on the framed paintings mounted on the wall, people might think Dick had an obsession with dead white guys painted in dramatic poses. Two presidents, a general in battlefield garb, an arrogant-looking man sitting behind a big desk, and a sailor standing in a small boat holding an old-fashioned harpoon. Obviously, Dick wasn't a big fan of landscapes.

When Trevor finally turned his attention to Dick, he noted with pleasure that the director looked a little pissed off sitting there behind his ridiculously large desk. If Trevor was lucky, maybe the man would blow a gasket the more he aggravated him. Then again, Trevor might not get the chance to hang around here long enough to do that. There was a good possibility Dick had called him in here specifically to fire him.

Trevor sauntered over to the empty chair in front of Dick's desk, passing his other least favorite person, Thomas Thorn, on the way. The well-dressed former senator was leaning casually against the edge of a low bookcase, regarding Trevor with something more than mild interest.

Regardless of the man's posture, there was nothing relaxed and casual about Thorn. While Dick liked to think he could make himself more impressive with a fancy office and a big desk, Thorn demonstrated that truly powerful people needed none of those things. You could put this guy in green tights and a pink tutu, and while he might look ridiculous, there would be no doubt in anyone's mind about which man was in charge…and which one was more dangerous.

Thorn was nearly sixty years old but could easily have been mistaken for a man ten or fifteen years younger. He was very fit, with a head of dark hair that didn't have even a sprinkling of gray in it yet, although that could have been because he dyed it. His dark eyes were as sharp and intense as a hunter's, and he had no problem giving away the fact that he was studying Trevor as much as Trevor was studying him. But while Thorn exuded the pure charm and charisma that many politicians possessed, he also had the cold, detached aura of a psychopathic killer. Thorn might not have set off the bomb that killed John, but he'd ordered the hit.

Until recently, Thorn and his head of security had never hung around the DCO training complex, but since John's murder, they'd both become regular features. Their excuse was that, in times of crisis, the DCO needed superior guidance and leadership. That was bullshit of course. Thorn was hanging around to make sure his plans—whatever those might be—went off without a hitch.

It was difficult seeing Thorn and knowing what the man had done, not just to John, but to the whole DCO. One friend was dead, and the rest were on the run for their lives, all because Thorn wanted them out of the way. The urge to rip out the man's throat was frigging hard to resist. The only thing that stopped Trevor was the knowledge that killing Thorn wasn't what John would have wanted.

A slow, evil smile curved Thorn's lips, as if he realized the struggle going on inside Trevor. The arrogance in the man's eyes damn near pushed Trevor over the edge, and he felt his canines elongate, aching to tear into some meaty part of this a-hole's anatomy.

Trevor took a deep breath and forced his fangs to retract, pushing down the urge to kill and instead turning his attention to the woman sitting in front of Dick's desk as he sat down beside her.

She was undeniably attractive, with long, strawberry-blond hair tied back in a professional-looking bun, perfect fair skin, and some seriously pink bee-stung lips. She also had the most unusual green-blue eyes he'd ever seen. They were kind of mesmerizing, actually.

Since she was seated, he couldn't tell exactly how tall she was, but he was guessing five ten or so. While he couldn't be sure of her height, he was definitely sure the woman worked out a lot. Not even the professional-looking pantsuit she had on could hide the fact that she had long runner's legs.

She also had the familiar scent of smokeless gunpowder clinging to her. It was mostly covered up with some kind of fruity bodywash and a flowery shampoo, but he could smell it. She'd fired a weapon recently, probably that morning. She was almost certainly a field agent of some kind, though what the hell any of this had to do with him, Trevor didn't have a clue.

He turned back to Dick. "Someone mentioned you wanted to see me? I would have come sooner, but they were serving hot dogs in the cafeteria."

Dick's jaw tightened, and for a moment, Trevor thought the man might explode, but instead, he got a grip on his anger and gestured to the woman. "Trevor Maxwell, meet Alina Bosch."

Trevor glanced at her. "A pleasure."

Alina nodded in return, but before she could say anything, Dick spoke again.

"She's former CIA and your new partner."

Trevor waited for the punch line. Because one had to be coming. There was absolutely no way in hell Dick was ever going to voluntarily put him back in the field, so why waste time giving him a partner? But after a staring contest with the man, he finally realized Dick wasn't joking.

He hated doing it, but he was gonna have to bite on this one. The curiosity was just too much for him. This was like giving in and admitting you couldn't find your four-year-old nephew during a game of hide-and-seek—it just plain sucked.

"Okay, Dick. I admit, getting someone out of the CIA is a big win for the team," Trevor said, giving him a thumbs-up. "But why partner her up with me? I mean, you've had me on the bench for a while." He threw Alina a glance. "No offense. I'm sure you're a wonderful agent and all. Your parents must be very proud."

Alina shrugged. "No offense taken. You're not exactly my first choice in partners, either."

Snarky and blunt. Two qualities he appreciated in a woman. Throw in the fact that she was also hot as a blowtorch, and Trevor had to admit he was disappointed she was on Thorn's payroll. It made him wonder if the man had chosen Alina through the use of some crazy software program that said she possessed all the qualities necessary to trick him into being stupid in her presence, because she definitely did.

"Oh, and just to be clear," she continued, "my parents don't know I'm CIA. They think I'm a barista at a coffee shop."

Out of the corner of his eye, Trevor saw Thorn regarding him and Alina with the same detached expression he probably used when pulling the wings off flies.

"You're right," Dick said. "I have been keeping you on the shelf lately, and with good reason. We just had six of our best shifter teams conspire to kill the former director of this organization. I haven't been able to bring myself to put you out in the field since John's murder because I simply don't know where your loyalties lie."

The fact that Dick was even having this conversation with him and bringing up the subject of trust was significant. The man instinctively didn't want to trust Trevor because he was a shifter, but something else was going on that had him questioning that. Something serious enough to make him pair Trevor up with a new partner and put him back into the field.

Trevor had no idea what that something was, but if it meant getting out from under Dick's constant surveillance—even for a little while—it would be worth it to play along.

"You want to know where my loyalties lie?" Trevor asked bluntly. "That's easy. They lie with John Loughlin, the man who recruited me and taught me most of what I know. The man who was killed by a bunch of fucking cowards that I'd do anything to hunt down and gut like the pieces of crap they are."

Dick didn't say anything, but his heart sped up a little. No doubt because Trevor had let out a menacing growl at the end there as his anger got the best of him. Then again, maybe Dick's heart was beating a little faster because he knew Trevor was pointing those threats directly at him.

After a moment, the director looked at Thorn, who gave him a barely perceptible nod.

Dick opened a drawer along one side of his desk and took out a thick file folder, dropping it on the desk in front of Trevor with a thud.

"As I'm sure you already know, the DCO has expended a tremendous amount of time and resources in the hunt for the rogue shifters, especially Ivy and Landon, whom we consider the ringleaders of the conspiracy. Unfortunately, those efforts have been a failure. Regardless of our commitment to finding John's killers, the time has come to realize that our traditional agents simply don't have the tools necessary for the job."

Trevor almost laughed. Considering that the operatives Dick had sent out weren't even real agents but hired muscle, it was an understatement to say they didn't possess the tools to catch Ivy and Landon. Hell, those meatheads weren't just missing the right tools to catch a shifter; they didn't even own a fucking toolbox.

"So you want me to track them down?" Trevor asked, figuring that was what Dick wanted to hear.

"No, I want you and Agent Bosch to track them down," Dick said. "Together."

Trevor turned to regard the former CIA agent sitting beside him. Alina returned his gaze. There was only one reason Dick would team them up—so she could keep tabs on him. That meant she was already deep in Dick's pockets—or Thorn's. While he seriously wanted the chance to get out and do a little digging on John's killer, he wasn't thrilled at the idea of having to deal with a partner who'd be on the phone reporting everything he did to Dick five times a day.

"Before you bother asking what Alina brings to the table, I'll clarify that point right now. She's very good at digging out traitors," Dick said succinctly, and Trevor had to wonder if that was a little jab at him. "It's one of the things she's excelled at the past few years in the CIA."

Trevor didn't say anything. This was obviously a done deal. If teaming up with Alina was what he had to put up with to get back in the game, he'd make it work.

"Fine," he said. "If it's settled then, I'd like to head out immediately. I have a couple of leads I want to look into this afternoon."

"What leads?" Dick asked.

"I've heard rumors about some people down in Fredericksburg who got into a scuffle in a restaurant with a couple of guys they described as…odd. I think it might be the rogue shifters."

Dick eyed him doubtfully. "Why the hell would any of the rogue teams stay this close to the DCO training complex? That seems incredibly foolish."

"That's only because you seem to think they're out there running scared," Trevor said. "They're not. Ivy and Landon would almost certainly have left at least one team close to DC so they could keep an eye on what we're doing. I'm sure you've already realized they likely still have people on the inside feeding them info, right?"

Trevor felt a slight twinge telling Dick this kind of stuff, but it wasn't like it was a big secret. Dick might be a moron, but Thorn was smart enough to know at least some of the shifter teams were likely nearby. Part of staying on with the DCO was playing the game and making it look like he was actively engaged in catching his former coworkers.

Not that he was really leading Dick anywhere near his friends. In truth, he wanted to get down to the Fredericksburg area so he could check out a guy that Evan had stumbled across while reviewing video foot-age from the DCO's front gate on the morning of the bombing. The guy had only started working for the DCO three weeks before John's death, had driven onto the complex insanely early that morning, and had quit two days after the bombing. Even better, the man had a direct connection to Thorn. He'd worked IT support at one of the local Chadwick-Thorn subsidiaries before showing up at the DCO. With his background, Trevor doubted he was the man who'd built the bomb that had killed John, but he definitely could have been the one to plant the device in the director's office.

It was someone they should have looked at a long time ago, but it had taken forever for Evan and Skye to find him, since they were dealing with their own trust issues within the remains of the DCO analyst section. It was a given that some of the people who'd stayed there were on Team Thorn. Any digging they did had to be accomplished slowly. But if this was the man who'd delivered the device that had killed John, it would be a good first step toward finding that link to Thorn.

Dick threw one of those what-do-I-do-now glances in Thorn's direction. The former senator responded with another imperceptible nod. Thorn should rig up some marionette strings for the director. They could take their act on the road.

"Do it," Dick said in his best imitation of a man who knew what the hell he was doing. "But I want you two to keep me informed of everything you're doing at all times."

Trevor snorted. "Of course you do—since you trust me so much now."

Dick didn't take the bait. "I don't trust you. And I won't until you give me reason to. Until then, you two should consider yourselves on a short leash."

Chapter 2

"I THOUGHT WE WERE GOING TO FREDERICKSBURG?" Alina asked as they passed straight through the town and kept going until they hit Highway 2 and headed south.

After leaving Dick Coleman's office, Trevor had told her he'd meet her in front of the admin building, then disappeared. When he showed up fifteen minutes later in a black Suburban, she'd noticed he'd changed out of the black tactical uniform he'd been wearing and into cargo pants and a button-down.

Trevor glanced at his rearview mirror before giving her a smile. "We did go to Fredericksburg—and now we're leaving. I figured since it's such a nice day, why not enjoy ourselves with a leisurely drive through the country?"

She lifted a brow. "That's what this is all about…a nice drive in the country?"

"Yup."

"Yeah right," she muttered as he checked the mirror again.

Sighing, Alina turned her attention back to the fat file folder on her lap. It was stuffed full of reports related to all the places Ivy, Landon, and the rest of the rogue shifters had supposedly been sighted. Dick had told her they were a slippery bunch, but she found it difficult to believe they could move from location to location as fast as the DCO agents trying to track them down claimed. It was like they'd put a map up on a wall somewhere and thrown darts at it.

She flipped the page, frowning as she read over the various performance records of the operatives Dick had called "shifters." To say it read like something out of a movie was putting it mildly.

"Okay, I'm just going to come out and say it," she told her new partner. "I'm not so sure I buy all this shifter crap. Dick made it seem like it was the real deal, but I gotta tell you, it sounds like BS to me."

"It's real," Trevor said.

Alina waited for him to elaborate, but he didn't. "Show me."

He slanted her a look. "Excuse me?"

She closed the folder and tossed it in the backseat. "You're supposed to be a shifter, right? So show me what the heck the big fuss is all about."

Trevor's jaw flexed. "I'm not a trained monkey at the circus. I don't do tricks."

Okay, maybe demanding he perform for her had been uncalled for. She would have said as much when she caught him checking the rearview mirror again. She wanted to ask him who he thought was following them but decided that would be a waste of time. Trevor obviously didn't trust her enough to tell her what time of day it was, much less who might be following them.

That was okay, because she wasn't sure she could trust him much either.

It was one more thing that had her once again questioning her decision to leave the CIA. Taking a job in a classified department of Homeland Security she'd never heard of was bad enough, but chasing rogue government agents with a partner she didn't know the first thing about and couldn't trust was completely insane.

But then she remembered how much she'd hated her job at the Agency. She'd gotten so burned out on the crappy work they'd had her doing lately it was a miracle she hadn't gotten herself—or someone else—killed. That's when she took a breath and told herself that while her first day at the DCO was going a little rocky, she'd made the right choice leaving the CIA. She probably should have done it a long time ago, right after Jodi and the rest of her team had been killed.

"You okay?" Trevor asked suddenly as he drove down the tree-lined rural road.

Alina looked at him, not sure where his question had come from. "Sure. Why wouldn't I be?"

He shrugged. "I don't know, but your heart rate just shot through the roof, so I figured I should ask."

All she could do was stare at him in confusion, not sure what the hell he was talking about. "How do you know how fast my heart is beating?"

"It's a shifter thing," he said casually, as if he were talking about the weather. "My hearing is good enough to pick up the beating of your heart, and it's going a little crazy about now."

She eyed him skeptically, wondering if he was messing with her. Dick had tried to explain the basics of the shifter genetics, but he'd made it sound like they were part animal. None of it made any sense to her. Now she wished she'd asked more questions.

She and Dick had talked for quite a while about Trevor before he'd shown up for the meeting. While Dick hadn't gone into great detail about what a shifter was, he'd told her repeatedly that she couldn't trust Trevor and that there was a good chance her new partner was in league with the rogue DCO agents who'd murdered the previous director. After hearing that, she'd expected Wade's double to walk through the door.

But Trevor wasn't anything like her old teammate—at least not physically. Wade had been average in every way possible. Trevor was anything but. He was tall and athletic with a wiry build and short, black hair that seemed to be in a permanent state of casual bedhead. Alina had met men who spent a lot of money to get their hair to look like that, but Trevor's seemed to be completely natural. With lips that quirked constantly, a little scruff covering his jaw, and mischievous, hazel eyes, he seemed like a man who rarely took things very seriously. He'd definitely vexed the crap out of Dick, and even if he was supposed to have been part of a conspiracy to kill the former director, Alina had had a hard time keeping the smile off her face as he'd poked and prodded his boss.

By the time the meeting was over, she was ready to admit that Trevor was an attractive man with a nice body, an infectious grin, and a razor-sharp, wry sense of humor. While she had no idea what the shifter stuff was about, she'd had a hard time seeing him as a traitorous, cold-blooded killer. Then again, she'd never seen a traitorous, cold-blooded killer when she used to look at Wade either, and he'd betrayed the entire team and killed Jodi in the most vicious manner he could. All in all, she was a crappy judge of character.

"Your heart's beating faster again," Trevor murmured as he drove past the same gas station they'd passed twice already. "You sure you're okay?"

"I'm fine," she snapped.

Dammit, he was right. Her heart was thumping harder than normal. It always did when she thought about Wade.

"I'm just going to toss this out there," Trevor said. "But can I assume you're nervous about being in a vehicle with someone like me?"

Alina did a double take. "No, that's not it at all. I don't have a problem with you."

He arched a brow and gave her a look that said she was full of crap. "So you're telling me your heart starts racing at random moments for the heck of it?"

She opened her mouth to tell him it was none of his damn business, but closed it again. There was a good chance they could be walking into a dangerous situation when they got to wherever they were going. She'd rather not do that while in the middle of an argument. But she also wasn't in the habit of giving up personal info without getting anything in return.

"Why should I tell you anything?" she demanded. "It's not like you've been exactly forthcoming with me. You still haven't told me where we're going or what a shifter is. For all I know, you could be making up this stuff about being able to hear how fast my heart is beating."

Alina expected Trevor to say something suitably snarky, but he surprised her.

"Fair enough," he agreed. "We're going to talk to a guy who lives in Bowling Green. He worked in IT at the DCO training complex and went into work two hours before his normal duty time on the day of the explosion."

"You think he was working with the rogue DCO agents who killed John Loughlin?"

While the idea made sense, it wasn't exactly in line with what he'd told Dick.

"I think it's possible the guy might have brought the bomb onto the complex," Trevor said.

Alina waited for him to say something else about the man, but he fell silent. That left her with a lot of questions, the first one being why no one had already talked to this guy. Surely, the people investigating the bombing would have done that right off the bat. More importantly, why had Trevor lied to his boss about where they were going and what they'd be doing?

"You told the director you wanted to talk to some people who'd gotten into a scuffle with two men you thought might be the rogue agents," she reminded him.

He glanced at the side mirror this time. "Yeah, I did."

There was a lot of stuff he wasn't telling her, including who he thought was following them. She decided not to push on those two subjects…yet. He was talking, and she wanted to keep that going. Time to move on to a different topic and see what else he'd tell her.

"Back to the shifter thing for a minute," she said, trying to sound casual. "Dick said something about you having animal DNA, but that's just an expression, right? Like when someone says a person is as mean as a junkyard dog or strong as an ox."

Trevor didn't say anything for a long time, and Alina thought she'd pushed too far.

"I'm a coyote shifter," he finally said. "I have canine DNA mixed with my own. When I shift, I take on certain physical characteristics of a coyote."

All Alina could do was stare. What could she say to a man who'd just claimed to be part coyote?

"Are you serious, or are you just messing with me?" she demanded.

In answer, Trevor took one hand off the wheel and placed it on the center console between them. As she watched, his fingernails extended until they turned into five sharp claws almost an inch long and deadly looking as hell.

Alina stared. It had to be a trick.

She opened her mouth to ask how a human could possibly have claws but stopped cold as he turned to look at her with eyes that were glowing yellow and a pair of elongated canines protruding out over his lower lip.

Crap on a stick.

She jerked back so hard, she almost snapped her neck, then immediately regretted her reaction at the flicker of disappointment that crossed his handsome face. Before she could say anything, the claws, fangs, and glowing eyes disappeared.

Trevor put his hand back on the wheel and focused once again on the twisting, turning country road. "Enough about me," he said casually, as if having long claws poking out from under his fingernails was an everyday occurrence for him. Hell, maybe it was. "Now that I've told you where we're going and demonstrated the shifter stuff isn't BS, let's get back to you. Why was your heart beating so fast before?"

Alina didn't answer. She didn't like confiding in a stranger, even if he was supposed to be her partner. But he'd answered her questions, so she supposed she owed him something.

"A mission went wrong a couple of years ago in the CIA. I try hard not to think about it, because when

I do, I get upset. That's probably why you heard my heart racing."

She tried not thinking about the fact that her heart was probably racing all over again simply from making that confession, and she prayed he wouldn't push for more details.

"Are you wondering if you made a mistake getting out of the CIA?" he asked.

Her first instinct was to say no. Then again, that was always her first instinct. But instead, she nodded.

"Yeah. I'd be lying if I said I wasn't wondering that. But then I realize I did the right thing. It was time for me to leave," she said.

She looked out the passenger window, waiting with a slight sense of dread for his next question, the one where he asked her exactly why she'd left the Agency.

Nothing had been the same after the operation in Turkey. In the immediate aftermath of the ambush that had killed her entire team, she'd been so furious that all she could do was think about spending the rest of her life hunting Wade down and making him pay. The need for revenge was like a fever that raged day and night.

The Agency had done everything they could to help her find Wade at first. But after about a year of scouring the globe, the search had started to lose steam as other events took priority. The Agency moved Wade's cold-blooded betrayal to the back burner, he was placed on a watch list with thousands of other high-value targets, and Alina was told to let it go. She hadn't, and it had cost her.

Initially, the Agency had allowed her to stay in the field, but over time, her fixation with finding the man who'd killed her team had made her coworkers and supervisors uncomfortable. They began to think she was unstable, obsessive, and a risk to other agents. To some degree, maybe she was. Because for a long time, all she cared about was getting revenge.

Finally, the big shots at Langley had decided to put her zeal for catching traitors to good use and transferred her to the CIA's version of Internal Affairs. Instead of chasing after bad guys, she'd been chasing dirty agents. It wasn't something an agent should ever be asked to do, and Alina had hated it. So when the director of the DCO had approached her out of the blue about a new job— one that included a promise to jump-start her search for Wade—she'd hadn't even had to think about it. That brilliant move had gotten her a partner who had claws and glowing yellow eyes.

Well, she'd wanted a chance to get out and do something different. From now on, maybe she should be more careful what she asked for.

"You going to be able to focus on what we're doing here?" Trevor asked, pulling her out of her reveries.

Alina gave herself a shake and realized they were in the parking lot of a nice little apartment complex with well-trimmed hedges and perfectly manicured lawns. Around them, the other spaces were filled with electric cars. It wasn't exactly a place that screamed "cold-blooded killer hideout."

"I'll be fine," she assured Trevor, then added, "assuming you're actually planning to tell me what we're doing here. Who's this guy we're looking for, and do you have anything linking him to the bombing besides the fact that he happened to come into work early that day?"

If Trevor was involved with the people who'd murdered John Loughlin, why act like he was hunting down the killer? And if he wasn't involved with the rogue agents and honestly wanted to find who'd done it, why was he so reluctant to talk to her?

"His name is Seth Larson," Trevor said, shutting off the engine. "The DCO brought him in to specialize in cybersecurity and data protection. Like I said before, he was hired three weeks before the bombing and quit two days later."

As if that explained it, Trevor opened his door and stepped out of the vehicle. Alina quickly unbuckled her seat belt and jumped out, practically running to catch up with him as he headed for the apartment building.

"You do realize that when he started working at the DCO could easily be a coincidence, right?" she asked as she fell into step beside him. "And as far as quitting right after the bombing, I'm betting a lot of people bailed after that."

Alina took his silence as confirmation as they entered the building and climbed the stairs.

"Do you have anything else on this guy?" she asked. "Some indication of a payment, a personal beef with Loughlin, a connection with the rogue agents who went on the run?"

Trevor shook his head as he stopped in front of apartment 231. "Nothing like that. But Larson was previously employed by a man John had been trying to apprehend for years."

"What man?"

"An extremely powerful man who has used other people to do his dirty work. As it happens, he's also the same man who got Seth Larson the job at the DCO."

That didn't tell her much. And while Trevor appeared to be searching for the bomber, he didn't seem to be trying to find any of the rogue agents.

She opened her mouth to ask him about it, but before she got a chance, he reached out and pushed the doorbell. He immediately followed that up with a few knocks that were louder than the bell.

The door was jerked open so fast, Alina automatically reached for the sidearm on her hip but stopped at the last second at the sight of a young guy in jeans and a T-shirt with wire-rimmed glasses and at least three days of stubble on his face, a little blond boy standing behind him.

"I heard the bell," the man said, clearly pissed off. "You didn't have to knock, too."

Trevor frowned and opened his month to say something no doubt abrupt and snarky, but his words were cut off by a soft, frightened voice.

"Daddy, do you have to go away again?"

Larson glanced over his shoulder at his son. The little boy, who couldn't have been more than eight, was close to tears.

"No, Cody. Daddy's not going anywhere. I'm just talking to some old friends."

Cody moved closer, studying her and Trevor, his blue eyes curious. "Friends?"

Larson looked at them, a pleading expression on his face. "You two are friends, right?"

Alina smiled at Cody. "Yes, we're friends of your dad. We worked with him a little while ago."

That seemed to satisfy the little boy, who turned without another word and headed back into the living room. When he was out of earshot, Seth Larson frowned at them.

"I don't remember seeing either of you from the time I was at the DCO, but I'm guessing that's where you know me from," he said.

"Yes," Trevor said, his tone softer than Alina would have expected. "I'm Trevor Maxwell, and this is my partner, Alina Bosch. We'd like to ask you a couple of questions about the morning the bombing happened."

Larson threw a quick glance at his son, as if he was afraid Cody might have heard, but Cody was lying on the floor coloring and didn't even look up. "Sure, I can talk. Just...don't use that word—*bomb*. I don't think Cody knows what it means, and I really don't want him to. He's autistic, and sometimes he gets upset easily."

Alina nodded. Beside her, Trevor did the same.

Larson led them into the small, tidy apartment, past an eat-in kitchen, and into the living room. There was a couch against one wall, with a TV and bookshelves opposite it. A fancy computer sat on the coffee table, some kind of accounting spreadsheet showing on the screen, but Alina barely took notice of any of it. Cody was far more fascinating.

Spread out on the floor around him must have been nearly a hundred completed pictures torn out of coloring books. Every one of them was absolutely amazing. While the colors were unusual—trees in blues and purples, people in every shade of the rainbow, skies in yellow with orange clouds—there wasn't a single crayon mark out of place or outside the lines. In a word, they were breathtaking.

Seemingly oblivious to them, Cody finished the picture he was working on, then carefully pulled it out of the book and set it aside before starting the next one.

Larson motioned them toward the couch. "You two want a soda…or water? Sorry, but that's all I have in the house."

Alina shook her head as she sat. "No, I'm good."

Trevor declined the offer as well, moving carefully around the pictures on the floor as he grabbed a place beside her on the couch and pulled out a pen and spiral notepad from a cargo pocket. Larson sat down on the floor with Cody, making sure to move his son's artwork aside first.

"To be honest, I'm kind of surprised no one stopped by before this," he said.

That confirmed what Alina had thought. It shocked the heck out of her at the same time. She was an agent, not a cop, but talking to every single person who'd been in the complex at the time of the bombing seemed like common sense.

"On the day of the…incident…you showed up for work two and a half hours before your normal duty time," Trevor said. "Mind if I ask why?"

Larson's gaze went to his son, a smile curving his mouth. "I went in early so I could grab a few hours before Cody got out of bed. He loves his grandma—she watches him for me when I'm at work—but he can be a handful sometimes." He frowned at them. "My boss— Lisa Marino—said it was okay. I'm sure she'll confirm that if you ask her."

Beside her, Trevor visibly relaxed. "Lisa left the DCO two weeks ago. I'll try to get in contact with her, but that could take a while."

"How about Karl Thomas? Is he still there?" Larson asked. "He knew about me going in early."

Trevor nodded. "I think he's still there. I'll check."

Larson looked at Cody again, his expression thoughtful this time. "I guess a lot of people left after what happened."

"Is that why you quit when you did?" Alina asked. "Because of the…incident?"

Larson was silent for a moment as he watched his son color. Tears formed in his eyes, and he blinked.

"I had to," he said, turning back to them. "I loved the work, and the people there were amazing, but the hours were already getting tough on Cody…and his grandma. Trying to go to work early might have helped a little, but a full day at work was still too long to be away from him. When the other stuff happened, I realized that if I'd walked past the admin building forty-five minutes later to get that cup of coffee from the cafeteria, I could have been caught up in…in everything that happened. Then Cody wouldn't have anyone except his grandma, and she's too old to care for him full time. I couldn't take that risk."

"How long have you been taking care of Cody on your own?" Trevor asked.

"About a year," he said, then cleared his throat. "I guess Kristy just couldn't deal anymore. She bailed one day while I was at work. I was mad at her for a long time, but I finally gave up on that. I know now that she did the best she could."

Alina glanced at Cody to see if he'd react to the mention of his mother, but he continued to color like he hadn't heard a thing.

"Do you stay home with him full time?" she asked Larson.

Larson nodded. "Pretty much. Like I said, my mom comes over to take care of him now and then, but he doesn't like me to be out of his sight for long." He gestured to the laptop on the coffee table. "I do a little consulting work long distance to help pay the bills, but it's tough. I really thought I'd struck gold landing that job with the DCO."

Alina remembered thinking something very similar when Dick had offered her a job there. That reminded her of what Trevor had said before they'd knocked on the door, about there being an extremely powerful man involved in getting Larson hired at the DCO.

"Can I ask how you heard about the job at the DCO?" she asked Larson.

"I'd done some work for a subsidiary of Chadwick-Thorn back before Kristy left, then some consulting work in April for the main corporate office over near Anacostia-Bolling, installing and networking a fancy security system," Larson said. "While I was there, I got the opportunity to meet with Thomas Thorn, and after the security gig was done, he offered me an IT job at the DCO. It had everything I was looking for—good hours, great pay, amazing medical benefits, challenging work. It was mostly internal security stuff like monitoring DCO employees to make sure none of them were inadvertently sending classified material over unclassified computer systems. Things like that."

Interesting. Was Thomas Thorn the man Trevor had been talking about? The one John Loughlin had been trying to put in jail for years? If so, no wonder Trevor hadn't wanted to say anything. The previous director of the DCO had been chasing a man who was not only the CEO of one of the biggest and most politically connected defense contractors in the world, but also a former senator? There was something scary big going on here.

She was still thinking about that interesting tidbit of information when she realized Trevor was asking something else. Alina forced herself to focus on what her partner was saying.

"You mentioned that you were near the admin building forty-five minutes before the…incident…getting coffee. Did you see anyone else around?"

Larson thought about it for a moment, then nodded. "Yeah. I mean, it was still dark at that time, but I saw three or four people around the main building."

"Did you recognize them?" Trevor asked.

"I hadn't worked there long enough to learn almost anyone's name outside the IT section," the man said. "Sorry."

Trevor frowned, but Alina wasn't ready to walk away from the potential clue just yet. "Do you think you could ID the people you saw if we gave you some photos to look through?"

"Yeah, I guess," Larson said. "But do you think you can bring the photos here or email them to me so I don't have to leave Cody with my mom?"

"Of course," she agreed.

While Alina added his name and email to the contact list in her phone, Trevor scribbled something in his notepad. She thought he was writing down notes on what they'd talked about, but then he tore the paper out of the pad and held it out to Larson.

"Give this guy a call in a few days," Trevor said. "I think he can set you up with some IT work you can do from home. Tell him I sent you. I put my number on there, too, just in case you need anything."

Alina glanced at Larson's little boy as she stood. "Bye, Cody."

Since Cody didn't look up from his coloring book, she thought he hadn't heard her, but just as she and Trevor followed Larson to the front door, the boy jumped up and ran over with one of the pictures he'd made. When he held it out to her, she saw it was the one he'd been working on when she and Trevor had first gotten there, the one with the yellow sky and the orange clouds. She took it very carefully.

"Is this for me?" she asked.

Cody didn't say anything. Instead, he turned and went back to his coloring book, starting another page.

"Thank you," she said, but he was already lost in his work.

She glanced at Trevor as they headed outside to their SUV. "What was that all about?"

He pushed the button on the key fob to unlock the doors. "What was what all about?"

"That number you gave Larson. Do you always give suspects the name and number of prospective employers?"

Trevor shrugged. "I think it's obvious that guy isn't a suspect. He's just someone who might have seen something. Besides, he could use a little help."

Alina couldn't argue with any of those things. "It was a nice thing to do."

He only grunted in answer.

They didn't talk much as they headed north on Highway 2 back toward Fredericksburg and the interstate. It wasn't dark yet, but the sun was low on the horizon. It would be nightfall by the time they got back to the DCO complex.

As the last few beams of the sun's light slipped through the trees lining the road, Alina replayed the day's events. To say she was confused about everything she'd seen and learned was an understatement. Her new partner wasn't anything like Dick had described. Other than the fact that he was very closed-mouth when it came to sharing information, Trevor seemed like an okay guy. Well, there were the fangs, claws, and glowing gold eyes. Those were going to take a while to get used to. Even so, she wasn't ready to brand him the traitor the director of the DCO claimed him to be—yet.

Chapter 3

"Keep your eyes closed and just relax."

Tanner Howland frowned even as he said the words. He wasn't sure he was the best person to help another hybrid get a handle on their inner animal, especially since he was still trying to figure it out most of the time himself, but Sage Andrews, the woman the DCO had rescued from a lab in Tajikistan a while back, was in a really bad way. Besides, he couldn't say no to anything Zarina Sokolov asked him to do. Meeting the beautiful Russian doctor had been the only bright spot in his dark existence since he'd been captured and turned into a beast over a year ago. If not for her, he probably wouldn't even be alive right now.

He, Zarina, and Sage sat on the floor in the small living room of Sage's dorm room/prison cell on the DCO complex while two armed men stood guard outside the door.

"That's it," he said. "Breathe in and out, nice and slowly."

As Sage inhaled and exhaled, Tanner looked for any sign that the beast inside her might take over and she was about to lose it. Beside him, Zarina did the same. He would have preferred her to watch this exercise from farther away, like on a closed-circuit television in another room. But Zarina insisted she needed to be close in case Sage lost control.

When he'd tried to argue, Zarina had folded her arms—a sure sign he wasn't going to change her mind no matter what he said. "Who taught you how to control your inner beast?" she asked. "Me, that's who."

But while that was true, Tanner didn't like the idea of Zarina putting herself at risk. He'd been watching out for her ever since she'd saved his life in Washington State after a pair of psycho doctors had injected him with a serum that turned him into a hybrid like Sage. He wasn't about to stop now.

Across from him, Sage's brow knit, like she was fighting for control. Tanner tensed, but after a moment, she relaxed again. While he'd had more than his share of episodes since being turned into a hybrid, sometimes it seemed like Sage was more beast than human. If there was any doubt of that, all a person had to do was take a look at Sage's living arrangements, and the truth was obvious.

Since she was prone to violence, staying in one of the normal dorm rooms like he did was out of the question, so John Loughlin had turned one of the outbuildings into a small efficiency apartment of sorts. Her bedroom, bathroom, kitchen, and living room took up the back half of the building while the front was part medical facility, part guard station. In between the front and back sections was a wall of steel bars as thick and heavy as anything you'd expect to see in a real prison.

It wasn't the nicest way to treat a woman who'd never asked for any of this to happen to her, and Tanner hated it more than anyone, but there wasn't anything else they could do. Sage gave in to her animal rages once every few days. The deep scratches along the walls and floors were a testament to that. A petite, slender girl with long, wavy, dark hair and expressive gray eyes, she looked like she wouldn't hurt a fly. But when the animal inside took over, Sage turned into something extremely dangerous.

That was why Dick kept two armed guards there 24-7. Currently, both men were standing outside the steel bars of Sage's cell watching them, disdain on their faces. They both hated and feared Sage. The only reason they treated her halfway decently at all was because the DCO might be able to use her later. That said, the thought of Sage escaping and going on a rampage through the training complex terrified the new director.

Honestly, it terrified Tanner, too. If she got out of here, it would be up to him to stop her, and he wasn't sure if he could stop a raging hybrid without losing control of his own inner animal.

"We're going to do the door exercise again, Sage," he said quietly. "Just like we've been doing for the past few weeks, okay?"

Sage gently wrapped her graceful fingers around the silver cross on a chain around her neck, her lips moving in a silent prayer. She'd told Tanner that she had grown up in a very religious family and that her father was a pastor of a church back in her hometown. In fact, the first things she'd asked for after she'd calmed down enough to talk to anyone were a cross and a Bible.

After a few moments, Sage nodded, letting him know she was ready.

"I want you to imagine that you're standing in front of a door in a dimly lit room. It can be any kind of door you want. It doesn't matter, as long as it's something you can easily remember."

She frowned, then relaxed again.

"Do you have the door set in your mind?" Tanner asked.

"Yes," she said, the tips of her fangs clearly visible.

"Relax, Sage," he said softly. "We're in no rush. Take a minute and center yourself. Concentrate on the door as you breathe in and out."

That was the thing with Sage. All it took was a word or a noise or a bad memory, and the beast was off and running.

"Can you describe the door for me?" he asked.

Sage nodded. "It's a white door with a pink unicorn hand-painted in the middle, like the one to my sister's bedroom. I can see it so clearly I feel like I can reach out and touch it."

Tanner glanced at Zarina. She looked just as concerned as he was about Sage's choice of imaginary doors. This wasn't the one Sage usually described.

He didn't know much in the way of details when it came to what Sage had been through during her captivity, because she refused to talk about it, but he was almost certain she'd watched her younger sister die a painful, horrible death as a result of being injected with a previous version of the hybrid serum. Focusing on her late sister's bedroom door probably wasn't a good idea for a hybrid who wanted to stay in control, but there wasn't anything Tanner could do about it now. With the image already in her head, there was no way Sage would be able to forget it, even if she wanted to.

"That's good, Sage," he told her. "Remember that on your side of the door, you have a handle that you can open or close. On the other side, there is no handle. That's where the beast is. It can't get through the door unless you open it. You're in charge, okay?"

Sage nodded.

"Can you feel the beast on the other side of the door?" he asked.

"Yes," she whispered, her fingers tightening around the cross. "It's always there."

"It's okay," he said soothingly "You're in control. And to prove that, I want you to open the door a crack."

Sage tensed visibly but kept her eyes closed. "I thought you were going to show me how to keep it locked away forever?"

"That's not something I can do," he said. "You need to learn how to get the beast under control."

"I can't," she said brokenly.

"Yes, you can."

Sage chewed on her lower lip. "Maybe we should wait until Derek is here."

Staff Sergeant Derek Mickens was the Special Forces soldier who had risked his life to save her from a burning building in Tajikistan. She only seemed truly in control of her animal side when she was with him or even talking to him on the phone. But Derek was deployed more than he was home, and he couldn't be around as much Sage needed him. Even calling regularly could be difficult as hell for him.

"Sage, you need to learn how to do this on your own," Tanner said gently. "Derek can't be with you all the time. Now that he's on deployment, he might not be back for a long time."

Tanner realized he shouldn't have said that the moment the words were out of his mouth, but by then, it was too late to do anything about it. Sage's heart rate spiked immediately, and her body went as rigid as if she'd been hit with a live electrical wire.

Oh shit. She was going into full hybrid mode.

"Zarina, get out of here!" he ordered, jumping up.

Across from him, Sage did the same, claws out and eyes glowing bloodred.

"I can help," Zarina insisted, getting to her feet.

"Get out," he growled. "Now!"

He hadn't intended the words to come out that way, but knowing Zarina was trapped with him in a prison cell with an out-of-control hybrid made his control slip a little.

Zarina looked like she wanted to argue but then turned and ran for the door. Tanner expected the guard to immediately jerk open the door, but when he glanced that way, the man was still fumbling with the keys on the ring, searching for the right one.

"Open the door, dammit!" Tanner shouted.

A flash of movement coupled with a growl had Tanner spinning around to see Sage rushing toward him, her curved claws ready to slash him to ribbons.

Tanner tried to stay in control, tried to let just enough of the animal out to allow his feline reflexes to kick in, but with Zarina still in danger, that control slipped away like sand through his fingers.

Claws and fangs coming out, he blocked Sage's right arm, then shoved her back, knowing he had to put some distance between them before he shifted all the way and lost complete control. Sage charged at him again, rage filling her glowing red eyes as she yowled in frustration. While she would probably never hurt him, the beast in charge at the moment sure as hell wanted to.

He blocked another slash, fighting the urge to strike back. If he landed a blow with his larger claws, he'd tear the smaller woman nearly in half. Instead, he reached deep down and found the control to retract his claws.

Sage blinked at him, like she was almost as shocked as he was that he'd done it. He thought for a moment the move would be enough to get her to calm down and back off. But then something behind him caught Sage's attention, and her eyes went feral again.

Tanner glanced over his shoulder, and his heart lurched. Both guards had come into the cell, one holding a Taser, the other a dart gun that Tanner knew was loaded with a sedative. The only problem was that the idiots had left the cell door open behind them. If Sage got past the men, she'd be through it in a flash. Then the only thing standing between her and freedom would be Zarina.

Zarina, heaven help her, was standing resolutely in the open doorway like she thought she could stop Sage by sheer willpower.

As Sage poised to leap at the guards, the guy with the Taser froze, while the one with the dart gun was shaking so much it looked like he was about to wet his pants. Sage was going to get through those two before they could blink. Then she'd be on Zarina.

Fury overwhelmed Tanner like a tidal wave. One moment, he was standing there, wondering what the best move would be. The next, he'd shifted completely and let out a roar loud enough to shake the walls. Claws extended to their full length, he went for Sage.

She backpedaled, the red glow disappearing from her eyes.

At the same time, Dart Guy dropped his weapon and really did piss himself, while Taser Man jerked back

and fired his stun weapon into the ceiling, burying the
high-voltage electrodes in the soft acoustic tiles.

Sage ran for her bedroom, sobs tearing from her
throat instead of growls, while both men made a beeline
for the cell door.

Zarina ran past Tanner, hurrying after Sage before
he could stop her. Now that Sage was back in charge
of her body, all she'd be interested in doing was hiding
away from the rest of humanity in horror and shame.
Tanner knew what it felt like to lose control, especially
in front of people you considered friends. Hopefully
Zarina could console Sage and remind her that she'd
done well—right up until Tanner had slipped up and
mentioned Derek.

He took a deep breath and got himself under control.
A few moments later, his fangs and claws retracted,
leaving him feeling drained and weary. Outside the cell,
the two guards stared at him in revulsion. Abruptly realizing he was aware of their attention, the men turned and
headed outside. But the distance wasn't great enough to
prevent him from hearing what they said to each other,
especially the part where they muttered about having to
babysit those *damn freaks*.

Those two might have been total d-bags, but it still
reminded Tanner that in the eyes of most of the people
left at the DCO, he and Sage were little better than
poorly behaved animals. It made him wonder how much
longer Dick would tolerate their presence.

—∞—

Tanner was still sitting on one of the benches overlook-
ing the obstacle course when Zarina finally came out of

Sage's cell an hour later. He'd spent the time thinking about all the ways the situation in Sage's holding cell could have gone wrong—and there were a lot of them. Worst among them wasn't the possibility of Sage getting past those guards but the fact that he might have been the one who put the men down—right before he lashed out at Zarina. The thought chilled him to the core.

Zarina walked over to join him, sitting down on the wooden bench with a sigh. Some of her long, wavy, blond hair had come loose from its bun to hang down around her face, and it was all he could do not to reach out and gently take the silky strands between his fingers.

"How's Sage doing?" he asked.

"She feels horrible. But at least she's not sobbing uncontrollably now," Zarina said. "I told her that she did very well on the exercise, but she's still upset she lost control and attacked you."

He shrugged. "She got her animal side back under control pretty fast."

Zarina pinned him with a look. "You know that's not true, and so does she. Sage only gained control because you roared at her. If not for that, she would have tried to attack those two guards and probably me, too. She's terrified she might kill someone while her animal side is in control."

Tanner didn't say anything. He knew exactly how Sage felt. He was afraid of the same thing.

"It's so strange to see the obstacle course completely empty," Zarina said in that soft, beautiful accent of hers. "It's like this place is falling apart in front of our eyes."

Tanner couldn't help but think that there was more to Zarina's words than the literal interpretation. While the facilities were already showing signs of neglect, it was like the soul of the DCO was rotting away from the inside out as more and more good people left to be replaced with dirtbags. Soon, there'd be nothing left to show for all the work John had put into this place. Over a decade of hard work gone in the blink of an eye.

"The new teams don't do a lot of training," Tanner said.

Zarina let out a delicate snort. "The new teams don't do anything but sit around and eat. And the only time they leave the complex is to go traipsing off to some far corner of the world chasing after Ivy and Landon or one of the other teams. If Dick and Thorn knew just how close they really are to the DCO complex, they'd go crazy."

Tanner chuckled. She was right. Dick in particular would pass out if he knew that almost all the shifter teams were hiding less than two hours away from the Washington, DC, area.

"Speaking of Ivy and the others," Zarina said, glancing at him, "do you think you'll be seeing Kendra and Declan anytime soon?"

Kendra MacBride and her bear shifter husband were expecting twins any day now, so it wasn't really the best time to be on the run. Tanner looked around before answering. He doubted anyone could have snuck up on them without him knowing, but he checked anyway. "I won't risk going to see them. Not unless they call me, which I doubt they will."

Zarina frowned. "I'd feel a whole lot better if I could give Kendra a checkup myself. She's a week past her due date already. I should be with her."

Tanner sighed. Zarina still wasn't thrilled that he

was the only person in the DCO to know where Landon, Ivy, and the rest of the fugitives were hiding. Or that he was the only one who'd gone to see them. She knew they were somewhere close by because of how long Tanner had been gone the last time he'd taken Kendra something to help her deal with muscle spasms related to her pregnancy.

"You know that isn't possible," Tanner said as gently as he could. "They're watching you too closely. While you're an amazing woman, you're not a covert agent. Thorn's people would find you."

It was Zarina's turn to sigh. "I know. It's just hard thinking about Kendra and the others being out there on their own. I hate that Thorn's goons are always following me."

Zarina wasn't the only one being watched. Thorn had people following some of the other DCO employees as well, including Trevor. The coyote shifter was under almost constant surveillance.

Fortunately, Dick and Thorn ignored Tanner. For whatever reason, they considered him nothing more than a dumb animal, too out of control to be trusted to do anything covert or complicated. That was fine with him, since being invisible made it easy to slip away and get messages to his friends whenever Dick was closing in on them. It also made it simple to snoop around Dick's office, talk to his secretary, and listen in on private conversations that people had no idea he could hear so he could figure out what the hell Dick and Thorn were up to. With John out of the way, Thorn would be making his big move, but no one had a clue what it was.

"Can you at least tell me if Ivy is with Kendra?" Zarina asked. "If Kendra goes into labor without a doctor there, I'd feel a lot better if Ivy were around to help."

Tanner shook his head. "You know I can't tell you anything. It's safer for everyone if you don't know."

She made a face at him, sticking out her tongue. He chuckled, unable to help himself. Clearly, living in the United States was having a profound effect on her. She would never have done anything like that when she'd first arrived here.

"Why?" she demanded, her blue eyes flashing. "Because Adam says it is? What do we even know about this guy? Hell, he doesn't even have a last name! He popped up as a voice on the end of the phone a couple of days after John died, and we all did exactly what he told us to do. How do we know we can trust him?"

Zarina was only echoing what Tanner had thought the first time the mysterious shifter named Adam had called. He'd given Landon, Ivy, and the others places to hide, new identities, money, and even burner phones Tanner used to keep in contact with them.

"We know we can trust him because Landon and Ivy trust him," Tanner said. "According to them, Adam had been working behind the scenes with John for years trying to find something to pin on Thorn. Adam hasn't done anything to steer us wrong yet."

Zarina's mouth tightened. "So Ivy and Kendra aren't together?"

Tanner lifted a brow but didn't answer. Zarina rolled her eyes and turned her attention back to the obstacle course again.

The funny thing was that Zarina was right. The DCO agents had split into three groups and were hiding out at separate locations. Ivy and Landon weren't with Kendra and Declan.

"Are you going to tell me what happened in there?" Zarina asked after a moment. "I haven't seen you lose it like that in a long time."

That was only because she hadn't been in Costa Rica when he'd completely gone animal during a rescue mission and had run off into the forest like a lunatic. When his team found him, they'd had to tackle him, then practically sit on him for thirty minutes until his rage subsided.

Since then, Tanner had thought he had his inner animal well in hand. Now, he realized any semblance of control he'd been experiencing was nothing more than an illusion. The moment he'd thought Zarina was in danger, he'd completely lost it. Even now, he could feel the beast in the back of his mind, prowling around, looking for a way to slip out again. It was like the thing had been encouraged by that minor bout of freedom.

"Sometimes I imagine this is what an alcoholic or drug addict must feel like," he said softly, staring down at the grass in front of their bench. "Knowing that there's this monster inside you, ready to slip out and attack the second you give it a chance."

"You're not an alcoholic or an addict," Zarina said firmly. "You were given a serum that made drastic changes to your DNA and your hindbrain, which is the part that controls our most primitive functions, including survival instincts, aggression, and your fight-or-flight response. That's why you sometimes lose control in stressful situations."

He appreciated how Zarina always tried to make it

seem as if all his issues were related to the hybrid serum he'd been given, but they both knew it was more than that. He'd already been a basket case long before he'd been given those drugs. The rage issues, memory blackouts, and panic attacks had started somewhere between his fourth and fifth deployment in the army and had only gotten worse once he was out of the Rangers. That was why he'd been living alone in the woods of Washington State to begin with. So he wouldn't lose it and hurt someone.

When he didn't say anything, Zarina reached out and rested her hand on his jaw, turning him to look at her.

"Tanner, the things that are happening to you aren't your fault. But you're dealing with them. *We're* dealing with them."

The touch of her hand on his face was enough to warm his whole body, and it was all he could do not to turn ever so slightly and press a kiss to her palm.

He wished he could tell Zarina exactly how he felt about her, because right now, he was happier than he'd ever been in his life. But it would have been unfair to tell her that he loved her, then in the next breath admit he was almost certainly going to have to walk away from her.

"Sometimes I think it would be better if I went back to the forests where you found me," he said quietly. "So I could get away from all of it."

Zarina looked confused at first, but then an expression of overwhelming pain filled her eyes. "Away from me?"

Seeing the sorrow on her face hurt him worse than anything he'd ever experienced, even the searing agony he'd felt as the hybrid drug had first burned through his bloodstream all those months ago, tearing his DNA apart from the inside out.

He loved her more than his own life. Which was why what he was doing felt so completely right.

He gently trailed his hand over her cheek. This was the first time he'd touched Zarina like this, and it almost took his breath away.

"Away from you more than anyone," he said. "I'd die if I ever lost control and hurt you."

"You'd never hurt me."

"You can't be sure of that."

"I am sure. Tanner, I'm close to finding a cure." She reached up to grab his hand and squeeze it tight. "The serum I gave Jayson wasn't perfect, but it counteracted the effects of the crap Dick gave him. All I need is a little more time, and it will be ready."

"You've been working on that antiserum for almost a year and a half," he pointed out. "You might be close, or you could be another year or two away."

She shifted on the bench so she could face him squarely, shaking her head vigorously. "It won't take that long. I'm sure of it. You have to promise you won't leave before I have a chance to finish it."

That wasn't a promise he could make. He had no idea when he was going to leave, since he still needed to help Sage, but he couldn't ignore the risk he posed to Zarina and the other people around him. At some point, he'd lose control at the wrong time, and someone he cared about would pay the price. He refused to stay here and let that happen.

But before he could tell Zarina that, she suddenly leaned forward and wrapped her arms around him, squeezing him tightly. He froze, shocked by the move. But after a moment, he enfolded her in a hug.

"Don't answer right now," she whispered. "Just think about it for a while…before you do anything."

Tanner closed his eyes, holding her like he'd wanted to for so long, torn that it couldn't always be like this. But he wasn't the man Zarina needed in her life. At some point, she was going to have to figure that out.

Chapter 4

ALINA STEPPED OUT OF THE SHOWER AND ABSENTLY dried off with the fluffy towel she took from the rack as she tried to figure out what was going on with Thomas Thorn. She'd found it strange enough that the man had been lurking during her initial interview with Dick Coleman, but now that his name had shown up in connection with the bombing, she had no idea what to think.

Tossing the towel in the hamper, she slipped into her standard bum-around-the-house-and-chill-out clothes—yoga pants, a tank top, and a cardigan. Considering it was summertime, she didn't really need the sweater, but cardigans were soft and cozy, and she liked wearing them regardless of what time of year it was. Forgetting about work wasn't really an option right now, though.

As she walked through the living room and into the kitchen, she went over everything she knew about Thomas Thorn, which wasn't a lot. Not that there was a reason she should know much about the man. She'd spent the past twelve years of her life buried in the CIA, where she'd focused on international threats—and Wade. She'd never been interested in DC politics. Hell, she couldn't remember the last time she'd voted.

Even so, she knew the obvious stuff. Thorn had been a senator up until a couple of years ago, when he'd stepped down to run his international defense corporation. He was filthy rich, owned more homes than she did shoes, and still wielded a tremendous amount of influence within political circles. She was also fairly certain he could have stepped into almost any executive-level job in the government if he'd wanted. Heck, she could see some president tapping him to be secretary of defense in a heartbeat. He was that well connected.

Which made her wonder why he'd been there that morning when she'd talked to Dick. From the looks the director had thrown Thorn's way, it was obvious he had some influence within the DCO. Why a man as powerful as Thorn would bother getting involved in a small covert organization that no one else in the world had ever heard of didn't make a lot of sense to her.

Then there was the stuff Trevor had said about the former DCO director attempting to send Thorn to prison. Her new partner had implied it was the real reason behind the bombing that had killed John Loughlin.

That was a pretty serious claim, and she would have appreciated Trevor getting into the details. Unfortunately, he'd refused to discuss the subject. She'd spent a good portion of the drive up from Bowling Green badgering him for information, and all she'd learned was that her new partner couldn't be badgered. She hadn't been ignored like that since she was an awkward teen in high school. Crap, Trevor could be irritating as hell when he wanted to be.

She walked over to the island in the kitchen and picked up the picture Cody had made. She couldn't help smiling. It was sweet of him to give it to her.

On impulse, she walked over to the stainless steel fridge and moved a few takeout order magnets around until she'd made a space for the picture, then used the magnets to hold it in place. She stepped back and admired it. The picture definitely brightened up her rather drab kitchen. Then again, she hadn't known her kitchen was drab until she'd put Cody's picture up.

Alina suddenly found herself thinking about how her life would have been different if she'd turned left instead of right after college and gotten a normal, ho-hum job, met a nice guy, settled down, and had kids.

She laughed at how crazy that was. Even though she'd had this apartment in Del Ray for years, she typically wasn't there more than a week or two at a time. She'd spent most of her time traveling around the world, sleeping in hotels, on planes, and in the backseats of cars while surveilling targets. The biggest factor in renting in Del Ray was because it was so close to Reagan National. If she was going to spend half her life at the airport, she might as well live close to it.

The notion that things could have been different, that she could have been a wife and a soccer mom with two-point-three kids and a minivan was fun to imagine. Looking at Cody's picture on the fridge, she wondered if she'd be the kind of mother who'd keep kids' artwork taped all over her kitchen. Probably.

She was just digging through the freezer for a frozen pizza that wasn't encased in frost older than the last ice age when she heard a quick knock immediately followed by the sound of the door opening, then the scrabble of doggy nails on the hardwood floor.

"You decent in there?" her friend Kathy McGee called as Molly bounded into the kitchen with a silly grin on her face.

"Yeah," Alina called. "In the kitchen."

Dropping to her knees, she gave her beautiful baby a big hug. Molly was a blue heeler cattle dog she'd rescued during a snowstorm five years ago. It was probably crazy for a woman doing fieldwork for the CIA to have brought in a stray, but there was no way in hell she was going to let the dog freeze to death. And once Molly had gotten comfortable in her apartment, it hadn't seemed right to give her to someone else. Fortunately, her next-door neighbor Kathy had offered to babysit Molly anytime Alina needed.

"How're you doing, girl?" She playfully ruffled Molly's long ears, then ran her hands through the short fur covering the dog's flanks. "Did you have a good time with Kathy today? Did you behave yourself and play nice with Katelyn?"

Katelyn was Kathy's cat and, against all rational explanation, Molly's favorite playmate. Which worked out well, considering how much time Molly spent in Kathy's place.

Her dark-haired friend came into the kitchen and leaned one shoulder against the wall but didn't try to interrupt the happy reunion, which pretty much went the same way regardless of how long Alina had been away. Kathy's presence didn't stop Alina from talking to Molly like she was a two-year-old.

"Did you miss your mommy?" she said in her best baby voice.

Molly let out a soft bark, then butted her head into Alina's hands, demanding more attention and pets. Alina couldn't help but laugh. Then again, that's what dogs were all about. They made you happy.

"You're a good girl, aren't you?"

Molly let out another soft bark. She wasn't a noisy dog, but she always got talkative when Alina acted all goofy. Alina had a sudden vision of Trevor watching her kneeling down on the floor, talking like this. He'd probably think she was a big dope.

"Molly wanted to come right over and find out how your first day on the new job went, but I told her she had to wait until you had a chance to clean up and relax a little," Kathy said.

Alina gave Molly one last pat on the head, then stood. "Oh, so Molly's the one who's all eager to hear about my first day at the office, huh?"

Kathy smiled and nodded, her blue-green eyes teasing behind her glasses. "Definitely. But if you're going to tell her about it, I guess I can hang around and listen in, too."

Alina gave up on the idea of nuking a frozen pizza and instead grabbed a box of Cheerios from the cabinet, a carton of milk from the fridge, and a bowl and spoon, then headed into the living room with Kathy following close behind.

"So tell me! How was your first day?" Kathy asked eagerly, kicking off her slippers and getting comfy on the couch.

Alina almost laughed at the excitement in her friend's voice but restrained herself. Kathy worked from home selling socks on the Internet and often said she lived vicariously through Alina's covert adventures.

Kathy was more than a next-door neighbor and her best friend. She was Alina's confidante, the only person she'd ever been able to talk to about her life in the CIA. She'd never told her friend anything classified of course, but Kathy was familiar with the stuff that had happened to Jodi and the other members of Alina's team. She'd also known how much Alina had come to dislike her job at the Agency. In fact, Kathy had been the one to convince her to accept the DCO's offer.

Molly hopped up between them on the couch and did a few circles before lying down with her head near Alina's hip. The dog immediately closed her eyes and went to sleep, happy as a clam now that she was with her mommy.

Alina dumped some cereal into the bowl, then added milk. "If I had to sum today up in one word, I guess that word would be...interesting."

Kathy tucked her sock-covered feet underneath her. "Okay, interesting is a good start. Tell me everything— starting with what your new partner is like. You did meet whoever it is today, right? Is it a man or a woman? Or are you part of a team with several hunky guys? Please tell me that's it."

Alina did laugh this time. Kathy could be a bit melodramatic.

"Yes, I met my partner. His name is Trevor Maxwell."

Kathy leaned forward expectantly. "And?"

"And what?" Alina knew exactly what Kathy was asking but figured she should make her friend work for it a little bit.

Kathy glared at her. "Don't even try it. You know exactly what I'm talking about. What's he like? Is he nice, good-looking, well built...married?"

Alina shook her head. "Kathy, he's my partner."

Her friend made a face. "Seriously? I sit at home all day looking at socks on the Internet, and you think I'm going to let you get away with that nonanswer? I'm not buying it. Spill!"

Alina laughed. "Okay, okay. I admit, I may have noticed that Trevor is attractive. He has dark hair that seems permanently tousled and dark eyes. He's maybe a year or two older than I am, isn't married that I know of, and is funny in that sarcastic, dry-wit sort of way. Oh, and he's definitely tall and well built."

"How tall and how built?" Kathy asked.

Alina shrugged. "Six four, two hundred and twenty pounds maybe."

"Whoa." Kathy's brows rose. "He sounds hot."

Alina didn't say anything as she spooned cereal into her mouth. She couldn't help wondering what her friend would think if she knew Trevor had claws and fangs.

"So I'm guessing you two hit it right off?"

Alina grimaced. "Unfortunately, no."

"Really? Why not? Did you get into a fight or something?"

Alina shook her head. "I wish it was as simple as that. But I don't think you can consider a complete lack of trust in each other a fight."

In between eating, Alina described her first day at the DCO, starting with the meeting she'd had with her boss.

"The man flat-out told me Trevor was involved with the murder of the organization's previous director," she said. "He as much as said the reason he hired me was because he thought I'd be able to dig out the traitors behind the conspiracy—Trevor being at the top of the list of suspects. My boss wants me to spy on my own partner the first day on the job."

Kathy didn't bat an eye at the mention of murder and

spying. She'd listened to Alina talk for so long that stuff like this was old hat to her. But she did grimace at the fact that the DCO was asking Alina to do the very thing that had made her quit the Agency.

"I don't remember you mentioning this as part of the job description when I suggested you take this job," Kathy muttered.

Alina shook her head. "I think this falls under the category of 'additional duties as assigned.' The worst part is that it's obvious Trevor knows I've been assigned as his partner simply to keep an eye on him. He'll barely talk to me."

"Okay, that sucks," Kathy said. "Do you think your boss is right? Is Trevor involved in murder? Do you trust him?"

Alina considered that. "I want to trust him."

"You know that's not really an answer, right?" Kathy pointed out. "To any of the questions I asked."

Alina sighed. "I know, but the reality is I don't know what to think of Trevor. He's my partner, and working with him is going to be tough if we can't trust each other. But after what happened with Wade, I'm not as quick to trust people as I used to be."

"That's understandable," Kathy said. "Let me ask you something. Besides your boss's suspicions about Trevor being involved, is there anything you've personally seen or heard that has you doubting him?"

Alina wondered if her friend had been a shrink in a previous life, because Kathy was definitely good at getting her to look at situations from a completely different perspective. But after replaying the day's events in her head, she realized Trevor had actually given her a few reasons to trust him, first by opening up about shifters, then telling her why they were going to see Seth Larson. Despite that, there was still one thing hanging over their partnership that made her reluctant to have faith in him.

"I suppose the thing that's bothering me the most is this gut instinct I have that Trevor is hiding something from me," she told Kathy. "I have no idea exactly what it is or why he's doing it, but I'm having a hard time putting my faith in someone when I know they're keeping secrets from me."

Kathy nodded. "What are you going to do?"

Alina didn't have to think about it very long. There was no way she was going back to the Agency, and she wasn't yet ready to walk away from the DCO. She wasn't sure why, but the same instincts warning her that Trevor was keeping stuff from her were also screaming that she couldn't bail on her new job.

Alina shrugged and set her empty bowl on the coffee table. "I'm not making any decisions one way or the other right now. Not until I have more information to work with."

Kathy's brow creased with worry. "What if you and Trevor have to walk into a dangerous situation? How do you do that if you don't trust him? Isn't that begging for trouble?"

"Yeah, I guess it is." Alina flopped back on the couch. "But right now, I don't have any other options. Until I know who the good guys are in this situation, I'm going to have to cover my own back."

⁓

Shit, he was tired.

Not surprising, Trevor thought as he walked upstairs

to his Woodbridge apartment. Between Dick putting him back out in the field with Alina and discovering the Seth Larson lead wasn't likely to go anywhere, things definitely hadn't gone the way he imagined when he'd woken up that morning.

Which was probably why he didn't realize there was someone in his apartment until he unlocked the door and pushed it open. Normally, someone breaking into his apartment would have had him reaching for his weapon, but in this case, he knew who his visitor was. The steady heartbeat combined with a complete and total lack of scent meant it could only be one person—Adam.

Closing the door, Trevor tossed his keys on the table inside the entryway. Adam stood in front of the big window in the living room, gazing out at the jogging path behind the building. He turned as Trevor flicked on the light, his hazel eyes quickly adjusting to the sudden brightness. Tall, with dark-blond hair and angular features, he wore a long duster even in the heat of summer. Considering it was August, Trevor should have been able to pick up the smell of sweat coming off the shifter from across the room, but he couldn't.

After the secretive shifter had shown up at his place for the first time weeks ago, Trevor quickly figured out the man wore some kind of cloaking spray that made it nearly impossible for him—or any other shifter—to pick up his natural scent. The only way Trevor could smell Adam's odor was if he got really, really close to him.

Not that it helped much. Adam didn't smell like any other shifter Trevor had ever been around. He smelled like a lizard. Thing was, Trevor had never heard of a reptile-based shifter. Then again, Trevor had seen the man's eyes shift once, and the pupils had been slitted.

Freakiest crap he had ever seen.

"You know, if you're going to break into my apartment, you could at least make dinner," Trevor said drily as he walked around the peninsula that separated the living room from the kitchen.

Adam lifted a brow. "Would you really eat anything I cooked?"

Considering Adam had been an assassin in his former life, probably not. "Good point."

Opening the fridge, Trevor grabbed two bottles of beer, then gestured at Adam. When the other shifter shook his head, Trevor shrugged and put one back.

"How was your trip down to Bowling Green?" Adam asked.

Trevor unscrewed the cap and swigged his beer. How the hell had Adam known where he and Alina had been earlier that day? He hadn't even known he was going down there until after lunch, and as far as anyone else knew, they'd been in Fredericksburg, not Bowling Green.

He didn't bother asking, knowing Adam wouldn't say. Besides, he was more concerned with other things — like the fact that Dick had bugged his apartment. He motioned around the room, then pointed to his ear.

"I've intercepted the audio going to our friends on the other end of the wires," Adam said casually. "They think you're watching ESPN while you make dinner."

Of course. Trevor wasn't sure why he worried. Adam had known his apartment was bugged before he had.

Adam had first shown up three days after John's murder, letting Trevor know Landon, Ivy, and the others were safe, then asking him to be his eyes and ears in the DCO. The other shifter had said he and the former director were friends, and that they'd devoted the past decade to putting Thorn in prison. Trevor had spent most of his adult life catching spies and traitors, so he was good at knowing when people were lying to him, and his gut told him Adam was on the level.

"It wasn't a complete loss," Trevor said. "The man I went down there to see—Seth Larson—isn't the one who brought the bomb onto the DCO complex, but he saw several people around the main building right before the explosion. I'm sending him photos from the DCO personnel records to look through. If we're lucky, we might get an ID on the person who set the device."

"Seems like a long shot," Adam said.

Trevor couldn't disagree with that. But until he had a chance to look into a few other leads he'd been working, it was the only shot he had to go on.

"Any word on Kendra?" Trevor asked.

"Tanner saw her a few days ago and said she's close to having her twins," Adam said, and Trevor could have sworn he saw a smile tug at his lips. "Declan is terrified he'll have to deliver the babies."

Trevor chuckled. He could just imagine the big bear shifter trying to deliver the twins while worrying about protecting Kendra at the same time. He was glad Tanner was in a position to help. The big lion hybrid might have control issues now and then, but there was absolutely no one else in the DCO who possessed his heart and compassion when it came to helping people in trouble.

But then the seriousness of that situation struck him. If Kendra went into labor suddenly, Tanner wouldn't be able to help with that. "All humor aside, she isn't going to have to have her kids in that B&B where they're staying, is she?"

Adam shrugged. "She'll have to. I'm trying to bring in a doctor and a nurse to take care of her, but I have to be careful. Thorn knows Kendra is close to giving birth, too, and I'm afraid if I use anyone in the area, he'll catch wind of it."

Shit. Being in the middle of giving birth to twins while worrying about Thorn's goons finding you had to be scary as hell. No wonder Declan was freaking out.

"How was your first day with your new partner?" Adam asked.

Trevor frowned. "You knew I was getting a new partner? And you didn't think that was something you might have mentioned to me?"

That slight smile crossed Adam's face again. "I didn't want to put you in the position of having to fake your emotions during your first meeting with Agent Bosch. You know what they say—you never get a second chance to make a first impression."

"Yeah right," Trevor said. He might have a hard time picking up Adam's scent, but he knew bullshit when he smelled it.

"So what's your first impression of her?" Adam prodded.

Trevor pinned him with a look. "If you know so much about her, why don't you tell me what she's like? I'm sure you have a complete file on her already."

Adam returned his look with those disquieting eyes of his. "Actually, I do have a complete file on your new partner. But those are just facts on a piece of paper. I'd much rather get your personal gut reactions to her. I tend to place a lot more faith in those kinds of assessments."

Trevor ground his jaw, fighting the urge to tell Adam to kiss his ass. The man could irritate the crap out of him sometimes.

"Well, for one thing, Alina strikes me as very competent," Trevor said. "Something tells me she was very good at the job she used to have at the CIA. Dick said something about her digging out traitors, so I suppose that's what she did there."

He waited for Adam to confirm or deny that last part, but the other shifter didn't say a word.

"She didn't lose it too badly when I did a partial shift in front of her, so I guess that earns her a few brownie points," Trevor added, taking another swig of beer. "But Dick obviously paired her with me at Thorn's urging, which means she's dirty."

Once again, Adam didn't say anything one way or the other about that. For some stupid reason, Trevor had hoped the other shifter would tell him that he was wrong, that Alina was one of the good guys. Kind of stupid, considering the facts of the situation.

The afternoon he'd spent with the former CIA agent had left him conflicted. His head told him that Alina was completely up to her neck in Dick's and/or Thorn's pockets, but after the conversation they'd had on the way down to Bowling Green, not to mention seeing the way she'd handled Larson—and Cody—he kept getting this weird feeling that there was something more to her than he suspected.

Unfortunately, he wasn't sure what that *something more* entailed. He couldn't even be sure if it was *something good* or *something bad*. His shifter instincts, which were usually reliable when it came to judging people, seemed to be withholding their opinion on the matter of Alina Bosch for the time being. A fact that pissed him off to no end.

"Anything else?" Adam asked.

Trevor shook his head. "Not really. I tried to hide that I was investigating Thorn's involvement in John's death, but the fact was probably impossible for her to miss. She handled that revelation better than I thought she would, though, so I'll have to admit, I'm torn. Part of me thinks I should trust her, but there's another part that's just as sure she's playing me. I don't suppose there's anything in that file you have on her that suggests one way or the other whether I can trust her?"

"Unfortunately, nothing written on a piece of paper can answer that question. You're right to worry about Alina," he said. "Dick actively pursued her and brought her in to be your partner. We have no idea what he said to her or what he's asked her to do. All I can suggest is that you protect yourself and not trust her any more than you have to, at least until she earns it."

"How am I supposed to know when that is?" Trevor muttered.

Since coming to work at the DCO, Trevor had had two partners—Ed and Jake. Trust had never been an issue with either of those men. It had just come naturally.

It was funny. He'd spent a good portion of his adult life living the life of spies and espionage, going undercover for months at a time to sniff out other people who were living the same way. Now his new teammate might be someone he couldn't trust.

"I'm not sure how you know when it's time to trust somebody," Adam admitted quietly. "I trusted my partner years ago when I worked for the DCO, and he ended up shooting me in the back. John trusted a lot of people, and it got him killed."

Trevor didn't know what the story was with Adam and his partner, but he certainly understood the reference to John's murder. The implications were clear. If he put his faith in Alina, and that faith ended up being misplaced, he was probably going to end up dead, too.

"I'll be in touch," Adam said.

"You might get a call in the next day or so from Seth Larson," Trevor said as the shifter headed for the door. "He's good with computers and security systems. In fact, I think he set up the security system at Chadwick-Thorn that Ivy and Landon had a problem with."

Adam lifted a brow, like he was waiting to see what any of that had to do with him.

"Anyway, the guy's in a tough situation, and I mentioned that you might be able to find him some work he could do from home," Trevor continued. "He has a kid with special needs he has to be around to take care of, you know?"

Adam regarded him for a long time before finally nodding. "I'll see what I can do to help him, but stop giving my number out like I'm your cousin who does plumbing work on the side, huh?"

With that, Adam turned and walked out.

As Trevor took another drink from his bottle of beer, he toyed with the idea of calling Adam in the middle of the night and leaving a message about a leaky toilet.

Chapter 5

"I DON'T CARE IF DICK SAID YOU'RE ALREADY CERTIFIED for fieldwork." Sabrina Erickson pinned Trevor with a look before turning her glare on Alina. "The two of you need to spend some time training together as a team before you get into the field and find out you have zero chemistry, because it'll be too late to do anything about it then. You're going to sweat now so you don't have to bleed later."

Beside Alina, Trevor grabbed his paintball gun from the table and grumbled something under his breath about hating training officers who spouted clichés. Alina hid her smile as she loaded her own paintball gun. Sabrina was a force of nature, that was for sure.

The woman had intercepted her and Trevor in the cafeteria an hour ago and joyfully informed them they'd be training all morning. Trevor had protested, saying he had some leads related to the bombing he needed to run down. Alina noticed he hadn't said *we have leads to track down*, which confirmed her assumption he planned to bail on her. Even though she knew there was a serious trust issue between her and Trevor, it still bothered her anyway. She hated not being trusted. It made her feel like the enemy. Like Wade.

The trim, athletic training officer hadn't batted an eye but simply smiled sweetly at Trevor and informed him that he could hunt down leads to his heart's content—after she was done with them. Something told Alina she was going to like this woman.

So they'd spent an hour at the pistol range, where Sabrina had each of them blaze through almost five hundred rounds of ammo with their issued sidearms, then come over here to the shoot house.

"You'll be doing a scenario involving a hostage," Sabrina explained.

Alina glanced up from loading another paintball. The black-and-silver gun had a long, slender barrel sticking out the front, a plastic tube full of bright-pink paintballs attached to the top, and a small bottle mounted below the handgrip. It looked like something out of a Star Wars movie and probably cost more than her car.

In all the time she'd been in the CIA, she'd never fired a paintball gun as part of her training. Hell, while she'd done a lot of tactical room clearance, she'd never taken part in any kind of hostage-rescue training either. That wasn't part of her normal CIA mission, so she'd never spent any time on it.

"Jaxson and Jake will be playing the part of the opposing forces," Sabrina continued. "You'll need to deal with them as well as any pop-up targets in the house in order to reach the hostage. The pop-up targets will make the alarms on your vests go off if you fail to take them out in time."

Trevor snorted, earning him a frown from the training officer.

"Something funny?" Sabrina asked.

He shrugged as he slipped a few extra tubes of paintball ammo into the cargo pocket of his uniform pants. "You realize I'm a shifter and that I can get through this scenario easily, right?"

Sabrina's lips curved. "Maybe, maybe not. We'll see. Besides, the objective for this training is for both you and your partner to make it through and rescue the hostage. If you get through but Alina doesn't, you start over. Teamwork—remember?"

Trevor scowled at that but didn't say anything.

"I'll be watching from the overhead catwalk," Sabrina called over her shoulder as she headed into the house. "The training event will start when the alarm rings the first time. If you haven't completed the course before it rings a second time, you fail and have to start over." She turned and gave them a pointed look. "By the way, keep your goggles on at all times. I wouldn't want anyone to lose an eye in there."

Okay, maybe she wasn't going to like this woman, Alina decided as she slipped her goggles down from her forehead. She got the feeling Sabrina had a trick or two up her sleeve for dealing with Trevor and his shifter abilities.

At first glance, the building looked like a normal, everyday house, albeit in need of a fresh coat of paint. Then Alina realized there were no windows on the second floor and that the glass in the first-floor windows was bulletproof. The walls were probably reinforced as well. She hadn't seen many tactical training shoot houses in the CIA. This kind of stuff was normally reserved for special operations forces. At least she and Trevor weren't using live ammo. That would have been a little crazy. Then again, crazy seemed to be kind of the norm around here.

After Sabrina disappeared inside, Alina turned to Trevor and held up the paintball gun. "What the heck do I do with this thing? I've never fired one before."

If Trevor was surprised by that admission, he didn't let on. "The gas pressure bottle under here propels the paintballs when you pull the trigger," he said, pointing it out with his finger. "The tube on top holds ten paint-balls. Think of it like a magazine and reload accord-ingly. People who do this paintball stuff seriously use containers that hold fifty to a hundred at a time, but the training officers rarely let us get away with that."

"I don't know why," she quipped. "I personally always like to have a lot more ammo than I think I'm going to need."

Trevor smirked but didn't laugh. "This is the safety. It operates just like the one on your normal sidearm. Just take the weapon off safe and pull the trigger when you're ready to fire."

Without another word, Trevor turned and headed for the door of the shoot house.

"Don't you think we should talk about how we're going to do this before we go in there?" she asked, hur-rying to catch up with him. "This could get ugly if we don't have a plan."

He shrugged. "I'll take the front of the room as we go in. You cover me and deal with the back side of the room. It shouldn't be that complicated. I'll be able to smell and hear Jake and Jaxson long before we get to them."

Alina opened her mouth to ask what the heck he expected her to do while he was sniffing around like a bloodhound when a loud buzzer went off.

Trevor lifted his foot and kicked in the door with the heel of his boot.

Alina cursed and followed him inside. The first room had three doors leading off in different directions but was otherwise empty. Before she could even begin to wonder which room they should start with—or why the hell the place smelled like a litter box that hadn't been cleaned in a week—loud music filled the house.

She did her best to ignore both the blaring techno beat and the god-awful stench, moving quickly to cover the blind spots to the left and right of the door they'd come in. It would have been a lot easier if she'd been working with a partner who was interested in communicating—and working as a team.

Fortunately, the first room was clear, so the fact that she had no idea which direction Trevor was going to move as he crossed the threshold didn't come back to bite them in the ass.

Alina shook off her irritation, waiting for Trevor to figure out which direction he wanted to go. He paused, and she assumed he was sniffing for a clue. There were three doors to choose from. But then she realized he was standing there with a pissed-off look on his face.

"What's wrong?" she shouted.

Trevor cursed. "It's Jake. The damn guy knows exactly how shifters work—me especially. Between the loud music and cow piss he dumped all over the place, he's taken away any advantages I have. I can't hear or smell a damn thing."

"Cow urine?" Frowning, she looked around and realized the floor and walls were suspiciously wet. "Okay, that's officially gross."

"The clock is ticking, people!" Sabrina called out from the dark catwalk above them. "Get a move on before you get the hostage killed!"

Alina looked questioningly at Trevor.

He shrugged. "I guess we do this the old-fashioned way."

Heading for the closed door on the far side of the room, he kicked it open, leaving her no choice but to scramble to catch up. She turned her attention to the right side of the room just as a man-shaped silhouette popped up from the floor with the picture of a bad guy with unkempt hair on it.

Alina aimed her gun and squeezed the trigger twice in rapid succession, popping the target right in the center of the chest with pink paint. She was thinking the gun was surprisingly accurate when two more colorful splats hit the same target, even though it was her responsibility.

She threw Trevor an irritated look just as a green paintball exploded in the center of his chest. She spun in the direction the shot had come from, only catching a brief glimpse of a dark-haired man as he jerked back around a corner and disappeared. A split second later, she felt something smack into her upper back.

Crap on a stick.

She didn't have to see the green paint dripping on the floor to know she'd been hit. All because she hadn't been paying attention to anything except how annoying Trevor was. Her new partner had gotten her shot!

"Don't bother starting over!" Sabrina shouted. "You haven't made it far enough even to count as a good beginning. Keep going."

Trevor growled and wiped his hand across the green dye painted all across his chest. His eyes were blazing yellow, and she could see the tips of his fangs extending over his lower lip as a rumble of anger continued to vibrate out of his chest.

He slammed his foot into the center of the next door, completely ripping it off the hinges and sending it flying across the next room.

Alina blinked. Apparently, Trevor had a temper. Well, at least after getting hit with a paintball. She couldn't blame him. She was damn pissed—not to mention embarrassed—they'd been taken out so easily.

She followed him but was once again forced to scramble to try and cover her partner, knowing the whole time she probably couldn't trust him to do the same for her. Instead of working as a team, they were two people trying to work through a shoot house scenario completely on their own.

As expected, the results were a complete disaster.

Alina and Trevor moved from room to room, so worried about Jake and Jaxson they missed nearly every pop-up target in the house. The damn alarm buzzer on her vest rang nearly nonstop, and on those rare occasions when she was able to focus on her surroundings enough to hit the targets, Jake or Jaxson would pop out of the nearest doorway and smack them with a green paintball.

"You two are never going to make it through this house unless you start to work as a team!" Sabrina cajoled from the catwalk. "You need to stop worrying about your own butt long enough to cover your teammate's back. That's the only way this is going to work."

Even though Alina knew Sabrina was right, she still had the urge to shoot a few paintballs in the woman's general direction on the off chance of hitting her.

On the upside, Sabrina didn't tell them to go back to the start. Why bother? They were doing so poorly, it wouldn't have helped anyway.

As she and Trevor continued to move through the house, they did a better job of shooting the targets, but when a flash of movement from the left caught their attention in the fourth room, both of them turned that way, leaving their right flank wide open again. Jake stepped out and popped both of them, then darted out of sight before either of them could react.

Alina let out a sound of frustration that rivaled Trevor's growls. She wouldn't have been surprised if Sabrina called a halt to the exercise.

By the time they reached the room where the hostage dummy was seated at a table with a picture of an angelic little kid taped to its face, Alina was more than ready for the training to end. She and Trevor needed a reset. Hell, they needed to get outside and talk over the possibility that they might be the worst team in the history of covert operations.

Alina was so focused on that, she didn't see Jake until he slipped up behind her and draped one arm around her shoulder and neck, yanking her back against him. At the same time, he put the barrel of his paintball gun against her head.

"Drop your weapon, Trevor," he called loud enough to be heard over the music. "You two are toast."

Trevor spun around, pointing his weapon in her direction. For a moment, Alina thought he was going to say the hell with it and start blazing away. But before her partner could decide one way or the other, Jaxson slipped into the room behind Trevor and pointed his paintball gun at Trevor's back.

"Drop it, Trevor," Jaxson said. "Seriously. It's over."

Trevor's eyes blazed bright with fury. He wasn't

the only one. She'd never performed this poorly in any training she'd ever attempted, not even when she was a rookie going through the academy at Quantico. She hated getting beaten like this, all because she and Trevor didn't trust each other.

This crap had to end.

Alina caught her partner's eye and held it. She and Trevor hadn't been working together long enough for him to read her body language, so she hoped he realized what she was doing. Because she flat-out wasn't going down without a fight. She was about to do something crazy, and if he didn't play his part, she was going to get a splat of bright-green paint to the side of the head.

She relaxed against Jake, like she was giving up. At the same time, she tossed her paintball gun to the floor, slightly to her left. Far enough away that it was out of easy reach but close enough for her to get to it when she had to.

The moment she felt Jake loosen his hold the slightest bit, she moved. No hesitation, no concern for what Trevor might or might not do. She just reacted, stomping down on top of Jake's right foot with the heel of her boot. At the same time, she brought the edge of her right hand down in a groin strike, whacking Jake in the balls. It wasn't as hard as she could have hit him—she didn't want the man writhing on the floor in pain—but it was enough to make him jerk away. Protecting the family jewels was as instinctive for a man as breathing.

Reaching up, she grabbed the hand he had draped over her shoulder, twisting it away from her body and torque-ing his wrist until she swore she heard it creak. He had no choice but to let her go…or let her break his wrist.

Alina lunged forward and to the left just as Trevor's

gun went off. Hitting the floor, she tucked into a roll then grabbed her paintball gun and came up shooting.

Jaxson had been caught off guard by her sudden move, and he wasted half a second trying to decide if he should shoot her or Trevor. That delay cost him. Alina came up on one knee and popped him three times in the chest.

She continued moving, spinning around to face Jake, not sure what she would find. But she was delighted to see him standing there where she'd left him, a fluorescent pink paint splat right in the middle of his forehead. He looked pissed.

She turned to confirm that Jaxson was down as well and found Trevor regarding her, his gaze both thoughtful and approving.

"See how well it works when you trust each other?" Sabrina called from the catwalk. "Took you long enough!"

Alina ignored the training officer, focusing on Trevor as he continued to study her intently. It was impossible to say how she knew it, but something had just changed between them.

"Don't stand there looking all impressed with yourselves!" Sabrina shouted. "Head back outside so we can see if you can be a team for more than ten seconds at a time. And Jake, wipe that paint splat off your face. You look ridiculous."

Alina and Trevor made their way toward the front door. As she screwed another pressure bottle onto the bottom of her paintball gun, Trevor motioned toward the building with his chin.

"How about we try something different this time?" he suggested. "You take lead, and I'll cover you."

She didn't answer right away, wondering if there was

going to be a catch. When there didn't seem to be one, she nodded.

"Okay. I can do that," she agreed.

Before she could say anything else, the start buzzer went off again.

Alina shoved open the front door with her shoulder, forcing herself to trust her partner. They moved from room to room much faster this time, dealing with pop-up targets and the occasional appearance by Jake and Jaxson. Sometimes, they missed a target and got dinged for it; other times, Jake and Jaxson got them. But throughout the whole thing, she and Trevor worked together and covered each other. By the time they rescued the hostage, she and Trevor were that much closer to becoming a real team.

It was crazy how good that made her feel, considering that, according to the director of the DCO, Trevor was the enemy.

—◊—

Trevor hadn't realized how hungry he was until he and Alina walked into the Pizza Place in nearby Dumfries and he breathed in the aroma of garlic and freshly made tomato sauce coming from the kitchen. Damn, he could eat a whole pie himself.

He and Alina had finished up training two hours ago, then spent another thirty minutes hanging around talking with Jake and Jaxson before getting cleaned up. Alina had been fine with grabbing something for lunch at the DCO cafeteria, but Trevor hadn't felt like sitting there while his coworkers stared at him like he was some kind of freak. Plus, this place made fantastic pizza.

Spotting an empty booth toward the back of the dining room, Trevor pointed it out to Alina, then gestured for her to lead the way.

The excellent food wasn't the only reason he'd wanted to get off the complex. He also wanted to talk to Alina in a setting a little more private than the cafeteria. This morning's training had made him curious about her. Once again, he had this crazy feeling he'd pegged her all wrong.

They both ordered iced tea when their server came over to drop off their menus. Alina glanced at hers for all of five seconds before looking at him.

"You want to split a medium pepperoni?" she asked, her expression hopeful.

"Let's make it a large," he said. "I'm pretty hungry."

Their server brought their drinks, then disappeared with their order, leaving an awkward silence in her wake. Trevor added sweetener to his tea, searching for the best way to start the conversation. Across from him, Alina suddenly seemed very interested in the old pictures mounted on the wall above the booth.

Damn, this was so much easier when he was teamed up with Jake and Ed. Then again, training with them had been a whole hell of a lot less difficult, too.

This morning had been ugly, at least at the start of the shoot-house exercise. He was man enough to admit that a good portion of the blame for that train wreck rested squarely on his shoulders. Yeah, he'd been thrown for a loop by Jake's trick with the noise and cow urine, but the biggest reason they'd done so poorly was because they'd flat-out refused to trust each other. With his shifter hearing and sense of smell taken out of the equation, he'd been dependent on Alina to watch his back as they'd moved through the house, but his suspicions of her made that leap of faith impossible.

It had taken Alina doing something extraordinary, like putting her complete faith in him and risking a paintball to the side of the head, to get him to realize he was being stupid. Dick might have hired her, but that didn't have to define her. Maybe that's what his gut had been trying to tell him. Maybe there was more to Alina than the job she'd been hired to do. While he wasn't ready to trust her completely, he'd at least give her a chance.

"I guess you like pizza, huh?" he asked lamely, finally breaking the silence that had gone from merely awkward to seriously uncomfortable.

Alina turned her attention away from the photos on the wall to give him a sheepish look. "Yeah. When I was growing up, Friday was pizza night at our house. Mom and Dad made a big event out of it, so I always associate pizza with family and good times." A smile curved her lips. "Now, it's my number one go-to comfort food. My freezer is stuffed full of them, and the front of my fridge is covered in magnets from all the local delivery places."

Trevor sipped his iced tea. He'd always considered pizza the ultimate food. "Were you being serious yesterday when you said your parents don't know what you do for a living?"

Alina's eyes sparkled with mischief as she shook her head. "I was just messing with you. Of course my parents know I worked for the CIA. Though to be truthful, they refuse to talk about it."

He was about to ask for details, but their server came

over with their pizza just then. It was an absolutely drool-worthy collection of cheese, pepperoni, and excess grease. In other words, perfect. The woman placed the big pizza on the table between them along with plates, utensils, and a load of napkins.

Trevor contained his curiosity about Alina's family while they each helped themselves to their first slices of pizza. He watched in amusement as she used some of the paper napkins to soak up the excess grease, then practically emptied half a bottle of Parmesan cheese on her slice.

"You plan on having any pizza with that?" he teased as she poked the slice a few times with a fork as if she thought that would help all the added powdered cheese stay in place.

Alina shrugged. "I like Parmesan cheese on my pizza. Is that a crime or something?"

"Nope, not a crime at all." He picked up his slice and took a few bites. "Back to your parents. What's the story behind them refusing to talk about you being in the CIA?"

Alina hesitated long enough to take a bite of her own pizza before answering. "My family is what you'd describe as politically active. They've been involved in state and city politics for generations. City council, state senate and assembly, state cabinet positions, campaign management and fund-raising—you name it, and someone in my family has done it. With my background, everyone assumed I'd go into politics, too."

He snagged another slice of pizza and sprinkled some Parmesan cheese on it. "You didn't want to?"

"Actually, I did. I never saw myself running for

office, but I thought about doing the behind-the-scenes stuff, maybe managing a campaign or working on some-one's staff. I even went to college for political science."

"How did you go from being a poli-sci major to join-ing the CIA?"

She ate a few more bites of her pizza, nibbling all the way down to the back of the slice but not eating the crust there. When she was done, she tossed the pizza bone to the side and got another piece, drowning it in powdered cheese.

"There was a small Agency recruitment effort on campus," she explained. "A lot of my friends didn't want to have anything to do with them, but I went and listened. This was sometime in 2003, and the intelligence failures of 9/11 were all anyone talked about those days. What they told me changed my entire outlook. I signed up a few months later and went straight into the CIA right after graduation. With my background, I thought I'd be doing analyst work, but I ended up in the field instead."

Trevor had still been in the army at that time and clearly remembered what those years following 9/11 were like. Those events had changed a lot of people's outlooks.

"What did your family think of your career choice?" he asked.

Alina sipped her iced tea. "My brothers and sister weren't thrilled, but they respected my decision. But when I told my parents I was joining the CIA, well, let's just say they were disappointed. I think they had visions of me running around the world, inciting coups, toppling governments, kidnapping people, and assassi-nating world leaders. There was a period of time in the beginning when both of them stopped talking to me."

Trevor winced. "And now?"

"It's better," she admitted. "But now, when I visit for the holidays, my profession is strictly off-limits. I don't talk about what I do, and no one brings it up."

Damn. That sounded really screwed up. "Must make for some tense dinners."

She laughed. "Not as bad as you might think. I love my family to pieces, but sometimes they act as if the real world doesn't exist. They're comfortable believing everyone and every situation, anywhere in the world, can be handled through reasonable political debate and a nice, civil voice. You and I both know that, sometimes, things don't work out like that. My family would simply rather not talk about those things. They're comfortable not knowing what I do, and I'm comfortable not telling them."

Alina might have seemed cool about the whole thing, but the slight elevation in her heart rate told Trevor she wasn't as chill with her family's opinion of her chosen career as she might try to suggest. He could get that. Family was family. If you knew they were disappointed in you, it was hard to act like it didn't matter.

"Are you from the DC area, or did you move here after the DCO hired you?" he asked.

"I grew up in Sacramento, but the Agency had me based out of DC for the past five years. I have an apartment in Del Ray, near Reagan National."

He reached for another slice of pizza. "Del Ray? That's practically at the end of the airport runway. You don't mind living near all that noise?"

She shook her head. "It's not that bad. I don't even notice it anymore. Besides, it was really convenient while I was in the Agency, since I practically lived in the airport."

He chuckled. "I feel ya. Sometimes I think it'd make more sense to live in an RV. That way, I could park it at the airport whenever I go somewhere. Any plans to move closer to the DCO training complex at Quantico so you won't have to deal with that morning commute?"

"No. I like my apartment, and my neighbor is my best friend. No way am I going anywhere." She shrugged. "Besides, I still have no idea if this gig in the DCO is going to work out. It would be stupid to move then find out I don't like the work that much." She motioned at him with her half-eaten slice of pizza. "How about you? Do you live near Quantico?"

"Yeah. I have an apartment in Woodbridge that I was lucky enough to get into called Kensington Place. I can stumble to my car ten minutes before work and still make it there in time."

She blinked. "I've heard of that place. It's kind of fancy, isn't it?"

"It's a little pricey, I admit. But shifters do get a bonus over the regular GS wage scale. The DCO actually found the place for me."

She laughed. "The perks of having fangs and claws, I guess."

Trevor didn't sense a trace of bitterness in her words, which was what he usually got from a lot of the other regular agents working in the DCO when they found out that the freaks got paid more than they did.

"Okay, now that you know all about me, what about you?" Alina asked. "How'd you end up in the DCO?"

He wiped his mouth with a napkin. "It's a long story."

She gestured at the pie in the center of the table. "We still have half a pizza left to polish off, so feel free to take your time."

"Well, in that case, I suppose I should start with the fact that I was born to be a cop," Trevor said, grabbing another slice.

Alina lifted a brow. "That seems like a tough burden to put on a newborn, don't you think?"

He chuckled. "I'm serious. My dad, uncle, all three of my brothers, and my sister are all cops in Portland, so I'm not exaggerating when I say my life was planned out for me. From the time I was ten years old, it was a given that I'd either go in the army and serve as an MP, then get out after my first tour so I could become a cop like everyone else in my family, or I'd go to the local junior college and get my associate's degree in criminal justice, then get a job as a cop like everyone else in my family."

Alina made a face. "Crap. And I thought my life had been tightly scripted out for me. That had to have been a little claustrophobic."

"Yeah, no kidding," he agreed. "But it turned out that in my case, I had even fewer options than that. See, I was a wide receiver for our high school football team, and I was good enough to get some attention from the local universities. I got a couple of looks from recruiters at both Oregon and Oregon State during my junior year, and everyone was talking a full scholarship if I could make it through my senior year without getting injured. I have to admit I was kind of psyched about going to a big school and playing in front of thousands of fans. Unfortunately, my mom and dad weren't planning on letting me get near any of the big schools.

They'd already locked their sights on Western Oregon University. It was only an hour and a half from home, and it offered a bachelor's degree in criminal justice and a full scholarship. Dad was practically salivating at the thought of his youngest son hitting the detective ranks before the age of thirty. So at that point, even the military was off the table."

"I'm hearing a *but* coming," Alina said, taking a bite of pizza.

"Yeah. It was definitely coming." He waited for their server to refill their teas and leave before continuing. "Because in between my junior year and senior year of high school, I went through my first shift. In a flash, my whole life changed."

Alina stopped chewing and swallowed quickly. "Wait a minute. I naturally assumed you were born a shifter. It didn't happen until you were seventeen? Did something happen to bring it on or whatever?"

"I *was* born a shifter, but shifter abilities usually don't start appearing until sometime in our late teens."

She nodded in interest, pizza apparently forgotten. "Did you freak out that first time?"

He snorted. "Hell yeah, I freaked. I thought I was turning into a werewolf or something."

"So how did it happen?" she asked, her eyes bright with anticipation. "Did you wake up in the woods naked under a full moon, or was it something really scary like finding yourself raiding the fridge and eating raw meat in the middle of the night?"

Trevor laughed. Those were exactly the kind of snarky questions he would have asked if she was the shifter and he was the curious normal guy.

"You watch way too many movies," he said.

Her cheeks took on a slight flush, and he had to remind himself this was his partner he was talking to, not a woman he was dating. That was tough to remember, since he couldn't help but notice how damn sexy Alina looked when she blushed.

"It wasn't anything that dramatic," he finally said, taking mercy on her. "I woke up in the middle of the night dripping with sweat. Every muscle in my body was worn out like I'd just finished running a marathon in full pads and a helmet. I went into the bathroom to throw some cold water on my face. Then I looked in the mirror and...well, I guess you can imagine how seeing fangs and claws could be a little tough for a seventeen-year-old to deal with."

"Did you tell anyone? Your parents or brothers or sister...a friend?"

He shook his head. "No. I thought I was turning into a monster. There was no way in hell I was going to tell anyone."

She frowned. "That must have been difficult to keep secret."

"Tell me about it." He washed a bite of pizza down with a swig of tea. "When you first shift, it can take a while to gain control. I was on the verge of sprouting fangs and claws whenever I smelled a girl, got nervous or frustrated or angry, even when I got hungry. I hid it the best I could and tried to act like nothing was going on, but everything went to crap when I showed up for football practice and blew past the fastest cornerback on our team like he was standing still." He shook his head, remembering it like it had been yesterday. "That's when I knew I couldn't play anymore."

"Why not?"

"Because someone would have figured out something was going on with me. Or assumed I was on performance-enhancing drugs. Plus, it seemed wrong playing football when there was no one who could keep up with me."

Alina looked at him in surprise. "Wow. That's a mature way to look at the situation for a high school kid. There'd be a lot of seventeen-year-olds who would have tried to take advantage of those physical abilities to make themselves look good."

"Yeah, that was me," he quipped, "very mature for my age."

"So what'd you do?"

"What could I do?" He transferred another slice of pizza from the tray to his plate, then reached for the Parmesan cheese. "I dropped out of football and started hitting the science classes pretty hard, hoping to figure out what the hell was happening to me. When that didn't work, I made the decision to get the hell out of town before anyone noticed how much I'd changed. I joined the army and headed to basic training the day after I graduated from high school. I signed up to be an MP, which was something of a consolation prize for my dad. My mom was a little freaked out, though. This was back when everyone thought Iraq was hiding nuclear and chemical weapons and the UN inspectors were being denied access to all kinds of suspicious facilities. Mom thought we'd be going back to war any day and was sure I'd get pulled into it. That didn't happen, but she was a mess at the time anyway."

"I think it's nice that your mother worried about you

so much." Alina's voice took on a wistful tone. "My mom knows what I do is dangerous, but since we don't talk about it, she treats it like a tree that falls in the forest."

"If there's no one there to hear it, did it really make a sound?" Trevor finished for her.

"Exactly." Alina sipped her tea. "How did you manage to keep your shifter side hidden in a whole unit full of MPs?"

"It wasn't as difficult as I thought it'd be." He took a bite of pizza, chewing before answering. "Being completely exhausted throughout basic training helped, but mostly, I got better at controlling both my abilities and my emotions."

"How long were you an MP?"

"A few years," he said. "As I got better with my abilities, I started getting good at figuring out when people were lying to me. They start sweating, their breathing gets all erratic, their heart rate spikes, their muscles tighten up—stuff like that. When I was assigned to Fort Carson in Colorado, I ended up catching a couple of high-vis bad guys, including a contractor who was trying to drive out the gate with a trunk full of classified documents. My commander put my name in for a transfer to CID—the army's criminal investigative command—and the next thing I knew, I was reassigned as an investigator at Redstone Arsenal, a big R&D base in Alabama, where they had me watching for civilians and contractors trying to steal government secrets."

"O-kay. Don't take this the wrong way, but that sounds boring as hell."

"Some of my coworkers thought it was," he admitted. "But for me, it was always about getting into that other person's head and trying to figure out what they were going to do before they even decided to do it. Besides, my dad was over the moon about it. He figured I'd get out of the army soon, and he'd be seeing a detective in the Maxwell family in the very near future."

"I hear another *but* coming," she said.

Trevor chuckled. "You're getting good at this. Yeah, my skills got me noticed by some people in DC, and I was transferred to the Defense Intelligence Agency without ever being asked whether that was something I wanted to do. I was put on a team responsible for tracking down traitors selling military intelligence and the foreign agents trying to recruit them."

"So basic counterespionage and counterintelligence?"

He nodded. "Yup, spy versus spy."

She continued eating. "What did your dad think of that?"

"He wasn't thrilled. I liked it, though. Up until that point, I'd been limited to one little base, waiting for a government employee to do something stupid. But with the DIA, I went all over the world, anywhere there was a threat against the Department of Defense. I enjoyed the freedom to pursue just about anyone I wanted. And as a shifter, I was very good at finding those people."

"What changed?" she asked. "How did you end up in the DCO?"

"What changed? Nothing really. That was the issue." He shook his head. "No matter how many criminals I caught, no matter how much good I did, I knew in the back of my mind that I could never be myself. I was a freak, and I could never let anyone know it. I was alone in a sea of people. That was a shitty thing to have to live with, and there was a part of me that was unhappy as hell. I was seriously close to saying *screw it* and moving back to Portland to be the cop that my parents always wanted me to be."

"And then?" Alina prompted.

"And then John Loughlin found me." Trevor tried to ignore the stab of sorrow that came with saying his boss's name but wasn't very successful. "He found me and helped me realize that I wasn't a freak, that there were other people like me, and that I didn't need to keep living in secret. It was the most amazing thing anyone had ever done for me."

Alina's face clouded. "And then someone killed him."

He swallowed hard. "Yeah. Someone killed him. The only reason I'm still at the DCO is so I can figure out exactly who did it and make sure they pay."

Chapter 6

ALINA FIDGETED IN THE PASSENGER SEAT OF THE BIG Suburban as Trevor waited for an opening in traffic, then changed lanes. It was well after rush hour, but I-95 was still packed.

"Does the dress fit okay?" he asked, glancing at her.

She fought the urge to squirm again. "Yeah. It fits fine. It's just that this is the first time I've worn a dress like this on a mission. I'm so used to working in pant-suits that wearing a dress feels…odd."

Not that she was complaining about the dress. A shimmery, black evening gown with a sexy neckline and a little slit up the side that showed off just enough leg to be interesting without being over the top, it was probably the most gorgeous dress she'd ever seen. Normally, she would never have worn anything like it on a mission, but Trevor said she needed to look the part for the undercover role they were playing that night, so she'd agreed, even though she didn't have a clue what the hell they were up to this evening.

All she knew for sure was that they were heading to Baltimore and that almost no one else in the DCO—most especially their boss—knew what they were doing. Why the hell she trusted Trevor so much was a shock to her, but the shoot-house training they'd done yesterday had demonstrated they could be good together—when they trusted each other.

Trevor looked over at her, eyeing her up and down before turning his attention back to the freeway with a shrug. "If it helps, I think you look frigging awesome."

She appreciated the compliment probably more than she should have, but that didn't keep her from pointing out the obvious. "Mind telling me why you get to wear a suit and tie while I have to wear something that shows off more than it covers?"

He glanced at her again. She didn't miss the way his gaze lingered on the nice amount of cleavage she was displaying before he met her eyes.

"Well, for starters, my suit would be way too big for you," he said. "For another, I think I'd look absolutely ridiculous in that dress. Finally, there's a good chance that a distraction will be called for during this mission." He gave her another once-over that had her skin warming alarmingly. "And trust me—you are definitely one serious distraction."

She felt her face heat and was glad it was nighttime. Until she remembered Trevor could see in the dark.

"Speaking of where we're going," she said, "don't you think you might want to let me in on the big secret? Since I was nice enough to wear this dress for you and all. I'm trying to trust you here, but that's hard if you're going to keep me completely in the dark."

Trevor was silent for so long, Alina thought he wasn't going to answer. She wouldn't have been surprised. He'd been completely mum on the subject the whole time a behavioral scientist who worked for the DCO named Skye Durant had picked out Alina's disguise for the mission. She'd been too busy being amazed that the DCO had a clothing and prop department that included expensive cocktail dresses to press him on the subject then, but she couldn't contain her curiosity any longer.

"We're going to an out-of-the-way restaurant near the Inner Harbor called the End of the Road," he finally said. "The place pulls in enough business to make the establishment look legit, but the restaurant is a front for a high-stakes gambling operation that they run out of the back of the place."

She thought about that for a moment, replaying everything she'd learned on their trip down to Bowling Green on Wednesday, then combining it with what Trevor had told her yesterday over pizza.

"Something tells me we won't be looking for the fugitive shifters and their teammates playing poker in this backroom joint," she said.

Trevor didn't look at her. "No. We're looking for the man I think built the bomb that killed John. My sources say he likes to gamble there."

Clearly, Trevor had no intention of going after his fellow shifters. Apparently, he didn't believe they had anything to do with John's death.

"Any chance Skye and that nerdy guy I saw her talking to might be your sources?" Alina asked.

Trevor didn't answer her.

No shock there. Trevor was obviously going behind Dick's back on this manhunt for the bomber who'd killed John, which was almost certainly going to get him into trouble if the director ever found out. If Thomas Thorn really was behind the bombing, that trouble might just be of the fatal variety for everyone involved. If Skye and that guy—who was definitely an analyst type if Alina had ever seen one—were the ones passing Trevor his intel, her partner struck her as the kind of man who would do anything to protect them.

The fact that Trevor didn't want to talk to her about any of this meant he was worried she'd run off and tell Dick. After yesterday's training, he might trust her more than he had before but apparently not enough to put anyone other than himself at risk.

Even though she understood why he'd do that, it still hurt a little. She couldn't help wondering if he was simply being careful out of habit or because he knew Dick had cornered her in the main building this morning.

The director had waylaid her the moment she'd walked in the door, pulling her into his office and grilling her for over thirty minutes about what exactly she and Trevor had done down in Fredericksburg on Wednesday and why she hadn't reported to him already.

Since she hadn't been able to come up with any convenient lie—and knowing he'd check up on anything she'd said anyway—Alina told him they'd gone to Bowling Green and talked to Seth Larson. She'd done a good job of downplaying the whole thing, making it seem like Trevor had simply been looking for proof that one of the shifters had been around John's office at some point prior to the explosion. Dick had been curious about Larson, but Alina had kept her answers vague. She didn't want to make trouble for Larson. He already had it hard enough.

"I want to know when Trevor takes a piss," Dick said, fixing her with a stern look. "Don't forget why I hired you, Agent Bosch."

The mere thought of spying on her partner had Alina twisting anxiously in her seat again.

"You sure that dress isn't bothering you?" Trevor asked. "Is it chafing or something?"

She couldn't help but laugh. "No, it's fine. Trust me, dresses this expensive don't chafe."

He threw her an amused glance as he turned off I-95 onto 395, getting closer to the Inner Harbor. "I just figured maybe there was something under the dress that was too tight, or...I don't know...pinching somewhere."

That went to show how little men knew about what women had to go through to look this good. "Sorry to burst your bubble, but with a dress this formfitting, wearing panties isn't an option."

Trevor glanced her way, his eyes automatically going to the juncture of her thighs. He looked away quickly, like he didn't want her to realize where his mind might have been, but it was a little late for that. The heat she'd seen there—and the little flash of yellow glow if she wasn't mistaken—gave him away.

Beside her, Trevor suddenly seemed very interested in something in his side view mirror. Knowing he was attracted to her should have pissed her off. What kind of work relationship could they build if he saw her as a woman instead of a partner? But for some reason, she couldn't quite muster up as much outrage as she probably should have. In fact, she found his attraction to her...interesting. Definitely something she was going to have to talk to Kathy about.

As Trevor turned off the interstate and hit the side streets a little while later, she realized he was still checking his side mirror as well as the rearview every few seconds. Then she recognized the same gas station they'd already passed. Trevor was driving in circles and checking his mirrors to see if they had a tail. She checked her side mirror but didn't see anything suspicious.

She was about to ask if he did when he suddenly turned into the parking lot of the Horseshoe Casino and began driving up and down the rows of parking spaces. She glanced over her shoulder to look behind them but still didn't see anyone.

"Are you lost and refusing to ask for directions, or are you worried we picked up a tail?" she asked, turning back around.

She wasn't sure who the hell might be following them, but if she had to guess, she'd say it must have been someone Dick sent to keep an eye on them. That wasn't good.

"I don't think anyone's following us, but I wanted to make sure," Trevor said, pulling out of the parking lot. "As far as getting lost, you don't have to worry about that. As a shifter, it's genetically impossible for me to get lost."

Alina was still wondering if Trevor was serious or not when he turned onto a street called Worchester and headed toward an area near the train tracks that looked a little run-down. Surprising, considering they weren't all that far off the main thoroughfare. They kept going until the road ended in a big parking lot in front of an equally large industrial building. Looking at it, you'd never know the place was a restaurant if it hadn't been for the glitzy lights along the front and a big neon sign proclaiming it to be *The End of the Road*. Looked like a dive to her.

There were more fancy cars in the parking lot than she expected to see. Even a few limos that looked seriously out of place. As did the two big guards standing by the front door wearing suits that were working overtime in their attempt to cover up all the muscles and the handguns both men were carrying in underarm holsters.

"You're telling me the police never realized what's going on around here?" she asked Trevor.

He pulled into a parking space and turned off the engine. "I'm sure they know. But as long as no one causes problems, they apparently look the other way."

Alina nodded. On some level, that made sense.

Beside her, Trevor flipped down the visor and adjusted his tie in the mirror. Damn, he looked good in the expensive silk suit Skye had picked out for him. And the light stubble along his jawline made him look even better. Then again, she'd always had a thing for guys with scruff.

"Who's this guy we're looking for, and why do you think he's connected to John Loughlin's death?" she asked.

"These days, he goes by the name of Doug Smith." Trevor reached into the backseat, coming up with a thin manila folder. He flipped though the file until he came out with a photo of a man in his early forties with dark hair sprinkled with a little bit of gray.

"His real name is Dokka Shishani," Trevor continued. "He's from Chechnya, where he fought for years in the Chechen-Russian conflict. It's also where he learned his trade as a bomb maker. He moved to the States in 2008, becoming a naturalized citizen in 2014. Since then, he's been implicated in a few assassination-style bombings in South America and Asia, but nothing that's ever stuck. He does a good job blending in with the local Russian community, which must be hard as hell considering how much Chechens and Russians dislike each other."

Alina had spent some time over in Chechnya during the early part of her career in the CIA. The war there had devastated the country for nearly twenty years, and it was just now starting to crawl out from under the massive destruction. It was a tough place to live but an even tougher place to get out of.

She picked up the picture and studied it, committing the man's face to memory. "With a background like his, I'm surprised he was allowed through immigration. The State Department normally would have flagged somebody like him long before he ever got a green card."

"You'd think so, wouldn't you?" Trevor agreed.

Stepping out of the SUV, Trevor came around to her side to open her door. She took the hand he offered her, telling herself that she did it simply because the guards might be watching. But as she slipped her right leg out of the SUV, flashing a good amount of thigh, she admitted to herself that maybe she did it because it gave her a chance to get a rise out of him.

And yeah…he looked. All the way from thigh to ankle and back up again.

"You really do look amazing in that dress," he murmured, pushing the door closed.

"You look pretty damn good yourself," she said as she rested one hand on his arm and let him escort her across the parking lot. She actually appreciated the assist. It had been a while since she'd worn heels this high. She was out of practice.

"You were saying something about how our guy got through immigration?" she prompted softly.

Trevor's mouth twitched. "I do remember vaguely saying something about that. Before you derailed my train of thought."

She laughed. Damn, he could be seriously smooth when he wanted.

"It turns out Mr. Shishani had a sponsor with enough power to pull the right strings," Trevor explained. "That sponsor got our guy in the country with limited State Department review, accelerating his naturalization paperwork and getting him through in record time."

Alina noticed the two guards watching them as they approached the front doors. The muscle-bound suits were eyeballing them so hard the building could have fallen down behind them and they probably wouldn't have noticed.

"And what's the connection between this guy and John?" she asked.

Trevor stopped, turning to look at her. "None between Shishani and John, but the guy who sponsored Shishani and got him into the country? Yeah, there's definitely a connection."

She blinked in surprise. "You're saying Thomas Thorn brought a Chechen-born bomber into the United States and paid him to kill John Loughlin?"

Trevor didn't answer but merely started for the entrance again. The guards opened the doors for them without a word. Once they were inside the little hallway that led to another set of double doors and the restaurant beyond, he stopped.

"There's no indication Shishani ever came onto the training complex, but he definitely had the know-how to make the bomb, and the attack matched his style perfectly. Throw in his connection to Thorn and the fact that he's been spending money like it's going out of style the past few weeks, and that makes him somebody worth checking out."

Alina let that sink in for a moment. "I would have preferred to hear some of this stuff before we'd gotten here, but for now, let's assume everything you think you know is right. What do you hope to get out of this guy? I'm pretty sure we're not going to get a spontaneous confession from him."

Trevor shrugged as he motioned her forward and opened the door for her. "I can be very persuasive when I want to. You'd be amazed what you can get out of people when you say *please*."

Alina would have called him on that, but the smell of cigar and cigarette smoke hit her so hard, she couldn't breathe, much less talk. So much for a smoke-free Maryland.

She scanned the bar along the right side of the room, then the booths on the left, and the tables and chairs filling the space in between. Beyond the bar, she could see a nondescript door, which could just as well have led to a storage room or an office if it wasn't for the big, muscle-bound bouncers standing on either side of it.

"What's the plan here?" she asked Trevor quietly as the restaurant's patrons eyed them curiously. "Because I don't see anyone warming up to us enough to invite us into the back room."

"We're Trevor and Alina Hoffman, a filthy rich, newly married couple from Silicon Valley," Trevor said, glancing around as if taking in the ambience. "We've been on an extended honeymoon for the past few months and are currently heading for a trans-Atlantic cruise out of New York City. We decided to do some gambling and got tired of dealing with all the crap at the local casino."

"You think they'll buy that?" she asked as he led her across the room toward the door with the guards.

"You sell the fact that we're a newly married couple, and I'll make them believe I'm a rich guy with a gambling addiction."

She could do that. Then she realized one big flaw in their cover story. "If we're a newly married couple, shouldn't I be wearing a ring?"

Trevor gave her a sidelong glance. "What makes you think you aren't?"

She looked down at her hand in confusion and almost fell off her stacked heels as she saw the monstrously large diamond he'd somehow slipped onto her ring finger when she wasn't looking. Oh crud, it was huge! And as beautiful as any she'd ever seen.

"When did you put this on? More importantly, is this thing real?" she whispered.

Thank goodness she had his arm to keep her steady. She was feeling faint at the idea of wearing a diamond that was probably worth more than her entire apartment.

"I put it on you when we were married on the first of June in Monaco," he whispered back. "And of course it's real. I would never put something fake on the love of my life."

"Trevor, I'm serious," she said.

He made a face. "Okay. I slipped it on your finger when I was helping you out of the SUV. And yes, it's real, so don't lose it. I had to sign my life away to get it out of the DCO safes."

She gulped. "How much is it worth?"

"Nothing compared to you, sweetheart," he said in a romantic tone as they stopped in front of the two guards.

The bouncers working this door were a little bit more professional than the ones outside.

"Can I help you?" one of the men asked in a deep, rough voice that made Alina wonder if he chewed gravel for fun.

"Someone told me a man might be able to find a friendly game of poker somewhere near here," Trevor said casually. "I don't suppose you two might be able to point my wife and me in the right direction for a game like that?"

The two men regarded him suspiciously.

"I think you're talking about the Horseshoe Casino," Gravel said. "It's nearby, very clean and friendly."

Trevor chuckled. "The Horseshoe is very friendly. But the place doesn't have the quite the atmosphere we're looking for. It's a little too…what's the word?… sanitized for our liking."

Gravel studied Trevor for a moment, then glanced at the bar, giving someone there a nod. Ten seconds later, a slim man in an expensive suit appeared at their side.

"My name is Teddy," he said in a cautious yet friendly tone. "What can I do for you?"

"I'm Trevor Hoffman. This is my wife, Alina. We're getting ready to head out on a cruise in a few days and decided to do some gambling while we're in town. Someone told us this place runs a clean game, so I thought I'd spend some money here."

Teddy surveyed them with a practiced eye, taking in the cut of Trevor's suit and her expensive gown, not to mention the big honking ring she wore. He must have liked what he saw, because he nodded.

"If I could get some identification and a credit card from you, Mr. Hoffman, I can quickly check your credentials and set you up with a line of credit."

Alina tensed as Trevor handed over the requested ID and credit card. They could be in trouble. The fake ID and credit card by themselves would have taken quite a bit of time and money to pull off. Coming up with an Internet background to support that would take even longer.

"What are they going to find when they run your name and that credit card number?" she whispered as he slipped his arm around her and casually urged her away from the two men guarding the door.

"Relax." He flashed her a grin. "They'll find us with all the relevant financial and societal tidbits one would expect to see when looking at the rich and bored."

She glanced at Teddy. He typed something into a computer just out of sight behind the bar. A moment later, he lifted his head and frowned in their direction.

"Something's wrong," she whispered.

Even the two guards were eyeing them funny now. She was starting to wish she had a weapon. If things went bad, they were in trouble.

"Alina," Trevor said softly as he tightened his arm around her waist and tugged her closer. "Now's the time for you to sell the newlywed thing."

She opened her mouth to ask him exactly how he suggested she do that when he pulled her even closer.

She wished she could have said it was years of CIA training that took over and made her kiss him. But that wouldn't have been true. Instead, it was a totally different kind of instinct. The kind that made a woman want to kiss a hot guy.

She weaved her fingers possessively into his dark hair, parting her lips and inviting his tongue in to play. Trevor slid one hand down her back, molding her so tightly against him she could feel the outline of every muscle in his amazing body.

"Mr. and Mrs. Hoffman."

It took a minute for Teddy's voice to register, and when it finally did, Alina reluctantly stepped away from Trevor. She swayed a little on her feet, suddenly breathless. If Trevor's arm hadn't been around her, she might have melted into a puddle on the floor. She'd never been affected by a kiss like that before.

Teddy smiled at them. "I've started you with a hundred-thousand-dollar line of credit. If you step this way, security can clear you. Then I can take you in so you can start enjoying your evening."

I was already enjoying my evening, Alina thought.

Trevor looked at her, his mouth curving into a sexy grin, as if he'd been thinking the same thing.

Teddy and the two guards might have thought the flickering yellow glow that rimmed Trevor's eyes was a reflection of the light. But Alina knew better. As he stood there gazing at her while the guard waited with the handheld metal detector, she couldn't help but wonder what that flash of gold had meant.

—ww—

Trevor couldn't believe how badly he wanted to bail on the mission and spend the rest of the night kissing Alina. He'd thought she was attractive the first time he'd seen her, but holding her in his arms and feeling her body against his, knowing she wasn't wearing anything underneath that dress, damn near made him burst into flames.

But then he remembered he might be only a few feet away from the man who'd built the bomb that had killed John. He couldn't let this opportunity to get something on Thorn slip away, not after all the work Skye and Evan had done to track Shishani down. He owed John that much at the very least.

He took a deep breath and got his inner animal under control. He hadn't been quite sure about bringing Alina with him tonight, but Skye had convinced him that he stood a much better chance of getting into the place with the cover she'd concocted. Flat-out, a lone man trying to weasel his way into a private gambling establishment was an uphill battle, no matter how rich he was supposed to be. Besides, Skye had already created their fake identities and set everything up. According to her, it had been too late to change the plan. Trevor was pretty sure she'd been working him.

In the end, though, Trevor hadn't needed anyone to twist his arm to get him to go along with the plan. His head still wasn't a hundred percent sold on his new partner, but his gut told him to trust her.

"Just hand your credit chit to the dealer at the first table you choose," Teddy said as he escorted them into the private gaming area.

Trevor thanked the man, fighting back the growl clawing its way out of his throat as Teddy gave Alina a long, lingering look before he walked away. The urge to rip the guy's face off for having the balls even to lay eyes on her was so strong, his claws actually extended.

He cursed under his breath and forced them back in. His animal nature was merely trying to lay claim to someone who didn't belong to him. Alina was his partner, not his wife. That kiss, amazing as it had been, had just been part of their cover.

"Chill the hell out," he muttered to himself.

"What was that?" Alina asked, raising her voice to be heard over the cheering at the nearest craps table.

"Nothing," Trevor said. "I was just saying it's nicer in here than I imagined."

She turned slightly to survey the room, giving him a nice glimpse of cleavage. Couple that with the intoxicating pheromones she was putting off, and it was enough to make his inner coyote howl.

Get a fucking grip! What the hell is going on in your head?

"Is that him?" Alina asked, pulling Trevor out of his daydreams.

Trevor dragged his gaze away from her and looked over to see Shishani standing at one of the craps tables, dark eyes intent on the bets his fellow gamblers were placing while he sipped the drink in his hand.

"Do we keep an eye on him until he leaves, then follow him?" Alina wanted to know.

Trevor shook his head. "No. As much as he likes to gamble, he could be here until this place closes. I sure as hell don't feel like waiting around that long to talk to him."

"You have a better plan?" she prompted.

"Yeah, I do. One that revolves around you and your distracting beauty."

She grimaced. "I hesitate to ask."

Trevor gave her a smile as he reached into the inner

pocket of his suit jacket and came out with two very fancy-looking pens. She watched curiously as he turned toward the wall so the security cameras couldn't see what he was doing, and started taking the pens apart. One held a tiny vial…like one of those tubes that sample perfumes came in. The other contained a tiny piece of plastic, not much bigger than the eraser on a pencil.

"Don't worry. It's nothing too extreme. Which, I admit, is rather disappointing for me." He motioned off to the left with his chin. "The restrooms are down a hallway over in that direction. At the end of that corridor is an emergency exit. As you can imagine in a place like this, the hallway is covered by cameras, and the door is heavily alarmed."

He held up the small piece of plastic. "Step one of the plan involves me planting this device in the hall-way. When I activate it, it will momentarily pause the cameras and trip a piece of software code in the security system that will disengage the door lock and alarm. Once I activate the device, it should give us about thirty seconds to get Shishani out the door and into the alley out back."

"Nice toy," she murmured, looking at the tiny device. "But I have a question. How are we going to get Shishani into that hallway so we can get him out the door?"

Trevor held up the small glass vial. "That's where this—and you—come in."

"You want me to drug him?" she asked in confusion. "Don't you think security will get suspicious when Shishani starts stumbling around as we lead him toward the restroom?"

Trevor chuckled. "It's not that kind of drug. It's a

powerful diuretic designed to make him have to go to the bathroom really badly—as in really, really badly. We simply need to follow him casually down the hall when that happens and take him right out the back."

"Not a bad plan. You need me to slip the drug into his drink?"

Trevor shook his head. "I can do that. I need you to distract him—and anyone else who might be looking our way—long enough to let me do it."

She looked doubtful. "What if I can't distract him, or anyone else, long enough for you to slip it in his drink?"

Trevor arched a brow as he slowly scanned her up and down. "Something tells me that's not going to be an issue. If anything, you'll have so many guys after you, we'll never make it to the back hallway without a bunch of them following you like lovesick puppies."

She laughed. "You're really good for a girl's ego, you know that?"

"Just one of the many services I provide." He flashed her a grin. "You ready to go work your way close to him at the craps table while I slip off to the bathroom and plant this device? It will be easier for you to get close to him if I'm not with you at first."

"Okay," she said. Giving him a smile, she flipped her long, red-gold hair over her shoulder and headed for the table and the man who had almost certainly made the bomb that had killed John.

Trevor followed, then turned toward the back of the club and the security bug he needed to set up. The sooner he did that, the sooner he could get back here and keep an eye on Alina, because suddenly, the idea of leaving her alone anywhere near Shishani didn't sit well with him.

Chapter 7

TREVOR COULDN'T BELIEVE ALINA HAD BEEN CONCERNED she wouldn't be able to distract Shishani—and most of the other men around the craps table. All she had to do was smile and laugh at Trevor's quips, and she had almost every person around looking her way. When Alina turned and asked the table in general why a certain bet had been made, it was insanely simple to step closer to Shishani and slip the drug in his drink.

From that point forward, it was simply a waiting game, though he had to admit he didn't like the way their suspect kept leaning over to try and engage Alina in conversation. Yeah, she wasn't really his wife, but Trevor still had a nearly uncontrollable urge to rip the man to shreds. And no, it had nothing to do with being this close to one of the men responsible for John's death.

He took an almost perverse pleasure in watching Shishani squirm when the drug started kicking in. A minute later, the man excused himself from the table and made a beeline for the bathroom. Alina gave Trevor a questioning look, but he shook his head. Let the guy do his business first. They'd grab him as he was coming out of the bathroom.

Trevor purposely made a lousy bet, then announced he was going to try his hand at roulette, grabbed Alina's hand, and headed for the nearest table. Halfway there, he veered toward the back of the club instead.

Trevor activated the bug the moment he and Alina stepped into the hallway, and Shishani stepped out of the men's restroom. Fortunately, there was no one else in the corridor or anywhere nearby, which would make this a whole lot easier.

The man's eyes lit up when he saw Alina, but then his expression changed to one of confusion when he saw Trevor, too. The crazy urge to renovate the man's face reared its ugly head, and it was all Trevor could do not to snarl.

Keeping his inner coyote in check, Trevor walked straight up to the bomber and wrapped his hand around the back of the man's neck, slinging Shishani face-first into the opposite wall. It wasn't hard enough to knock the guy out, but it was enough to knock a dent in the sheetrock and send Shishani bouncing backward like a pinball. Alina had the door open by the time Trevor grabbed his arm and shoved him out into the night.

The alley behind the building butted up against a high fence that separated this part of Worchester Street from the train tracks. It was pitch-black and reeked of spoiled food, spilled beer, and nasty Dumpsters. One end of the alley led toward the parking lot, while the other meandered through trash and other junk.

Trevor dragged Shishani a little farther down the alley so no one peeking out of the club would see them. Alina hung back and kept an eye on the door just in case.

He thumped Shishani up against the wall of the building, behind a tall Dumpster that smelled like it was used to store zombie bait for the coming apocalypse, and gave the man a shake.

"Wakey, wakey, Mr. Shishani," he said. The guy

might not be unconscious, but he was so woozy he might as well have been. "Time to talk about a bomb you recently made."

The man's eyes fluttered open, and he looked at Trevor in confusion for a moment. Then his eyes went wide.

"I don't have any money," he said in a damn good imitation of a Northeast accent. No wonder he'd blended in so easily after coming here from Chechnya.

Trevor wrapped his hand around the man's neck and lifted him off the ground, holding him pinned to the wall. "Don't bother pretending you didn't hear what I said, Mr. Shishani. I'm not buying it."

Shishani mumbled something that sounded like okay, but with his hand around the guy's neck, it was hard to tell.

Trevor let the guy slide down the wall. "Talk."

Shishani threw Alina a desperate look. "Lady, you have to help me. I was just smiling at you. I had no idea your husband was the jealous type. I swear I don't know who this Shishani guy is you're looking for. My name is Smith…Doug Smith."

Trevor growled softly and picked Shishani up by the throat again, holding him there while Alina moved closer.

"You might as well kill him. He's not going to talk," she said calmly. "No one will find him for weeks back here. They certainly won't smell his body, that's for sure."

Shishani's dark eyes widened as Trevor continued to hold him prisoner. When Trevor dropped him this time, the man was much more cooperative.

"What do you want?" Shishani asked. "I don't even know who you are. I haven't done anything to you."

"You didn't do anything to me, but you did do

something to a friend of mine," Trevor growled. "You built a bomb that killed a federal agent near Quantico a month ago. I want to know who paid you."

The man's eyes bulged as he shook his head. "I can't talk about that. It would get me killed."

Trevor tightened his grip on the man's throat again but didn't lift him off the ground this time. Beside him, Alina made a show of looking down at her shoes like she was worried she was getting something nasty on them.

"You might be killed if you talk, but you definitely won't be making it out of this alley if you don't," Trevor said. "Your call."

Shishani glanced at Alina to see if there might be some help coming from that direction. When that didn't work, he threw a quick look at the parking lot at the end of the alley. No luck there, either.

"Okay, okay. I made the bomb," the man admitted. "But I swear I didn't plant it. I didn't even know who the target was. I got a call on the Sunday before the bombing and was told that I'd be given a large sum of money if I could build a powerful bomb—fast. When I said I couldn't do it quickly because I had no explosives, I was given the address of a warehouse near Woodbridge. When I went there, I found C-4 plastic explosives, blasting caps, and electronic parts. They were all military-grade material. The best I've ever worked with. I didn't sleep for three nights so I could get it done in time and finished just before I got a call early on Tuesday morning. I delivered the finished bomb in an empty copier paper box to a facility near Quantico. Then I went home. I didn't know that the bomb had been used to kill someone who worked for the U.S. government until later the next day. Even then, the news did not say who the person was, just that it was someone who worked there."

"Who did you deliver the bomb to?" Trevor demanded.

It had been one thing when he'd *thought* Shishani had made the bomb. Now that he *knew* for sure, it was difficult not killing the piece of shit on the spot.

"I never saw who picked it up," Shishani said. "I dropped it off behind the visitor's center just outside the gate. There was no one in the parking lot when I left, so I have no idea who took it."

"Who paid you for the bomb?" Trevor asked, his voice coming out in a barely disguised growl.

Shishani looked like he was about to waffle, but whatever he saw in Trevor's expression must have changed his mind.

"It was Thomas Thorn." He wet his lips. "I have done many jobs for him over the years. He pays well. He would likely pay you, too, if you keep your nose out of this."

Trevor glanced at Alina. She looked stunned. He couldn't blame her. It was one thing to suspect a man like Thorn, but to have actual proof was something else entirely.

"Thorn won't be paying me anything," Trevor announced. "Because we're going to take you straight to the nearest federal attorney's office, and you're going to tell them everything you just told me. Word for word."

Smith shook his head wildly. "I'm not going to do that. It would be suicide!"

Trevor was about to point out that not testifying would be suicide as well, but before he got the chance, the back door slammed open, and heavy footsteps echoed on the ground. He cursed, pissed that he'd been so focused on Shishani that he hadn't paid attention to what was going on inside the club. He barely had enough time to breathe before four big bouncers raced around the side of the Dumpster, their hands on the weapons holsters behind their backs, their bodies tense and ready for violence.

The sight of Alina standing there in her fancy cocktail dress slowed them for a moment, but then Shishani cried out for help.

Trevor cursed as the armed men whipped out their pistols. It would have been a lot easier if he and Alina had been carrying weapons, but there was no way they would have gotten them past the metal detectors. That meant he had to improvise.

Grabbing a handful of Shishani's suit jacket, Trevor spun around, tossing the man at the bouncers, knocking two of them down in a tangle of arms and legs and sending the other two backpedaling to avoid going down in the heap. The two bouncers on the ground fired their weapons, sending bullets zinging around the alley.

Shit.

Knowing he had to move fast, Trevor shifted, allowing his claws to slip out a little bit so he had at least something to fight these trigger-happy psychos with. He was about to launch himself at the men on the ground when he caught sight of one of the other bouncers turning his big handgun in Alina's direction.

Twisting that way instead, he lunged forward with a growl, slashing at the man's arm, tearing through the suit fabric and slicing the flesh underneath open to the bone. The man cried out and immediately dropped his weapon. Trevor kicked him in the chest, sending him flying backward to bounce off the fence. The man's head hit one of the metal support poles with a thud, and he dropped to the ground, out cold.

Trevor spun to face the other bouncer who was still on his feet, worried he'd shoot Alina, and found her kicking the guy's ass. She'd obviously ditched her high heels at some point, because she was barefoot as she spun and lashed out with her lèg, the slit in her gown making it easy for her to pull off the complex Taekwondo move. Even so, the urge to run to her defense was nearly impossible to ignore. When she planted her heel in the center of the guy's face, Trevor decided she had the situation under control. He turned to deal with the two men he'd left sprawling on the ground a few moments earlier and found one of the bouncers pointing his weapon straight at him.

Trevor jumped to the side just as the man fired, avoiding a fatal gunshot but still feeling a line of fire cut across the right side of his rib cage as the bullet grazed him. Letting out a growl, he charged forward, closing the distance between him and the asshole before the guy could get off another shot.

He could easily have laid the man's throat open, but he didn't. The guy was simply out here doing what he thought was his job, even if it was for an illegal gambling operation. So instead, Trevor closed his hand into a fist and popped the guy a blow across the jaw that staggered the big man. Before the guard could collect himself, Trevor grabbed him and tossed him toward the Dumpster. The man hit the heavy metal bin so hard it slid a couple of inches, then he dropped to the ground unconscious.

The last remaining bouncer must have decided the

odds didn't look so favorable anymore, because he turned and hightailed it for the back door of the club.

Alina started to go after him, but Trevor caught her arm. "Forget it. Let's get Shishani, and get the hell out of here before anyone else shows up."

She nodded. But when they turned to look for Shishani, they found him lying on the ground where Trevor had tossed him earlier, a single bullet hole through the center of his chest. Their chance to put Thorn away had died along with him.

"Fuck," Trevor growled. "A stray round from one of those trigger-happy buffoons must have hit him."

Alina crouched to check the man's pulse anyway. A moment later, she stood up. "Do we call the cops?"

Trevor shook his head. "We can't. It would tip off Thorn to what we were doing. As bad as it sounds, we need to bail. Chances are the police will never find out about this. Dead bodies aren't exactly good for business, and this isn't the kind of establishment that can handle the scrutiny of a murder investigation. In an hour, this place will be cleaned up, and the body will be gone. It will be like none of this ever happened."

Alina didn't seem thrilled with the idea of leaving, but there wasn't much else they could do. Nodding, she started down the alley, slowing only long enough to pick up her discarded heels and tiny evening bag.

Trevor looked down at Shishani's body. He couldn't find it in himself to care that the man was dead. His bomb had killed John. But he was pissed to be back at square one in his search to pin something on Thorn. Almost pissed enough not to notice how badly the right side of his rib cage burned.

As he turned and jogged down the alley after Alina, a realization struck him. He'd assumed *he* was back to square one, but after tonight, maybe it was time to start thinking about *them* being back to square one.

Alina reached for her door handle the moment Trevor pulled into a space in front of her apartment complex. She was still annoyed at him for hiding that he'd been shot. She'd only realized it because he'd grabbed a T-shirt from the duffel bag behind the seat and pressed it to his ribs.

"It's just a scratch," he'd insisted when she asked how badly he was hurt.

The amount of blood on the T-shirt said otherwise. Ignoring the fact that he was driving, she'd reached across the center console and yanked his jacket open, then pried the makeshift compress away from his ribs so she could see for herself. It was a hell of a lot more than a scratch. His white dress shirt was soaked with dark red blood. She'd wanted to head for the first hospital they could find, but he'd refused.

"The doctors would immediately recognize it as a bullet wound and call the cops," Trevor said. "There's no way I could explain how I ended up this way, and even if I could, I wouldn't want to risk word of it getting back to Dick or Thorn. I promise I'll be fine. I'll fix myself up once I get home."

Then he'd told her that his idea of fixing himself up included pieces of old T-shirts and duct tape.

"No, you're not," Alina had said. "We're going to my place, and I'm going to bandage you up."

The moment Trevor put the SUV in park, she was out and heading for the driver's side. She needn't have bothered. He was already coming around to meet her like he wasn't injured at all.

"Couldn't someone at the DCO complex have looked at you?" she asked as they headed upstairs to the second floor. "They have doctors and a medical facility there, right?"

"Yeah, but again, I can't go there without taking a risk that Dick or Thorn would hear about it."

Alina shook her head. Trevor had some serious trust issues, bordering on paranoia. But if all this stuff they were learning about Thorn was true, maybe he had good reason to be paranoid. She only hoped she wouldn't get him upstairs to find out that his injuries were worse than he thought. Then what the heck was she going to do?

They made it upstairs without running into anyone. Once on the second floor, she practically tiptoed passed Kathy's door, praying Molly didn't smell her and want to come right over. That was all Alina needed, a curious Kathy asking all kinds of complicated questions while Molly jumped around like a crazy dog, wondering who the hell this new guy in her apartment was.

"Take off your jacket and shirt," she ordered as soon as they were inside. "I'll get the first aid kit."

Trevor headed into the kitchen, shrugging out of his jacket as he went, while she darted into the bathroom. Her supplies weren't anything a military medic would be impressed with, but there was definitely a lot more stuff than would be found in a typical home first aid kit.

When she hurried into the kitchen a few moments later, she found Trevor over by the table, attempting to wipe the worst of the blood off his torso with the remains of his expensive button-down.

Alina stopped, transfixed by the sight of her partner standing there with his shirt off, blood oozing from a long horizontal gash along his right side. For a second, she flashed back to an image of Fred lying in her arms, blood soaking through his shirt as he bled to death. That visual shook her so hard, she could barely breathe. Cursing under her breath, she got a grip on herself. Her partner was bleeding, and she needed to help him.

"Don't bother with that," she said.

Taking the bloody shirt out of his hands, she dropped it in the trash can. It was ruined beyond all possible repair.

She grabbed a hand towel off the hook by the fridge and soaked it under the faucet, then pulled a chair out at the kitchen table and sat.

"Move closer," she instructed. "Let me get you cleaned up and see how bad this wound is."

"I'm fine, Alina. The guy barely nicked me," Trevor protested but obeyed. "Most of this blood is from right after it happened. It's probably already stopped bleeding."

"Right," she muttered as she gently began cleaning the skin around the gash across his ribs with the washcloth.

Damn, it looked more like he'd been torn open with a dull chainsaw blade than hit with a bullet. It must have skipped along the muscles and bones instead of going straight through. She supposed that was a good thing. Still, the slice seemed deep. Any rational person would have been in an emergency room right now, demanding sutures and pain meds.

Trevor was right about one thing, though. The worst of the bleeding had stopped. If anything, it looked like the gash was actually starting to seal itself with new flesh. That was hard to believe, considering how severe the wound had been. She'd never been one to get queasy at the sight of blood, but since her partner was the one bleeding, it got to her a little more than usual.

"Talk to me," she said as she used the towel to wipe up a fresh dribble of blood running down his lower ribs. "So I don't have to think about what the hell I'm doing."

"What would you like to talk about?" he asked. "Other than my inability to avoid getting shot, I mean."

She couldn't believe he was cracking jokes. "I don't care. Anything."

When he didn't respond, she decided to ask him about something that had been on her mind ever since she'd seen the way he moved tonight.

"Why don't you tell me about what else you can do as a shifter? I'm not sure why, but I'd assumed that your abilities were limited to keen senses, claws, and fangs. But after seeing you fight, I'm guessing there's more to it than that?"

He shrugged, making the gash start bleeding again. "You've pretty much seen the majority of what I can do." He paused as she tossed one bloody towel in the trash and grabbed a fresh one. "Beyond all the enhanced senses, I'm faster than a normal person, both in speed and reflexes. I'm stronger than someone twice my size, and I can take a lot more punishment as well as heal faster. Within a couple of hours, this"—he pointed at the wound—"will be closed up completely, and in a few days, it'll look like it's months old. It won't be long before you'll have to know it was there to even find it."

"That must come in handy," she said, wishing like

hell her teammates in the CIA had been shifters. Maybe some of them would still be alive.

"I won't lie and say my healing ability hasn't saved my ass a time or two," he admitted. "But I try to use my coyote instincts to keep from getting into screwed-up situations in the first place. Trust me, I'd much prefer to be clever and tricky and not get shot at all."

"I'm all for that," she agreed.

Thankfully, the gash had stopped bleeding for the most part. It was still painful looking, but she breathed a sigh of relief knowing he was going to be okay.

"So what happened tonight?" She tossed the second towel in the trash and picked up a third to clean off the dried blood from the rest of his torso. "Why didn't your coyote instincts for trouble keep you from getting hit?"

"I don't know. I guess I was a little distracted."

Trevor didn't elaborate. Then again, he didn't need to. Alina was well aware of the fact that he'd taken a bullet because he'd been worried about one hitting her. She'd seen him jump to take out that big guard as the man had been about to shoot her.

"Thanks for covering my back," she said softly. "I know you got hit because you were more worried about me than yourself, so...thanks."

He shook his head. "Don't worry about it. We're partners."

Trevor might have been making light of what he'd done, but Alina appreciated it more than she could put into words. She hadn't had a real partner since Turkey, and it wasn't until now that she realized the biggest thing she'd missed was knowing she had someone who'd watch her back.

Tears suddenly filled her eyes, and she forced herself to finish cleaning off the dried blood on Trevor's
stomach. It was while she was absorbed in the meticu-
lous task of wiping down every square inch of exposed
skin that she became aware of the fact that he was an
extremely fit man. It was hard to miss when her face was
only inches from his very well-defined abs.

Well, she'd been looking for something else to
focus on so she wouldn't start crying, and Trevor was
definitely a distraction. Her partner had the body of a
Roman god, with shoulders, pecs, and arm muscles that
made it obvious he worked out a lot. But he also had
that lean, ripped look to him that make her think more of
Tarzan than a weight lifter. And the way those rippling
abs disappeared into his beltline, showing off just the
sexiest hint of happy trail was definitely interesting.

As she lightly traced the wet towel back and forth
across his lower abs and that absolutely mouthwater-
ing trail of manliness, it dawned on her that she was
in a somewhat compromising position. Seated in front
of Trevor, her hand inches from his belt buckle and
the very obvious bulge in his dress pants, thoughts
of tending to his wound suddenly took a backseat to
the memories of what it had been like kissing him
tonight. And the stuff she was remembering weren't
the kind of thoughts she should have been having
about her partner.

Alina knew it was supposed to have been a fake kiss
as part of their cover, but if it had been fake, then her
real sex life clearly sucked, because she'd never been
that turned on from a kiss in her life. She'd actually
gotten excited from a thirty-second make-out session in

the middle of a crowded club, which was completely crazy. She wasn't a teenager. She wasn't supposed to get all tingly from a simple kiss. If they hadn't been on a mission, she could only wonder how far she would have been willing to take things.

Crap, she was getting tingly all over again, simply thinking about Trevor's lips on her. Not to mention the feel of his strong, muscular body under her fingers.

Strong, muscular body under her fingers. Say what?

Alina gave herself a shake and discovered that at some point, she'd tossed the last washcloth in the trash and was running her hands back and forth across Trevor's drum-tight abs, getting damn close to the danger zone around his belt buckle.

"I'm pretty sure you've gotten all the blood off," Trevor said from above her.

She jerked her hands away as if he were on fire. Which, she guessed, he kind of was. Because she was definitely going to get burned if she kept playing this game. And he definitely hadn't missed her unprofessional grope fest.

She didn't dare look up at him as she took out a handful of sterile pads and a roll of gauze bandage from her first aid kit. Knowing she was probably blushing furiously, she kept her head down and focused on wrapping the stretchy gauze tightly around his ribs. But focusing was harder to do than she imagined, because she was getting turned on as hell. She was more aroused than she'd been in a really *really* long time.

What the hell was wrong with her?

She'd never been the kind of woman to go all gaga over a guy, no matter how hot his abs happened to be.

Yet here she was in front of her partner, telling herself it wasn't okay to hump his leg or yank open his belt buckle.

She determinedly forced her hormones back under control. Thankfully, Trevor had no idea what he was doing to her. She would have been mortified if he'd known how turned on she was.

Alina finished the wrap, then added some surgical tape to keep everything in place. Whether she wanted to or not, it was time to stand up and look her partner in the eye.

"I think we're good here," she said softly as she rose to her feet.

Trevor stood there, barely a foot of space between them, his naked chest and shoulders so close that it was hard not reaching out and touching them. His dark eyes were thoughtful, and Alina waited for him to say something snarky...or teasing.

He didn't do either of those things. Instead, he stepped a little closer so all those spectacular chest muscles were mere millimeters away from her breasts.

"We certainly are good here, aren't we?" he said, his voice warm and smooth, like melted chocolate, almost making her melt in return.

Alina's breath hitched. Trevor was going to kiss her. Just like he had back in that club in Baltimore. Except this time, there wasn't anything to interrupt them.

Chapter 8

ALINA DIDN'T CARE THAT KISSING HER PARTNER WAS crazy. Telling the tiny rational voice in the back of her head urging her to be cautious to shut the hell up, she placed one hand on that beautiful chest of his, licked her lips, and prepared to meet his lips head-on.

Then the door to her apartment opened, immediately followed by the sounds of running doggy feet.

Trevor had already stepped back a few inches by the time Molly rounded the corner and raced into the kitchen in her exuberant fashion. Catching sight of Trevor, she stopped cold with the oddest expression Alina had ever seen on her dog's furry face.

"You decent in there?"

Kathy came around the corner…and stopped cold with the oddest expression Alina had ever seen on her friend's nonfurry face.

"O-kay, apparently not," Kathy said after a few moments, one brow arched high as she took in Trevor's naked chest, Alina's sexy dress, the bandages around his torso, and the scant distance between the two of them.

"Should I come back later?" she asked coyly. "Like in the morning, with two cups of coffee and a box of doughnuts?"

Alina forced out a laugh. "Very funny, Kathy. But it's not like that."

Kathy nodded slowly, still looking pointedly at her. "No?"

"No," Alina insisted. "Trevor got a little nicked up while we were working tonight, and I was applying some first aid."

"Uh-huh," Kathy said, giving her a knowing look.

That was when Alina realized her hand was still resting casually—even possessively—against Trevor's chest. Refusing to let her friend see her squirm, she slowly took her hand away from all that muscle.

"You two have obviously figured this part out, but to make it official, Kathy, this is my new partner, Trevor Maxwell. Trevor, this is my best friend, neighbor, and long-term dog sitter, Kathy McGee."

"That's Kathy with a *K*," her friend said, not even trying to hide the fact that she was blatantly ogling his naked upper body as she stepped forward to shake his hand. "It's so nice to meet you finally. I've heard a lot about you. Though I must admit, in the stories Alina told me, you were fully clothed."

"Kathy!" Alina said. "Are you trying to embarrass me to death in front of my partner?"

Her friend held up her hands in mock surrender. "Okay, okay. I'm just having a little fun. Sheesh. Remember, I work from home, so I don't get a chance to see half-dressed men that often."

Alina wanted to ask if that disappointing fact included Kathy's boyfriend, Armen, but decided not to go there. Kathy very well might tell them more than they really wanted to know.

Silence descended over the crowded kitchen, and for a moment, Alina was worried Kathy might open her unfiltered mouth and say something else completely inappropriate. Fortunately, Molly chose that moment to point out that no one had bothered to introduce her to the new man in the room, so she walked up and wedged herself firmly in between Alina and Trevor, looking at him with her head tilted sideways in obvious confusion.

"This is Molly," Alina said. "She's my fur baby, though she spends most of her time with Kathy."

As Trevor squatted down to ruffle her dog's ears, Alina wondered if Molly had somehow picked up on the fact that there was something different about him... that he was a shifter. It definitely seemed like it. Molly sniffed Trevor's hands like crazy in between regarding him with a clearly baffled expression, as if her nose and eyes were telling her two different things.

Regardless of Molly's confusion, it was safe to say she was captivated by Trevor. Even after he stopped petting her and stood up to slip back into his suit jacket, Molly sat there in front of him, her tongue hanging out in joy and her tail wagging a hundred miles an hour.

I feel you, Molly. There's definitely something about him that really gets to you, isn't there?

Alina caught movement out of the corner of her eye and saw Kathy wander over to take a look at the first aid kit still on the kitchen table. Fortunately, the last towel she'd tossed in the trash had been relatively blood-free and covered up the worst of the mess in there. Kathy would lose her mind if she saw all that blood.

"I've heard rumors about the federal government running on a tight budget these days, but don't tell me they expect you two to provide your own medical care?" Kathy asked.

Trevor chuckled. "No. I could have gone to the hospital, but the paperwork would have been horrendous. I didn't want to deal with it, since it was a little scratch. I was going to ignore it, but Alina wanted to bandage it up."

Kathy laughed. "Well, at least she's getting some use out of the kitchen. It's not like she cooks in here."

"That's not true!" Alina protested. "I cook."

"I'm not talking about the kind of cooking I just walked in on," Kathy said. "I meant the kind with food, pots, and pans. And before you say it, poking the buttons on the microwave doesn't count."

Alina's mouth fell open, not sure if she was more offended by Kathy's sly sexual innuendo or the fact that her best friend had just outed her complete lack of cooking skills. She was about to blast Kathy with a snappy comeback—as soon as she came up with one—only to be interrupted by her partner.

"So, Kathy, you take care of Alina's dog every day, even when she isn't traveling? How do you pull that off and work too?"

Kathy smiled. "I work from home, so it's not a big deal."

When Trevor returned her smile with one of those roguish grins of his, Alina thought her friend might melt right there on the spot.

"Do you telecommute or own your own business?" he asked.

"Kathy owns her own business," Alina answered quickly. Her friend didn't like to talk about how she made a living. "She sells socks on the Internet."

Trevor looked back and forth from her to Kathy and back again, as if he expected one of them to start laughing and say, *just kidding*. When neither of them did, he turned to Kathy.

"Socks...seriously?"

"Yes. I sell socks on the Internet," Kathy admitted, slightly indignant, before turning to shoot Alina a vindictive glare. "And I'll have you know that I sell a lot of them, thank you very much."

Trevor glanced at Alina, who shrugged. "I have to admit, she's right about that. As crazy as it sounds, she makes a buttload of money selling socks."

"So how exactly does one get into the sock business?" he asked Kathy, his face completely serious. Which was a good thing, since Kathy could get rather irate if she thought people were ragging on her chosen line of work.

"Purely by accident," Kathy explained. "A couple of years ago, I went to this outlet center down near Potomac Mills specifically to buy these thick, warm socks that I loved. They were cozy to wear around the house or in bed but were also perfect with the shoes I wear. I'd go through a dozen pairs a year, I wore them so much."

Trevor frowned in confusion. "Okay, not seeing the start of a thriving new business yet."

Kathy held up a finger. "I'm getting there."

He leaned back against the kitchen counter, a move that only served to tighten his abs and make him look more delicious than ever. And yeah, Kathy noticed. She almost lost her place in the story as her gaze was drawn to that rippling display of muscles just above Trevor's belt.

What was it about tight abs that did it for almost every woman on the planet?

"So," Kathy continued, "I go to this outlet store I'd been going to three or four times a year only to find out they no longer sold my favorite socks. I completely freaked! And I wasn't the only one. There were three other women there who were as upset as I was. But the manager of the store said the company discontinued the entire line and told me there was nothing she could do about it."

"That must have been traumatic," Trevor said, still somehow managing to keep a straight face.

"It was," Kathy agreed, apparently not noticing how hard Trevor was fighting to keep from grinning.

"So I came home and ended up finding the socks I liked online being made overseas. The only problem was that I had to buy in bulk—a hundred pairs. I was desperate, so I bought them, figuring I could sell some of the extras to other people I knew who loved the socks as much as I did. Those friends and acquaintances ended up buying every single pair I'd ordered before they even arrived. So I ordered more, and people bought those, too. The next thing I know, I'm quitting my day job so I can stay home and sell socks on the Internet." She smiled. "Honestly, I couldn't do any of it without my boyfriend, Armen. He's the one who makes most of the deliveries to UPS."

"He drives a minivan," Alina pointed out, not because she thought Trevor would be interested in that fact, but because she liked to tease her friend about it.

"What's wrong with minivans?" Kathy demanded.

"Nothing at all," Alina said before turning to Trevor with a mock whisper behind her hand. "She won't admit it, but I think Kathy has a thing for guys who drive minivans."

Kathy rolled her eyes. "Oh yeah. Minivans really get me going. And guys who drive minivans? You just can't get any hotter than that."

They all laughed at that, then talked a little more about minivans, socks, and working from home before

Kathy announced she needed to head back to her place and get some work done before she went to bed.

"Besides," she added with a smile, "I'm sure you two would probably rather get back to what you were doing before I interrupted."

Alina laughed, but now that she thought about it, having Trevor all to herself again might be fun.

"See you in the morning," Alina said to her friend as she held the door open for her. "I'll drop Molly off at the normal time."

"Really?" Kathy whispered as she stood in there in the doorway, glancing at Trevor, who was still in the living room playing with Molly. "Any chance you two might, you know, sleep in a little late tomorrow?"

Alina wasn't sure how to answer, especially considering the fact that Trevor had probably heard every word of it. Finally, she shook her head and went with the safe response, just in case.

"Like I said. Trevor's my partner. It's not like that."

Kathy nodded but didn't seem convinced. "We'll see."

Alina closed the door and turned to find that Molly had hopped up on the couch and assumed her normal comfy position to one side of the cozy sectional. But this time, instead of staring at the TV waiting for Alina to turn it on, her fur baby was staring intently at both of them, apparently waiting to see what was going to happen next. Alina had to admit, she was curious about that, too.

Trevor walked over to meet her as she crossed the living room, and for a second, she thought her partner was going to sweep her into his arms. But instead, he stopped a few paces short and nodded toward the door.

"I should be going, too. I have to get up early to

make it up here in time to pick you up and get us to work on time."

She was confused for a moment, not sure what he meant by that. Then she remembered her car was still down at the DCO training complex in Quantico, nearly an hour away. Crap, she'd completely forgotten that.

"You sure you don't might driving up here to pick me up in the morning?" she asked. "The traffic coming north will suck if you're not here early."

He grinned and took a step closer, and suddenly, the possibility of a kiss coming her way was back on the menu.

"I don't mind," he said softly. "Something tells me I'm not going to get a lot of sleep tonight anyway."

Her breath caught at the implication in his words. She guessed he'd been having more than a few unprofessional thoughts of his own this evening. For some insane reason, that made her happy.

She licked her lips, ready for what she was sure was coming next, when Trevor's damn cell phone rang.

Crap, if they were interrupted one more time, she was going to scream.

Trevor growled as he pulled out his phone. He glanced at the number, frowning as he answered it.

"Hold on a second," Trevor said. "Alina's with me. Let me put you on the speaker."

A moment later, Seth Larson's voice came over the phone. "You gave me your number and said I should call if I needed to. Well…I needed to."

"What's wrong?" Alina asked. "Is Cody okay?"

"Yeah, he's okay, just a little freaked out. Earlier tonight, some thugs from the DCO came to visit. They were real assholes, asking me all kinds of questions regarding what you and I talked about, what I'd seen that morning, who else I might have talked to."

"What'd you tell them?" Trevor asked.

"As little as possible. I mentioned you guys thought I might have seen something the morning of the bombing, but I told them I didn't see anyone. I didn't even bring up the employee photos you sent to me. I kind of got the feeling you wouldn't want me to say anything about it."

"That's good," Trevor said. "Did Cody have a problem with them being there?"

On the other end of the line, Seth sighed. "Yeah. They got a little physical with me, and Cody didn't handle it well. It took two hours to calm him down."

"I'm sorry, Seth," Trevor said, his jaw tightening in anger. "I didn't intend for any of this to come back on you."

"I know. Don't worry about it. We'll be okay. The only thing that bothered me is that they showed up at my place. How did those guys know you'd come to see me?"

Trevor looked at Alina. "I'm not sure, Seth. I guess the information must have fallen into the wrong people's hands."

Alina winced. It was obvious Trevor had a good idea where those thugs had gotten their information. She'd told Dick, and Dick had sent some goons down there to check out her story. She hadn't told Dick anything specific, but it had been enough to put Seth Larson on the man's radar.

She was angry at herself, but more than anything else, she was disappointed. It sucked knowing she was the reason those men had shown up and scared Cody. And it double sucked that Trevor, a partner she'd been getting closer to by the minute, was looking at her like she'd betrayed him.

"Hey, before you get the impression that it's all dark clouds and spilt milk," Seth added in a lighter tone, "I also called you to say I talked to that friend of yours. He lined me up some pretty cool IT work. He's even going to come in and set up a home office with a secure computer network for me. It sounds like a pretty sweet deal, so I just wanted to say thanks. I really appreciate it."

Trevor's mouth edged up. "I'm glad to hear that. If anyone has earned the right for something good to happen in their life, it's you."

Seth didn't think that was true, but he said he wasn't going to turn down the job offer regardless. "I'm too desperate to stand on principle."

They talked for another minute or two, then Seth hung up after promising to let them know if anyone else from the DCO showed up. Alina expected Trevor to immediately ask her who the hell she'd told about Seth. He had every right to. She'd screwed up.

But he didn't say a word. Instead, he gave her a nod and headed for the door, his face an expressionless mask. That was ten times worse than anything he could have said to her.

"See you tomorrow morning?" she asked as he turned the knob.

He hesitated for a moment but didn't look back at her. "Yeah, I'll be here."

Then he was out the door and gone, leaving Alina feeling like ten pounds of crap as she wandered over and collapsed on the couch beside Molly. Her fur baby put her head on Alina's lap with a sigh, as if she completely understood what Alina was going through.

"What the hell am I going to do, girl?" she whispered. "I was hired to figure out if Trevor was a bad guy, but right now, I'm the only one betraying anybody."

Molly lifted one brow, then the other, apparently as torn as her human happened to be. Clearly, there wouldn't be any advice coming from her canine companion.

Alina sat there caressing Molly's fur and trying to figure out what the heck she was going to do. She'd spent the past three years hating Wade for betraying her team, and yet here she was, doing the same thing. No, she hadn't gotten anybody killed, but she still felt like crap on a stick.

She was still staring restlessly at the wall when she heard her phone ringing from nearby. It took her a moment to remember she'd tossed her little purse on the couch when she and Trevor had come in. She looked around and realized that Molly was lying on it.

After yanking the purse from under her, Alina dug out her phone, hoping it was Trevor. But it wasn't her partner. It was Dick.

Alina groaned. She'd completely forgotten Dick said he wanted updates from her every night. Her thumb hovered over the green button, but she just couldn't tap it. Between kissing Trevor, confirming Thorn's involvement in the bombing, seeing their witness to that fact die right in front of them, then discovering Dick had sent men to harass Seth, there was no way in hell she was going to tell her new boss anything.

She let the call go to voice mail, then stood. She was exhausted and needed to get cleaned up before going to bed. She doubted she'd get much sleep, but she might as well try.

"Come on, Molly. Let's get ready for bed. If nothing else, at least I can watch you sleep."

———∽∽∽———

Tanner wasn't sure if the preseason football game he was watching on the TV in his DCO dorm room was happening in real time or whether it was a replay. Considering it was nearly one in the morning, it had to be the latter. Not that it mattered. It wasn't like he was paying attention to the game anyway. As usual, he was thinking about Zarina.

He ran his hand through his mane of dark-blond hair and took another long drink from his fourth bottle of Mountain Dew for the night. While there were no bars on the windows or padlocks on the door of his small efficiency apartment, he was as much a prisoner here as Sage was in her cell. The only difference was that his imprisonment was self-imposed. He could walk away at any time, but for reasons he was only now starting to explore, he stayed here surrounded by people who considered him to be little more than a monster.

At first, he'd told himself it was so he could get a handle on the hybrid rages that happened whenever he got angry. To be truthful, he'd succeeded in that. Until this most recent slipup with Sage, he hadn't lost it in months. But instead of leaving, he'd convinced himself if he stayed a little longer, Zarina might actually find a way to rid him of his animal side. It was a long shot, but it allowed him to justify staying.

Staring at the TV now, his mind a thousand miles away from the football game, he finally admitted it wasn't his control issues or the cure for them that kept him here. It was Zarina. And the fact that he loved her so much it hurt.

Tanner took another swig of soda and glanced at the big throw pillow Zarina liked to hug when she curled up on the couch and watched TV with him. While their nightly get-togethers were frequent, no one would call them dates. But he enjoyed the time they spent together, even if all they did was talk about football and why anyone would play a game where the men in the striped uniforms were throwing their hankies on the ground all the time—Zarina's words, not his. It was fun and casual and made him feel like he was a normal guy.

He was anything but normal, though. It was about time for him to accept that and move on with his so-called life, so Zarina could move on with hers. And he needed to do it sooner rather than later.

He was still considering that when he heard footsteps outside his door. For a crazy half second, he thought it was Zarina. His heart beat faster at the possibility, but then his hybrid instincts took over, calculating the weight of the person from the heavy thud of their foot-falls and their height by the interval in between strides. It was a tall man, wearing dress shoes. A moment later, he picked up Trevor's scent.

Tanner was off the couch and across the room before Trevor could even knock. As he opened the door, he was about to point out it wasn't a good idea for people to see them together, but one glance at the coyote shifter's face, and he changed his mind. The guy looked like shit.

He took in the suit Trevor wore, his nose wrinkling at the whiff of fresh blood coupled with the subtle flowery scent of a woman's perfume.

"Nice fashion statement, dude," Tanner remarked as Trevor walked in. "Don't think I've ever seen anyone wear a suit without a shirt. I'm pretty sure it's not going to catch on."

Trevor didn't answer but simply flopped down on the couch.

"I'd offer you something alcoholic, because you sure as hell look like you could use it," Tanner said, closing the door. "But Zarina thinks it's a bad idea to mix hybrid and booze. So the best I can do is a Mountain Dew."

"That's fine," Trevor said.

Tanner grabbed two bottles of soda from the fridge, then handed one to Trevor before taking a seat on the other couch. When he'd first come to the DCO, he and Trevor rarely crossed paths, mostly because Trevor and his counterespionage team had always been on missions. Since John's death, they'd both committed themselves to helping their friends who'd been implicated in his murder as well as finding the real killer, so they'd become friends in addition to allies.

"Shitty night?" Tanner asked.

He knew Trevor had gone to Baltimore to look for a person who might have info on the bomb that killed John but not much more than that.

"You could say that." Trevor opened the bottle of soda and downed half of it in a few big gulps. "I had the guy who made the bomb right in my hands. He came out and admitted Thorn paid him to make the device and deliver it to the visitor's center at the main gate of the DCO on the morning of the explosion."

"Which confirms our worst fears, that someone who works with us picked up that device and put it in John's office."

Trevor shrugged. "Yeah. Unfortunately, a bunch

of muscle-headed bouncers from the club came out
and thought we were robbing the guy. The idiots got
trigger-happy and killed him before he got a chance to
tell anyone." He shoved a hand through his dark hair
and let out a growl of frustration. "I had Thorn's balls
right in my fucking hand, then it all went to shit."

"Is that how you got shot?" Tanner asked.

Trevor nodded. "Yeah. I got distracted at the wrong
time, and one of the d-bags creased my ribs. It's nothing."

Distracted wasn't a word Tanner would usually associate with his friend. Trevor was the kind of man who
seemed to be able to focus on the details in the middle
of the biggest shit storm.

"Alina okay?" Tanner prompted.

"Oh yeah, she's wonderful. Peachy, in fact."

Tanner wasn't the most perceptive guy on the planet
when it came to picking up nonverbal cues, but even he
figured out something was going on here.

When he asked, Trevor was silent for so long, Tanner
thought he wasn't going to answer. Finally, his friend
took a deep breath and took the plunge.

"Alina isn't turning out to be the person I thought
she was."

Tanner wasn't sure if that was good or bad.

"I thought she was supposed to spy on me and tell
them everything I'm doing," Trevor continued.

"Now you don't think so?"

Trevor let out a short laugh. "Oh, she's almost certainly reporting back to Dick. Two days after we talked
to Seth Larson, Dick sent someone to rough him up and
find out what he knew. The only way Dick could have
known about Larson is if Alina told him."

Tanner frowned. "Okay, so you've confirmed that she's a spy for Dick."

Trevor shook his head. "Yeah, but you should have seen the look on her face when she realized I'd figured out what she'd done. She seemed genuinely contrite, like she knew she'd made a mistake."

Tanner lifted a brow.

"I know what you're thinking." Trevor held up his hands. "That she's playing me. I admit, the thought has crossed my mind more than a few times. But I do this spy-versus-spy thing for a living. I usually know when people are playing me. I'm telling you, something else is going on with Alina. Sometimes it seems like she's actually on our side."

Now Tanner was even more confused. Either Alina was working with Dick, or she was one of the good guys. "Speak English, would you? What the hell are you saying?"

Trevor told him what happened at the club, saying he and Alina had fought well together, and how she'd brought him back to her place to fix him up afterward.

"If she was simply doing Dick's dirty work, she didn't need to do any of that. Hell, she could have let those guys kill me," Trevor added. "My gut's telling me that while she might have told Dick about Larson, she had no idea what he was going to do with that information."

"That doesn't mean she's on our side," Tanner pointed out.

Trevor turned back to the TV, his breath coming out in a rush. Tanner was tempted to call it a sigh, but since real men didn't sigh, it had to be something else.

"We kissed," he said quietly.

Tanner tried not to overreact—and failed. "You *what*?"

Trevor shook his head. "It wasn't like that. Well…it wasn't supposed to be. Alina and I needed a cover to get us into a club in Baltimore, and Skye and Evan set us up as a couple of newlyweds. One thing led to another, and before I knew it, we were put in a position where we had to act like a man and woman who'd just been married. So we kissed."

"And?"

"And all it was going to be was a quick peck. Just part of our cover. But while it might have started out tame, it sure as hell didn't finish that way. I've never had a kiss like that in my life."

Tanner took a long drink of Mountain Dew as he considered that. "It might have been that way for you, but what about Alina? Maybe it really was part of your cover for her."

"I thought that at first, too," Trevor admitted. "But when Alina was tending to my gunshot wound later at her place, she kept running her hands over my chest and stomach long after she'd cleaned off all the blood. She was definitely into me."

"How do you know?" Tanner asked. He hated to be obvious, but he got the feeling Trevor wasn't seeing the situation clearly.

"Because I could smell her arousal."

"Oh," Tanner said.

Okay, that was definitely TMI. There was a reason men didn't share this kind of stuff with their friends.

"Up until that point, I'd assumed Alina was very good at deception and that she was playing the role Dick had given her. But you can't fake arousal, no matter how good you are."

Tanner couldn't argue with that. "What are you going to do?"

"I have no frigging idea." Trevor dropped his back on the couch and stared up at the ceiling as if the answer was written there. Or maybe he was simply looking for divine inspiration. "I want to ignore what my head is saying, just go with my instincts, and trust her. I want to believe this thing that seems to be going on between us is real. But at the end of the day, how do I toss aside all my doubt and trust her completely, knowing that if I do, and she's dirty, it won't be me paying the price? It will be our friends."

Tanner would have answered, but he had no idea what to say. He sucked at relationships almost as much as he did at giving personal advice. Fortunately, Trevor's phone rang, relieving him of the responsibility of solving his friend's dilemma.

Trevor pulled out his phone and looked at it warily, as if he was worried it might be Alina calling to ask if they were talking about her. After a moment, he thumbed the button and put it to his ear.

"No, Evan. It didn't go well tonight," Trevor said in a deadpan voice. "Is there another reason you called?"

Evan must have said something interesting, because Trevor told him to hold on. "I'm putting you on speaker so Tanner can hear." He pressed the button. "Go ahead."

"Vivian just called," Evan said. Vivian was the receptionist at the main office in DC. She acted as their eyes and ears at that facility, even though there wasn't much going on there lately. "Thorn booked one of the classified conference rooms at the DCO office in DC. He didn't give her an exact time but just told her to reserve the room for the next two days."

Trevor frowned. "Why would he bother using one of our classified conference rooms? He must have at least half a dozen of them at Chadwick-Thorn."

"I was wondering the same thing," Evan said. "The only reason I can think of for why he might want to use one of our rooms instead of his is if what he's discussing is so secret he can't risk anyone at Chadwick-Thorn overhearing it. Their secure facilities are good, but ours are better."

"Anything that classified is something we're going to want to hear," Trevor said.

"That's what I was thinking," Evan said. "Which is why I called you."

"Is there any way we can get someone into that meeting?" Tanner asked.

He'd only been to the DC office once. While it was hidden in the basement of the EPA building on Pennsylvania Avenue, it was fancy as hell, not to mention secure.

"Not a chance," Evan said. "Thorn will almost certainly have his own security people there to keep people out. If we're going to hear what they're saying in there, it's going to have to be covert."

Trevor chuckled. "Fortunately, we work for a covert organization that's damn good at snooping on people. See if you can find someone you still trust in IT, and ask if they have a listening device we can get into the conference room."

"Getting a wire that can do the job won't be the problem—it's getting it into the room," Evan said. "If Thorn's people are any good, they'll sweep the room before the meeting, so we can't put the listening device in there ahead of time. It will have to go in at the last minute, and that might be tough."

"Leave that to me," Trevor told him. "You get the bug and make sure we find out exactly when Thorn is holding the meeting."

"I'm on it."

"You think this has something to do with this big move we've all been waiting for Thorn to make?" Tanner asked after Evan hung up.

"I hope so," Trevor said. "Because if not, I'm not sure how else we're going to get the son of a bitch. We've dug into every lead and gone down every rabbit hole looking for something to put the man away. I don't know what else to do."

Tanner wanted to put Thorn away as much as Trevor did, but it was looking less likely with every passing day. Even this classified meeting was a long shot. For all they knew, Thorn merely wanted a fancy place to hold one of his weapons program briefings for the DOD.

He and Trevor sat there in silence for a while, watching the fourth quarter of a game that even the fans in the stadium had given up on and walked out.

"So what are you going to do about Alina?" Tanner asked as the ref finally—and mercifully—announced the game was over.

Trevor shrugged. "Pick her up for work in the morning, then take it from there."

Tanner considered suggesting Trevor try talking to Alina instead but thought better of it. Trevor was as crappy at talking to women as he was, so it would be a train wreck. Better to pray and hope for the best.

Chapter 9

MOLLY RAN STRAIGHT IN TO SAY GOOD MORNING TO Katelyn the moment Kathy opened the door.

"So how'd everything go last night after I left?" Kathy asked Alina. "Judging by how tired you look, I'm guessing it went very well. Tell me everything, and don't even try to spare me the details. I'm a big girl. I can handle it."

Alina was tempted to make something up so Kathy wouldn't be disappointed, but she didn't. Not only did she hate lying to her friend, but she was simply too tired to come up with anything.

"If you want to know how the night went, that's easy. It sucked."

Kathy looked surprised for a moment, then hustled her into her apartment and closed the door. Alina had been there enough times to know what the place looked like by heart. The layout was the same as her apartment, with most of the furniture nearly identical too. The only major difference was the pile of small cardboard boxes stacked up against the living room wall. Most likely socks waiting to be sent out in this morning's deliveries.

"What happened?" Kathy asked.

Alina was in the middle of giving her friend the synopsized version of last night's events when her cell phone rang. She dug it out of her pocket. It was probably

Trevor telling her he wasn't coming to pick her up and
that she needed to take an Uber down to Quantico.

It wasn't Trevor. It was Dick, no doubt wanting to
know why the hell she hadn't returned any of his calls.
In addition to calling her several times the previous
night, he'd already called twice this morning.

She sighed and let this call go to voice mail, too, then
shoved her phone back in her pocket.

Kathy must have seen the look of displeasure on
Alina's face, because she led her over to the couch and
plunked her down, then sat beside her.

"What's wrong? You haven't had this new job long
enough to be hating the thought of going to work in the
morning already."

"It's not that," Alina said.

Picking up last night's story where she'd left off,
Alina explained about Seth Larson and how she'd told
her boss about the meeting.

Kathy frowned. "I don't see the problem here. Dick is
your boss, right? Why wouldn't you tell him about it?"

Alina sighed. "This is going to sound crazy, but I'm
getting the feeling my boss isn't exactly one of the good
guys. There's a lot going on that I don't understand, but
my instincts are telling me that Dick is in league with the
person who had the previous director murdered. From
everything I've seen over the past few days, Trevor is
trying to get the evidence to prove it."

Kathy grimaced. "And you just told the bad guy
exactly what Trevor is up to."

Alina nodded. "Yeah. I didn't realize what I was
doing, and by the time I did, it was too late to do anything about it. Then last night, Larson called and said

Dick sent some guys to pay him a visit. They roughed Larson up and scared the hell out of his autistic kid. I felt like crap knowing it was my fault, but then felt ten times worse when I saw the look in Trevor's eyes. He didn't say anything, but he knows it was me. I feel like I betrayed him."

Hell, she *did* betray him.

Kathy considered that. "Well, the first thing you need to do is stop talking to Dick. Second, talk to Trevor, and tell him exactly how you feel. Tell him that Dick duped you into spying on him and that you had no intention of betraying him."

Alina almost laughed at the simplicity of Kathy's plan. Leave it up to her friend to uncomplicate the situation and say what needed to be said. Considering the way the tension left her body the moment she heard her friend's idea, Kathy was probably right on.

"You're suggesting I blow off my boss's calls? Ignore the man who signs my paycheck?"

"I remember you telling me that you always felt there was something off about Wade," Kathy said. "That your instincts had screamed at you for months there was something sideways about him. You were furious you'd let your head overrule your instincts and promised me you'd never do anything like that again."

Alina sighed. She vaguely remembered that late-night conversation with Kathy and the promise she'd made. Right now, those instincts were telling her Trevor wasn't the bad guy in this equation. If anyone was— besides Dick and Thorn—it was her.

She nodded. "You're right."

"Of course I'm right," Kathy said. "If talking to Dick

feels wrong, it is. Tell the guy the battery on your cell phone died or that you dropped it in the garbage disposal. It worked for that quarterback. It'll work for you."

"It didn't really work for him, Kathy," Alina pointed out. "He was found guilty, got suspended, and lost millions of dollars in pay."

"Well, yeah, I guess. You don't have millions of dollars, and it's not like your boss can be as evil as the football commissioner, so you should be fine." Kathy shrugged. "Besides, you lie much better than that cute quarterback. His face is too honest to pull off a good one."

Alina laughed at the image of Dick losing his mind when she told him she missed his calls because her phone fell in the garbage disposal. But her amusement disappeared as another concern took center stage.

She'd lain awake a long time last night trying to understand why she'd been so strongly affected by a simple kiss. She'd known since her first day on the job that she and Trevor had some kind of connection. And that connection was getting stronger than she'd ever experienced with any other partner or team member she'd ever had.

Who the heck was she kidding? The thoughts she'd been having about Trevor last night weren't things she'd ever thought about any teammate she'd ever had. Those had been I-want-to-get-you-naked-and-wrestle-with-you-on-the-floor kinds of thoughts.

"Earth to Alina."

Alina jerked out of her musings to see Kathy waving her hand in front of her face. "Sorry."

"You've been sitting there grinning like an idiot for the past two minutes," Kathy said. "What's so funny?"

On the floor, Molly and Katelyn seemed interested in knowing the answer to that, too. They'd stopped playing with each other and were eyeing her curiously.

"Oh, it's nothing," she said.

"Don't give me that," Kathy said. "I've known you long enough to recognize when you're hiding something."

Alina picked a nonexistent piece of lint off her pant-suit. "It's possible I'm starting to feel things for Trevor that I shouldn't necessarily feel for my work partner."

Kathy gaped at her. "Wait a minute. Are you saying you're falling for him romantically? I mean, not that I blame you. Trevor is definitely hot. I haven't seen abs like that since the Chippendales tour came to town. And he's attractive as sin. Like that guy on that show."

"What show?" Alina asked, knowing she shouldn't.

Her friend was always saying someone looked like an actor on TV or in the movies, but she could never remember the actor's name, so it usually devolved into a big game of twenty questions.

"You know, the one on the Syfy channel."

Alina sighed. "Kathy, the Syfy channel has a lot of shows."

Her friend waved her hand. "I don't know the name of it. I don't think it's on anymore, but I'm sure you know exactly what I'm talking about. It was the show about the people who go through the gate in time. They're surrounded by water, and there are spaceships and soul-sucking aliens with white dreadlocks. He was the good-looking one with the quirky smile."

Alina had absolutely no idea what show Kathy was referring to, much less what guy. Her work schedule over the years hadn't left her a lot of time to watch TV.

But she let it go. The name of the show would pop into her friend's head at some point.

"Okay, regardless of which movie or TV star you think Trevor looks like, I'm not falling for him romantically."

Kathy looked doubtful. "You sure?"

Alina was about to declare that of course she was sure, but then she realized that would be something of a lie. "Okay, maybe I am…a little. But I didn't intend for things to get out of hand like they did last night. It just happened."

Kathy's eyes widened. "What got out of hand? Are you talking about the way you were groping him when I walked into your apartment last night?"

"I was not groping him," Alina insisted. "I was rendering first aid."

Kathy snorted. "I'm pretty sure what I stumbled in on last night isn't the kind of first aid they teach down at the local YMCA."

"Whatever," Alina said. She refused to engage in that line of conversation. "Besides, that's not what I'm talking about. While we were undercover, we kissed. It was supposed to be a little smooch as part of our cover, but it ended up being hot, and I got kind of turned on. Things got even more sexually charged when we got back to my apartment. When you walked in on us last night, I was damn close to jumping him."

Kathy blinked, clearly too stunned to speak. "Wow," she finally said. "Not that I don't envy the heck out of you, but doesn't what happened last night complicate things? If they weren't complicated enough already, I mean. I don't suppose you have a clue if he felt the same way about the kiss?"

Alina shook her head.

Kathy thought a moment. "Remember before when I suggested you tell Trevor how you feel? Maybe you should leave out the part about wanting to have sex with him. At least for right now."

Alina couldn't disagree with that logic.

She would have asked if Kathy had any other suggestions, but then she heard a knock from across the hall. "That's Trevor. I have to go."

"Good luck," Kathy said as Alina headed for the door.

"Thanks."

After last night, she had the feeling she was going to need it.

Alina wanted to ask how Trevor's gunshot wound was doing, but the silence in the SUV was so deafening she was almost afraid to break it. Not that his wound was the only thing she wanted to talk to him about, but damn, if she couldn't talk about something that simple, how was she going to confess to betraying him?

Telling Trevor the truth had sounded so easy when Kathy suggested it earlier, but sitting beside him in the Suburban on I-95 south, it felt like the words were stuck in her throat. She had to say something, or she was going to go insane.

"Trevor, there's something I need to tell you," she said quietly.

"What's that?" he asked, not looking at her.

"I owe you an explanation."

He glanced at her, his expression unreadable. "You don't owe me anything."

She winced. Clearly, he wasn't going to make this easy. Why should he? This was her screwup, not his.

"I told Dick about Larson," she admitted in a rush. "I never dreamed he would go and harass the guy—or Cody. I'm sorry I did it, and I'm sorry I didn't trust you."

Alina expected questions, a furious rant, or at least an angry look. Instead, Trevor gave her nothing. He stared straight ahead as traffic jammed the highway.

She took a breath and decided to dive into the deep end of the pool. "Dick recruited me specifically to keep an eye on you, but I didn't know that when I agreed to take the job. It was only afterward, during our first meeting in his office—when Thorn was there—that Dick told me you betrayed the DCO and had either helped murder John or were protecting those who had. I didn't really know until later that I'd been set up and lied to."

Trevor finally looked at her, his face guarded, almost thoughtful. He gazed at her for so long, she started to get uncomfortable, both at the intensity in his eyes as well as the lack of attention he was paying to the road.

"Aren't you going to say anything?" she finally asked.

He turned his attention back to the highway. "What would you like me to say?"

"I don't know, but say something," she said in exasperation. "Tell me you believe me, call me a liar, say you couldn't care less about my excuses. At least acknowledge you heard me."

When Trevor still didn't say anything, Alina thought her whole confession had been a waste of time and breath. But then suddenly, he jerked the steering wheel to the right, crossing two lanes of traffic and steering the SUV onto the shoulder of the road. Behind them, cars squawked and blew their horns, but her partner ignored them as he slammed on the brakes and turned to face her.

"Why didn't you walk away from the job the minute Dick told you what he expected you to do? Why work with a partner you thought was a traitor?"

Alina blinked. Of all the things she expected he could have asked her, why she'd taken the job wasn't one of them. But it was a question. And she had wanted him to say *something*. This was a start at least.

"I wasn't lying when I told you it was time for me to leave the CIA," she said. "Going back wasn't an option. And in reality, there was some stuff in my past at the CIA that makes going after a traitor a very tempting offer. Dick obviously knew that when he recruited me."

"What the hell does that mean?" Trevor demanded. "What stuff in your past?"

She took a deep breath. It was time to tell him about Wade and why she'd left the Agency, but before she could open her mouth to spill the secrets she'd never planned to tell anyone, Trevor's cell phone rang. He cursed and dug it out of his pocket.

She expected him to ignore the call, since what they were discussing was kind of important, but instead, he thumbed the green button.

"Maxwell." He listened for a moment, then frowned. "Slow down, Zarina. I can't understand what you're saying."

Whatever the woman had to say, it must have been bad, because Trevor tensed.

"What's wrong?" Alina asked.

Trevor eyed her for a moment, his gaze calculating, like he was trying to decide if he could trust her. Alina fully expected him to tell her it was none of her business, so she was surprised when he hit the speaker button on the phone.

"Zarina, can you repeat that? I just put you on speaker so Alina can hear."

There was a slight hesitation, then a woman's accented voice came on. "Sage has escaped and is running loose through the wooded area outside the complex. I'm doing the best I can to keep it quiet while Tanner and Jaxson try to get her back. If Dick figures out she's missing, that will be all the excuse he needs to send someone out to kill her."

Alina might not have known Sage, or Zarina and Tanner for that matter, but that didn't stop her from getting a bad feeling in the pit of her stomach. The concern on Trevor's face told her she was right.

"Which way is Sage heading, and how much of a head start does she have?" Trevor asked.

"Tanner said she's heading northeast, with at least a fifteen-minute head start."

Cursing again, Trevor threw the Suburban into gear and floored it, making the other drivers honk and swerve as he merged onto the interstate.

"We'll try to get ahead of her," he said as he weaved in and out of traffic. "Hopefully we can keep her from reaching any heavily populated areas outside the Quantico boundary."

"Hurry," Zarina said. "Sage hasn't interacted with more than a handful of people the whole time she's been here. I'm not sure how she'll deal with the outside world."

"No kidding," Trevor muttered. "I'm going to call Tanner. We'll let you know something as soon as we can. Do anything necessary to keep Dick from finding out about this."

"Who is Sage?" Alina asked after he hung up. "And why do you think Dick will have her killed?"

Trevor's jaw tightened, but he didn't answer.

"Dammit, Trevor!" she snapped. "I admit it. I screwed up, and I betrayed you, and I'm sorry about that. But right now, I need to know what's going on if I'm going to help you find that girl. Unless you intend to kick me out and leave me stranded on the side of the road."

He glanced at her. "Alina, this isn't some damn game. This isn't about you and me and how much—or how little—we might trust each other. This is about a terrified woman who needs help. If you tell Dick about any of this, he'll have her executed, plain and simple."

Hearing Trevor say he didn't trust her hurt more than she wanted to admit. "I'm not going to tell him anything."

Trevor was silent for a moment, but then he nodded. "Okay. I'm trusting you, not just with Sage's life, but with Jaxson's, Tanner's, and Zarina's as well. If Dick finds out what they've been doing, getting fired will be the least of their problems."

Alina grabbed the roll bar handle as Trevor took the next exit at warp speed and turned on state road 234 along the northeast side of the Prince William Forest. The wooded area served as a buffer along the northern edge of the Quantico training facility. Trevor must have been trying to get north of Sage and stop her before she got out of the forest.

Trevor handed his phone to her. "Hit the third number on speed dial."

She looked down at the phone and realized there

wasn't a single name listed in the contacts list. Just a collection of ten speed-dial numbers. It was clearly a burner phone. Containing her curiosity for the moment, she poked the third button, then put the phone on speaker. When the call connected, all she heard was a garbled mix of what sounded like the pounding of feet.

"Trevor?" a male voice shouted over the din.

"Yeah, it's me, Tanner," her partner said. "Alina and I are on Highway 234 heading toward the northeast side of the boundary. Where are you and Jaxson?"

"I'm tracking Sage on foot through the forest, maybe ten minutes behind her. Jaxson is in an SUV trying to keep up with me as best he can. Hold on, and I'll pull him into the call."

A few moments later, the roar of an engine came over the line, interspersed with a lot of expletives.

"I'm a little busy trying to read a map and drive at the same time, guys," Jaxson said. "It's not really the best time to chat."

"Then just listen," Trevor told him. "Tanner, do you think you can catch up with Sage before she reaches the perimeter fence?"

"Not a chance," Tanner said. "Sage is really frigging fast. Probably as fast as I am, which is kind of painful to admit. She's making a beeline for the northeast boundary and will probably come out somewhere around Independent Hill. She's barely five minutes from the fence."

Trevor swore and floored the gas. "Alina and I will try to get in front of her and keep her from getting too far into town. Hopefully we can keep anyone from seeing her."

"Approach her slowly so you don't freak her out," Tanner warned. "She's just scared."

"It's not her I'm worried about. It's the civilians she runs into. I don't want someone calling the cops," Trevor said. "You have any idea where she's ultimately going or what she's trying to do?"

"If I had to guess, I'd say she's trying to find Derek," Tanner replied.

Trevor muttered a curse. "I'll call you guys when we reach the outskirts of Independence Hill."

He nodded, and Alina hung up.

"I already know Jaxson," she said. "Who are Zarina and Tanner?"

"Good friends who are willing to risk their lives to help someone."

She was hoping he'd say a little bit more than that, but okay. "If you're all friends, why is Sage running from them? More importantly, what's the big deal if someone sees her?"

Trevor passed several cars on the four-lane road before answering. "Did Dick tell you about hybrids?"

Alina shook her head. "Not really. He mentioned them, but from the way he said it, I assumed it was another word for shifter. He also used the acronym EVA once, but he never said what it meant."

Trevor grunted. "Figures. Dick likes to paint all of us with the same brush. EVA means extremely valuable asset. It's the bureaucratic term the DCO came up with to describe shifters. As you can imagine, it's not a term we think much of."

She could understand that. "Okay. So what's a hybrid, then?"

"Hybrids are man-made shifters. It's an attempt by some evil people to create shifters in a laboratory by giving normal, everyday people a chemical cocktail to twist their DNA around and force their bodies to exhibit the same traits shifters possess. It's a violent, dangerous, and incredibly painful process that can have a ton of unintended side effects, especially when it comes to a person's self-control."

Alina already knew she wasn't going to like where this was going. It sounded like something out of a horror movie.

"Sage was kidnapped from her home in Canada and given who knows how many different hybrid drugs," Trevor continued. "On top of that, she was shuffled all over the world from one clandestine lab to the next, where she was experimented on. Sage isn't the first person to fall victim to those psychopaths, but she's by far the most unstable one we've been able to rescue. She's hanging on to her sanity by a thread. We hate doing it, but we have to keep her locked up in a small apartment-slash-cell on the complex."

"The most unstable one you've been able to rescue?" Alina repeated, getting a sinking feeling in her stomach. "Do you mean there have been others that you couldn't rescue?"

Trevor nodded. "Unfortunately, there have been a lot. Many never survive the hybrid serum to begin with. Most of those who do live become so violent and insane we've had no choice but to kill them."

Alina shook her head. "Who would try to play God like that?"

Trevor didn't say anything, the same impenetrable wall shutting her out.

"Answer me," she said. "Who did this?"

He gave her a quick glance before focusing again on the road they were speeding down.

"It was Thorn," he growled. "That asshole has been trying to build a hybrid army for years, and Sage is just one of the many casualties that have occurred along the way."

Chapter 10

Jaxson and Tanner were waiting for them outside a tiny Catholic church located on the outskirts of Independent Hill.

"She's inside," Jaxson said the moment Trevor and Alina got out of the SUV.

Trevor muttered a curse. The hope that they'd catch up with Sage before she reached the town had evaporated when Tanner had called a few minutes ago to say she'd already jumped the fence and that he'd tracked her to the church.

"Please tell me she's alone," Trevor said.

Secretly, he didn't think they could possibly get that lucky, but hey, this was a church, so maybe his prayers would be answered.

Tanner shook his head. "Afraid not. The good news is that there's only one other person in there with her. I assume it's the priest."

Trevor glanced at Jaxson. "Did you bring them?"

"Yeah."

Jaxson opened the back of his SUV and took a hard plastic case from the backseat. Placing it on the hood, he lifted the lid to reveal four dart guns. It was amazing how much these things looked like the paintball guns he and Alina had used the other day. All things being equal, Trevor would much rather have been back in the shoot house getting shot with green-dye rounds.

"We're going to tranquilize her?" Alina asked, looking back and forth between Trevor and the other guys.

"None of us want to, but we might not have a choice," Trevor told her.

He appreciated the fact that even though she'd never met Sage, Alina was clearly uneasy about the idea of shooting her with a tranquilizer dart. It made him feel a little better about bringing Alina on this rescue mission.

When she'd first confessed to spying for Dick, he'd just about lost it. But after she'd admitted Dick had made it seem like he was a traitor and a murderer, Trevor had cooled off a bit. He'd known Dick for a long time, so he knew what kind of manipulative SOB the man could be. That said, he still wasn't ready to trust Alina completely. They had a way to go before they could get there. But his gut told him they were on the right track. That was good enough for now.

Trevor pushed those thoughts aside for the moment, needing to focus on Sage and getting her back to the complex before Dick or anyone else discovered she was gone.

"No one wants to shoot her," Tanner was telling Alina. "But we can't take the chance Sage might lose control in there and hurt the priest or one of us. Trust me when I tell you this. Hurting someone is the last thing Sage wants to do. It would tear her apart."

"We'll try and talk her down first," Trevor promised as he slid the dart gun inside his belt at his lower back. "We only pull the weapons as a last resort, understood?"

Giving Tanner and Jaxson a nod, he and Alina headed around to the back of the church while Tanner and Jaxson took the front.

They passed a tiny house attached to the rear of the church that was most likely the priest's residence, then made their way over to the back door of the church. Trevor hoped like hell she hadn't gone into a rage and killed the poor man already.

"A hybrid's eyes will turn bright red when they're on the verge of losing it," Trevor told Alina. "When they get like that, it's nearly impossible to get through to them. That's when they're really dangerous. If you see her eyes turn red, get the hell out of the way, okay?"

Alina looked like she wanted to argue, but then shook her head. "Fine. But how about we make sure it doesn't come to that?"

"That's the plan," he murmured as he pushed open the door. "But everyone knows what they say about plans."

Giving Alina a nod, Trevor led the way down the hall, his footsteps silent on the marble floor. Thankfully, he didn't pick up the scent of blood. Maybe it meant Sage was fully in control.

When they reached the end of the hallway, he heard soft voices coming from the main part of the church. Trevor couldn't be sure, but it sounded like someone praying.

He stepped into the main part of the church, Alina right behind him. Sage was sitting in the front pew beside an older priest dressed in traditional black garments. Their hands were clasped in front of them as they recited a prayer together.

Sage's head immediately came up, her eyes glowing as red as two Christmas tree lights. Trevor's heart sank. If that wasn't bad enough, her claws and fangs were out, too. Crap, she was in full-on hybrid mode.

Why the hell wasn't the old priest freaking out?

Unless he was blind, he had to have figured out that there was something seriously different about Sage. But the guy simply sat there, softly praying as if he were the only person in the church.

Sage shot to her feet, a growl slipping from her throat. Beside her, the priest's prayers stumbled to a halt. He looked up, his eyes filling with alarm when he saw Trevor and Alina. He slowly shook his head, like he was trying to get them to back off.

Noise from the front of the church startled Sage, and she whipped her head around to look over her shoulder at Tanner and Jaxson as they slipped through the big double doors and fanned out to either side.

Trevor held up his hand, motioning for them to stay where they were. Taking a deep breath, he stepped a little closer to Sage, hoping she'd turn her attention back to him. As he moved, he caught the priest's eye, trying to get him to slip away from Sage, but the old guy seemed intent on remaining where he was. It was like he thought Sage was the one in danger.

"It's okay, Sage," Trevor said gently. "We're here to help. No one's going to hurt you. We're all friends here."

Sage didn't seem to believe that. Eyes blazing, she took three quick strides in his direction, her long, sharp fangs bared in a snarl. Hybrids might not have had much in the way of control, but they definitely had some serious fangs on them. If Sage ever truly lost it and sunk those teeth into someone, it would be all over.

He hadn't seen Sage much since he and the others had brought her back from Tajikistan, but she looked like she hadn't slept in days. From the wetness on her cheeks, it was obvious she'd been crying, too.

Trevor's heart went out to her, it really did, but that didn't stop him from slowly reaching behind his back for the tranquilizer gun. With her hybrid strength and reflexes, Sage was already close enough to attack. Even if he darted her in midair, the sedative wouldn't take effect for fifteen to thirty seconds. A hybrid could do a lot of damage in that amount of time. He could probably survive an attack like that, but if Sage turned on Alina, his partner probably wouldn't be so lucky.

The thought of Alina getting hurt bothered him a hell of a lot more than he ever would have expected.

"Alina, start backing away slowly," he whispered. "Things are about to go all kinds of bad."

He'd already figured out a while ago that his partner was stubborn, so he wasn't surprised when she hesitated. But he didn't expect her to completely ignore him, much less step in front of him to put herself between him and Sage.

Trevor's gut reaction was to grab her and drag her behind him, but he knew if he did, it would only freak Sage out even more.

"Alina, what the hell are you doing?" he demanded.

"Sage, my name is Alina," his partner said calmly. "You don't know me, but I promise that I won't let anything bad happen to you. We need to get you back home. It's not safe for you to be out here like this."

Sage growled, flashing her fangs again. But she made no move to pounce. In fact, he could have sworn the red glow in her eyes dimmed a little. Maybe Sage responded better to women than men? Or maybe she simply responded to Alina. He had to admit she seemed to have a way about her that put people at ease.

Alina must have taken Sage's hesitation as a good sign, because she stepped closer and held out her hand, palm up. "Will you let me take you home, Sage?"

The gesture seemed to shock Sage as much as it did Trevor, and she took a step back. "It's not my home," she growled in a tone that was filled with anguish. "I don't want to go back there."

Trevor held his breath as Alina moved closer to Sage again. This was frigging insane.

"Where would you like to go instead, Sage?" Alina asked. "If you could go anywhere, where would it be?"

"I want to go wherever Derek is," she wailed. "Can you take me to him?"

The look of heart-wrenching despair that crossed her face as she said Derek's name nearly ripped Trevor's guts out. He'd expected her to say she wanted to go back to her family in Canada, but Tanner had been right. Her instinctive need to be with the man who'd saved her in Tajikistan was stronger than the urge to go home.

Alina gave Trevor a questioning look, no doubt wondering who the hell Derek was and how they could get him here. Unfortunately, that was going to be tough. The man was still active duty Special Forces. He was lucky to see the States more than a month or so out of the year.

"He's a soldier," Trevor said. "He's probably…"

He'd been about to say Derek was probably deployed, but then he caught sight of Tanner waving his hands and shaking his head. Okay, maybe he wouldn't talk about that.

"Derek's currently…hard to reach," he said instead.

Tears welled up in Sage's eyes. "Can't I just talk to

him on the phone? Please? If I could hear his voice, that
would be enough."

Alina looked at Trevor again. All he could do was
shrug. How the hell could he get hold of a deployed
Special Forces soldier when he wasn't even sure where
in the world the man was?

"I promise that when we get back to the complex, I'm
going to find Derek and get him on the phone," Alina
told Sage firmly. "I don't care what I have to do. You're
going to talk to him today. I swear it."

Sage regarded Alina silently, as if trying to decide if
she should believe her. Trevor tightened his grip on the
tranquilizer gun behind his back. But as he watched, the
last of the red glow slowly faded from Sage's eyes, her
claws and fangs retracting. Then she threw herself into
Alina's arms, tears coming hard and fast.

Alina wrapped her arms around the girl, squeezing
her tightly and promising she'd keep Sage safe and get
her back with Derek as fast as possible. The heartache
pouring out of the poor girl in great racking sobs was
difficult for Trevor to watch. Damn, he hated seeing a
woman cry. It drove a spike right through his frigging
heart. Sage was like a wounded animal who was lost
and confused and in pain, not knowing why it was all
happening to her. He couldn't imagine how the girl even
held it together.

One arm still around Sage, Alina guided her over to
the first row of pews and sat down with her, rocking the
girl back and forth and making soothing sounds in her
ear as she caressed her dark hair. Trevor had to admit
that trusting Alina enough to bring her with him had
been one of his better ideas.

Releasing his grip on the dart gun, Trevor gestured for the priest to follow him out of the church. Tanner joined them while Jaxson stayed inside to keep an eye on Alina and Sage. Considering the man had seen everything, Trevor was going to have to do some serious damage control.

"I've never seen a shifter lose control like that," the old man said once they were outside. "Is she ill?"

Trevor gaped. Beside him, Tanner looked just as surprised.

"You know about shifters?" Trevor asked cautiously.

The priest nodded. "Yes. The church has been aware of the existence of these very special people for a long time. Our histories say they were poorly treated at first, but once the clergy finally realized they're no more evil than any of God's other creatures, the church took on the role of protecting them and their identities."

Trevor exchanged looks with Tanner. Okay, he hadn't expected that. "So you're not going to tell anyone about this?"

The priest smiled. "The girl came into my church seeking solace and peace. She was so scared that it was difficult to understand what she was saying, but I did glean from her words that churches have always represented safety and sanctuary to her. The girl's secret is safe with me…and the church." He regarded Trevor thoughtfully for a moment. "You never answered my question about whether or not the girl is ill."

"No, she's not ill," Trevor said honestly. He couldn't exactly lie to a priest. "Sage wasn't born a shifter. Someone gave her a drug to turn her into one against her will. The out-of-control behavior you saw is a result of those drugs. We're trying to help her, but she's having a hard time of it."

The priest's mouth tightened. "Besides helping her, I trust you're doing whatever is necessary to make sure the person who did this horrible thing isn't allowed to do it again?"

Trevor nodded. "We're trying very hard."

The priest looked like he would have said more, but just then, Alina and Jaxson came out with Sage. The girl was practically glued to Alina's side, and while she'd stopped crying, she still seemed emotionally and physically drained.

"We can take her back to the complex in my vehicle," Jaxson said. "I should be able to get us through the gate without anyone paying too much attention."

Alina hesitated, looking in Trevor's direction. He was about to tell Jaxson that he'd take them in his vehicle and let the other man run interference at the gate, but then his frigging phone rang. He pulled it out to see who it was, intending on letting it go to voice mail. Then he saw who it was.

Holding up his finger to tell Alina to wait, he moved to the side to take the call. "What's up, Evan? This isn't exactly the best time to talk. I'm kind of busy."

"Well, you're about to get even busier," Evan said. "Vivian just called. Thorn is heading to the DC office right now for that classified briefing. If you want to hear what he says, you need to be there in an hour."

Shit.

Trevor glanced at his watch, trying to calculate how long it would take him to get into the middle of DC at this time in the morning. With traffic, it was going to be close. "Did you talk to IT and figure out a way to get a set of ears into the conference room?"

"Yeah, I have a way to do it. I just don't know how we're going to make it work," Evan said. "You never explained how the hell we're going to get the bug in the room with them."

That was because he hadn't given it one second of thought. "Like I said, let me worry about that. I'm leaving now, but it's going to be tight. Any chance you can rig up a way to slow things down if I'm late?"

There was a long sigh on the other end of the line. "Dammit, Trevor. I'm an analyst, not a field agent. I sit around a soft, cushy cubicle all day and play with a computer. I don't know how to *rig* anything."

"You'll figure it out," Trevor said, trying to be as encouraging as he could. "Keep it simple, and you'll be fine. I'll be there as fast as I can."

He hung up and gave Tanner a nod, knowing the hybrid had heard the entire phone conversation.

"What was that about?" Alina asked.

While he'd been on the phone, she'd gotten Sage into the back of Jaxson's SUV and somehow convinced her to stay put. Through the open back window, Trevor could see the girl looking anxiously at Alina.

"Did Dick go after Seth and Cody again?" Alina prompted when he didn't answer.

He shook his head. "No, nothing like that. I just need to be someplace."

"Do you want me to come with you?"

Trevor's first instinct was to say yes, but the word got stuck in his throat as his head spoke up and urged caution. Letting her help with Sage was one thing; bringing her to a meeting where Thorn might finally reveal something damaging was a completely different world. He hated himself for doing it, but that didn't keep him from shaking his head.

"No. I'd rather you help Jaxson get Sage back to the complex and settled. You and she seem to have a connection, and what I'm doing isn't a big deal. I'll take Tanner with me and catch up with you later."

Disappointment flashed across Alina's face for a brief second before she nodded and climbed in the backseat of Jaxson's vehicle with Sage.

Trevor had no doubt his partner knew he'd fed her a line of crap, and he could tell it bothered the hell out of her. It bothered the hell out of him, too, especially considering what she'd just done for Sage. But until he knew for sure that she wasn't playing him, he couldn't take the risk of telling her what he was doing.

As Jaxson pulled the Suburban out of the church parking lot and drove away, Alina threw Trevor an angry look. It occurred to him then that he might have burned down the already shaky bridge that had started forming between them.

—⁓—

Vivian met Trevor and Tanner in the lobby of the DC office. With its big reception desk and black-and-white photos of well-known landmarks like the Washington Monument and the Capitol Building on the walls, it wasn't all that remarkable. It certainly didn't scream covert organization.

"Thank God you're here," she said softly. "Thorn and the people he's meeting with have been here for a while, and poor Evan is about to blow a gasket."

Trevor could believe it. While Evan might be on the verge of passing out, Vivian seemed cool as a cucumber as she led them down a deserted hallway. Considering the leggy blond had never done anything other than receptionist work for the DCO, that was a little surprising. Then again, maybe she was a ninja receptionist? He could see John hiring someone like that to work the desk of the organization's clandestine headquarters.

"Who's in there with him?" Tanner asked.

"I don't recognize them," she said over her shoulder. "No one from the Committee or the DCO, that's for sure."

"Not even Dick?" Trevor asked.

The DCO's new director was rarely far from Thorn when anything important was going down.

She shook her head. "No. They're all scientist types."

"How do you know that?" Tanner asked.

"Trust me," Vivian said. "I know a nerd herd when I see one."

Trevor frowned. If Vivian was right about them being scientists, this meeting could very well be about another hybrid project—or whatever Thorn had decided was the next step in hybrid evolution.

"Man, am I glad to see you guys," Evan said when they walked into the office where the analyst was waiting for them. "I was able to delay the start of the meeting for a few minutes by popping the circuit breakers, which made all the computers in the conference room have to reboot, but I couldn't get away with that more than once."

"Sorry about that. Traffic was a bitch, as usual," Trevor said. "Did you get the wire I asked for?"

Evan nodded and held out a small plastic and metal device that looked kind of like a miniature flash drive, except the USB adapter on the end of it didn't look quite right.

"Who'd you get it from?" Trevor asked.

"Karl in IT tech support." Evan handed it to him. "He said all you have to do is press the base in and hold it for a few seconds to turn it on. Then just get it somewhere in the room, and it will do the rest. It'll pick up anyone talking as well as capture the video feed going into the overhead projector. And before you ask, I didn't tell him what we needed it for, and he didn't want to know."

"Which conference room are they in?" Trevor asked.

Evan's eyes widened. "You're not going to be able to just walk in there."

"Why not?" Trevor shrugged. "I'll act like I walked into the wrong room, drop the device under a table, then be out of there before they even realize I slipped a bug in the room."

Evan exchanged looks with Vivian. "It's not that," he said. "Thorn put two guards on the door, and one of them is Frasier."

Trevor cursed. His plan would be infinitely more difficult with someone guarding the door, but Douglas Frasier's presence made it damn near impossible. Frasier flat-out hated his guts. Then again, it seemed like Frasier hated everyone's guts, but especially shifters'.

In addition to being Thorn's head of security, Frasier also ran certain special projects for the former senator. Which was a nice way of saying the man killed people his boss wanted dead. Trevor didn't know a lot about the guy, but he knew Frasier had worked for the DCO years ago and that he'd been paired up with the first shifter the organization had ever discovered—Adam. Trevor wasn't sure what happened between the two of them, but considering what Adam had said about his partner shooting him in the back, Trevor had a pretty good idea. Whatever it was, it forced Adam to go off the grid while Frasier had landed a cushy job working for Thorn. The man was never going to let him get within ten feet of the conference room his boss was in.

Trevor glanced at Tanner. The hybrid had even less chance of getting past Frasier than he did. That left only one option.

He stared at Evan, trying to come up with something to say to convince the analyst he had it in him to bluff his way past Frasier and the other guard and figure out how to slip the device into the room.

"Why are you looking at me like that?" Evan asked suspiciously. Then his eyes widened as it dawned on him. "No way! I can't go in there. Frasier would know I'm lying. He'd shoot me."

Shit. Evan looked like he was about to start hyperventilating at the mere thought of going in the conference room. Trevor opened his mouth to point out it was highly unlikely Frasier would kill him, but Vivian cut him off.

"I'll do it."

Well, damn. He hadn't even considered suggesting she do it. Which was rather sexist, he realized. "You sure about this?"

"Will this help catch the people who killed John and Olivia?" she asked.

Trevor nodded.

"Then I'll do it. Olivia was my friend long before I

started working here. She even got me the job interview. As for John, he was the best boss I've ever worked for and an even better person. If putting a bug in that room will get me a little revenge, I'm in. I want those bastards to pay for what they've done."

"How are you going to get it in there?" Trevor asked as he handed the device to her.

"Carefully" was all she said, then she left the room.

Evan let out a breath. "What do we do if they catch her?"

"We go rescue her," Trevor said.

Evan seemed a little nervous at that idea but nodded. "I'll get the computer set up. That way, we'll know what's happening in there."

Taking a laptop out of his backpack, Evan placed it on the table, then slipped something that looked like some kind of wireless mouse adapter into one of the computer's USB ports and began poking keys.

"You want to pick up the pace a little?" Trevor said. "At this rate, Frasier could knock Vivian out and drag her out to the trunk of his car before you get any sound on that thing."

"Hold on." Evan's fingers flew over the keys. "I'm praying she remembered to push the adapter to turn it on, or this will all be a waste of time."

A few moments later, muffled noise came out of the computer's speakers along with the sound of something heavy thudding together.

Evan threw Trevor a nervous look. "What the hell was that?"

Trevor held up his hand for silence, trying to figure out what the hell they were listening to.

"I thought everyone would like some coffee and Danish," Vivian said over the speaker. "Nothing like a little caffeine and sugar to get you through a morning meeting."

"Thank you, Vivian."

Thorn's deceptively sweet voice made Trevor's teeth ache.

"Of course, Mr. Thorn. If you need anything else, just let me know."

"Damn, she's smooth," Tanner said as Vivian left the room. "John should have put her in the field."

Trevor chuckled. "No kidding. Maybe he intended to. John was always ten steps ahead of everyone else when it came to knowing who'd be a good field agent."

"He was good when it came to seeing other people's futures," Evan said softly. "I wish he had spent a little more time worrying about his own. Then maybe he would've foreseen somebody planting that bomb."

The mood in the small office immediately changed as the humor that had been there a moment ago disappeared. They stared at the blank screen of the laptop, listening to the men in the conference room drink their coffee and talk about whether they preferred cheese or apple Danish.

"I'm surprised you didn't bring Alina with you," Evan said. "Zarina told me she helped get Sage back, so I figured she was a newly accepted member of our little rebel alliance."

"She wanted to stay behind to take care of Sage," Trevor said, the lie sliding wet and slimy off his tongue. Great, now he was lying to Evan like he'd lied to Alina. At this rate, he was going to end up no better than Thorn and his a-hole friends.

"But everything is good with her, right?" Evan probed. "She's on our side, isn't she?"

Trevor didn't know how to answer that. His head was still advising him to proceed with caution, while his instincts shouted at him to trust her. That disconnect had him tied up in knots, not sure what to do. Why the hell did this have to be so difficult?

He shrugged. "I'm leaning that way, but in truth, I'm not sure."

Evan frowned in confusion, while Tanner gave him a look that said he thought Trevor was full of crap. He knew the feeling. He was confused, too, and pretty sure he was full of shit.

Thankfully, the door opened, and Vivian stuck her head in, saving him from fielding any more questions about Alina.

"We good?" Vivian asked.

Trevor motioned at the laptop. "We have audio, but it remains to be seen if we're going to grab any video from the projector. Regardless, you did good."

Before she could say anything, the screen on Evan's laptop flickered to life.

"We've got video," the analyst announced excitedly.

Vivian nodded. "I need to go out and man the desk in case anyone else walks in late for the meeting. Hope you get what you need."

"Me, too," Trevor said. "Thanks again."

As she closed the door behind her, an image of some kind of chart appeared on the laptop screen. The timeline along the bottom stretched back at least four years, while the rest of the slide was filled with a bewildering array of stars, numbers, and various

horizontal lines. It didn't look like some kind of dia-
bolical scheme concocted by Thorn to take over the
world—or whatever the hell he was up to. In fact, it
looked like something involving a weapons development schedule.

Trevor cursed. This was probably going to end up
being a huge waste of time. He'd screwed the partnership he'd been building with Alina for nothing.

A man's voice came through the speaker. Even with
the guy explaining the chart, Trevor was still lost. All
the scientific terms might as well have been Greek as far
as he was concerned.

"The program has grown in leaps and bounds since
the minor setback we experienced at the end of May
when our test subject was unable to sustain a full transi-
tion," another man said.

The picture on the screen changed to a man lying
twisted and motionless on an exam table.

Trevor did a double take. Shit, that was Aaron
Moore. He'd been an agent at the DCO right up until
the moment he'd volunteered to take the hybrid serum
Thorn's doctors whipped up in their test tubes and died
in horrible, screaming pain as a result.

Now the chart made a whole hell of a lot more
sense. It outlined how long they'd been working on
the hybrid serum.

"We still don't know why Agent Moore responded so
poorly to the serum," the man continued. "While it was
a reduced dosage, Agent Harmon displayed absolutely
zero side effects when given the same treatment. In fact,
it appears the serum failed completely in Harmon's
case. I admit, having a test subject die from such a small

tweak in the formulation continues to confound our failure review team."

Trevor ground his jaw at the total disregard for
human life apparent in the man's voice as he talked
about Moore's death. Former Special Forces lieutenant
turned DCO agent Jayson Harmon should have died, too.
What Thorn's doctors didn't know was that Zarina had
injected Jayson with her own experimental drug minutes
before they'd administered the hybrid serum. Only her
drug hadn't been meant to turn him into a snarling beast
with a mouth full of fangs. It'd been meant to counteract
the serum.

Unfortunately, Zarina didn't have a chance to inject
the same drug into Moore, since no one had a clue the
guy was going to do something as stupid as volunteer
for the protocol before anyone had even figured out if it
worked on Jayson.

"As a consequence of the failure with Agent Moore,
the team made the decision to go back and restart the
project with raw hybrid material gathered by operatives
in Tajikistan," the man explained.

Trevor bit back a growl. That confirmed something he'd been worried about ever since the mission
to Tajikistan back in March. The entire purpose of it
had been to wipe out the last remnants of the hybrid
research program, but two members of the raid—Moore
and another dirty agent—had obviously taken samples
from the facility before destroying the place.

"Starting from square one worked to our advantage,
because we now have a successful formulation," the
man said.

"You're telling me the serum finally works?" Thorn

said. "You've created completely functional—and stable—hybrids that possess the same abilities as the naturally existing shifters?"

"That's exactly what we've done," the doctor said, pride evident in his smug voice. "In fact, it's possible we've made a few improvements over the original, as I think this video clip from our research facility on the farm will demonstrate."

Trevor glanced at Tanner and Evan to see them standing there with the same shocked expressions on their faces. He was damn stunned himself.

"He's exaggerating, right?" Tanner asked. "There's no way he could create hybrids that good."

Trevor could understand Tanner's reluctance to believe what he was hearing. Every hybrid variant created up to this point, in Washington State, Costa Rica, Tajikistan, or Maine, had all been stricken with some level of aggression, rage, or control issues. Unfortunately, that included Tanner and Sage. If Thorn's people had overcome that, this was a complete game changer. It meant Thorn no longer had to pretend to be interested in keeping natural shifters around. He could wipe out every one of them on the planet if he wanted to.

On the computer screen, a video replaced the slide presentation. At first, all they could see was what appeared to be an obstacle course, but as the doctor continued to narrate, four large men dressed in military camo appeared on the screen. As the camera followed their progress through the course, it was obvious they weren't normal humans—or normal shifters.

They snarled as they moved, exposing more

razor-sharp teeth longer than any shifter possessed. They looked like frigging sharks. They ran fast, too, making jumps and leaps that few but the most agile shifter could pull off. And when they extended their perfectly matching long, curved claws so they could scale a vertical wooden wall thirty feet high, Trevor knew Thorn's doctors hadn't exaggerated.

They'd made hybrids that somehow combined the strength and power of a bear shifter like Declan with the agility and claws of a feline shifter like Ivy, all in a fully controlled package.

Trevor waited for one of the men to say where this testing was being done, but other than a couple more references to a "farm," no one said anything useful.

"And the test subjects are all taken from among my most elite paramilitary units?" Thorn asked. "They're loyal to me?"

"Yes, Mr. Thorn," the doctor said quickly. "The minute we had the new formula worked out, we started our recruitment effort with volunteers who'd spent at least ten years working on your various black-ops teams. Additionally, our psychology assessment process placed the highest emphasis on those who demonstrated loyalty specifically to you. These men represent exactly what you're looking for. They're highly trained, fast, strong, dangerous, fearless, and completely loyal to one person and one person only—you."

That seemed to please the hell out of Thorn. He continued to pepper the doctors with questions regarding the strengths and weaknesses of the hybrids and when there'd be enough of them to proceed to phase two of the project. The doctor seemed to think these new super soldiers had no weaknesses and suggested that phase two could be ready as soon as Thorn gave the word.

"You have it," Thorn said. "Accelerate the timeline, and proceed the moment you think the team is ready."

"What the hell does *phase two* mean?" Evan whispered.

"No idea," Trevor said. "But I'm guessing this is the move we've all been waiting for."

After the meeting was over, Evan transferred a copy of the briefing onto a flash drive and handed it to Trevor.

"Get back to the complex, and start scouring the video for anything we might have missed—where the farm is, who these doctors are, who these new hybrids are, and what the hell phase two of Thorn's plan is," Trevor told him. "Everything and anything you can find."

Evan nodded. "Will do."

"What are you going to do?" Tanner asked after the analyst left.

"Get this information to Adam," Trevor said.

Tanner nodded. "You want me to come with you?"

"No. We can't risk someone seeing us together. Besides, I have something more important I need you to do."

"What's that?"

"Take another run at Dick's office," Trevor said. "Now that we know what we're looking for, maybe you can find something that will tell us where the hell Thorn is cranking out these hybrids and what he plans on doing with them."

Tanner groaned. "Why don't I go talk to Adam while you sneak into Dick's office? I'm a former Army Ranger. I'm no good at all this snooping and spy work."

Trevor shook his head. "No way. To get into his office, I'd have to sneak past that guard dog secretary of his. She hates my guts. You, on the other hand, she seems

to like. Which confuses the hell out of me. I always figured she didn't like me because I'm a shifter, but that
prejudice doesn't seem to apply to you."

"She probably doesn't like you because you're
always such a smart-ass around her," Tanner muttered.
"Besides, it's Saturday. Phyllis won't even be there."

"Phyllis is always there," Trevor said. "The woman
probably has a hideaway bed under her desk."

Tanner frowned and crossed his arms over his chest.
"I've been snooping around Dick's home and office for
weeks with nothing to show for it. Hell, considering the
fact that he wasn't invited to this meeting, it's possible
he may not even know what Thorn is doing."

Trevor found that hard to believe. Dick and Thorn
had been working hand-in-hand since the inception of
the DCO. The idea that he wouldn't know about something this big seemed impossible. Then again, if there
was one person on the planet better at manipulation than
Dick, it was Thorn.

"Dick knows something," Trevor insisted. "Root
through his office looking for reference to a farm. If
Evan can come up with the names of those doctors we
listened to or a facial recognition ID on those hybrids,
look for them, too. Based on what we just heard, Thorn's
plan is going down in less than a week. If we're going to
stop him, we need to have intel now."

Tanner let out a breath. "I'll try, but I'm not promising anything. I suck when it comes to searching through
computer files."

"Then figure out another way to get the information
we need," Trevor said. "Before it's too late to do anything with it."

Chapter 11

JAXSON HAD GOTTEN ALINA AND SAGE BACK ON THE complex without being noticed, then Zarina distracted the guards while Alina slipped the girl back into her room. After that, all three of them had moved heaven and earth to get in contact with Derek's Special Forces team down at Fort Campbell. Luckily, the sergeant and his team had just come back from a field exercise, so he'd been able to talk to Sage on the phone.

Sitting on the edge of the bed while Sage lay on her side, her pillow tucked under her head, a wistful smile on her face, Alina had to admit the effect Derek had on her was nothing short of amazing. Sage was as relaxed as if she'd taken a Xanax. Alina had never seen anything like it.

"How did you and Derek meet?" Alina asked softly.

"He saved my life in Tajikistan," Sage said. "I didn't know that's where I was, of course. Actually, I was barely aware of anything. I only knew I was filled with terrible pain and rage every minute of the day. I'd been like that for so long, I wanted it all to be over with. When the building where I was kept prisoner caught on fire, I thought my prayers were going to be answered and that I would finally get some peace. Then Derek was there, risking his life to save mine, even though I didn't want him to. I even tried to kill him, but he wouldn't give up. He got me out and brought me here."

Alina wanted to ask what had happened to her over there but didn't think that'd be a good idea. Sage had been experimented on and turned into a monster. That wasn't exactly something a person would want to talk about.

"How many times has he come to visit you since then?" she asked instead, figuring that was a safer subject.

"Twice." Sage rolled halfway onto her back, her smile disappearing as she gazed up at Alina. "I know it's hard for him, because he's always working and rarely home, but he calls as much as he can. That's almost as nice as him being here."

Alina's lips curved. "You like Derek a lot, don't you?"

Sage nodded, a smile lighting up her face again. "He has the most amazing, gentle voice, and when he looks at me, I can almost believe he doesn't see a monster. Sometimes, it seems like Derek is the only person who can save me. I ran off because I wanted to be with him."

Alina was no expert on relationships, but investing so much of yourself in a man you've only met a couple of times didn't seem healthy to her. Then again, Alina wasn't a hybrid, so she had no idea what the girl was going through. Who the hell was she to judge?

"Do you know where Fort Campbell is?" she asked.

Sage shook her head with a laugh. "No, not really. I just knew I had to find him."

She rolled onto her side again, and they both fell silent. A little while later, Sage fell asleep, a smile still curving her lips.

Alina couldn't help but hate the people who had hurt the fragile, vulnerable girl. Knowing Thorn was behind the hybrids, and that Dick would exterminate Sage if it proved convenient, pissed her off so badly, she wanted to hunt both men down and shoot them the same way she'd wanted to hunt Wade down and shoot him after he'd murdered her teammates.

Sage reminded her a lot of Jodi. She had the same tough outer persona wrapped around a gentle inner soul, and Alina promised herself she'd never let anyone hurt her the way Jodi had been hurt. That would almost certainly mean going up against two of the most powerful and dangerous men she'd ever met and aligning herself completely with Trevor and his friends.

Unfortunately, Trevor still didn't seem ready to trust her. She couldn't blame him for keeping her at arm's length. He was playing a game of intrigue and espionage at the very highest level, personally taking on Thorn and Dick in their own backyard. One screwup on his part and not only would he be dead, but so would a lot of other people.

As far as Trevor was concerned, Alina was an outsider. He'd been wary of her from the start, and her actions since then had only confirmed his worst fears. He'd thought she was a spy, and she'd behaved like one.

Even so, it'd still hurt like hell when he'd told her he'd rather do whatever he was off doing with Tanner instead of her. She'd known he was full of crap when he'd tried to convince her it was nothing. She'd seen the look on his face when he'd gotten that phone call. Something serious was going down, but he'd decided he'd rather face the threat with Tanner than his own partner.

Damn, that stung like a bitch.

Alina sighed. She didn't know how, but she was going to figure out a way to make Trevor trust her. Not only because he was her partner, but because he was quickly becoming something more to her.

—◦◦◦—

Trevor pulled into the parking lot of the motel in Falls
Church, Virginia, two hours later, then sat in his SUV
for another thirty minutes to make sure he hadn't been
followed. Getting out of the vehicle, he walked across
the parking lot and knocked on the door of room 105.
It swung open by itself. That was when he noticed the
piece of tape over the lock.

Trevor pushed it open the rest of the way, then pulled
the tape off and locked it behind him. Adam was sitting at the small, round table, waiting for him. Trevor
walked over and set the thumb drive on the table without
a word. Adam picked it up and slipped it into the pocket
of his signature duster.

"What's on it?" he asked.

"A video of Thorn's new hybrids," Trevor said.
"They're completely in control of themselves and demon-
strating abilities that no shifter has ever possessed. Thorn
already has a plan for how he intends to use them. I have
no idea what it entails, but I know he's moving on it soon."

Trevor expected Adam to ask for more details, but
instead, he simply nodded.

"There's something I need you to do," Adam said. "It
might not seem important given what you just told me,
but trust me when I say it is."

Trevor got a distinctly uncomfortable sensation in his
stomach. Adam had asked him to do very few things
directly, other than staying in the DCO and keeping an
eye on Thorn and Dick.

"What is it?" he asked hesitantly.

"I need you to track down some people who have

popped up on the radar. My sources say they're planning to hit the ammunition supply point on Aberdeen Proving Ground tonight."

Trevor frowned. Adam had his own operatives he could send out to do basic reconnaissance work like this. Why ask him to do it?

"We finally get some clue about the fucked-up game Thorn is playing, and you want me to chase ghosts around a military base in Maryland when we're this close to nailing the son of a bitch who murdered John?" Trevor demanded.

Adam didn't blink. Then again, the man rarely showed any outward sign of emotion. That cold, detached persona convinced Trevor that Adam might very well share his DNA with a reptile.

"John is the reason I want you to do it," Adam said.

Trevor bit back a growl. "That makes no damn sense whatsoever."

"John never got so focused on Thorn that he forgot the threat posed by every other asshole out there," Adam said. "If these people are stealing military-grade weapons, John would be the first one to say they have to be stopped, even if it means putting your vengeance against Thorn on hold."

"If you're so worried about someone stealing weapons from the army, why don't you just drop an anonymous tip to the base military police? Let the MPs stop the damn heist."

"Because it's possible some senior army personnel on the base are involved," Adam said without missing a beat. "If we alert the army, we'll tip our hand that we're onto them. We need to stop these people now."

The other shifter stood, reminding Trevor how tall he was, which was one hell of a trick, considering Trevor was six four.

"If I have to, I'll send some of my own people, but they're nowhere near your level of training, and they know next to nothing about the army or military munitions." Adam's eyes glinted. "They'll do the best they can, but chances are they're going to get killed. I guess you're okay with that, though, because you have better things to do, right?"

Trevor cursed. He didn't miss the passive-aggressive heat in Adam's voice or the fact that the other shifter was calling him out. In the end, Trevor would never let someone else walk into a dangerous situation in his place. And Adam knew it.

"Okay, I'll check it out," Trevor said. "You do realize I probably won't be able to do more than a little recon, maybe identify these people if I'm lucky."

Adam nodded. "Identifying them and figuring out what they're up to will be more information than we currently have. Since you spoke in the singular, I assume that means you won't be taking Alina with you?"

"I thought you didn't trust her," Trevor pointed out.

Adam's face was as unreadable as ever. "I never said I didn't trust her. I simply told you there was good reason to protect yourself until you knew if she had your back or not. I'm asking you to sneak onto a military base and do something that might involve you getting shot at by a lot of people. It would be good to have someone you trust backing you up."

Trevor didn't say anything.

Adam reached inside his coat and pulled out a large

envelope. "Everything you need to get onto the base is in here."

With that, Adam walked out of the hotel room, closing the door behind him. Trevor opened the envelope, dumping two military ID cards, travel orders putting him and Alina on temporary assignment to Aberdeen, and a collection of pictures and maps of the base's ammunition supply point, or ASP.

He picked up the green ID card with Alina's picture on it. It was a good photo, way better than you typically saw on military identification. Then again, Alina was very photogenic. Where the hell had Adam gotten this picture anyway? It definitely didn't look like a driver's license photo. More like something you'd see on a Facebook page.

Trevor stared at the photo, wondering what to do about his partner. Did he trust her enough to take her with him on a mission like this?

Chapter 12

"CRAP, THESE GUYS ARE GOOD," ALINA SAID, WATCHING through a set of night-vision binoculars as two men got to work on the heavy-duty lock of an earth-covered bunker five hundred feet away from where she and Trevor hid behind a similar bunker. "They've broken through three high-security locks in less than five minutes."

"And since this area isn't being overrun with MPs, I'm guessing they've disabled the alarm inside each bunker as well," Trevor added. "Which means they're better than good—or they have the frigging security codes."

Alina turned her attention away from the dozen men in army camouflage who were working fast to load four large military cargo trucks with crates of ammo and looked at Trevor crouched beside her in the darkness. "You seriously think someone on this base gave these guys access to military weapons?"

Trevor shrugged. "My source said there might be high-level military personnel involved. Considering how easily these guys slipped on base, the fact that there was nobody manning the gates of the ammunition supply point, and the way they seem to know exactly which bunkers to break into to find what they're after, I'd say he was right."

Alina itched to ask Trevor who the hell his source was but restrained herself. By including her on this mission, he was obviously willing to extend the proverbial olive branch to her. She wasn't going to push her luck now and mess everything up. She'd said she was going to do whatever was necessary to win his trust. Right now, that simply meant trusting him first.

"I don't know. We didn't seem to have any problems slipping onto the base, either," she pointed out. "Maybe they bought their fake IDs from the same place you got ours."

Trevor chuckled softly. "Somehow, I doubt that."

She waited for him to say more, but he didn't. Not surprising. Trevor might have trusted her enough to bring her along, but that didn't keep him from being tight-lipped about the mission, especially about who'd given it to them. He'd simply shown up at Sage's prison dorm and told Alina he needed her help slipping onto an active duty military installation on the off chance that a group of thieves might show up and steal some military weapons.

At first, she'd thought he was joking. She couldn't understand why the DCO would send the two of them onto an army base to confront people who sounded an awful lot like terrorists. What the heck did Dick expect them to do?

But on the drive up to the sprawling military research and development base located two hours north of DC, it dawned her on that this probably wasn't a DCO mission at all. She wanted to ask Trevor if this had something to do with Thorn but decided to trust him. After everything she'd seen the past few days, trusting Trevor was becoming easier by the minute. She hadn't trusted anyone in a long time and had been afraid she never would again. She was glad to see that wasn't the case.

"We need to move closer," Trevor whispered. "See if we can identify who these people are and what they're taking."

"Then what?" she asked. "Are we going to try to take them down?"

"I don't know," he admitted. "We're seriously out-numbered, so I guess it's going to depend on how heavily armed they are. If we have to, we'll stick a tracking device onto one of their vehicles and see where they lead us, then call in the cavalry once their guard is down."

Alina nodded, liking the sound of that. She wasn't thrilled about letting these guys off the base with four truckloads worth of ammo and explosives, but it was better than getting into a gunfight and losing.

She climbed to her feet and followed Trevor around the back of the bunker they'd been hiding behind. As they moved in a wide circle toward the bad guys' trucks, they used other bunkers along the way to conceal themselves when they could, keeping to the heavy shadows anytime they had to cross open ground. Hopefully, the men stealing the ammo were too focused on what they were doing to notice anyone sneaking up on them.

Alina would have preferred to have the SUV closer, in case they either had to run like hell or chase someone, but it would have been too risky, so they'd left it half a mile back. As they approached the trucks, Alina checked out the scene with her night-vision binoculars, looking for any details she could see. That's when she realized there was something odd about some of the crates the men were loading into the trucks. She wasn't an expert on army munition containers, but she'd seen enough in her former job to know there was something unusual about the stuff they were stealing.

"Why do those ammo boxes look bigger than the U.S. ammo containers I'm used to seeing?" she whispered to Trevor as they both dropped to one knee.

Trevor's eyes flared vivid yellow, then went back to their normal color. "Because they're foreign."

"What do you mean, foreign?"

He didn't take his eyes off the scene in front of him. "You probably can't see the writing from here, but I can. It's Russian. Mostly infantry type stuff—small arms ammo, hand and rocket-propelled grenades, and explosives."

Okay. That didn't seem right. "What's Russian ammo doing in an American depot?"

"The army stores lots of foreign ammo at Aberdeen," he explained. "It's held for intelligence exploitation, to train Special Forces teams, even to support overseas operations conducted by our allies in places like Syria and Iraq."

Huh. She'd never thought about where ammo like that was stored.

They moved closer, but after a few dozen feet, Trevor put out his hand to stop her.

"What is it?" she asked softly.

Trevor sniffed the air, then looked at her, his eyes glowing yellow again.

"I swear I smell shifters, but the scent isn't quite right."

Her jaw dropped. "Crap! If you're smelling them, do we have to worry about them smelling us, too?"

He shook his head. "We're approaching from downwind, so we should be good. But stay quiet. If I'm right and there are shifters here, we have to be worried about them hearing us."

Up ahead, several of the men climbed into two of the trucks. As she and Trevor ducked down in the grass along the edge of the road, the vehicles cranked up with a loud rumble and headed toward the gate of the ammo area.

"We have to move," Trevor whispered. "Before the other two trucks get loaded up and take off."

Alina pulled her pistol out as she rose to her feet. She and Trevor picked up the pace, closing the last twenty feet between them and the nearest truck. It sounded like there were still at least half a dozen men on the other side of it. Maybe this was even crazier than she'd thought. What the hell were they going to do against six men, especially if one—or more—of them were shifters?

"Move a little closer, and see if you can get a good look at these guys while I plant a tracking device on the truck," Trevor said. "Then we'll pull back and follow them."

She was in complete agreement with that plan. She made her way to the front of the big five-ton truck while Trevor headed for the rear of the vehicle. She was just about to lean down and poke her head around the high bumper when a tall figure stepped out from around the front of the truck right into her path.

She froze, her blood going cold.

Wade.

He was taller and broader than she remembered, but it was him. A hundred different emotions rolled through her all at once—shock, denial, anger, fear.

Wade seemed just stunned as she was, and they stood there for what seemed like forever, staring at each other. Then a slow smile spread across his face, revealing a mouthful of long fangs.

"I was wondering when we'd see each other again," he said, his eyes flaring red.

Her eyes widened as his arm came up and he aimed his gun at her. She tried to get her weapon up in time, but Wade was so much faster than she was. Faster than she could imagine anyone being.

Something slammed into her side, knocking her off her feet just as Wade pulled the trigger. The bullet missed her, hitting the asphalt where she'd been standing.

She braced for impact, expecting to hit the pavement, but instead, Trevor tucked her to his chest and hit the ground rolling.

They ended up in the shallow ditch alongside the bunker access road. Trevor immediately came up to return fire against Wade and the other men who had raced to join him. Alina quickly got her act together and came up on one knee. For a second, everything flashed back to that same desperate and futile stand she and her old team had made in Turkey so many years ago. Even the zing of the bullets zipping right past them sounded the same. Any moment, Trevor would go down, just like Rodney and Fred and Jodi.

No, dammit! Things weren't going that way. Not again.

Firing a few more rounds in Wade's direction, she turned and put several bullets through the big gas tank mounted beneath the cab of the truck. Fuel sprayed everywhere, quickly followed by a whoosh of flames.

The men near the truck scrambled away as fire engulfed the vehicle. Wade pulled back, too, but kept shooting in her direction. She heard him growling in anger as he yelled at the other men not to kill her.

"She's mine!"

Alina stood and moved toward him, climbing out of the slight protection of the ditch, screaming right back at the man who had killed her teammates three years ago. She had no idea what she was shouting. All she knew was she couldn't let this man—this monster—get away.

Strong arms wrapped around her, yanking her off her feet and carrying her away from the burning truck. Some part of her mind recognized that it was Trevor, but she fought against him anyway, not understanding why he was trying to stop her from getting to Wade.

Then the truck exploded, picking up both her and Trevor and tossing them in the air like an angry giant. They hit the ground hard, slamming the breath out of her and sending pain jolting through her body. She felt the heat from the fire wash over her back a second later, making her wonder if her clothes might burst into flames.

She crawled to her feet, ignoring the ammunition in the back of the still-burning truck as it continued to explode, throwing metal fragments and flaming debris everywhere. There were two bodies lying near the center of the blast, but she doubted either of them was Wade. He was too evil to go down that easily. She moved to the side, in the direction he'd disappeared, trying to get an angle where she would have a shot at the bastard.

She caught sight of him climbing in the passenger door of the last truck as it pulled away. She fired the few remaining rounds in her weapon, dropped the magazine, reloaded, then started to fire again as fast as she could. She put at least nine rounds into the cab of the rapidly departing truck, sure she must have hit Wade at least once.

"We have to get out of here!" Trevor shouted, taking

her hand and yanking her farther away from the burning truck, the fire, and the ammo that was still cooking off in the flames like giant pieces of popcorn.

She knew he was right. If one of the chunks of steel zipping out of the flames hit them, they'd be dead. Even realizing that, it was damn hard to let him pull her away.

She kept shooting as they backpedaled away, putting one round after another as it disappeared from sight, praying she'd hit something in the cargo area and make it explode just like the first one had.

No such luck.

When she ran out of ammo, she practically screamed in frustration. She looked at Trevor. "Should we chase them?"

He shook his head. "No. By the time we get back to our vehicle, they'll already be halfway across the base. Besides, we're both out of ammo. What would we do if we catch them, throw harsh words at them? We need to get out of here before the MPs show up and start wondering what the hell happened here."

Dammit. She'd had Wade right in front of her, and he got away. But she nodded and started jogging with him toward their vehicle.

"At least tell me you got the tracking device into their truck," she said.

"Damn right," Trevor said. "Unfortunately, I attached it to the underside of the truck you decided to blow up, so I don't think it's going to help us very much."

"Crap on a stick!"

He glanced at her as they ran. "I'm guessing you know that guy pretty well?"

"Yeah, you could say that. He got my entire CIA

team killed a few years ago. I've been hunting him ever since."

Trevor looked at her in surprise, his expression suggesting he was waiting for her to say more. Instead, she saved her breath so she could run faster. This wasn't the right time or place for a conversation. They needed to get the hell out of there.

When they got to the SUV and climbed in, Trevor cranked the vehicle, then floored it, spinning through the grass and squawking the tires as they reached the asphalt, and racing for the gates of the ASP.

"Silly question, but I'm guessing that guy wasn't a hybrid when you were working with him back in the CIA?"

"No. I think I would have noticed the fangs. They kind of stand out."

"Yeah, they do."

He didn't say anything else for a while, not until they were out of the ASP and hauling ass through the narrow back roads that crisscrossed these remote parts of Aberdeen. Only when they were far enough away from the ammo depot and weren't likely to get rolled up in whatever perimeter the MPs might put around the area did Trevor finally look at her.

"You're probably not going to believe this, but we actually got what we came here for tonight."

Alina frowned. "I'm not sure if you noticed, but those guys got away with a lot of ammunition and explosives."

"Yeah, they did," he agreed. "Three truckloads worth without us getting a tracking device on them. And the guy you were trying to kill got away, too. I know that bothers you even more."

Alina couldn't stand hearing that last part. "Yeah,

don't remind me. Just explain how you think we got what we came here for."

"Because, while I would have liked to stop those guys from escaping and get the man who killed your teammates, at the end of the day, we were sent here to get a look at these people and figure out what they were doing. We did that—and more."

"We did?"

"We know they were stealing Russian ammunition, you know the man who was running the operation, and we have undeniable proof the theft was conducted on the orders of Thomas Thorn."

She stared at him as they entered the main part of the base, then pulled off the road as MP vehicles and fire trucks sped past them, heading the other way. She was suddenly tired of not knowing what was going on in this organization...and on this team.

"What the hell does Thomas Thorn have to do with any of this?" she demanded. "Why does he want Russian ammunition, and how the hell is Wade connected to him? And for that matter, who sent us on this mission to begin with? Because it sure as hell wasn't Dick. And when the hell were you planning to clue me in to all these damn secrets you've obviously been keeping from me from the beginning?"

After the emergency vehicles passed them, Trevor could have pulled onto the road and kept going. But instead, he sat there. "You're right. I have been keeping a lot of secrets from you. Something tells me you've been keeping more than a few of your own, too. We can't do that anymore. It's time we go somewhere and have a discussion we probably should have had the first day we met."

"I can't believe Dick bugged my apartment." Alina glared at the tall glass filled with water and micro listening devices that was sitting on her kitchen counter. "That bastard."

"We can't be sure it was Dick," Trevor pointed out as he picked up the glass and tried to count the number of bugs that had been planted around his partner's place. He quickly gave up—it was like counting gumballs in a vending machine. If Alina had this many hidden microphones in her place, he could only imagine how many his apartment contained. "It could just as likely have been Thorn who ordered it. Though I do have to agree with you on one point—Dick is a bastard."

They'd only learned about the bugs because Trevor had called Adam on the way back from Aberdeen to give him an update on what had happened there and tell him that they were heading to her apartment.

"I'm going to tell her everything," Trevor had added.

"You know her apartment is probably bugged, right?" Adam had pointed out.

"Any chance you can do something about that?"

"I can," Adam had said. "As long as you realize you'll be tipping Dick and Thorn off that you're onto their surveillance. That may cause complications for both of you later."

Trevor was aware of that. But he and Alina needed to get a lot of stuff out in the open, and the best place to do that was somewhere she'd feel comfortable.

"Understood," he had told Adam. "Think you can have the place swept within the hour?"

Adam had assured him he would.

"What was that about?" Alina had asked when he'd hung up.

That was when he'd told her that her place had almost certainly been wired for sound from the moment she'd accepted the job at the DCO.

Needless to say, she hadn't been happy about it. Muttering under her breath, she'd texted her friend Kathy and said she was coming home but that she'd need some privacy for the night so she and Trevor could deal with some stuff, then asked if Kathy could keep Molly for a bit longer.

"How do we know this friend of yours was able to find all the bugs?" she asked now, taking the water glass from his hand and giving it a shake.

He took the glass back from her and set it firmly on the counter. "Adam, and the people he employs, are very good at what they do. If they say the apartment has been cleared, it's clear."

She regarded him thoughtfully for a moment, then nodded. "I guess that brings me to my next question. Do you work for Adam? Is he the one who's been sending us all over the place the past few days?"

Alina had been patient on the drive back to DC, asking a few questions but essentially waiting until they got back here to get into anything serious. He supposed now was finally the time to talk about it. But looking at Alina, her face and hair smudged with black soot from the fire, her clothes torn and burnt in places from the flying debris and the impact of being thrown to the ground, she looked tired. Judging by how slowly she'd walked up the stairs earlier, beat up as well. He'd be lying if he said he wasn't concerned about her. It was all he could do not to pull her into his arms. He shoved his hands in the pockets of his cargo pants instead.

"Maybe you should get cleaned up first," he suggested.

Alina didn't say anything, and for a moment, Trevor thought she might take him up on his offer, but then she shook her head.

"Not yet. We need to talk and get everything out in the open first. We've been hiding the truth from each other long enough. We can worry about cleaning up later. Right now, I just want to know what's really going on."

He nodded and motioned her over to the small table in the corner of the kitchen. He would have preferred the couch, but both of them were too dirty for that. They'd make a mess of her nice furniture if they sat there.

"First off, no, I don't work for Adam. He's a friend of John's and had been working with him for years, trying to find something that would put Thorn in prison. When John was murdered, Adam continued to try to find that evidence."

"Evidence of what?" Alina asked. "I keep hearing all this innuendo implying Thorn was involved in John's death, but if John and Adam were after him for years, he must have done something else. What's behind all this?"

Trevor shrugged. "I have no idea where it all started. I've heard some rumors that make me think Thorn broke the law around the time the DCO was getting started. I'm not sure what it was, but it was bad enough for John and Adam to commit themselves to putting the man away. I've only picked up on that kind of stuff recently, of course. John had kept most of us out of his personal war with Thorn, probably thinking it would keep us safe."

"What changed?" Alina asked. "Why suddenly pull you into it?"

"Tajikistan happened," Trevor said. "John called and yanked me out of the mission I was on in Jakarta, telling me to get my ass to southern Tajikistan in time to help Landon, Ivy, and some other DCO agents take down a hybrid research station. It's a long story, but the short version is that we confirmed Thorn had been behind the hybrid program from the very beginning. He'd been funding the project with money skimmed from the DCO's budget for years. He's the one who gave the order to start experimenting on shifters to see what made them tick and to kidnap doctors and scientists like Zarina to further his research, and when his people came up with the first hybrid serum, he was the one who ordered they use it on innocent people. We have no way of knowing how many people died during that testing, but it wouldn't be a stretch to say it was probably a couple hundred."

Alina flinched. "Tajikistan? That's where you rescued Sage, right? Thorn turned her into a hybrid?"

Trevor nodded. "Yeah. Out of all the people injected with various strains of the serum in Atlanta, Washington State, Costa Rica, and all across the globe, we know of only three who lived—Tanner, Sage, and a DCO agent named Minka Pajari."

"I'm having a hard time believing someone so evil could still exist in the modern world." She shook her head. "How is it possible no one has ever been able to pin anything on Thorn? I know he's a former senator and head of a weapons manufacturing company, but still, you'd think the DCO would have been able to make something stick by now."

Shit. She really had no idea.

"The DCO was started shortly after 9/11 by eight powerful senators and representatives who called themselves the Committee," he explained. "The existence of the Committee and the identities of the people on it are closely guarded secrets. Those eight people control all the money that flows into the DCO and dictate what missions the organization will pursue. They're the real power behind the scenes, and with that almost unlimited power, there's damn near nothing they can't do."

On the other side of the table, realization dawned on Alina's face.

"Thorn might be a former senator and CEO of Chadwick-Thorn, but he's also the senior member of the Committee," Trevor continued. "He's pulled the strings within the organization from the very beginning. That's why John and Adam were never able to get him on anything. Thorn is rich and powerful and has an entire covert organization full of agents at his beck and call to make sure he's always ten steps ahead of everyone who comes after him."

"Thorn is crooked, and he's in charge of the DCO?" Alina asked in shock. "How the hell did that happen?"

Trevor shrugged. "Thorn is one of those assholes who does what he wants simply because he can. And as far as what he wants, that seems to be hybrids."

"But what does he want the hybrids for?" She chewed on her lip as she considered that. "What's he trying to gain? Is this some twisted plan to get more agents for the DCO?"

"That's the part we haven't figured out," Trevor admitted. "He's been working on creating a perfect man-made shifter all this time, spending millions of dollars and throwing lives away like they're nothing, and we don't have a clue why. I'm willing to bet that whatever his endgame might be, we're getting close to it. Tonight proves it."

"You mean Wade, don't you?" she asked softly. "He's Thorn's perfect man-made shifter."

Trevor nodded. "I think so. The other day, when I left you to take care of Sage, it was because I got a tip that Thorn was holding a classified meeting with some people. We were able to slip a listening device into the conference room and heard his scientists announce they'd solved the hybrid problem. They're in the process of creating a whole squad of the damn things at a location they called the farm. These new hybrids are highly trained, deadly, and completely loyal to Thorn. The ones we saw during the briefing looked exactly like Wade, right down to the mouth full of extra teeth and red eyes. Wade definitely smelled different from any shifter or hybrid I've ever sniffed before, too. Like a blend of both. I think that guarantees Wade is one of Thorn's new pets."

"And you honestly don't have a clue what Thorn's going to do with these new hybrids?"

"No. But if he felt it necessary to get John off the playing field—and go to all the effort he's expended trying to wipe out almost every shifter the DCO has—it must be big."

"What can we do to stop him?"

Trevor lifted a brow. "You sure you want to get involved in this, now that you know who—and what—you'll be facing? You've probably figured this out, but

Thorn isn't exactly the kind of man you want to piss off unless you're ready to go all in. You take a swing at him and miss, and you probably won't get another chance. John found that out the hard way."

He'd known from the first day he met Alina that she wasn't the kind of woman to run from a fight, so he wasn't surprised when she nodded.

"After seeing Sage and understanding what Thorn did to her—and people like her—I'm ready to take my chances against him," she said. "If that's not enough, the asshole has Wade working for him. No way in hell I'm walking away from that."

His gut reaction was to tell her there was no way in hell he was letting her walk into it. But he couldn't do that. She was a trained field agent, the same as he was. Even so, the thought of her being in danger like she was tonight made it suddenly hard to breathe.

"Okay," he said. "I just wanted to make sure you were going into this with your eyes wide open."

She reached up to push her hair behind her ear. "So what do we do first?"

"Mostly, it's a waiting game at this point. I have a lot of people working on this, and we've given them a lot to work with."

"What do you mean?"

"Adam and the analyst you saw the other day—Evan—are looking into the Russian ammo angle, Wade's involvement, and Thorn's new hybrid squad to see if they can come up with anything to tell us what he's planning," Trevor said. "While they're doing that, Tanner is trying to learn where Thorn's hybrid farm is located. Plus, we still have Larson going through the

DCO employee files to see if he recognizes anyone from the morning of John's murder. In addition to that, I have an FBI contact named Tony Moretti out in Sacramento doing forensic work on the remains of the bomb I sent out there. With all those people digging, someone is going to find something soon. We just have to give them a chance."

Alina gazed at him thoughtfully. "You realize that I've just learned more about the DCO and what's going on around here in the past ten minutes than I have in the past four days, right?"

Trevor winced. "Yeah, sorry about that."

She shook her head. "Don't be. Dick hired me to spy on you. And even though my a-hole radar was pinging on high alert every time he said something, I still bought his crap. So if one of us owes the other an apology, it's me."

Trevor's mouth edged up. "There's enough blame to go around, so let's just call it even and go from here, okay?"

Alina smiled, and he felt something stir in his chest. Damn, the woman had a strange effect on him.

She leaned forward a little, resting her chin on her hand. "What changed? What made you start trusting me when you were so sure I was on Dick's side?"

He opened his mouth to answer, then realized he didn't know.

"I'm not sure," he finally admitted. "I guess it's one of those instinctive kind of things. I kept getting the feeling you weren't the person I thought you were. And after seeing you risk your life to go after Wade, that's when I knew it was time to trust you."

Alina gazed at him for a long time, and he felt his heart pound faster. Did she realize he was holding back a good portion of the story, that it wasn't just the way she'd thrown herself into a fight that had tipped the trust scale in her favor but the fact that he'd started feeling something for her? Or that it was the most powerful thing he'd ever felt and growing stronger by the minute?

"Well, thanks, whatever the reason." Alina reached across the table to cover his hand with hers. "Knowing that you trust me is more important to me than you can imagine."

Trevor looked down at her hand. She had beautiful fingers. Long and graceful, like the rest of her. She casually ran them back and forth over his knuckles, then slowly laced them through his. His heart thudded so hard in his chest, he could hear it.

He cleared his throat. "Yeah. Trust is pretty important to me, too."

Suddenly, his gums and fingers started to tingle like they did whenever he was on the verge of an uncontrolled shift. Shit, that hadn't happened to him since those early days in high school.

He probably should have pulled his hand away. That would have been the smart thing to do. But at that moment, he wasn't worried about doing what was smart. He was only interested in doing what his instincts told him was right.

What the hell was it about Alina that had him acting like this? And more importantly, did she know the effect she was having on him?

He lifted his head to see her smiling at him.

"Trust is definitely a two-way street," she agreed. "I think it's time I tell you everything."

Chapter 13

ALINA WAS SHOCKED AT HOW FAST EVERYTHING HAD changed between her and Trevor. Then again, almost getting blown up could force two people to set aside their differences surprisingly fast. Trevor had taken a huge risk telling her everything. If she'd actually still been a spy for Dick—or Thorn—her partner had given her more than enough to hang him and his friends. Trust like that deserved trust in return.

She hadn't realized she'd taken his hand in hers, not until the strength and warmth in his strong, sexy fingers seeped through her palm and all the way down to her toes. She marveled that something as simple as two hands touching could have such a profound effect on her, but the contact made her feel warm all over.

"I used to run a CIA direct action team," she said quietly. "There were five of us—Fred and Rodney, two guys I'd worked with my whole career, and Jodi, a new agent fresh out of Quantico and probably the closest friend I'd ever had in the Agency. Then there was Wade, a piece of crap the big shots at Langley put on my team, not because he was a good agent, but because he'd always talked a good game and knew the right people."

She hesitated, but Trevor didn't interrupt. Instead, he sat there and let her collect her thoughts, not seeming to mind that she was still holding his hand.

Once she started, the story flowed, and she told him

everything. How her team had been sent to southern Turkey to stop a group of terrorists from getting the chemicals necessary to make sarin gas. How Wade had taken the lead setting up the raid. And how Fred and Rodney had died in the ambush.

Talking about Jodi was harder, simply because it hurt to think about how young the woman had been when she'd been so viciously murdered. But for some reason, Alina found it easier to talk to Trevor about it than she had other people, even Kathy. Maybe because he never pushed her to keep going but instead allowed her to get the story out however she had to.

"You know what sucks nearly as much as losing my three best friends in the world?" she asked. "It's that less than five months after my team was wiped out, the Syrian town of Ghouta was hit with a sarin rocket attack. Over fourteen hundred men, women, and children died."

Trevor frowned. "I read about that but never heard who did it. Are you sure it was the same people you'd gone into Turkey to stop?"

She shrugged. "The UN investigated, but nothing formal ever found its way into the reports. Everyone in the CIA knew what happened, though. There were a handful of rockets loaded with military-grade sarin used in the attack, but the majority of the civilian deaths were contributed to lower-grade gas spread with several improvised explosive devices. That was the stuff my team was supposed to keep off the battlefield, and we failed. My team, and all those people, died because I didn't realize what Wade was up to until it was too late."

Alina appreciated that Trevor didn't pull out the standard *it's-not-your-fault-you-shouldn't-blame-yourself* crap. She'd heard that more than enough over the years. She didn't need it from him, too. But he seemed to sense she needed to talk about it without him trying to introduce logic into it. She was well aware all those deaths lay squarely at Wade's feet. That didn't make it hurt any less, though.

"I spent years looking for Wade," she admitted. "You could say I became obsessed with it. That obsession made it easy for Dick to recruit me into the DCO. All he had to do was promise to help me find Wade again, and I was hooked. It's kind of sad how easy I made it for him."

"Don't beat yourself up over that part," Trevor said. "Dick might look like a moron, but he's actually a master when it comes to manipulating people."

Maybe so, but she was still mad at herself for buying into his crap. On the flip side, it was amazing how good it felt to talk to someone who genuinely seemed to get it. It was like a weight had been taken off her shoulders.

"You want something to drink?" she asked.

After almost getting blown up and talking for two hours straight, he had to be as parched as she was.

"Yeah," he said. "Thanks."

Realizing she was still holding on to his hand, she reluctantly released it and got up from the table. Instead of waiting for her there, Trevor followed her over to the fridge and leaned back against the counter beside it.

"Thanks for listening to me vent," she said as she handed him a bottle of water. "I never realized I had so much baggage until I started unloading all of it on you."

Trevor grinned. Damn, he had a sexy smile.

"No problem," he said. "I'm glad you feel comfortable enough to talk to me."

She returned his smile, wondering exactly why she was able to talk to him so easily. They hadn't been working together that long, but she felt like she could tell him anything.

"I don't know why, but I'm more comfortable with you than anyone I've ever been around," she said. "I don't think I've ever felt this close to a guy."

That admission came out sounding a lot more serious than she'd intended, and in the silence that followed, she found herself gazing into Trevor's eyes for what seemed like a really long time.

"Is it just me, or is there something more going on here than just the beginning of a really good working relationship?" he asked softly.

Not trusting herself to speak, Alina could only nod, ridiculously glad she wasn't the only one having these thoughts. But was she ready to risk her partnership with Trevor simply because he made her feel all tingly when he looked at her?

"I've noticed that." She wet her lips. "And if we're being truthful, I suppose I should go ahead and admit I've been feeling something building between us for a while."

His eyes glinted gold, another smile spreading across his face. "Since we kissed up in Baltimore?"

Her lips curved. "The kiss, and what came later at my apartment when I helped clean you up. That was…interesting."

He chuckled. "Interesting is one word for it, though I probably would have gone with arousing."

She liked the sound of that. "Arousing, huh?"

He nodded. "Especially your scent."

She had no idea what that meant, and her confusion

must have shown clearly on her face, because Trevor laughed again. Setting his bottle of water on the counter, he reached out and gently ran a finger down her arm. That simple touch made her skin tingle like a brush with electricity. Talk about arousing.

"You probably didn't realize it, but my sense of smell is good enough to pick up any strong scent your body puts off," he said.

"Strong scent?" she asked, still not sure what he was getting at but thinking she might be in trouble.

He nodded. "Sweat, fear…arousal. I can smell those and more."

Alina was confused for all of a second, then remembered how excited she'd gotten that night while she'd been cleaning his wound and running her hands all over his well-muscled abs and chest. He'd smelled the scent of her body when she'd gotten wet.

She couldn't have stopped the blush that crept onto her face if she'd tried. "Okay. That's a bit awkward."

"It doesn't have to be," he said. "If it helps, I was turned on that night, too. If Kathy hadn't come in when she did, I probably would have stripped you naked right here in your kitchen."

His blunt admission surprised her. She hadn't picked up on any interest on his part, other than the kiss, of course. She'd never considered messing around with a coworker, but that seemed to be where this was going. As crazy as it sounded, the idea was appealing. A little scary, too, but not nearly as terrifying as she would have thought. Maybe getting tossed through the air by that explosion had rattled her more than she'd realized.

"Is this going where I think it's going?" she asked.

"Are we seriously going to take a chance at blowing up our partnership for a roll in the hay every now and then?"

Trevor pushed away from the counter to stand in front of her, his expression serious. "I don't want to go anywhere you're not comfortable going, but we have to face the fact that if we keep going up against Thorn, worrying about how our partnership will handle a move into the bedroom is the least of our worries. You've seen what Wade is now, and Thorn may have a dozen more just like him. When you come right down to it, we may not make it out of this alive."

Alina opened her mouth to tell him that she wasn't going to base a decision to sleep with him on the probability of surviving their next encounter with Wade or one of Thorn's other hybrids. But before she could get the words out, Trevor pressed a gentle finger to her lips, sending sparks of electricity dancing across her skin.

"Even if that wasn't the case, if we weren't facing any threat from Thorn at all and were assured of having a long, dull work relationship, I'd still rather take a chance at having something special and amazing with you instead of sitting around for the rest of my life wondering what could have been," he said.

Though he moved his finger away, she couldn't speak. He'd taken the words right out of her mouth... along with most of her breath.

"You know as well as I do—maybe better—that we aren't guaranteed anything in this life," he continued. "If we sit around and wait, telling ourselves that we should do the safe, mature thing, we're going to miss out on something that might be a once-in-a-lifetime chance. I don't know about you, but I'm more scared of wasting that chance than I am of what happens if we sleep together and find out we aren't good in bed."

Alina stood there in shock. She had a hard time processing that a man as rough and sexy as Trevor could be so damn romantic. Guys like him weren't supposed to exist.

She was still trying to form a response when Trevor's mouth quirked in a sexy little smile as he took a step closer.

"I'll assume that silence implies concurrence," he whispered.

Then he kissed her.

Alina immediately buried her fingers in his hair, kissing him back. She couldn't really say she'd ever taken the safe and mature path at any point in her life, so why start now?

Trevor's hand slipped into her hair, cradling the back of her head as he deepened the kiss. She moaned at how good he tasted. Like chocolate…but better. She tangled her tongue with his, encouraging him not only to keep going, but to go even further.

He wrapped his free arm around her, tugging her against him. He hadn't been kidding when he'd said her kiss the other night had gotten to him. She could feel the evidence of that poking her in the stomach, urgently requesting attention.

Unfortunately, she also discovered she'd been banged up more in that explosion tonight than she'd thought. While his hand roaming down her back and over her ass felt unbelievably good, she couldn't help wincing whenever he found a particularly sensitive spot.

Trevor pulled back, a look of concern on his face.

"I'm fine," she assured him. "It's just a few bumps

and bruises from getting bounced around earlier. If you think I'm going to let you get away with heating me up, then stopping because I have a boo-boo, you're crazy."

He flashed her a grin. "I wouldn't dare. I was going to suggest we get you in a warm shower first to relax those sore muscles."

She smiled, liking where he was going with this. "I think a warm shower would be perfect, but only if you join me."

He kissed her again, a long, slow kiss that promised a night of lovemaking she didn't think she'd ever forget. "That was the idea. Who else are you going to get to scrub your back?"

They kicked off shoes and boots in the hallway leading to her bedroom. Taking him into the adjoining bathroom, she flicked on the light, then reached for the bottom of his T-shirt. Just because they weren't getting busy yet didn't mean she had to keep her hands to herself.

Pulling his T-shirt over his head, she ran her hands up his strong chest and along his shoulders, reveling in the feel of his rippling muscles. She couldn't help noticing that the slice along his ribs where the bullet had grazed him the other night was completely closed up now. She ran her fingertips along it in amazement. It looked like a scar that was weeks, even months old.

Shuddering a little at the memory, she dragged her gaze away from it and went back to focusing on his chest, kneading the thick, powerful muscles there, enjoying the way his breath caught. She started to head south, intending to go for his belt, but he caught her hands.

"My turn," he said huskily.

Trevor stripped off her shirt, then made quick work

of her bra. A quiver went through her at the way his eyes flared bright yellow as he took in her rounded breasts with their dark pink nipples. He glided his hands up her stomach, gently cupping her breasts as he bent his head to kiss her again.

He trailed his mouth along her jaw and down her neck, nibbling here and there as he headed lower. While she definitely enjoyed what he was doing, she knew if he reached her nipples, they'd never get in the shower. Not that she minded making love right there, but something told her the anticipation would only make the finale even better.

Groaning, she weaved her fingers in his hair and pulled him away from her neck. Trevor gazed down at her with eyes so gold they were practically glowing. Knowing he was so aroused turned her on like crazy, and it was all she could do not to say the heck with everything and get busy on the bathroom vanity.

"We still have to take that shower," she reminded him.

Trevor nodded, apparently incapable of speech as she jerked his belt open. Gaze locked with his, she popped one button after the next until the front of his cargo pants was completely open. The urge to yank down his underwear and wrap her hand around his thick shaft was nearly overwhelming.

She resisted the urge, instead slipping her hands inside the waistband of both his pants and underwear and slowly shoving them over his hips and down his thighs.

Alina had to drop to one knee to get his pants all the way down, a pose that only put her in a better position to take in his absolutely perfect erection. He was so ready for her that his thick shaft was practically pulsing in time with his heartbeat. Mesmerized, she reached out to wrap her fingers around him, but he caught her hand and pulled her to her feet.

"More clothes, remember?" he said with a chuckle, kicking his pants out of the way. "Then a shower."

Now that Trevor was standing there completely naked, her resolve slipped a little. "Maybe just a little quickie before we shower?"

"I'd be lying if I said it wasn't tempting," he said, his hands finding her belt buckle. "But I want you relaxed and flexible for what I have planned later, and a hot shower is the best way to do that."

Alina was so intrigued by that image, she completely missed the part where he unbuckled her belt. She definitely noticed when he wiggled her pants and panties over her hips and down her thighs. Mostly because Trevor let out a sexy growl as her ass came into view in the bathroom mirror.

As Trevor reached out to turn on the water in her walk-in shower, she used her foot to push her clothes over to join his cargo pants. She wondered if he'd noticed how wet her panties were. But then she caught the way he was grinning at her and realized he knew exactly how aroused she was.

Taking her hand, he pulled her close, wrapping his arms around her and tipping his head down to kiss her again. Except this time, there was nothing between their bare skin...and one very hard cock. Not that she was complaining. She enjoyed the sensation of his hard-on pressing against her stomach as his tongue slipped into her mouth and teased hers.

When the water warmed up enough, Trevor led her into

the shower, closing the door behind them. Alina sighed with pleasure the moment the hot spray rained down on her. She could feel her muscles loosening up already.

It got better when Trevor filled his hands with shower gel and lathered up her whole body. She stood there, letting the water cascade over her back while his strong hands gently massaged, relieving aches and pains she hadn't even known were there.

"You have really great hands," she said as he began to massage her butt. "If you ever need extra money, I think I'd be willing to pay for this."

He chuckled. "Why would you pay me when I'm more than happy to do it for free?"

"Okay," she agreed. "Anytime you want to rub my ass, feel free. I certainly won't complain."

"I'm going to hold you to that," he whispered in her ear, making little shivers run up and down her spine at the promise in those words.

Alina was still thinking about that when Trevor wrapped his arms around her. Having his shaft nestled right against her ass was just about the best thing ever, second only to how amazing it felt when he reached around and teased her nipples with his soapy fingers. She whimpered and dropped her head back onto his chest. He murmured something she couldn't make out, pressing his lips to the curve of her neck and sliding his hand down between her legs to tease her clit.

While she would have loved to have stayed like that all night, it was time to return the favor. With that in mind, she reached behind her and wrapped her hand around his cock and slowly caressed him.

Trevor let out a sound that was half growl, half groan.

Alina wiggled her bottom against him in time with her hand. "You don't mind if I do this, do you?"

"Not at all," he said, his voice husky in her ear. "But before this goes too far, it might be a good time to ask if you might have a condom or two around?"

She was so focused on the movement of her hand on his cock and his on her clit, it took a moment to realize what he'd said. Then the importance of his question fully registered. Crap, they'd started making out without considering protection. What the hell kind of field operative was she? She was supposed to be able to think under pressure.

Her mind was drawing a complete blank. For a second, Alina was terrified she was going to have to call Kathy and borrow some from her.

Hey, neighbor, mind if I borrow a cup of sugar and a couple packs of condoms?

She could just imagine how that would work out. Fortunately, the thought of getting a lecture from her best friend on the dangers of starting something you couldn't finish allowed her to collect her thoughts and remember that she'd bought condoms the last time she'd gone out with a guy. Of course, that had been so long ago, she was seriously worried she might have exceeded the normal shelf life on a pack of condoms. She hoped not.

"There should be some in the medicine cabinet above the sink," she said over her shoulder. "But check the expiration date."

She shivered as Trevor opened the door and stepped out of the shower, taking his warmth with him. But he was back quickly, already rolling a condom down the length of his long shaft.

"Success." He flashed her a grin as he closed the door behind him and spun her around to face him. "Now, where were we?"

She smiled back at him. "We were in the middle of you giving me one hell of an all-over body massage, but judging from that guy"—she motioned at his condom-covered erection—"I'm guessing we're moving on to something else."

Chuckling, he pressed her back against the tiles, then cupped her ass in his hands and lifted her off the floor like she was a toy. She instinctively wrapped her legs around his waist as the head of his cock found her wet opening and lodged there, making her breath catch in her throat. She tried to pull him in deeper with her legs, but he refused to let her, using his hands on her butt to keep her right where he wanted.

"If you prefer, we could always go back to that massage," he murmured, his voice more of a growl than anything else.

She shook her head, barely able to trust her voice as his shaft slowly slid in deeper. "No, this is good. We can always get back to the massage later."

Much later.

Alina kissed him even as he drove his cock the rest of the way in. She gasped against his mouth as he filled her. If she hadn't known better, she'd have thought he was custom-made specifically for her pleasure.

She didn't miss the fact that Trevor's fangs were slightly extended. She could feel their sharp tips against her tongue as she kissed him. But instead of being distracting or scary, they felt amazing. There was something powerful and empowering about knowing he was so hot for her that he could barely stay in control. Trevor must have sensed her complete acceptance of his shifter nature, because he growled against her mouth, squeezing her ass tighter as he pounded into her harder.

As much as she wanted to keep kissing him, the pleasure soon became too much. She pulled away with a moan and buried her face against his powerful neck.

"Harder," she demanded, the word sounding husky to her own ears. "Just like that. Don't you dare stop."

Trevor hitched her a little higher on the tile wall and started thrusting into her so hard it almost knocked the air out of her. It also hit that perfect spot inside, shoving the orgasm that had been slowing building higher and higher right off the edge.

Alina screamed then, knowing the shower would make the sound ten times louder and not caring one little bit. She simply held on tightly and gave in to the pleasure, letting it wash over her.

She came harder than she ever had in her life. Thank goodness Trevor was holding her up, because if she'd had to depend on her own legs to do it, her butt would have been on the floor of the tub.

Trevor let out a deep growl, and she felt his body stiffen as he let himself go. Knowing he was coming with her was an intense feeling and only drew out her own pleasure that much longer.

Afterward, they stayed there against the tile wall for a long time, breathing hard and gasping for breath. At some point, Trevor reached over and turned off the water. She expected him to set her down, but he didn't. Instead, he kept his hands under her ass, kissing and nipping her neck and shoulder as the aftershocks of her orgasm bounced around inside her. She instinctively kept her legs locked tightly around his waist, not wanting to let him move. That had been the most incredible thing ever. She never wanted to let him go.

But then a voice in the back of her head started to whisper things, and she couldn't help but wonder if what they'd just done had also been a mistake. She had no idea where the thought had come from, but within seconds, the voice in her head began to get louder until she had no choice but to weave her fingers into Trevor's wet hair and pull his head back so she could look him in the eyes.

She searched his face, looking for any trace of doubt that would tell her this had all been a case of crazy attraction, and now it was over. While she definitely didn't feel that way, she needed to know what was going on in that head of his.

"What's wrong?" he asked softly, concern in his gold eyes. "Did I hurt you? Was that too hard on your back?"

She ignored his questions, still searching his eyes. They weren't glowing as much now, but they were still clear and bright, with no doubts that she could see.

"Alina?" he prompted, pulling away. "What's wrong?"

She tightened her legs around him, refusing to let him move. "Any regrets?"

Trevor gazed at her for a long moment. Then he leaned in close and rested his forehead against hers. "Never."

That single whispered word made all the doubts and fears in the back of her head immediately disappear.

"I regret many things that have happened since I met you, Alina," he said softly. "I regret putting you in a situation where you almost got shot when we were up in Baltimore. I regret not kissing you that first night we came back here after you taped up my ribs. I regret blaming you for Dick sending those guys after Seth and Cody. I regret leaving you to handle Sage on your own, instead of taking you with me when I spied on Thorn. Most of all, I regret not trusting you from the beginning and not listening to my instincts when they were shouting at me to stop thinking so damn much and go with my gut. But I can promise you, the one thing I don't regret is telling you exactly how I feel and making love to you. Of all the decisions I've made since meeting you, making love to you is the one I'm sure I got right."

Alina's heart did a crazy little cartwheel. Damn, he could say some seriously sexy and romantic stuff. If she'd been wearing panties right then, they probably would have melted right off.

She moved her forehead against his, kissing him softly. "Good. I just had to make sure."

He nodded, then, still holding on to her, turned toward the door of the shower.

"Hey, I didn't mean we had to stop what we were doing," she said, feeling crappy about ruining the mood, especially since she'd just had the best sex of her life.

He held her easily with one arm as he opened the shower door and stepped out with her still wrapped around him like a parasitic sex fiend. He snagged a towel off the hook on the wall and handed it to her.

"Who the hell said we were done?" he asked as he carried her into the bedroom. When he got there, he pulled back the blanket and sheet, then lifted a brow.

"Now, are you going to unwrap your legs from around my waist, or should we go at it again like this?"

That's when Alina realized Trevor was still buried deep inside and still hard as a rock. Okay, that was interesting. It also seemed to indicate she hadn't ruined anything.

"You sure you're not upset that I got a little serious there for a bit?" she asked, not making any move to unwrap her legs from around him. She knew she'd have to move at some point, if for no other reason than to swap out their latex protection. But for the moment, she was absolutely fine with where he was.

"I'm not upset," he assured her. "We're working without a playbook now. Sometimes, we might have to take a break and get a course correction to make sure we're both heading in the same direction."

She smiled. "Well, in that case…break's over. How about we get back to that massage you were giving me before?"

One second, she was wrapped around his waist, and the next, she was bouncing on the bed after he'd tossed her there. Then he was flipping her over on her stomach and straddling the back of her thighs, his big hands already sliding up her butt to the muscles of her lower back.

"As long as you realize that this might start with a massage," he rasped in her ear, "but that's not where it's going to end."

Her lips curved. "I should hope not. After all, I do vaguely remember telling you that anytime you wanted to put your hands on my ass, you should feel free."

He let out a sexy growl. "I remember. And before this night is done, I'm going to make sure there's nothing vague about your memory of telling me that."

———

"You sure we shouldn't be checking in with Adam or Evan? Or Tanner, for that matter?" Alina asked Trevor as she ate another spoonful of mint chocolate chip ice cream from the bowl resting on his chest.

She was naked, curled up beside him, supremely content to eat her favorite flavor of ice cream while her satiated body trembled in near exhaustion from the hours of lovemaking they'd just done in this very bed. Well, on the floor and atop her dresser, too. But it had been in the bedroom at least, so it all counted.

"Not at this time of night," he assured her, careful not to disturb her bowl of ice cream. She'd already made sure he understood how important mint chocolate chip ice cream was to her. "It may take days for them to find something we can use. We just have to be patient."

Alina ate another spoonful of ice cream. "What should we do in the meantime?"

Trevor took the spoon out of her hand, then moved the bowl of ice cream off his chest, sitting up at the same time.

"I was still eating that," she protested only to gasp as he let some of the melted green stuff dribble onto her breasts.

"Don't worry." Wicked glint in his eyes, he leaned forward and slowly and deliberately licked the ice cream with his warm tongue. "I'm not going to stop you. I just thought you might enjoy it more without the bowl."

Chapter 14

TANNER MUTTERED A CURSE AS HE LEFT A MESSAGE FOR Trevor. Where the hell was he on a Sunday morning?

He scrolled through the numbers on the burner phone and clicked on Adam's.

Tanner had waited until Sunday to snoop around Dick's office, figuring there'd be more of a chance it'd be empty. Since Tanner lived on the complex, he happened to know for a fact that Dick worked whenever the hell he wanted to. Fortunately, Dick wasn't there. Unfortunately, Dick's secretary, Phyllis, was. Worse, she spotted him before he could duck out. On the upside, Trevor was right about her liking Tanner. The minute she'd seen him, a smile spread across her face, and she sagged with obvious relief. She'd been trying to make a pot of coffee for the past thirty minutes with no luck.

The fact that the damn machine was so complicated it needed to have a control panel was half the problem. The other half was that it had apparently been built for use on the International Space Station. It had a cartridge that could be preloaded with filters so it could make twenty pots in succession—if the filters didn't run out… or get jammed. He'd seen industrial copiers that were easier to clear than that thing.

While Tanner fixed it, he made small talk with Phyllis. At the same time, he tried to come up with some way to get her out of the office. But short of asking her to look for some nonexistent part for the coffee pot, he couldn't come up with anything.

He was still thinking about that when Phyllis's phone rang. When he realized it was Dick, Tanner thought for sure the man was on his way into the office, but after eavesdropping on their conversation, he realized Dick wasn't in town.

"Dick away on business?" he asked when Phyllis had hung up.

She shook her head as she dropped her cell phone into her purse. "No. He just took the weekend off."

Tanner paused, coffee filters in hand. Could it be this easy? Maybe he wouldn't have to use the widget Evan had given him to decipher the password on Dick's computer at all.

"Is he down at his farm?" Tanner asked Phyllis, trying to sound casual.

Her brow furrowed. "Farm?"

"Yeah, his farm. I heard him mention going down to the farm a lot, so I assumed it was his. I have to admit, Dick doesn't strike me as the farming type. Just can't see him sitting on top of a tractor, plowing the fields."

Phyllis laughed. "Dick doesn't own a farm. As far as I know, the man has never been on a tractor in his life. The farm is the nickname for the Chadwick-Thorn research facility near Millers Creek, North Carolina. I think they call it that because it's built on the remains of an old chicken farm. Dick goes there a few times a year."

Well, damn. It really had been that easy.

Tanner shook his head, still amazed at his good fortune as he waited for Adam to answer. The shifter picked up on the second ring.

"I've got some information for you," Tanner said.

"It's going to have to wait," Adam said curtly. "I need you to bring Zarina to the safe house in Charles City. Now."

Tanner tensed, his fangs trying to come out as fear gripped him. "What's wrong?"

"Kendra's in labor. The doctor and nurse were supposed to be here an hour ago, and they aren't answering their phones. I'm worried Thorn's men got to them."

"Shit," Tanner muttered. "It's going to take me at least an hour and a half to get to Charles City. Maybe you should take Kendra to a hospital."

"We can't risk it," Adam said. "If Thorn is onto us, the first place he'll be watching is the hospital."

Tanner felt his fangs extend. He closed his eyes for a moment and forced himself to calm down. "Okay. We're on our way. Tell Kendra to hold on."

Hanging up, Tanner dialed Zarina's number, praying she was working in the lab. Luckily, she was. He explained the situation as he raced across the quad in the center of the complex. She was ready and waiting for him near her car by the time he got there.

"I'll drive," he said.

Zarina didn't argue, simply tossed him the keys and jumped into the passenger seat.

Even without a lot of traffic, the drive to the bed-and-breakfast seemed to take forever. Tanner heard Kendra's screams of pain the moment he got out of the car. He glanced at Zarina to see her looking just as concerned as he was.

"We have to hurry," Zarina said, dragging a big duffel bag full of medical gear out of the backseat and shoving it in his direction.

They ran for the big wraparound porch, hurrying up the steps. Declan, wolf shifter Clayne Buchanan, and Adam met them at the top.

"What the hell took you so long?" Declan demanded. The huge, blond bear shifter looked like he was about to kill someone. "Kendra has been screaming like this for hours."

"It's been fifteen minutes," Adam and Clayne said in perfect harmony as Zarina pushed past them, running into the foyer and up the stairs to the second floor.

When another scream of agony came from up there, Tanner thought for sure Declan was going to shift completely. He'd only seen the big guy in grizzly bear mode once before, in Costa Rica when Kendra's life had been in danger. He could be frigging scary.

"I'll stay down here," Tanner called out after Zarina's disappearing backside.

"No, you won't," she said over her shoulder. "I might need your help, and it's obvious that no one else down there is going to be of any use."

Tanner blinked. The mere thought of being in the same room as Kendra while she was giving birth scared him shitless. "But—"

"Get up here!" Zarina shouted, her tone suggesting that if he didn't come up on his own, she was going to come back down and get him.

Tanner looked at the other men for help, but they seemed more than ready to let him throw himself on this particular grenade. Cursing under his breath, he ran up the stairs before he went into hybrid mode and ripped a hole through the nearest wall so he could escape.

He almost turned and ran back down the stairs again

when he rushed into the bedroom and found Kendra lying on the floor with Clayne's wife/partner, Danica, on her right and Zarina kneeling between her legs.

Zarina glanced at him. "Get behind her, and help her sit up when it's time to push."

Tanner nodded. That didn't sound too bad. At least Zarina wasn't suggesting he assume a quarterback stance between her legs and help catch the babies on the way out. Just the thought of that made him queasy. Shit, he'd done emergency first aid on the battlefield, seen men and women with body parts completely blown off, and he'd never felt like this.

"Shouldn't Declan be up here instead?" he asked as he walked in.

"He was," Kendra said in between breaths. "I sent him downstairs. He was about to pass out."

Tanner knew the feeling. Swallowing hard, he moved around behind Kendra. He was about to ask something completely lame like how she was feeling when another contraction hit and she cried out again.

His fangs extended in automatic response to the primal sound. *Oh shit*. He was going to lose it.

"Can't you give her something?" he asked. "Make the contractions stop until later? When she's more ready?"

Zarina didn't look at him. "She's ready. She's fully dilated, and the first baby is in the birth canal. This is happening right now. Help her sit up a little. She'll be able to push better in that position."

Tanner got on his knees behind Kendra, then wiggled forward so she was leaning against his thighs. When he placed his hands on her shoulders, she screamed, pushed, and reached up to clamp one hand around his wrist so hard he thought she might break bones.

He was about to suggest again that Declan should really be the guy up here doing this when he heard a booming roar that shook the windows, quickly followed by the rapid *pop, pop, pop* of an automatic weapon. Glass broke, and wood shattered.

Shit. Someone was shooting at the house!

Danica jumped up and ran to the window. "Dammit! It has to be Thorn's men. I guess we know what happened to the doctor and nurse now. That son of a bitch got them and made them talk."

There was more shooting downstairs, this time from inside the bed-and-breakfast. It was followed by a long growl that Tanner immediately recognized as belonging to Clayne. The wolf shifter's howls of rage were unmistakable.

"There must be a dozen or more of them out there." Danica turned to them. Dressed in jeans and a tank top, her dark hair up in a ponytail, she looked more ready to go sightseeing than take down bad guys, but she was a seriously skilled agent. "More than the guys can handle on their own."

Kendra was in midcontraction but nodded. "Go. I'll be okay up here with Zarina and Tanner."

Danica didn't hesitate. Pulling her pistol from behind her back, she sprinted for the stairs.

"Maybe I should go help, too," Tanner suggested.

Zarina shook her head. "No. We have to deliver these babies before any more of Thorn's people show up, and I need your help to do it."

Tanner nodded. While getting Kendra and her twins

safely through this was their top priority at the moment, something told him Zarina was more worried about him losing control and going full hybrid if he went downstairs. She was probably right. But if Thorn's men got through Declan and the others, Zarina trying to protect him from himself wasn't going to account for much. If he had to fight people up here to protect Kendra and Zarina, he had no doubt his inner lion would take over.

Kendra gripped his wrist more tightly as another contraction hit. They were coming closer together. That had to mean she was close to delivering the babies, right?

"I see the head!" Zarina announced.

After that, everything happened a lot faster than Tanner thought it would. Within minutes, Zarina was cradling a tiny, little human. It wasn't exactly the clean little package they show on TV all the time, but it definitely seemed healthy if the defiant cry it cut loose was any indication.

Zarina wrapped the little boy in a bath towel and quickly handed him to Tanner. He almost suggested that Kendra should probably hold the child, but she was still gasping and pushing, so maybe that wasn't such a good idea. He grabbed the baby like a football and held on for dear life as Zarina turned her attention to the boy's twin.

Downstairs, the sound of shooting intensified, as did the growling and snarling. Tanner itched to run down and help, even if it meant going hybrid. The thought of his friends facing such overwhelming odds without him made his claws come out and his hands ache with the need to rip someone to shreds.

He was so focused on fighting down the urge, he didn't realize Zarina had delivered the other baby. It was only as Zarina placed the carefully swaddled but very messy baby in Kendra's arms that he realized the shooting had stopped. He was still trying to figure out whether that was a good thing when Kendra glanced up at him expectantly. He quickly leaned over to hand her the little boy he'd been holding.

The infant gave him a curious look for a second, then must have decided he liked his momma's arms a lot more than Tanner's, because he closed his eyes and snuggled against her.

Footsteps pounded on the stairs, interrupting the sudden silence. Tanner picked up Declan's scent long before he reached the bedroom. Tanner looked up to see the big bear shifter standing in the doorway, his look of concern quickly replaced by one of wonder.

Zarina smiled at him. "You're the father of a set of perfectly healthy twins—a boy and a girl."

Declan stood there, not saying anything, just gazing at Kendra and their two children. Then he slowly moved to his wife's side and dropped to his knees beside her. "Are you okay?"

Kendra's lips curved. "I am now. Is everyone okay downstairs?"

Declan nodded, then leaned close and put his forehead against wife's, closing his eyes as he breathed her in. "Everyone's fine. Well, except for Thorn's men. Some got away, but most of them are dead."

Declan pulled back to gaze down at the twins, a goofy smile crossing his face.

"Do you have names picked out?" Tanner asked.

Kendra nodded. "Chloe and Noah, after my grandmother and Declan's grandfather."

Tanner would have commented, but Adam stuck his head in the room.

"Sorry to break up the joyous moment," he said, "but we need to get packed up and out of here before the cops—or more of Thorn's men—show up."

———————

Alina clutched the sheets, her whole body quivering as Trevor slowly moved inside her. His thrusts were almost casual, like he had all the time in the world. Or maybe he simply enjoyed driving her insane. Not that she was complaining. If there was a better way to start off the day than with a gorgeous man between your legs, she couldn't imagine what it could be.

Trevor's eyes flared brighter, as if reading her mind. Giving her a sexy grin, he bent his head to kiss and nibble her neck until she was panting and writhing so much beneath him she thought she might orgasm just from that. After the number of ways he'd made her climax last night, anything was possible.

When her orgasm hit, she wrapped her arms and legs around him tighter and bit down on her lower lip to keep from screaming too loudly. The move didn't work any better now than it had the other times they'd made love.

Only when Trevor was sure she was coming did he let himself go, nipping her neck a little with his sharp fangs as he climaxed with her. She kept her legs wrapped tightly around him afterward. She wanted him to stay right where he was, between her legs, buried deep inside her forever.

"I could get used to this," she said softly, pushing a stray hair away from his forehead.

He chuckled. "That's the idea. I want you to get used to it. Why do you think I'm working so hard?"

She smiled. "I'm not sure I would call anything we did last night *work*. If so, then sign me up for overtime."

"Okay," he admitted. "I have to agree with you about the work thing, but I'm definitely doing my best to impress you."

She kissed him. "Consider me impressed."

That kiss led to another, then another. That was about the time she felt him get hard again.

She gave his shoulder a playful shove. "Okay, that's it. No more kissing for the rest of the morning. It just leads to more sex, and we can't have any more sex until I get something to eat."

Trevor groaned but rolled off after one more quick kiss. "I'll shower first. If we both go in there, I can't promise to keep my hands to myself."

Alina sighed as she watched his naked backside disappear into the bathroom. Considering she'd gotten a grand total of two hours of sleep last night, she should be a complete zombie. Instead, she felt amazing. Great sex could do that.

She was still lying there when she realized she hadn't heard the water turn on. Trevor might be fast in the shower, but he couldn't be that fast. Rolling out of bed, she headed for the bathroom.

She found her partner standing in front of the vanity completely naked and staring at his phone, an intent— dare she say worried—expression on his face.

"Did you miss a call?" she asked. "I never heard it ring."

He nodded absently. "Yeah. Tanner called earlier, but he didn't say what it was about, and his phone went to voice mail when I called him back. There's an email from Seth Larson, too, but I haven't read it yet. I got caught up in a text from that friend at the FBI I told you about—Tony Moretti."

That caught her attention. "The one doing the bomb analysis? What did he say?"

"It's a long report," Trevor said, scrolling his finger down his phone. "But the most interesting thing is that the bomb was made with military grade C-4 and military blasting caps. Tony was able to use the chemical markers they put in the C-4 to track the explosives back to a specific lot number, most of which are from the black-ops world."

"You mean like the CIA?"

He looked up at her. "Or the DCO."

She frowned. "Okay, that is scary. Anything else?"

"Nothing that will make you feel any better." He scrolled through the report some more. "There was a partial lot number on one of the blasting caps as well. It traces back to the black-ops world, too, except a friend of his at the CIA is sure they consumed all of those caps in training years ago, so Tony doesn't think our bomber could have gotten them from the Agency."

She considered that. "So either his friend at the CIA is lying or we're looking at a blasting cap that might have been issued to the DCO?"

He shrugged. "Maybe."

She walked over to lean around him so she could look at his phone. "Any way we can check?"

"I'll never get anywhere near the DCO's ammunition inventory system, not without raising a bunch of red flags," he said. "But maybe Jake could. One of his additional jobs in the DCO used to be helping with the monthly inventories before everything went to crap and he got labeled as persona non grata thanks to his association with me."

"Call him," she urged. "Let's see what he can do."

Trevor's brow furrowed. "I've been trying to keep him out of this, so he won't get any more screwed over than necessary."

Alina nudged his big, strong shoulder. "How about you let Jake decide that? I'm pretty sure he wants to catch John's killer as much as anyone."

Trevor sighed but didn't say anything.

She nudged him again. "So are you going to call him?"

He nodded. "Yeah. Let me see what Seth has to say first, then I'll call Jake. Why don't you go ahead and jump in the shower? This might take me a second."

Alina had barely stepped in the shower and gotten the water turned on before she heard Trevor curse. She opened the glass door and looked out. "What's wrong?"

"Seth identified three people going into the main DCO building about thirty minutes before the blast. John Loughlin, his secretary, Olivia, and this guy."

Trevor turned his phone around, showing her a photo of a guy with dark hair cut military style and blue eyes.

"Who's that?" she asked.

He turned the phone around and stared at it, as if to assure himself he was seeing straight. "It's Ed Vincent, my former teammate—the one who quit the DCO within days of the bombing without ever bothering to tell me. Oh, and by the way, Ed used to help with monthly ammo inventories, too."

Alina gaped. "Wait a minute. Are you suggesting

one of your former teammates provided the explosives that Shishani used to make the bomb? That Ed's the one who brought the thing onto the complex and put it in John's office?"

Trevor frowned. "I don't want to believe it, but what the hell am I supposed to think? There's no reason Ed should have been there at that time of the morning. Hell, he shouldn't have been anywhere on the DCO complex. He was supposed to be with Jake, doing some kind of training that week. It's one of the big reasons they didn't go with me on that mission up in Maine."

Alina wanted to ask what the mission up in Maine had been about but decided against it. There would be time for that later, after they dealt with this.

She turned off the water and stepped out of the shower, then placed her hand on his chest. His heart pounded beneath her fingers. "You need to call Jake and get him on this. Because right now, we're merely guessing."

Trevor nodded, his brow still furrowed. "All right. I'll call him now. But I can promise you, Jake isn't going to like this. Go take your shower."

Alina cleaned up as quickly as she could. Over the running water, she could hear her partner arguing with Jake. Apparently, Jake wasn't happy with the idea of checking up on an ex-teammate. After Trevor told Jake why he was suspicious, the other man must have calmed down and agreed to do a little digging, because Trevor hung up.

She turned off the water, then grabbed a towel from the hook and wrapped it around herself.

"Jake said he'd do a quick check of the DCO ammunition inventory system, then call us back." Trevor sighed. "I pray you're right and that I'm seeing stuff that's not really there."

Alina hoped so, too.

She finished up and was drying her hair when Trevor's phone rang. Her partner had already showered and dressed and was waiting with phone in hand.

"What do you have?" he asked Jake.

Trevor listened, jaw clenched. Finally, he hung up with barely a grunt of acknowledgment. For a minute, she was sure he was going to sling his phone across the room.

"Well?" she prompted, setting the dryer on the vanity.

He took a deep breath. "The ammo inventory system is a complete train wreck now that so many people have left, but Jake was able to confirm that there's a box of electric blasting caps and a case of C-4 missing. It looks like the stuff disappeared early Sunday morning of the weekend before the bombing. It's not like Ed signed for the crap, but his passcode was used to turn off the alarm in the bunker, so it's pretty damn evident."

Crap on a stick.

Trevor shook his head. "Fuck, he really did it. Ed stole the explosives and gave them to the bomber. Then he brought the damn thing on the complex and put it in John's office. No wonder he left. He knew we'd figure out his code had been used to get into the storage bunker at some point."

"What do we do now?" she asked softly.

"We go after him," Trevor said, his voice as soft and low as hers.

"You know where Ed is?"

"I don't, but Jake does," Trevor said. "Turns out he's talked to him a couple of times in the past few weeks. He didn't tell me, because I always seemed so pissed at the way Ed left. Ed's been working private security under a fake name at an industrial place outside Gainesville, Virginia."

Alina twirled her hair up in a twist, then hurried into the bedroom to put on some clothes.

"Are we going to arrest Ed…or something else?" she asked as she pulled on her jeans.

Trevor didn't flinch. "That all depends on him."

Chapter 15

"If Ed was so worried about the DCO figuring out he was behind the bombing, why hang around the area and get a job?" Alina asked. "Why not flee the country?"

Trevor shrugged as he and Alina approached the address Jake had given him earlier, momentarily distracted as he realized the place was a decrepit-looking hazardous material storage site. Of all the jobs he could imagine his former teammate taking, security guard at a hazmat site wasn't one of them. The operation was nothing more than a large collection of mismatched metal warehouses surrounded by endless piles of beat-up drums and long sections of rusted chain-link fence. Not only that, but it stunk to high heaven. Trevor's nose was already burning, and they hadn't even gotten inside yet.

"Ed and I worked espionage cases for a long time together, digging out sleeper agents and moles who had been hiding in plain sight for years," Trevor said as he slowed the SUV. "Maybe Ed thought changing his name and blending into a sea of humanity was the best way to disappear. He's seen it work in the past."

"Okay. But then why contact Jake?"

Trevor didn't have a good answer for that. "No clue. Unless he thought Jake might be willing to clue him in when trouble was on the way."

Trevor pulled up to the gate of the hazmat complex, expecting to see guards there—maybe even Ed—but there was no one around. Just a wide-open gate and an empty guard shack. The hair on the back of his neck stood up, and his senses began to tingle. This place was like a ghost town. Something didn't feel right.

"Are you sure this is the address Jake gave you?" Alina murmured as he drove through the gate. She took in the discarded, rusty drums stacked up against a few of the buildings. "It doesn't look like there's anyone here."

Trevor was thinking the same thing. "It's Sunday, so maybe the place is closed."

Alina made a face, clearly not buying that idea. "More likely the EPA shut everything down, and everyone who used to run the place is in jail. Maybe Ed is watching this place until the feds send someone in to clean it up."

Considering that his eyes were practically tearing up from all the strange chemical odors, Trevor could believe that.

He stopped in front of a building that looked like it was the main office and climbed out of their vehicle. Alina did the same. They were confronted with rows of squat, metal buildings marked with various hazmat signs, warning the structures contained everything from flammable liquids and gases to poisons, corrosives, and explosives. He could see why they needed guards in a place like this. It wasn't exactly the kind of facility you'd want people wandering around in. Which begged the question, why had the gate been left open? And if there were guards around, why hadn't anyone challenged them yet?

"Are we wasting our time here?" Alina asked.

Trevor was tempted to say yes. Then he looked down the row between two of the buildings and spotted a truck with a security decal plastered on the side. The driver's side door was open, and it was parked in front of a big two-story building with flammable signs posted on both sides.

He caught Alina's eye and jerked his head in that direction. She nodded, falling into step beside him. As they got closer to the truck, he expected Ed to step out of the big warehouse and ask them what the hell they were doing here, but there was no one in sight. The big, sliding double doors of the warehouse were open, a rusty lock hanging off the hasp and heavy petroleum fumes rolling out of the building in waves.

"Can you smell Ed's scent in the truck?" Alina asked. "At least confirm he's here?"

Trevor leaned and took a sniff. With the fumes, he could barely smell anything. He thought he was picking up a man's scent, but it didn't seem familiar. With this stench, he simply couldn't trust his nose.

He shook his head. "I can't be sure." He motioned toward the warehouse. "But we're here now—might as well check the place out."

The interior of the building was dark, the only light coming from the overhead skylights and a few windows scattered along the upper and lower floors. The windows might have let in a bit more light if they hadn't been filthy—and covered with heavy-gauge security wire.

The second level seemed to be more catwalk than actual storage area, with its only apparent purpose being to provide access to the various overhead hoists and to let people move around the stuffed warehouse more easily.

The fumes were worse inside, making Trevor's nose tingle and eyes water more than they already had been.

He closed his eyes and focused on his sense of hearing, trying to shut out the stench long enough to figure out if he and Alina were alone.

His eyes snapped open when he heard a creak of metal somewhere in the back of the place.

"Which way?" Alina asked.

She had her sidearm out and had clearly been covering him while he'd been standing there with his eyes closed. Maybe her instincts were saying the same thing his were, that there was something strange going on in here.

Trevor pulled his own weapon out as he motioned with his chin toward the rear of the building. "That way. It sounded like footsteps."

They carefully made their way between stacks of barrels and boxes, every one of them marked with either a flammable-liquid or flammable-gas label. Trevor hoped no one started shooting in here. This wasn't the environment for it. One shot into the wrong box or drum, and this place would go up like a Roman candle.

Trevor scanned the dimly lit rows and aisles between the boxes and drums as well as the second-floor catwalk that ran around three sides of the building and overlooked the main floor. If there was someone in here, he couldn't see them.

He tried to move and listen at the same time, straining to catch the sound of another creak—or better, the sound of a heartbeat—but he didn't pick up anything. Maybe that was because the space was large, and sound bounced around funny because of all the metal.

Or maybe it was simply because there was no one here.

He and Alina were near the back wall when he picked

up a scent that didn't belong. It was hard to believe he could smell anything with all the petroleum odors cloying his nose, but this odor was peculiar enough to grab his attention. It smelled a little like blood mixed with something seriously nasty.

Trevor turned and headed in that direction, letting his nose lead him. Alina followed silently. The stench only got stranger the deeper they went into the building. It was definitely blood. And it smelled fresh. At least he thought it did. It was hard to tell with the other odors nearly overwhelming it. Shit, what the hell was that smell?

When he rounded a stack of boxes, Trevor discovered exactly what it was—and really wished he hadn't.

There were two metal containers in the center of the floor, filled with viscous, yellowish-green liquid. Inside each was a decomposing body. One looked fresh, still mostly recognizable and wearing the remains of a dark-blue security uniform. The other wasn't so fresh.

"Is that…acid?" Alina asked in horror.

Trevor couldn't blame her. He'd seen a lot in his time in the army, DIA, and DCO. But nothing like this.

All he could do was nod as he slipped his weapon back into his holster and stepped closer to get a better look. The fresher body wasn't too bad, but the other one was hard to look at. The acid had eaten away most of the guy's skin and organs. About the only solid parts left were one arm and a leg that had been too long to fit into the cramped space of the metal shipping container.

Trevor wasn't sure what the hell was going on here and wasn't sure he wanted to know. He hated to think it, but it looked like Ed had killed two of the security guards who'd worked here and attempted to dispose of their bodies. Why? He had no idea. Just like he had no idea why Ed had killed John and Olivia.

He was about to take out his phone to call the cops when a glint of something shiny along the badly decomposed man's leg caught his attention.

Ignoring the acid fumes and the horrible stench, he leaned over the container and took a closer look. A long, slim piece of metal was attached to the man's lower thigh bone just above the knee joint.

Shit.

Heart pounding, Trevor yanked his weapon out and spun to look around the warehouse space.

Alina spun around with him, her eyes trying to dart every direction at once. "What's wrong?"

"Ed broke his leg jumping out of a helicopter when he was in Air Force Pararescue. He had a long plate attached to his lower femur to stabilize it," Trevor said. "This body is Ed's. We've been set up."

Somewhere along the catwalk on the far side of the warehouse, a man clapped his hands in applause.

Trevor and Alina pointed their weapons that way as Jake stepped forward to stand in the beam of late-day sunshine streaming in through one of the overhead skylights. Wade and two other men were with him. Judging by their size and the telltale red eyes, they were hybrids as well.

"So you finally fucking figured it out, huh, Trevor?" Jake sneered. "Took you long enough."

Then the shooting started.

Trevor tried to stay with Alina, but as the four people up on the catwalk started blazing away at them with automatic rifles, that became impossible, and they both had to run for their lives. He turned and headed deeper into the warehouse, popping off an occasional shot at Jake and the others as they moved down the stairs from the second level. He hoped he could draw them away from his partner and give her time to get out of here.

"What happened, Jake?" he shouted as he ran, wanting to make sure they knew exactly where he was. "Ed catch you planting the bomb, or is there another reason you killed the man who covered your back for all those years?"

He didn't really expect an answer, not in the middle of a firefight, but Jake surprised him by laughing. From the sound of it, the man wasn't more than three or four rows away.

"He didn't catch me," Jake called out as he headed in Trevor's direction "But I knew he was onto me. The stupid idiot confronted me after the bombing. I had no choice but to kill him."

Trevor wasn't naive. Jake wasn't confessing out of the goodness of his heart. He and some of his hybrid buddies were probably trying to home in on Trevor's voice right this second. Knowing that, it would likely have been smart to shut up. But Trevor had never professed to be that smart, not when it came to dealing with a traitor. He was pissed, and he wanted Jake dead.

"You didn't simply kill Ed, you asshole," Trevor growled as he kept moving, luring Jake, and hopefully the others, in a great big circle around the warehouse. "You put him in a tub of fucking acid."

"There's no reason to be like that, man," Jake said. "It was nothing personal. Just business."

"Business?" Trevor snapped, doubling back toward

the place they'd found Ed's body. "What the hell does that mean? Whose business?"

"Isn't it obvious?" Jake asked, mirroring Trevor's movements. "I've worked for Thomas Thorn from the day the DCO recruited me," Jake admitted. "When he called and said it was time for John to die, I simply did what I was paid to do. Like I said. It was nothing personal. Just business."

Alina dove for cover behind four yellow drums covered in flammable-liquid labels. It wasn't the best place to hide. One spark, and it would all be over. But when you're getting shot at by your psycho ex-teammate turned hybrid monster, you take what you can get.

She turned, expecting to see Trevor right behind her, and barely caught sight of him running in the other direction. Alina moved to follow, but another burst of automatic weapon fire near her feet drove her back even farther, making her scramble for better cover.

She heard Trevor shooting at Jake, then practically taunting the man, and she knew exactly what her partner was doing. The damn heroic idiot was trying to get Wade and all the others to chase after him so she could get away. She could understand why he would do something like that—she'd do the same. But he had to know that, with her background, there was no way in hell she was ever going to leave him—even if they weren't already more than partners.

So she kept moving fast, avoiding the hail of gunshots coming at her from the catwalk above while trying to figure out where Trevor was at the same time. The moment she got a reprieve from the constant gunfire, she poked her head up to see where everyone was. As she expected, Wade and the other hybrids were coming down the stairs and splitting up to start searching the warehouse.

Seeing Wade up on the catwalk earlier had been bad enough, but realizing Jake, a guy she'd liked from the moment she'd met him, was involved in both Ed's and John's deaths was gut-wrenching. Knowing something about what it felt like to find out a team member had betrayed you, Alina didn't have to guess what Trevor would be trying to do once he thought she was safe. He'd be looking for revenge, and he'd do anything to get it—even if it meant risking his own life.

Alina had to figure out a way to help him. She needed to get Wade and at least one of those other hybrids to come after her and not Trevor. That would give her partner his best chance to deal with Jake—then get them both out of here.

It wasn't like she'd have to do anything special to get Wade to come after her. He hated her. Chasing her down would be fun for him.

Pulse racing at the insanity of what she was about to do, Alina hunkered down a little lower in her hiding place, trying to be as quiet as possible as she pulled her backup magazine out of her pocket and had it ready so she could reload quickly. When she had a chance to hit these guys, she needed to make it count. Because she wasn't merely fighting a collection of cold-blooded killers. She was dealing with hybrids who were stronger, faster, and ten times harder to kill than a normal person.

Yup, it was insane. But she was doing it anyway.

"I guess you're with Thorn now, too, huh, Wade?"

she yelled as she moved out from behind the protection of the boxes she'd been hiding behind, firing a couple of shots in the general direction of the stealthy hybrids.

When Wade didn't answer, she moved a little to the left, not even trying to be quiet, and poked him again. Not so much because she cared what he had to say, but simply so she could get his goat. Because that was one thing she always remembered about him...he hated losing at anything, even if it was just a bout of trash talking. He'd always wanted people to know he was the smartest person in the room and always had the answers.

"Did he buy you recently, or has he owned your balls all along? I know your loyalty has always been flexible."

That must have gotten his attention, because she heard him growl from somewhere to her right. Crap, he was a lot closer to her than she'd thought. She immediately started backing up, hoping he and the other hybrids—if they were coming this way—would follow.

"I started working for him a few weeks before Turkey," he admitted as he continued moving to the right. "As much as I disliked the four of you, I hadn't been planning to betray you. But when a man comes to you and drops a briefcase full of money in your lap, it's amazing how easy it is to change your plans. Thorn wanted the CIA out of the way so he could put sarin gas in the hands of certain rebel forces in Syria. You and your team had to go."

"Why would Thorn want something like that?" Alina demanded, just to keep him talking.

If he was talking, she'd know where he was. Of course, there was a very good chance he was just talking to distract her while his hybrid buddies circled around and took her out from behind. But that was a chance she had to take.

"Over a thousand people died in that sarin attack, Wade," she added. "Why would he pay you money just so a bunch of peasants would get killed? They were nothing to him."

On the other side of the warehouse, there was a barrage of automatic gunfire. Moments later, an explosion shook the building, and gouts of flame flew through the air, starting half a dozen small fires. Slower, individual shots followed, and Alina knew that meant Trevor was still over there dealing with Jake and maybe one of the hybrids.

"Oldest reason in the world—money," Wade said from somewhere close behind her.

He was trying to herd her toward one of his men, she realized. Her instincts screamed at her to fall farther back or try and loop around him to the left. But she knew she'd never beat these guys at this kind of game. They were better equipped to be the cats than she was to be the mouse in this scenario. She moved behind a stack of heavy crates, preparing to shoot the first person she saw coming her way, praying it would be Wade.

"I guess Thorn was hoping the attack would prompt the U.S. and European coalition to mount a full-scale invasion of Syria and topple the al-Assad government. If that had happened, Russia and Iran would have been drawn in as well, and Chadwick-Thorn would have made billions selling arms to every side."

Even though Alina was coming to understand how horrible Thorn was, her mind still rebelled at the idea that someone could be so greedy they'd start a war for money.

Movement out of the corner of her eye caught her attention, and she leaned out from behind her crate just enough to see one of the hybrids standing a few feet away. She held her breath as the man sniffed the air. While it seemed like he might be picking up her scent, it was obvious he couldn't pinpoint her location. The fumes must be confusing him.

She slowly lifted her weapon, getting ready to shoot. She would have felt better if she'd known exactly where Wade was, but she wasn't about to wait to see if he'd show up. She'd never get a better chance than this to take out one of the hybrids trying to kill them.

The hybrid must have seen her movements, because he snapped his head around in her direction at the last second, his eyes glowing crazy red. He started bringing his weapon around, but she got her shots off first, hitting him three times and dropping him to the ground. Even after being hit that many times, he still got right back up and scrambled away between two rows of boxes.

She started to move after him, but as she stood up, she felt the hair on the back of her neck rise. She spun around and popped off several shots at Wade before throwing herself to the side just in time to avoid the burst of gunfire slamming into the crates only inches from her head. She was sure at least one of her shots had gotten the man, but he barely moved in response.

When Alina hit the concrete floor and rolled behind the next row of drums without getting shot, she thought she'd been lucky. Then something exploded nearby, sending a firestorm of flames rolling right over her head, forcing her to quickly crawl on her hands and knees to get away from the heat. She heard Wade somewhere right behind her, laughing now that he thought he had her.

But then she heard him curse as he moved right to avoid the flames starting to eat into all the cardboard boxes and wooden crates around them. "You've always been naive, Alina!" he shouted. "That's why I couldn't stand working with you. You never understood how the world works and how vicious people really are. You think Thorn made me and all these other hybrids to save the world or something? Fuck no! He needs a squad of unstoppable soldiers to start his war. He tried it before with lesser men, but this time, he's not messing around."

Alina came to her feet, trying to get a shot lined up on Wade through the flames as he prowled around. But the fire grew out of control now, and he was forced toward the front of the warehouse by the spreading flames, away from her.

The urge to do something extreme, like jump through the flames and go after him, was hard to resist. But her need for revenge paled in comparison to finding out what he was talking about. If Thorn was going to pull something like that sarin gas attack again, she needed to know about it. She wasn't going to let more innocent people die because of her.

"You're full of crap. There's no war!" she shouted, praying his ego would force him to answer.

Wade smirked as he backed farther away, the flames making his eyes look even redder. "The crazy bastard is sending us to the eastern part of Ukraine. Wearing Russian uniforms and using those Russian weapons we stole, he wants us to go kill a couple thousand people in the nastiest massacre you've ever seen. And we're going to make sure Russia gets blamed for it all. You wanted to know what war I'm talking about? The big one—World War III. The United States and NATO will have to respond, and then Russia will counterattack. After that, it's all over. Just think of all the money to be made in a war like that."

Alina stood there in the raging fire as drums of flammable liquid began to rupture, spilling sheets of flames everywhere. Her stomach churned as she realized all of this really was about money. Raging mad, she lifted her weapon and fired three shots at Wade. He skipped aside, though, and she missed. She expected him to return fire, but he laughed and backed toward the exit.

"I would have preferred shooting you." He grinned. "But burning you to a crisp works, too."

With that, Wade turned and let out a loud growl, like he was calling to the other hybrids. Then he picked up speed and disappeared into the warehouse beyond the smoke and flames. A moment later, she heard movement on the catwalk above, and she caught sight of the hybrids racing through the smoke, leaping to the floor beyond the wall of flames that had cut her off from Wade.

Alina turned and ran toward the back of the warehouse. She hadn't heard many shots being fired from that direction, and she prayed that meant Trevor had already won and found a way out of here. The flames were spreading fast, and soon, the smoke building up in here was going to make breathing impossible.

She found Trevor and Jake standing beside the tubs where they'd found Ed and the security guard, fire burning all around them. She slid to a halt, coughing and choking on acrid smoke. Jake had some kind of wicked clawed crowbar in his hands while Trevor was empty-handed.

"It's over, Jake," Trevor said, and Alina had to wonder why he was trying to talk the man down. It wasn't going to happen.

"I don't think so." Jake adjusted his grip on the make-shift weapon. "I've hated you and all your damn shifter friends the entire time I've been here. There's no way in hell I'm letting one of you put me in jail."

Lifting the crowbar, Jake let out a shout of hatred and charged at Trevor.

Alina lifted her weapon to shoot, but before she could squeeze the trigger, Trevor reached out and grabbed Jake, flinging him into flames. There was a short shout of pain as Jake's body disappeared into the inferno, but the fire roared higher, snuffing out the sound.

Trevor stood there, motionless for a time, staring into the flames where his old partner had disappeared. Finally, he turned and saw her. He ran over to grab her hand. "Can we make it to the front of the building?"

Alina shook her head. "We'll never get that far. There's a wall of flame between us and the doors. Even if we could, Wade and the other two hybrids are probably waiting for us."

"Then we find a way out the back," Trevor said without hesitation, tugging her in that direction.

But by the time they were halfway to the back wall of the warehouse, thick, black smoke was working its way down from the ceiling, making her lungs feel like they were on fire. There was no way they could keep going in this direction. She opened her mouth to tell Trevor as much, but he'd already scooped her up into his arms and was running through the boxes and crates so fast they were almost a blur.

Alina couldn't see more than a few feet in front of her, so she had no idea where they were going. She only prayed they got there soon. Gas cylinders and fuel drums were exploding all over the place, puncturing the smoke with gouts of red and yellow flames. If they didn't escape soon, this whole place was going to disappear.

Through watery eyes, she saw a patch of light ahead of them. She had half a second to remember the dirty windows covered with the security grating. Trevor didn't even slow down. He simply tucked her to his chest and smashed his shoulder through the glass, metal screen and all.

They hit the ground outside, then rolled a few times before Trevor was up and running away from the building with her. They'd only gone about twenty or thirty feet before the warehouse blew outward, and a column of fire consumed the sky behind her.

Trevor didn't stop running for at least five minutes, probably worried about hybrids coming after them. But when it appeared that wasn't going to happen, he carefully lowered her to the ground and checked her urgently for injuries, his face so overwhelmed with concern she could have kissed him.

The hell with it.

Reaching up, she wrapped her hand around the back of his neck and dragged his mouth down to hers. Trevor seemed surprised at first but must have decided that meant she was okay, because he let out a sexy growl and returned her kiss full force.

Pulling away, he looked at her seriously. "You really okay?"

She nodded. "Yeah, though maybe we should stop putting ourselves in positions where you have to keep saving my ass like that. Not that I mind being swept off my feet now and then, of course."

He grinned. "I like saving your ass. It's a nice ass."

She laughed but then grew serious again. "I know you were busy, but did you hear what Wade said to me? It's possible he was full of crap, but considering he probably thought we weren't going to make it out of there, I don't see why he would have bothered lying. I think he was serious. I think Thorn means to start a war."

Chapter 16

IT WAS GETTING DARK BY THE TIME TREVOR AND Alina got to the address Adam had given them when Trevor called asking to meet with the reclusive shifter. Unlike the normal out-of-the-way places where they usually met, this one was bustling with people. Of all the places Trevor expected to meet Adam, an expensive loft-style apartment complex near the Navy Yard wasn't one of them. As they walked in, something told Trevor this meeting was going to be different from the previous ones.

The first floor of the building looked like an office of some kind, complete with desks, leather couches for visitors, and potted plants. Trevor looked for a sign on the wall indicating what kind of business it was but didn't see one. The employees—three men and a woman—looked up from their computers as Trevor and Alina entered. Trevor would never have known they were shifters if it wasn't for the fact that—like Adam—they didn't have a scent. He had heard Landon and Ivy refer to them as hidden shifters, because they could essentially hide in plain sight. While they possessed some level of animal ability, it wasn't enough to put them on the DCO's radar as potential agents. But they'd gained Adam's attention and now worked for him.

The woman pushed back her chair. In her midtwenties, she had long, wavy, blond hair and gray eyes that looked like they'd seen way too much for her age.

"You must be Trevor and Alina," she said. "If you'll come this way, I'll show you where you can wait. Adam will be with you soon."

She led them down a hallway lined with small offices, storerooms, and corkboards filled with worker's comp disclaimers and work schedules that Trevor suspected were there more to make this place look like an actual company than anything else.

He picked up the scent of his fellow shifters long before the girl opened the door to the room at the far end of the hall, so he wasn't surprised to see Ivy and Landon; Ivy's sister and fellow feline shifter, Layla, and her boyfriend, Jayson; Clayne and Danica; the newest DCO agent, former Special Forces soldier Angelo, and his fiancée/partner, Minka, the hybrid Thorn's doctors had created using Ivy's DNA; feline shifter Dreya Clark and her partner/boyfriend, Braden Hayes, a former detective from the Washington burglary squad; and finally Declan and Kendra and their newborns. Even Tanner and Zarina were in attendance.

"Are you going to introduce me?" Alina whispered.

Trevor grinned. Despite the fact that the proverbial shit was about to hit the fan, he was damn glad to see everyone alive and in one piece. "Yeah. Come on."

Taking her hand, he led her into the room with its pool table, big-screen TV, more video game consoles than he'd ever seen in once place, and gigantic sectional couch and made the introductions.

Trevor didn't miss the knowing look Ivy and the other shifters gave him. They almost certainly smelled his scent on Alina and hers on him. Not that Trevor cared if anyone knew he and his partner were sleeping together. Everything that happened at the warehouse only reinforced the connection between him and Alina. The entire time he'd been fighting Jake and the two hybrids, all he could think about was Alina's safety. She was quickly becoming the most important thing in his life.

"When did you guys become partners?" Landon asked. A former captain in the Army Special Forces, he'd taken on a leadership role the day John had recruited him into the DCO.

"About a week ago," Trevor said.

No one seemed surprised by that. Each of them had fallen for their significant others just as fast.

Ivy smiled. "Well, it's good to see that you two are working out so well together. Though I'm not sure how Ed and Jake are going to take that." She must have seen Trevor wince, because her eyes filled with concern. "What's wrong? They're okay, aren't they?"

Alina exchanged looks with Trevor. "It's complicated," she said. "It might be better if we wait until Adam gets here to explain it."

Since Adam didn't show up on cue like Trevor hoped, he used the time to catch up with everyone. The most shocking thing was learning Kendra had given birth to the twins while a gunfight had raged a few feet away.

"I helped deliver them," Tanner said proudly as Alina fussed over Noah and Chloe.

Trevor did a double take at that.

"Please," Zarina said. "He held Kendra up so she could push and nearly passed out doing that. He would much have preferred the babies to come out nice and clean and already dressed in their onesies."

Tanner shrugged unabashedly. "Yeah, maybe. But I also held Noah while you delivered his sister. I did a really good job of that." His mouth curved as he looked at the baby boy Kendra was holding. "He likes me."

"Yes, he does," Kendra agreed. "Which is important, since I plan on calling you and Zarina when we need a babysitter."

Tanner went a little pale, which made everyone laugh. Even Noah and Chloe seemed to find it amusing.

The lion hybrid was still trying to explain why he wouldn't be a very good babysitter when Adam walked in.

"Sorry I'm late." He offered his hand to Alina. "I'm Adam."

She regarded him thoughtfully as they shook hands. "It's nice to meet you finally. I'd introduce myself, but something tells me you know a lot more about me than I know about you."

"You're right. I do." Adam looked at Trevor. "You sounded worried on the phone. How bad is it?"

"Really bad." Trevor looked pointedly around the room. "Before we get into that, are you sure it was a good idea to bring us all here?"

Adam shrugged. "After seeing that video on Thorn's new hybrids, we knew we'd have to make a move on the farm as soon as we know where it is and what's going on."

Trevor frowned. "Who's *we*?"

The words were barely out of his mouth when he picked up a familiar scent coming from the hallway. At first, he thought he was imagining it, but then he saw the other shifters stiffen, like they smelled it, too.

It was impossible.

Then John Loughlin walked into the room.

Everything seemed to stop, Trevor's heart included. He'd seen the damage the bomb had done to the director's office. How the hell could John be alive?

But he was.

Trevor glanced at the other people in the room to make sure they were seeing the same thing he was. Everyone was staring at John with a stunned look.

Trevor was so focused on John that he didn't see the beautiful, dark-skinned woman and little girl who couldn't be more than ten with him, or the big bull of a man standing behind them like some overprotective bodyguard. Trevor had run into the guy while on that mission in Maine, so he knew the man was a hidden shifter. While Trevor had no idea what kind of animal DNA was in this guy's system, he was willing to bet it was something big. And if Trevor didn't miss his guess, the woman with John was a hidden shifter, too.

"How..." Ivy whispered, tears in her eyes.

Before John could answer, she ran over and hugged him. John's arms went around her, his eyes a little misty, too. After a moment, Ivy pulled away to look at him.

"Why did you let us think you were dead?" she asked.

John gave her a small smile. "Once I introduce you to some very important people, I think you'll understand."

Turning, he took the dark-skinned woman's hand. Tall and slender, she had long, dark, wavy hair and the most intriguing blue-gray eyes Trevor had ever seen. As John wrapped his other arm around the little girl's shoulders, Trevor realized her eyes were the same unusual color.

"Everyone, I'd like you to meet my wife, Cree, and

my daughter, Boo." John glanced over his shoulder at the big man. "And this is Morgan."

If Trevor had been stunned before, it was nothing compared to how he felt now. Realizing that John was alive was a shock to the system, but hearing that he'd been married long enough to have a kid Boo's age? That damn near bordered on insanity. How the hell had John been able to keep that a secret from an organization full of highly trained spies and covert agents for so long?

"How can you be alive?" Dreya asked, finally putting into words exactly what everyone else was thinking. "Braden and I were there. We saw you walk into the building right before it exploded."

John glanced at Adam. "I have Adam to thank for that. If he hadn't shown up when he did, I'd be dead right now."

Adam inclined his head. "It was luck more than anything. The weekend before the bombing, my people picked up some chatter on the wiretaps we had on Thorn and his security team. Nothing obvious. Mostly a lot of code speak and double-talk. When we thought John might be in trouble, I went to the complex to warn him. I smelled the explosives the moment I walked in, so I grabbed him and got him out of there."

"What about Olivia?" Landon asked, his voice uneven and a little hoarse.

Adam shook his head. "She must have been in another part of the building, then gone into John's office just as the bomb went off. If I'd known she was there, too, I would have tried to save her."

"That still doesn't explain why you didn't tell us you were alive," Trevor reminded John.

John exchanged looks with his wife, who in turn glanced at their daughter. After a moment, she shook her head.

"Perhaps we should take the rest of this conversation downstairs," John said. "There's a lot more we need to talk about, and this isn't the best place to do it."

Cree pressed a kiss to her husband's cheek. "Boo and I will stay up here and play some video games."

When Morgan seemed torn between staying with Cree and Boo and going with John, she laughed and swatted him on the shoulder. "Go downstairs. We'll be fine up here."

After giving her hand a squeeze and Boo a hug, John led the way out of the room and down the hall, Adam at his side. Suddenly stopping in the middle of the corridor, Adam pressed his hand to the wall. A moment later, a section of it slid back, revealing a set of stairs. Trevor followed him down the steps along with Alina and the others.

"Do the people who own the building know this is here?" Alina asked Adam over her shoulder.

"I own the building," Adam said when they reached the bottom. "The apartments upstairs provide good cover for all the people who live here. Plus, we're close to the DCO."

By close, Adam meant ten blocks from the DC office.

"How long have you been here?" Landon asked when he and Ivy caught up with the rest of them.

"About five years," Adam said. "I purchased the building shortly after leaving the DCO, but it took time to build all this."

"All this" turned out to be a huge underground

operation center that was bigger than the one the DCO had. There had to be thirty shifters manning the computers and digital map boards. One of them, a tall, slender, graceful woman who'd accompanied Morgan on the mission in Maine, walked over to whisper something in Adam's ear. Adam nodded, then grinned at her. She smiled in return, cupping his jaw in one elegant hand before walking back over to check something on the computer.

"Who's that?" Trevor asked.

"Milan," Adam said before leading the way to the big conference room on the other side of the room.

"Is he always so talkative?" Alina asked as they followed.

"No," Trevor said. "Normally, he's worse."

Once in the conference room, Trevor and Alina took a seat around the table with the other DCO agents, then waited for John to begin.

"First," John said as he moved to stand at the head of the table. "It was my decision to keep you in the dark and let you think I was dead. Adam was against it from the beginning, but I insisted."

"Why?" Kendra asked.

Of all of them, Kendra had worked the most closely with John. Keeping a secret like this from her had to hurt.

"Because I'm not naive," John explained. "Thorn chose to take his shot at me on the DCO complex because that was the easiest place to get to me, but he could just as easily have set that bomb in my apartment building. If he had, Cree and Boo and a lot of other innocent people would have died. I simply couldn't take that chance. As far as Thorn and the rest of the world was concerned, I was dead. I decided to let him think that, both for the safety of my family and because I thought it might finally make Thorn tip his hand."

"I'm fine with that," Ivy said. "But you could have told us. We're your friends."

John gave her an apologetic smile. "I intended to tell you eventually. As soon as the heat was off you or when we figured out what Thorn was up to."

Trevor wasn't thrilled with John's decision or his explanation of it, and from the looks on the faces of his coworkers, neither were they. But he understood why John had done it. Back at that warehouse, he would have done anything to get Alina out of there safely. He hadn't thought twice about jumping out of a second-story window, even though he hadn't known what would be waiting for him on the ground.

"Well, since Dreya and I had to sneak back into the United States, I'm guessing we're not here because the heat is off us," Braden pointed out. "Does that mean you've figured out what Thorn is up to?"

John looked at Trevor and gave him a nod.

Trevor gave him a nod in return. "Before I get into Thorn and his insane schemes, there's something I'd like to ask first. What started all this?"

John frowned. "All what?"

Trevor gestured around them, taking in the conference room and the command center beyond. "All this. Why is it here? What does it do? I know Thorn did something horrible a long time ago, but what was so bad that it put all this into motion and made you and Adam spend the past decade trying to put him in jail?"

On the other side of the table, Landon nodded. "I'd like to know that, too."

John regarded them thoughtfully, studying them one by one as if trying to decide whether they could handle the information. Finally, he looked at Adam and nodded.

"Most of you have probably already figured out by now that I used to work for the DCO," Adam said. "What some of you may not know is that I was the first shifter the organization *recruited* and that Frasier led the team I was placed on. In fact, he was supposed to be my partner."

Trevor didn't miss the way Adam emphasized the word *recruited*. From what he'd heard, Adam had been given a choice between a lifetime in a foreign prison where he'd never see the light of day again or working for the DCO. Adam had chosen the latter.

"I wasn't thrilled with the situation, but I tried to make the best of it," Adam continued. "At first, it wasn't as bad as I'd feared. The ten-man team I was on did some good things and stopped some bad people. But then one night in June of 2003, we slipped into a cozy, little mansion outside Roanoke, and everything changed. We'd been told before the mission that the man who owned the house was a cold-blooded killer selling military weapons secrets to China. The plan was to move in and execute him before he had a chance to take any of us down. I admit, killing people was something I was used to, so I didn't think too much about it. But the moment we walked in and I picked up the scent of children, I knew they'd lied to us."

When Adam fell silent, John picked up the story. "The house belonged to Walter M. Collins."

Trevor frowned. "Why do I recognize that name?"

"Collins was an up-and-coming congressman for the state of Virginia," John said. "While he'd made a name for himself in the House, he was exploring the idea of running for Senate. With his military background, voting record, and charisma, he had a good chance of unseating his rival in the upcoming election."

"Thorn," Landon surmised.

Adam nodded. "Thorn sent us in there to execute a political rival, plain and simple. When several of my teammates and I refused to do it, Frasier and the men who sided with him turned on us. Frasier shot me in the back, then wiped out the rest of the team. Worse, he executed Collins, his wife, and their three children."

Damn. Trevor had known Frasier was a piece of shit, but kids? There wasn't a level of Hell low enough for a man like him.

"By the time I recovered," Adam continued, "Frasier and Thorn had convinced everyone I'd gone rogue and killed the Collins family and my teammates on my own."

"I found out what happened and helped get Adam to safety," John said. "At the time, we had no proof Thorn was behind any of it, but I had my suspicions."

"I wasn't interested in proof," Adam said, his voice almost coming out as a hiss. "I was going to hunt down Frasier and tear pieces off his body until he told me everything I wanted to know, but John convinced me to do it his way. That's when I made the decision to start my own organization. Originally, we just intended to keep an eye on Thorn, but now, we watch over the DCO, trying to step in when they do something they shouldn't and picking up smaller missions they can't be bothered with. Depending on what you learned, maybe we've finally reached the point where we can stop Thorn once and for all."

Trevor was silent as he let everything sink in. Adam and John had been patiently waiting for more than ten years to catch Thorn doing something that'd put the asshole in jail for life to make him pay for ordering the execution of a politician and his family. Trevor wasn't so sure he could have been that patient. But now, they knew where Thorn's new hybrid army was being built, and they knew what he intended to do with them. All they had to do was stop him and make sure the man didn't weasel out from under all of this.

Leaning forward, Trevor explained everything he, Alina, and Tanner had learned, starting with the video on Thorn's hybrids.

"They're nothing like any hybrid we've ever seen before," Trevor said. "Somehow, Thorn's doctors have figure out how to counteract the rage. While I'm pretty sure they don't hear and smell as well as shifters—or Tanner and Minka, for that matter—that disadvantage is more than outweighed by the increase in strength, speed, and their ability to withstand injuries. They're damn near indestructible now."

When Tanner went on to explain how he learned the location of the farm in North Carolina, Adam stepped in to say he already had some of his people in the area watching the place.

"It's very well protected," Adam added. "None of my people could get close without risking detection, but there's a lot of activity going on. They're mobilizing for something big."

"They're planning to start a war," Trevor said, telling them everything he and Alina had learned at the warehouse earlier that day.

While everyone was stunned to hear what Thorn planned to do with his squad of hybrids, they were even more shocked when Trevor told them about Ed and Jake.

"Shit," John muttered. "I thought Jake was perfect for the DCO when I hired him."

Without knowing exactly how many hybrids they were up against, not to mention the other security Thorn was sure to have there, it was difficult to come up with a solid plan to raid the farm in Millers Creek. They didn't have much of a choice, though. It was still easier to strike there than try to stop them in Ukraine.

"We're going to be heavily outnumbered," Landon pointed out.

"I've already got that covered," John said. "I've contacted your former Special Forces team, Landon. They're sending as many people as they can. I have a helicopter picking them up now."

Trevor grinned. John was always one step ahead.

They were looking at the maps Adam's people had made of the farm, trying to figure out how to get in and take down the hybrids when they didn't know a damn thing about the place, when an alarm suddenly went off.

Trevor looked up to see three big TV monitors in the command center he hadn't noticed before light up. On them, a group of men dressed in black stormed into an office, automatic weapons blazing.

Adam cursed and ran for the door of the conference room just as Trevor realized the office on the monitors was the same one he and Alina had been in a few hours ago. The people getting shot were Adam's shifters. And one of the shooters was Frasier.

"Shit," he said. "They found us."

Trevor had been worried this would happen. There were too many people and cameras in this part of DC to hide from all of them.

He and the others raced up the four flights of stairs after Adam, weapons drawn. But by the time they got to the main level, Frasier and the other men were gone. Out on the street, people were screaming. Clayne, Danica, Dreya, Braden, Angelo, and Minka took off after Frasier and his buddies, but Trevor instinctively knew it was a waste. The assholes were almost certainly in vehicles disappearing into the crowded DC traffic.

Besides, there were injured people to worry about.

He and the others checked the four shifters lying on the floor. The three guys were dead from multiple gun-shot wounds to the chest, but the woman was still alive.

"Her pulse is weak, but it's there," Alina announced.

Ivy was already on her phone, calling for an ambulance.

A commotion from down the hall suddenly caught Trevor's attention.

"Shit," he muttered.

Jumping to his feet, Trevor ran down the hall to the room where Cree and Boo had been, Alina at his heels.

He slid to a halt when he saw John kneeling on the floor, his wife in his arms. Cree had been shot, but she was alive…barely. John's face was as pale as a ghost as he leaned over so she could whisper something in his ear. Morgan stood protectively nearby, looking just as torn up as John.

A moment later, Zarina wedged her way between him

and Alina, hurrying to Cree's side. Trevor only prayed there was something the Russian doctor could do. There was a lot of blood. Boo had nearly lost her father, and now she might lose her mother. For real, this time.

Trevor frowned. Where *was* Boo anyway?

He and Alina looked around the room, under tables, in closets, anywhere the little girl might be hiding. Trevor tried to pick up her scent, but it was harder than it should have been. It wasn't that her scent was cloaked like the hidden shifters, but every time Trevor thought he had a lock on her, it would disappear again.

"They took her," John said.

Trevor turned and saw John staring around in near shock, his shirt and hands covered in his wife's blood. He was still kneeling on the floor, Cree in his lap, her eyes closed, her body limp. For a moment, Trevor was sure she was dead. Then he heard a heartbeat. It was so faint, he almost missed it. But she was trying to hold on.

"It was Frasier and his men," John said quietly. "Cree heard them say they used traffic cameras to track Declan, Kendra, and the others from the bed-and-breakfast. They thought they'd ambush everyone but left when they couldn't find anyone."

Ivy dropped to her knees beside John. "What about Boo?"

John's eyes were wet with tears. "When Frasier shot Cree, Boo shifted and attacked Frasier. The fucking bastard knocked her unconscious, then told one of his men to take her. That Thorn's doctors might want to experiment on her."

Trevor stared, stunned. They'd all gone through their

first change during their mid to late teens. Boo was barely ten. It shouldn't have been possible for her to shift.

He was still trying to wrap his head around that when Declan came in with the injured girl from the front room so Zarina could monitor both of them. Then they all stood there while Adam tried to convince John that Cree was going to make it—and that they'd get Boo back.

"We'll worry about Thorn and his hybrids later," Adam said firmly. "Boo comes first."

John looked like he was going to say something, but then Minka came in leading the paramedics and their gurneys.

"There are a lot of cops out there," she whispered to Trevor. "Angelo, Landon, Clayne, and Danica are trying to control the situation, but this is going to get complicated fast."

Telling Alina he'd be back, Trevor went outside to help. With the wall to the secret command center back in place, the loft appeared to be nothing more than an office that had been shot up by a bunch of crazies.

Outside, he took lead selling that exact story to the cops, telling them men with automatic weapons had shot up the place while he and the other Homeland operatives had been in a nearby office holding a budget session. The fact that neither Trevor nor any of the other operatives had fired a round only supported the story.

A few minutes later, the paramedics rushed out with two gurneys. Cree and the small, hidden shifter had oxygen masks on their faces. John hurried after, followed by Adam and Morgan.

"I have to go with her," John told Adam. "Cree…might not make it. I need you to get Boo back *and* stop Thorn."

Adam opened his mouth to protest, but John cut him off. "If you don't stop him, there could be millions of deaths. We can't let that happen."

Without another word, John climbed into the ambulance with Cree and pulled the door shut behind him. Morgan stared after the disappearing taillights, his face ashen. But then he took a deep breath, regained his composure, and turned to face Adam.

"You stop Thorn," he said. "I'm with whichever team is going after Boo."

Adam nodded.

While the cops continued to investigate the scene, Adam pulled Trevor and the others into a back room so they could make plans. Except now, they'd split up and hit both the farm and the DCO complex.

"We didn't have enough people to hit the hybrids to begin with," Clayne pointed out. "If we split up, I don't think we're going to be able to do it."

"Then we don't split up," Jayson said. The former Special Forces lieutenant gave them a fierce look. "We get Boo back first, and we worry about stopping the hybrids second. Because I sure as hell don't like the idea of leaving John's kid in the hands of Thorn's wacko doctors. Not to mention Frasier."

While Trevor agreed, it would be like sending up a flare. Any chance of catching the hybrids by surprise would be gone. He opened his mouth to say just that when his damn phone rang. Cursing, he dug it out of his pocket. Evan's number flashed on the screen.

"The frigging hybrids are here!" Evan said the moment Trevor answered.

"What are you talking about?" Trevor asked,

holding the phone a little away from his ear so Alina could hear.

"The hybrids we saw on the video during the briefing. They're here at the DCO complex. I just saw them heading into the gym."

"Are you sure?"

Evan cursed. "Of course I'm sure. Fourteen of them are frigging impossible to miss. Thorn, Dick, and those asshole doctors are here, too."

It was Trevor's turn to let out an expletive. "What are they doing?"

"I don't know for sure. I got close enough to see them setting up map boards, projectors, and big terrain planning tables. I tried to see what was on the maps, but Dick intercepted me."

Sounded like they were doing some last-minute planning. "Are you still at the complex? Is Jaxson there with you?"

"Yeah. Jaxson is keeping an eye on Sage. She started flipping out the moment she smelled the hybrids. I'm watching the gym to see if I can figure out what's going on. I've been trying to reach Jake, but he's not answering his phone. Do you know where he is?"

Trevor glanced at Alina. She shook her head. Yeah, too complicated to get into over the phone.

"Don't worry about Jake right now," he told Evan. "Do me a favor? If you see Frasier show up with a little girl, give me a call ASAP, okay?"

"Um…yeah, okay."

Trevor hung up. "It looks like our issue resolved itself," he said to his friends. "We don't have to split up, because everything is going down at the DCO complex."

Chapter 17

As Alina moved slowly toward the DCO medical lab on the back side of the complex, she attempted to mimic Trevor, Milan, Adam, and Morgan, hoping to tread as quietly as they did. They were like ghosts compared to her. She didn't feel so badly about not being able to move as gracefully as Milan. The tall shifter was all legs and looked like she was made for this stealthy stuff. But it turned out that Morgan—who was six five and probably weighed close to three hundred pounds—was a frigging ballerina compared to Alina.

Sometimes, the world was so unfair.

Evan had called while they were on the way to the complex to tell them Frasier and two other men just arrived, an unconscious little girl slung over Frasier's shoulder. Frasier had headed straight for the medical labs. Alina shuddered at the thought of what they were doing to Boo. If what Trevor said was true, it didn't bode well for her.

Alina would have liked to bring more people with them, but since the other DCO agents had to deal with the majority of the hybrids as well as Thorn's men, it had made sense for more of them to go to the gym. She only hoped her team could get in the lab and grab the girl without much of a fight. If it turned into a shoot-out, the numbers weren't on their side.

So far, their luck was holding.

Just before they reached the double glass doors of the lab, Trevor held up his hand, stopping them.

"We might have a problem," he whispered. "I just picked up Frasier's scent heading that way." He pointed toward the main admin building several hundred yards away. "Thorn and at least one hybrid are with him."

Getting Thorn and Frasier out of the picture was a good thing, wasn't it? Unless…

"Wait a minute," she said. "Are you saying you don't know if Frasier still had Boo with him?"

Trevor shook his head. "I can't explain it, but the moment that little girl went through her shift, her scent changed so completely, I can't recognize it."

Alina looked at Adam, then Milan, and finally Morgan. "None of you can pick up her scent?"

They shook their heads.

"So do we split up?" Alina asked.

It was obvious that no one liked the idea any better than she did.

"We have to," Trevor said. "She might be in the lab, or she might be with Frasier and Thorn."

Milan and Morgan immediately opted to take the lab, while Adam said he'd go after Frasier and Thorn. Unfortunately, that split left her and Trevor in a tough situation. Alina would have preferred to stay with Trevor, but she wasn't so sure about sending Milan and Morgan into the lab by themselves. She didn't know the first thing about Milan, but the woman simply didn't look like a fighter. Morgan might have been a big, strong guy, but would he be able to handle himself in a hostage scenario, or would he be too concerned about Boo to make good decisions?

She could tell from the look on Trevor's face that he was thinking the exact same thing.

"I'll go with Adam," he said, albeit reluctantly. "Alina, you stick with Milan and Morgan. But don't do anything crazy. If you find Boo, call out over the radio."

Alina nodded. She had a crazy urge to kiss Trevor before he and Adam left but thought better of it. Probably not the right time and place for that. She settled for catching his eye and reaching out to give his hand a squeeze.

"Be careful," she whispered, trying to communicate by touch what she couldn't say out loud.

He nodded. "You, too."

Turning, he and Adam disappeared into the shadows like they'd never been there, leaving her alone with Milan and Morgan.

"All right," she said to them. "Let's go get Boo."

———

"You seriously think these guys are going to give themselves up simply because we ask nicely?" Clayne asked over the radio, his voice dripping with sarcasm.

Tanner didn't want to encourage the wolf shifter, but he had to admit, the guy had a point. The hybrids they were moving in on had been hand-selected by Thorn because they were killers willing to walk into a Ukrainian village and massacre people by the hundreds.

"To be honest, no," Landon said from beside Tanner as they and Ivy headed toward the entrance on the west side of the gym. "But we have to try, because the alternative is to walk in there and start shooting people in cold blood, and I don't think anyone here is ready to do that."

No one said anything.

"Clayne, hang tight outside the front doors with your team," Landon instructed. "Angelo, you and your team should be able move in through the back without anyone hearing you. If you do, try and take up position near the showers."

Tanner tried to visualize the building's floor plan in his head and which doors each of the teams would be using. If Angelo, Minka, Jayson, and Layla could get to the showers without being noticed, they'd only have about fifteen feet of hallway to travel before they'd get to the main part of the gym.

Clayne, Danica, Declan, Braden, and Dreya would have to cover more distance when they came in through the front doors. Since there was almost no chance they could slip in without being seen, the wolf shifter and his team would be fully exposed. Hopefully, the hybrids' attention would be completely focused to the north and west entrances by then.

"No one moves until I give the word. Clear?" Landon cautioned. "I want eyes on the main gym floor before this goes down."

"And then?" Clayne asked, still sounding doubtful.

"We move in and hit them from three sides at once. If these hybrids are as rational as Trevor and Alina described, they'll realize they're surrounded and give up without this turning into a bloodbath."

Clayne snorted over the radio. Clearly, he wasn't betting on the likelihood of that outcome. But he didn't complain, which was surprising. Clayne usually liked being difficult simply because he was so good at it.

"When you give the word, then," Clayne said. "Just

keep in mind, if Evan's count is right, there are at least a dozen hybrids who are nearly impossible to kill in there, plus maybe another dozen of Thorn's hired mercenaries. If things go wrong with your plan, it'll likely go very bad, very quickly."

"If we're lucky, Derek, Diaz, and the other guys will get here soon," Ivy said. "That should go a long way toward evening the odds."

"We're not going to be able to wait," Jayson pointed out softly. "Last we heard, their helicopter was still twenty minutes out. We have to be in position in the next few minutes in case Trevor and his team run into trouble in the lab. If the shooting starts, and we don't have these hybrids contained…"

Jayson didn't bother to finish the sentence, but nobody needed to hear it, including Tanner. Their best hope of dealing with these new hybrids was while they were all in one place, enclosed by four walls, with every exit covered. If they got out of the gym, and he and the others had to hunt them down one by one on the DCO complex or in the woods beyond that, it wouldn't go well for any of them.

"We don't wait then," Landon said. "Move into position now. We go as soon as I get a look inside and give the word—or the moment it looks like Trevor's team is in trouble."

———

Hearing over the radio that the other teams were moving on the gym, Alina picked up the pace, slipping into the med bay with Milan and Morgan. Alina wanted to be in a position to grab Boo—if the girl was there—in the event the shooting started early.

Trevor hadn't given an update since heading after Frasier and Thorn a few minutes ago. While that made Alina nervous as hell, she took it as a good sign. Hopefully that meant he and Adam hadn't run into any serious trouble. Her stomach clenched at the idea of him getting into a shoot-out without her there to back him up.

She also hoped that meant Boo was still in the med lab.

Alina didn't need a shifter's nose to pick up the antiseptic smell the moment she stepped inside the lab. The scent of disinfectant, alcohol, and the tangy, metallic odor of blood were hard to miss. She only prayed it wasn't Boo's blood.

They hadn't gone more than a few feet when Alina heard a series of sharp snarls and grunts from a room at the end of the hall. She froze. Beside her, Milan and Morgan did the same. Had one of the hybrids smelled them? Were they all about to come running out of the room with guns blazing?

Alina tensed, ready for the possibility, but the growls immediately subsided. She glanced at the two shifters with her. They nodded and motioned her forward.

She moved as slowly as she could, treading carefully and trying hard not to make any noise. She wished she knew for sure one way or the other how well these new hybrids could hear and smell. For all she knew, the hybrids were blissfully unaware there was anyone else in the building with them. Or conversely, they were waiting for them with guns pointed straight at the door of the room they were hiding in.

When she heard another low snarl, Alina decided it sounded more like someone grunting in pain. She didn't think Boo could make a sound that deep or that loud, but then again, she didn't know what kind of noise a child shifter made. The fact that Milan and Morgan still looked worried as hell didn't make her feel any better.

Alina stopped outside the door to the last lab on the right, the two shifters right on her heels. She took a deep breath, then peeked around the jamb to look inside.

There were two of Thorn's men and two hybrids in the room, along with a doctor. She recognized one of the hybrids as the guy she'd shot three times in the warehouse earlier that day. He was sitting on an exam table while the doctor dug around in his chest for the bullets. That explained what the snarls of pain were all about.

Movement on the other side of the room caught her eye, and she looked that way to see Wade leaning against the far wall. Part of his attention was on the doctor and his hybrid teammate, but mostly, he was focused on Boo.

Alina was relieved to see the little girl alive. She was also furious at the way her captors had treated her. Boo was strapped down to an exam table while two doctors stood over her with eager expressions on their faces, as if they couldn't wait to cut into her. Boo seemed to realize that, too. Her small claws and fangs were fully extended, and she looked completely terrified as she struggled against her restraints.

Alina pulled back and motioned Milan and Morgan back down the hall. Then she pulled her radio mic close.

"Trevor, we found Boo. There are three hybrids and two of Thorn's men in the room with her," she said softly. "But there are also two doctors who look like they can't wait to start experimenting on her. We need to get her out of there."

Milan's eyes widened at the mention of the two doctors. Terrified the slender woman might take off and try to save Boo on her own, Alina put a hand on Milan's shoulder. Then she covered her radio mic with the other.

"We need a plan," she said to Milan. "Those hybrids are too close to Boo for us to storm in there. And the doctors are even closer. They could kill Boo before we get ten feet into the room."

Milan and Morgan nodded their understanding and held their ground.

"We're on the way," Trevor said in her earpiece. "Be there in two minutes."

"Hurry," she whispered. "We may not have two minutes."

———

Tanner pressed his back against the brick wall beside the side entrance to the gym. The door was an emergency exit, so it was always locked. Ivy picked the heavy-duty dead bolt in seconds, then led the way inside. Landon followed, then Tanner. Over the radio, he heard Clayne calling out that his team was standing by the front entrance. A few seconds later, Angelo announced they were through the back door.

Ahead of Tanner, Ivy and Landon stopped, allowing him to take point. He moved quickly down the service hallway that opened up into the main part of the gym. They'd decided early on during the abbreviated planning for the raid that Tanner would go in first to do recon. If Thorn's new hybrids were able to smell better than Trevor thought, they might not pay attention to Tanner's scent. He was a hybrid, too, after all.

Just then, Alina's voice came over the radio saying they'd found Boo and were getting ready to rescue her. That meant the rest of them needed to hurry.

Tanner dropped to a knee by the door, only to freeze when he heard a long, drawn-out hiss. A moment later, two very familiar scents reached his nose. He knew who they belonged to without looking, but he leaned in to check anyway, praying his nose was wrong.

It wasn't.

Jaxson was lying on one hip in the middle of the floor, his right arm clutched awkwardly to his chest. From the bruises on his face and the slash marks on his arm, ribs, and back, it looked like he'd been punched a few times as well as sliced open with something razor-sharp. Dark blood soaked his T-shirt.

The hybrids surrounding him would probably still be going at the guy if one enraged feline hybrid wasn't keeping them away.

Sage was standing over Jaxson, her fangs and claws fully extended, eyes glowing scarlet red as she snarled and slashed at anyone dumb enough to get close to her and the man she was protecting.

Tanner was thrilled Sage had retained enough control to be concerned about Jaxson, but it looked like the hybrids were getting tired of their little game. Sage was never going to back down, even to protect herself.

He scanned the room and was shocked to see two DCO analysts standing alongside a big hybrid over by a folding table, studying the map spread out on it. They didn't look happy to be there, that was for sure. Thorn must have dragged them in to help, though what he intended to do with them later was anyone's guess.

The thought that a man like Thorn might simply make them disappear when they'd outlived their usefulness certainly came to mind.

Suddenly, the big hybrid by the table turned and strode toward Sage and Jaxson with long, purposeful steps. As he moved, he reached down to the holster he wore on his hip and pulled out a handgun as large as his oversized mitts. Growling a warning that scattered the other hybrids, he pointed his weapon at Sage's head. She snarled at him, refusing to move.

Shit.

"New plan, people," Tanner said into his radio mic. "We need to move now!"

Chapter 18

TREVOR HATED LEAVING ALINA WITHOUT BACKUP. It wasn't that he didn't trust Milan and Morgan. He'd have simply felt better if he were there with her. Being apart from her didn't feel right.

He and Adam were still trying to figure out if Boo was in the admin building when Dick sauntered down the hallway, heading to his office. Grabbing him by the throat and making him talk was tempting, but since he and Adam didn't want to tip him off to their presence yet, they ducked into the empty office near Dick's. Thorn and Frasier showed up a few moments later without Boo, three mercenary goons in tow.

Beside Trevor, Adam let out a low hiss.

"Frasier doesn't seem like the kind of guy to crack under interrogation, but you want to take a run at him anyway and see if he'll tell us where Boo is?" Trevor asked softly.

Adam's eyes flashed an orangey-gold color. "He'll talk. You keep Thorn and Dick busy."

Trevor could do that.

They were about to implement that plan when Alina got on the radio to say they'd found Boo—along with three hybrids and a few of Thorn's men. Trevor's gut clenched.

He and Adam turned to leave the room when Tanner announced over the radio that they needed a new plan. Then all hell broke loose as the shooting started.

Cursing, Trevor shoved open the door of the office and stepped into the hallway, popping the first man who turned their way. Then he headed for the back exit while Adam covered their six.

As the sound of gunfire grew louder, Trevor realized it was coming from both the gym and the lab.

Alina.

Trevor wanted to ask Alina what the hell was happening, but if she was in the middle of a gunfight, distracting her could get her killed. So he settled for running faster, doing everything he could to get to her, Milan, and Morgan as quickly as possible.

He and Adam rounded the outside of the building and almost ran over four of Thorn's goons. Adam grabbed one of the men and shoved him roughly into his buddy, knocking them both down. Then he leaped onto the brick wall and climbed sideways along it faster than should have been possible before hopping off to come at the men from the opposite direction.

"Go!" Adam shouted at him.

Trevor went.

The sounds of gunfire coming from the gym took away any chance Alina's team had of catching Wade and the other hybrids by surprise. They needed to go on the offensive.

Giving Milan and Morgan a nod, Alina stepped into the room, her finger on the trigger. A simple bullet wasn't going to keep Wade and his hybrid buddies down for long, but it'd give Milan and Morgan time to take out Thorn's men and rescue John's daughter.

She shot the hybrid closest to the table Boo was strapped down to first, once in the hip and once in the stomach. It wouldn't be fatal, but it obviously hurt like hell if his snarl of pain was any indication. More importantly, it forced him away from Boo.

With him out of the way, she turned and took aim at Wade and the other hybrid. They ducked behind a row of cabinets, and she missed.

One of Thorn's men pulled his gun and shot Morgan in the shoulder, but the big shifter ignored it. Charging forward, he slammed into the man so hard, Alina heard bones crack. Then Morgan picked him up and tossed him in the second man's direction, sending them both crashing to the floor.

Milan used the distraction to sweep in and go for Boo. The slim shifter might not have been a fighter, but she was fast. When one of the doctors slashed at her with a scalpel he grabbed from a nearby tray, Milan ripped it out of his hand and shoved it into his throat almost faster than the eye could see.

Even though they'd taken the bad guys by surprise, Alina knew she and the two shifters were in trouble. The hybrids were already regrouping, and with Wade leading them, they'd get it back together soon enough. Then Wade would put a bullet into Boo simply because he was an asshole—and he could.

She needed to put Wade down—or at least get him out of here. Since the first option probably wasn't going to happen easily, that left the second.

Taking aim, she put a bullet through his right calf where it stuck out from the corner of the table he was hiding behind. It was a lucky shot, but he didn't need to know that.

Wade stood, pure, unadulterated hatred in his blazing red eyes. The urge to shoot at him until she ran out of ammo was almost irresistible, but there was a good chance she could hit him multiple times and still not keep him from killing Boo.

No. She needed him out of here. And the best way to do that was to make him chase her.

With that in mind, Alina turned and ran. She hit the door outside the lab at a full run, shoving it open. She didn't know where she was going. She only knew she had to get Wade as far away from Boo as she could.

She barely got a dozen yards from the building when she heard the door bang open. Behind her, Wade let out a growl. He was following her all right.

What the hell was she going to do now?

———————

Tanner felt his control on his inner lion slipping as he surged across the gym floor and slammed into the huge hybrid who was about to shoot Sage. His M4 carbine went flying, but there was nothing he could do about that. The hybrid's weapon went skittering across the floor, too, so that made them even. Tackling the guy hadn't been his first plan, but with so many innocent civilians, they were having to get a lot more hands-on with this raid than they'd ever intended. Simply standing back and trying to deal with the hybrids from a distance wasn't an option anymore.

Tanner roared as he took the hybrid to the floor, his long fangs extending so far they made his jaw hurt. The hybrid didn't seem impressed and roared right back as he shoved Tanner away, then lunged at him with a mouth full of knife-sharp teeth. Tanner got an arm up under the creature's jaw, barely keeping those teeth away from his neck. The thing was incredibly strong and vicious as hell.

Out of the corner of his eye, Tanner saw his friends locked in combat with the other hybrids. Even with Clayne's and Angelo's teams in the fray, it was nearly impossible to take them down. There were too many of the hybrids, and they were too hard to kill.

To his right, Sage jumped on one of Thorn's men just as he was about to shoot Jaxson in the back. The man went down screaming in pain as Sage swiped at him with her claws. While she had to do it to save Jaxson, Tanner knew from experience she'd regret it later.

Tanner's momentary focus on what the hell was going on around him almost got him killed as the hybrid he was fighting clamped razor-sharp teeth down on his arm. Tanner roared in rage, but instead of jerking his arm away and causing even more damage, he shoved it deeper into the man's mouth as savagely as he could.

There was a crack as something in the hybrid's neck snapped. He immediately released his hold on Tanner. Ignoring the blood and pain, Tanner spun away, scrambling for his weapon. Even though his head was tilted at a slight angle, the hybrid came at him again.

Tanner grabbed his carbine and squeezed the trigger the moment he got it pointed at the psycho. His rifle round hit the man square in the center of the forehead, putting the hybrid down for good.

"Go for a head shot!" he shouted into his radio mic. "It's the only thing that will kill them."

Tanner heard a feline yowl behind him, and he immediately spun around, expecting to see Sage in trouble.

But it was Dreya. A hybrid had her pinned to the wall, his forearm shoved against her throat, trying to crush her windpipe. Tanner expected to see Braden coming to her rescue, but the cop-turned-DCO-agent was busy trying to keep two of Thorn's men from killing Minka and didn't even realize his partner was in danger.

Snarling, Tanner scrambled to his feet and charged across the gym toward Dreya and the hybrid, his control slipping a little more with every step.

Trevor was halfway down the hallway before his nose told him Alina wasn't in the lab.

"Alina!" he called over the radio. "Where are you?"

No answer.

Shit.

Torn between tracking her and checking with Milan and Morgan to see if they knew where she was, he raced toward the sound of fighting coming from the room at the far end of the hall.

Milan crouched down behind Morgan, Boo in her arms, while the big shifter tried to protect them from the lone hybrid taking shots at them from the other side of the room. Morgan had been hit multiple times and was already bleeding badly.

Trevor lifted his weapon and shot the hybrid in the head like Tanner suggested. The hybrid looked stunned for a moment, then toppled to the floor.

Morgan collapsed a split second later.

Trevor leaped forward, catching the big shifter and easing him to the floor as carefully as he could. Boo left Milan's arms, falling to her knees beside him. Long, dark curls framed her face as tears streamed down the little girl's cheeks.

"You're going to be okay, Uncle Morgan," she said. "You have to be okay. You're too big and strong to die. Please don't die. Please!"

The anguish in Boo's voice just about ripped Trevor's guts out, and he prayed against all rational hope that somehow Morgan would be okay. Boo had been through enough already tonight.

Morgan chuckled weakly. Even though he was bleeding like crazy, he still had the energy to take Boo's hand and give it a squeeze. "Don't worry, Little Peanut. I'll be okay. I'm just catching my breath. I'll be up and about in no time."

"Promise?" the little girl asked, her lips trembling.

"I promise." Morgan looked at Trevor. "Alina took off a few minutes ago so one of those big, nasty hybrids would chase her."

Trevor didn't have to wonder which hybrid it had been. Somehow, things had worked out to put her and Wade in the same room with each other.

Double shit.

"Which way did they go?" he asked.

"Out the door and to the right, toward the back of the complex," Milan said softly as she checked Morgan's injuries.

"Call Zarina and tell her to be ready to come onto the complex the second the shooting stops," Trevor said. "Morgan probably won't be the only one who needs medical attention."

Trevor was out of the room and heading for the exit when he heard Boo ask Milan about her mother. The

door of the med lab closed behind him before he heard
the answer. He shook his head. How the hell did you
answer a question like that?

The moment he got outside, he stopped and sniffed
the air, trying to pinpoint Alina's location even as more
gunfire came from the gym. Then he heard blaring
techno music throbbing through his earpiece, and he
stopped worrying about tracking his partner's scent. He
knew exactly where she was.

Alina ran toward the one place she knew would give
her the best chance of surviving a lone encounter with a
hybrid—the shoot house she and Trevor had trained in
only a few days ago.

She was kind of shocked she'd made it all the way
to the training area. She could run fast, but Wade was
faster. No doubt he was toying with her, wanting her to
think she could get away from him so he could enjoy it
that much more when he caught her.

If he wanted to play that game, fine with her. It'd
make it easier for her to turn this around on him.

She raced into the shoot house, pausing only long
enough to hit every single button on the operation panel,
flipping on the pop-up targets, alarms, strobe lights, and
even the thumping techno beat Jake had played when he
and Jaxson had trained with her and Trevor.

As she moved deeper into the building, she was
relieved the place still reeked of animal urine. Wade's
sense of smell might not be as keen as a shifter's, but it
didn't hurt to make sure her scent was masked.

It was strange moving through the building with the

lights flashing and targets popping up all over the place without reacting to them. She was only about three or four rooms into the building when she heard a door slam open. Wade's angry snarls were so loud, she could hear them over the music. Something told her he was done toying with her.

"You know how I told you it was just business when I took Thorn's money and set you and your team up?" he yelled.

Crap, he was already in the next room over. She picked up her pace and put a few more turns between them, then took up a position she thought would allow her to get a shot at him.

"It really wasn't just business," he continued. "I would have done it for half the money for a chance to put an end to you and your whiny, little team of punks. Getting the chance to kill little Jodi like I did was absolutely the best night of my life. That little bitch squealed like a pig after that, begging me to let her live, telling me she'd do anything I wanted. If I would've had the time, I might have taken her up on that. I always thought she had a sweet ass, you know?"

Alina had to bite her tongue to keep from shouting at Wade that he was full of crap. She'd been forced to listen to the entire ordeal on the radio, and it replayed through her head almost every night before she went to sleep. Jodi had never squealed or begged. Her friend had died telling Wade to go to hell.

Knowing all that still didn't make it any easier to hear. Wade was trying to mess with her head and get her so mad that she would do something stupid, and it was working. She was so furious right then that her knuckles creaked under the pressure she was putting on the grip of her weapon.

She turned and faced the direction Wade would be coming from, ready to put a bullet through his head the moment he walked into the room.

Alina was still looking that way when she heard a footfall behind her. Heart in her throat, she spun around just in time to see Wade lift his gun and point it at her head. Somehow, he'd gotten all the way around the room she was in and had come through the other door.

"I'm prepared to let your partner live," Wade snarled, his red eyes boring into her. "In exchange for a suitable amount of begging, that is."

Alina knew she was already dead, and normally, she would never beg him for a drink of water if she was roasting in Hell, but the threat against Trevor made her reconsider. She'd do anything for Trevor, even if it was likely Wade was lying.

She opened her mouth to tell Wade what he wanted to hear when a shot rang out over the heavy thumping music. Wade stumbled back a little and twisted around to see who'd shot him in the shoulder.

Trevor stood in one of the other doorways, his weapon still leveled patiently at Wade, his eyes gold in the near darkness.

Her former CIA teammate snarled and pointed his weapon at her new partner, a man who'd become much more than someone she worked with every day.

Alina pumped two rounds into Wade's stomach without hesitation, following those up with three more to the chest. The impact slammed him against the wall behind him, but he didn't fall.

"Those were for Jodi," she said as she lifted her weapon and aimed it at Wade's forehead. "And this one is for Rodney and Fred."

Alina pulled the trigger, killing the man she'd hunted for three years. She watched him tumble to the floor, waiting for some sense of closure—or satisfaction—to hit her. She'd dreamed of this moment every day since the night her teammates had been killed. She should feel something, right?

But after a few moments, she realized nothing special was going to happen. Jodi, Rodney, and Fred were still dead, and she still missed them like crazy. Worse, the guilt she felt over the part she'd played in their deaths was just as gut-wrenching as ever.

Had this all been for nothing?

Then Trevor was at her side, pulling her close and making sure she was okay. He murmured words in her ear she couldn't hear over the music, but that was okay. She liked him saying them anyway.

She leaned there against him, drawing on his warmth and support. This was what making Wade pay had been all about, moving on and finding a new reason to wake up in the morning. Now, instead of starting every day hoping to find Wade and kill him, she could think about making a life with Trevor. And that wasn't too bad of a life to look forward to.

But then the sounds of distant gunfire pulled her back to reality, and she looked up at him. "Boo?"

"She's okay," he said loudly. "But they're still fighting in the gym. We need to go."

Nodding, Alina turned and walked away from Wade's body without looking back.

Chapter 19

TANNER WATCHED AS DECLAN WENT DOWN UNDER two hybrid attackers. A split second later, one of Thorn's men swung an empty rifle at Danica, knocking her unconscious.

Up until now, Tanner had been too busy in hand-to-hand combat to pay attention to details, but he knew that more of his friends had already fallen. He wasn't sure whether they were alive or dead. All he could say for sure was that they'd fought like hell. The Special Forces soldiers showing up in time to help wasn't going to happen. They were all going to die long before then.

Something in Tanner snapped at that realization. Maybe it was the last little shred of his control, or maybe the silly notion of keeping his inner animal chained up didn't matter when nearly everyone he cared about was dying around him. Either way, the barrier he'd been holding in place between himself and the beast collapsed, and the raging thing inside came charging out.

Roaring loud enough to shake the rafters of the gym, he charged at the largest concentration of hybrids left standing, vowing to kill them all before the end.

He tore into them with his claws, sank his fangs into shoulders and necks, and smashed bones to dust with his fists. He'd lost his weapon somewhere along the way, but he didn't care. Using an M4 would have been beyond him at this point anyway.

Blood went everywhere, both his and that of those he killed. He didn't care about that, either. Some part of him recognized that killing was something he'd always done well. He was better at it now than before he'd been turned into a hybrid, but even in those days long past, this was what he'd always excelled at.

When he heard an increase in gunfire from behind him, he spun and faced it, rushing toward it before he knew where it was coming from.

He tried to pull up when he realized it was Derek, Diaz, and the other SF soldiers, but stopping wasn't an option. Lowering his head, he picked up speed, heading straight for Diaz.

The beast inside him was shocked when the soldier's eyes flared yellow and he leaped aside at the last second with a snarl and a flash of fangs.

Shit. Diaz was a shifter.

No matter how much Tanner fought the urge, the beast inside simply wanted to kill. If it was Diaz, that was okay, too. If anything, the beast reveled at the thought of fighting someone truly capable of fighting back.

Suddenly, a heavy body hit him, tackling him to the floor. He tried to twist out of Clayne's grip, but the wolf shifter pinned Tanner's arms to his side, and he couldn't free himself. Another body landed on him—Diaz—then another, and another, and another. They crushed him to the floor, and no matter how much he raged, they refused to let the beast move. The animal was trapped, just like Tanner, and the beast didn't like it any more than he did.

Tanner realized then that the shooting had stopped. He supposed that meant everything was over. For everyone but him. His fight would never be over.

—⁓—

Trevor slid to a halt on the sidewalk as an enormous roar
echoed from inside the gym. He threw a look of concern
Alina's way. He'd never heard anything so primal and
enraged. If that was one of Thorn's hybrids, he didn't
want to think about how badly it was going in there.

"We need to hurry," he told Alina, but she was
already running ahead of him toward the gym.

Trevor was so eager to get there, he didn't realize
the danger he and Alina were in until it was too late. By
the time he smelled Frasier, the asshole had stepped out
from behind the building they were running past and
grabbed Alina, yanking her to his chest. He put his gun
to her head with a smug smile.

"Now, how did I know we were going to find you
here?" Frasier snorted. "I told Mr. Thorn we should have
blown you up along with your boss. Of all the fucking
shifters, my gut always said you were going to be the
biggest pain in the ass. But he wouldn't listen."

Heart thumping in his chest and fangs extending,
Trevor pointed his weapon at Frasier's head, ready to
take the shot the moment he got the right angle, but the
man was too experienced to make it easy on him. The
piece of shit was careful to keep himself hidden behind
Alina. For the first time ever, Trevor had to question
why his partner had to be so frigging tall.

The only thing Trevor couldn't understand was why
Frasier hadn't already shot them both—unless he simply
wanted to crow a little first.

Alina didn't look as nervous as she probably should
have been. Instead, she calmly stood there with an

expectant look in her eyes, waiting for Trevor to do something to end this once and for all.

Yeah, well, she might not have been nervous, but Trevor sure as hell was. Frasier was a cold-blooded killer who wouldn't think twice about shooting Alina. And there was no way Trevor could get a clean shot at him. Right then, he didn't give a shit if Frasier shot him. Alina was the only thing he cared about.

"Did he just admit to killing John?" a familiar voice said as two other men stepped out of the same shadows Frasier had.

Trevor would have liked to say he was stunned to see Dick and Thorn, but he wasn't. No matter how many times you flushed, shit always floated to the top. The two men carried weapons, though Dick didn't look nearly as comfortable holding his. He didn't seem to know where to point it, either, instead moving it back and forth between Trevor and Frasier.

"Damn right he was behind the bombing in John's office," Trevor said as he backed up a bit to keep all three men in his sights. "Are you seriously saying you never realized what the hell Frasier was up to? Didn't you used to work for the NSA? Aren't you supposed to know all the secrets? They blew up John's office when they realized he was close to getting the evidence he needed to send Thorn away for life."

Dick's eyes widened as he snapped around to look Thorn. "Is that true? You had John killed?"

Thorn shook his head in disgust. "Of course I had him killed, you moron. Are you really that stupid? Or just that naive?"

Dick's mouth tightened. It was possible the man

might have said something that would have changed Trevor's whole opinion of him, but he never got the chance, because Frasier took his weapon off Alina for a second and shot Dick twice in the heart.

Trevor quickly darted to the side, trying to get a shot at Frasier, when suddenly, a large shadow dropped down from the second-story roof of the building beside them, knocking Frasier to the ground.

As Alina stumbled to the side, Trevor leaped for her, but Thorn got there first, yanking her close to him and using her as a shield. Trevor aimed his weapon at Thorn while keeping an eye on Frasier.

The dark shadow that had dropped down from above resolved itself into Adam's muscular frame. Frasier tried to get a shot at the huge shifter, but Adam ripped the weapon from his hand. In a blur, Adam leaned in and sank his fangs into the man's neck. Frasier cried out in pain, but Adam released him almost immediately, pulling his handgun and quickly stepping back to cover Thorn from a few feet to Trevor's left as if Frasier didn't exist.

Trevor wasn't sure who to cover—Thorn, who was trying to use Alina as a human shield, or Frasier, who was only a few feet away from his pistol lying on the ground.

Frasier took a step toward the weapon, but then froze, a bewildered expression on his face. After a moment, he slowly turned to look at Adam, his expression now one of fear. Then he started to shake. Just a little at first, but then more and more, until his whole body was spasming in what had to have been tremendous pain.

Adam didn't even look at him. Not even when Frasier fell to the ground and convulsed so hard that blood appeared at the corners of his lips where he'd bitten himself. Frasier opened his mouth, but no sound came out. It was like his throat was paralyzed. A moment later, he went still as the last breath left his body.

"You're supposed to be dead!" Thorn shouted, looking at Adam. "Frasier killed you."

Adam's eyes swirled orange and gold, the pupils elongating to slits. "He failed."

"It's over, Thorn," Trevor said, interrupting the happy reunion between the two men. "There's no getting out of this one. It's either jail for the rest of your life or a box in the ground. You need to decide quickly—or I will."

Thorn slowly backpedaled toward the parking lot, dragging Alina with him. "That's not going to happen. I'm walking out of here, and you're going to let me go. Or I'm shooting her. And don't even try to pretend you don't care about her. You missed one of the bugs I left in her bathroom. I heard everything you said to each other. Very touching, but also useful to me. Back away, or I'll kill her right now."

Trevor hesitated. He couldn't do anything that would risk Alina's life. She was too important to him.

Alina suddenly caught his eye, and he knew what she was going to do even before she did it.

He opened his mouth to stop her, but it was too late for that. Alina stomped down on the top of Thorn's right foot with the heel of her tennis shoe. At the same time, she brought the edge of her hand down in a groin strike, smashing the former senator so hard in the balls the man's eyes went glassy and his face paled. Before Thorn could move, Alina reached up and grabbed the arm he had wrapped around her shoulder and neck, twisting it away from her body and torqueing his wrist until the bone broke. Then she lunged forward, rolling across the ground.

Trevor took the opening she gave him, putting a single bullet between Thorn's eyes.

Alina scrambled to her feet as Thorn tumbled to the ground. Trevor ignored him and rushed over to her, pulling her into his arms.

"Are you okay?" he asked, looking at her closely to make sure for himself.

Having her at the end of a gun barrel so many times in one day was too much. If it happened again, he was going to lose his fucking mind.

She nodded and kissed him. "I'm good. Thanks for backing me up on that and with Wade, too. I never did get a chance to tell you."

"Always," he said simply, meaning it in every sense of the word.

"The shooting has stopped in the gym," Adam said softly, as if reluctant to interrupt them.

Alina turned to look at him. "Do you think that's a good thing?"

Adam shrugged. His eyes were back to their normal color. "I guess the only way to know is to go in there."

As they left the three dead men behind, Trevor couldn't help glancing at Frasier. His body was still twisted into that bowstring taut position he'd been in before, two small punctures on his neck. They had barely leaked any blood. In fact, they looked almost harmless.

"Is your bite poisonous?" Trevor asked Adam as they made their way to the gym.

"Apparently," Adam said.

Trevor would have loved to hear more, especially about what kind of frigging shifter Adam was that allowed him to do something like that. But then another thought struck him.

"How do you…you know…kiss a woman with a mouth like that?"

Alina shot Trevor a look like he was crazy, but Adam chuckled.

"Carefully. Very carefully."

"What the hell are we going to do with her?" Alina whispered to Trevor as they sat back against one of the walls in the gym, her gaze on Sage, who was presently curled up in Staff Sergeant Derek Mickens's arms, sleeping. "It's not like Derek can hold her like that for the next three days until we figure out what to do with the hybrids and other prisoners we had to put in her room."

Trevor sighed and wrapped his arm around her, pulled her closer. "One problem at a time. Sage is calm right now. That's as much as we can ask for at the moment."

He was right. They'd dealt with enough problems for one night. Seeing so many of his friends seriously injured had taken a lot out of Trevor. He might have been trying to act like he wasn't upset, but Alina knew he was hurting. Sighing, she turned her gaze back to the feline hybrid and the only person who seemed to be able to keep her calm and accepted they couldn't solve every problem in one night.

It had taken hours for the chaos inside the gym to calm down enough for Alina to take a breath and allow herself to think for one second that maybe everything was going to work out okay. Maybe everyone they knew and cared about would make it out of this alive.

She, Trevor, and Adam had entered the gym carefully after dealing with Thorn, fearing the worst. But while the fighting was over, that didn't mean there wasn't anything left to be done.

First, there were the injured to care for—and there were a lot of them. No one had gotten through the battle unscathed. Declan had been clawed up so badly, he was in some kind of self-induced deep sleep hibernation mode that scared the hell out of Alina. He looked dead, but Trevor assured her he was healing and would be fine.

Danica had just regained consciousness a few minutes ago but still had a concussion. Minka, Dreya, and Braden were nursing broken bones. Jaxson had suffered multiple knife wounds and a dislocated shoulder. Clayne's thigh had been ripped open from knee to hip, nearly to the bone. And even though Alina had no idea how it had happened, Evan ended up with a gunshot wound to the shoulder. She hadn't even realized he'd come to help. As if all that weren't enough, Morgan was still passed out from losing so much blood.

Zarina had been waiting outside the gates of the DCO until the shooting had stopped, then rushed in as fast as she could. The Russian doctor hadn't bothered getting the worst of the injured to the lab but simply performed surgery right there on the floor of the gym, starting with Morgan, then moving on to Clayne, Evan, and Jaxson, one right after the next like some kind of machine. Only after she'd gotten the seriously wounded stabilized had she moved them to the lab for X-rays, casts, and stitches.

Landon had suggested calling in additional help, but Zarina had shaken her head.

"These are my patients," she told him. "I'll care for them."

While Zarina had been caring for the injured, Alina and Trevor had focused on secondary concerns. First, they'd convinced the local police and FBI agents who showed up at the front gate that all the shooting had been nothing more than a big training exercise. Unbelievably, the BS line had worked, keeping the place from getting overrun with law enforcement types who would have had a serious problem understanding why there were so many people in the gym torn to shreds. Alina had no idea how they were going to hide this, but step one was keeping it quiet.

Then they'd turned their attention to another dicey problem. Several of Thorn's hybrids and even more of his paid muscle had given themselves up, and no one knew what to do with them. Adam suggested they simply execute them, but neither Alina nor Trevor would allow that. Still, it wasn't like they could cart them off to jail, either. Trevor had used the threat of jail to try to get Thorn to drop his weapon, but she had no idea what the charges would have been. Conspiracy to start World War III?

While Thorn's men wouldn't have been much of a problem in prison, did they really want to turn a group of intelligent and lethal hybrids over to the justice system? Alina could imagine the CIA getting their hands on them so they could start up a shifter-like program of their own.

But they sure as hell couldn't let them go, either. As Alina had already learned with Sage, the DCO didn't have cells for holding prisoners, especially ones who could tear through walls with their fists. Left with no choice, Landon's Special Forces buddies had herded them into Sage's makeshift prison. Now they had nowhere to put the feline hybrid.

While Sage had held it together and even protected Jaxson and several of the analysts, after watching so many people get hurt, she'd lost control and started lashing out at anyone who came near her. If Derek hadn't been there, who knew what would have happened?

But like Trevor said, one problem at a time.

"To tell you the truth, I'm more worried about Tanner than Sage," Trevor said softly.

Alina glanced at Tanner. He wasn't physically injured beyond a really nasty bite wound on one of his arms, but the mental wounds he seemed to be suffering from were obviously severe. Right now, he was sitting on the floor by himself, his gaze fixed on the bodies of the men and hybrids he'd torn to pieces after he'd completely lost it. The expression on his face was so empty and lost, it was painful to see.

She couldn't imagine what he was going through. Sage might have lost control, but she'd never tried to hurt any of the people she knew. The same couldn't be said of Tanner. According to Landon, Tanner had turned on Carlos Diaz. The only reason Diaz had survived was because he was a shifter. While no one blamed Tanner for what happened, his actions still weighed heavily on him. Alina knew from experience that pain like Tanner was feeling couldn't be eased with a few words. He was going to have to deal with it on his own—at least until he was ready to let someone help him.

As if he'd been having those same thoughts, Tanner slowly stood up and headed for the front entrance of the gym. He must have felt Alina's eyes on him, because he stopped and looked at her as if wondering whether she might try to stop him. Part of her wanted to, but she knew deep down that he needed some time to get things straight in his head. After a moment, Tanner turned and walked out.

On the other side of the gym, Landon and Ivy were arguing with Diaz. Alina couldn't hear what they were saying, but it seemed to be getting heated.

"What's that all about?" she asked Trevor.

He followed her gaze, then chuckled. "Diaz thinks he was turned into a shifter because he was bitten by a hybrid last year. Landon and Ivy are trying to convince him that isn't possible and that if he'd give Zarina a sample of his blood, she could confirm that for him. Diaz doesn't seem thrilled with the idea."

Alina studied the Special Forces soldier. "Is that possible? Could he have been turned from a hybrid bite?"

"No. He's a full-blooded coyote shifter through and through. I've known since we went on that mission to Tajikistan together months ago."

Across the gym, it looked like Diaz had finally agreed to do what Landon and Ivy wanted, because he nodded.

Alina looked at Trevor. "You mention that mission to Tajikistan a lot. You ever going to fill me on the details?"

His mouth edged up. "As soon as the situation here is stabilized, why don't we head back to your place? That way, we can lie around in bed for the next few days and spend a lot of time filling each other in on all the things we haven't got around to."

She liked the idea of spending a few days in bed with him. But there was one thing that made her hesitate.

"Are we going to find that other bug Thorn mentioned first?" she asked. "Just in case there's still someone listening on the other end."

Trevor chuckled. "We can do that. Or we can give them something really good to listen to."

"I vote for option one," Alina said.

He shrugged. "Whatever you say."

Chapter 20

ALINA COLLAPSED FORWARD ON TREVOR'S CHEST, trying to catch her breath as the tremors of orgasm continued to ripple through her body. Molly hopped up and put her two front paws on the side of the bed, apparently checking to make sure her mom was okay after all the moaning and groaning. After confirming Alina was fine, the dog dropped back down to the floor and wandered off to the living room.

"I'm never going to get enough of this," Alina whispered in Trevor's ear, loving the way his muscular body quivered beneath her as her warm breath tickled him.

He chuckled, his arms coming up to wrap around her and keep her pressed tightly to his chest. "I certainly hope not. If you did, you might stop coming back for more."

She nipped at his ear. "Never. I'm your partner—you're stuck with me."

Trevor weaved his fingers in her hair and gently lifted her head to plant a firm kiss on her lips, slipping his tongue in and making her tingle all over again.

"There's no one I'd rather be stuck with," he murmured. "You already know that. Just like you know we're much more than partners."

Alina smiled down at him, knowing that was true. She and Trevor had spent a lot of time together in the three weeks since the battle with Thorn at the DCO training complex, and while they'd talked a lot about what their combined future might hold, they hadn't spent too much time putting a name to what they had going on between them. That was probably on purpose. In her case, she was afraid to jinx the situation by saying the words too soon. She had the feeling it was the same for him. They'd both lived most of their adult lives in a world where secrets were never revealed and the truth could only hurt you.

Maybe it was time for both of them to move beyond that world.

She pushed herself up a little so she could look at him. She was still straddling his waist very comfortably but now giving herself a little more perspective. Trevor certainly didn't seem to mind the view. He lay there with his hands behind his head, gazing up at her with heat in his eyes. She'd better get on with this before he distracted her with more orgasms.

"You're right. We are much more than partners," she said, carefully focusing on his face and not the other parts of his body that were begging for her attention. "Which poses an interesting question. If we're partners who are more than partners, what does that make us?"

Alina held her breath a little. She knew in general that guys tended to get a little squirrelly when these kinds of conversations came up, but she hoped Trevor would be different.

One second, she was straddling his waist, regarding him warily with a silly knot of worry growing in her belly, and the next, she was on her back with Trevor between her legs. Leaning over, he slowly kissed his way up her neck and along the curve of her jaw, then covered her mouth with his.

"I guess that makes us two very lucky people," he whispered in that soft, sexy voice of his as he gazed into her eyes "Because not everyone in the world gets a chance to find the person they're meant to be with, much less have the chance to work with them every day."

She smiled up at him. "Meant to be with. I like the sound of that."

He grinned. "If you like the sound of that, how about this? I love you, Alina Bosch…as my partner, as more than my partner, as the woman I'm going to spend the rest of my life with."

Something warm and altogether pleasant swirled in her belly and slowly spread throughout her whole body upon hearing him say those three little words. She'd known for a while they were in love with each other, but she was still surprised at how amazing it made her feel to hear him say it out loud.

"I'm kind of new at this, but I'm pretty sure this is the part where you tell me that you love me too, then declare your undying devotion or something like that," Trevor teased, a twinkle in his eye.

Laughing, she reached up and yanked him down, kissing him long and hard. "Of course I love you. I think I probably loved you from the day I met you. I've just been scared to tell you. I didn't want to pressure you to feel the same way before you were ready. I'm sorry if that meant we wasted time."

Trevor kissed her again. "We didn't waste a second. It simply took us a little while to get to where we needed to be. But we're here now, and that's all that matters."

Bending his head, he kissed and nibbled her neck, something that never failed to get her going. At the same time, she felt him rock slowly back and forth between her legs, his very hard cock teasing the opening of her pussy.

"Now, let's stop talking about how much we love each other," he growled. "And start showing it instead."

She sure as hell wasn't going to complain about that.

"We're going to be late for work again," Alina said as she buttoned her blouse an hour later.

Their quick display of love for each other had turned into a not-so-quick display, and now they were likely to be a good two hours late getting to the complex, especially since they'd spent the night at her apartment and were going to have to fight DC traffic all the way down to Quantico.

"Don't worry about it," Trevor said from the bathroom. "We'll work a couple of hours late to make up for it. Besides, who the hell is going to notice?"

Alina shrugged, agreeing. The DCO was still in a state of upheaval since that night three weeks ago, and none of that was likely to change anytime soon. Heck, right then, she wasn't even sure exactly who she and Trevor worked for.

One thing she knew for certain, it wasn't John.

After Cree had successfully made it out of surgery with the prognosis of a complete recovery, everyone assumed John would come back and take over the director's position at the DCO. But that hadn't happened. Alina and Trevor had stopped by to visit Cree at the hospital when John announced he was taking long-term leave. Seeing his wife severely injured and having his daughter kidnapped had changed his perspective on everything. Alina couldn't say she blamed the man. He'd been forced to hide the existence of his family from the world for nearly a decade. Maybe it was time for him to build his life around them for a while.

But John hadn't abandoned the organization completely. He'd worked with the DCO Committee— specifically Congressional Representative Rebecca Brannon—to appoint Landon as the deputy director. Landon hadn't been thrilled and had no desire to sit behind a desk, but he'd done it because John told him the organization needed someone with his solid reputation in place to rebuild trust and get some of the people who'd left during the Dick Coleman era to come back. It was going to take someone with a strong vision and a firm hand to make sure the DCO didn't go off the rails again.

It looked like putting Landon in charge was a good decision, as the DCO ranks had already started to swell with good people coming in once they realized someone with real field experience similar to John's was being put into a position of authority.

In addition to handling the day-to-day team management and field operations, Landon and his wife, Ivy, would still be partners and go on missions as needed, while Rebecca Brannon brought in someone else to deal with politics and budgets.

Rumors were already flying around that Brannon was bringing in a complete outsider to be director, some political mover and shaker from Massachusetts named William Hamilton. Alina had never heard of the guy, but apparently he was familiar with shifters already. In a bizarre twist of fate, it turned out Hamilton was the father of a woman Declan used to be engaged to a long time ago. That seemed a little strange—as in soap-opera strange—but both Declan and Kendra seemed to think there was some merit to bringing the guy in. Apparently, they'd seen him operate under pressure during some kind of kidnapping operation, and while they didn't necessarily trust him, they'd been impressed.

Besides, it wasn't like anyone could complain about any decision Rebecca Brannon had made up to this point. The congresswoman had somehow gotten Thorn's goons and the hybrids shipped off to a supermax federal prison—on God knows what charges. Apparently, she'd told them if they played nice and kept quiet, she'd see to it they got out before it was time to sign up for Medicare. Amazingly, they'd all agreed.

Even more impressive, she'd handled the situation with the media and Thorn's sudden disappearance like she was born to crisis management. She'd arranged for a few stories about Chadwick-Thorn being under investigation for DOD contract fraud to leak to the press the morning after the raid. Two days later, Chadwick-Thorn formally announced Thorn had fled the country along with a whole lot of company money, his head of security, several field agents, and a few of his lead medical researchers. The media had taken over from there, spinning tales of Thorn skimming millions from DOD contracts. There were reports of the former senator hiding out in South America as his company's stock tumbled. Alina had seen a story on the news last night that said Chadwick-Thorn was going to be broken up and its subsidiaries sold off at a loss. The name was even being changed back to Chadwick Defense.

"You want to stop by and see Evan at the hospital before we go in to work?" Trevor asked as he came out of the bathroom, all wet from the shower and looking good enough to eat.

Okay, she needed to stop having those thoughts right now, or they'd never get out of there.

"Sounds good. I'm sure he can use the visit," she said, trying to look at anything but the bulge under the towel wrapped around his waist. "Besides, it'll be a good excuse for why we're late."

Trevor flashed her a grin. "We can just tell everyone we were having sex. They'd buy that."

He was incorrigible. Alina ignored him and went into the kitchen to grab some small single-serving bags of chips. Evan liked when they brought him something unhealthy to eat. He'd been cooped up in the hospital recovering from an infection related to the gunshot wound to his shoulder, and he was going stir-crazy.

Fortunately, all the other members of the DCO had recovered much faster. Even Declan and Morgan were up and running around already. Hopefully, Evan would be joining them soon. The analyst didn't know it yet, but he was in line for a serious promotion. Landon had approved him to head up the intel branch.

The one dark spot in the entire aftermath was Tanner. When he'd walked out of the gym that night, he'd disappeared off the radar completely. The intel branch was turning over every rock looking for him, but so far, they'd found nothing. Alina expected Zarina to lose her mind completely, but instead, the Russian doctor had buried herself in her work.

Trevor had followed her out to the kitchen to grab

some coffee when the door opened and Kathy strolled in with a knowing look on her face.

"Hi, guys," she said cheerfully. "I figured I should come over to get Molly, since it seems like you forgot to drop her off."

Alina sighed. "Kathy, what did I tell you about locked doors?"

Her friend laughed and shook the key she was holding in her hand. "I don't know. Bring a key?"

Alina scowled.

"Seriously, Alina. How else am I going to get a look at your partner fresh out of the shower wearing nothing but a towel? Consider it back pay for all those years I babysat Molly for you."

Trevor chuckled and added sweetener to his coffee, then took his mug and disappeared back into the bedroom. Alina didn't know what the heck she was hiding. Kathy was well aware of the fact that she and Trevor were sleeping together. He'd been sleeping at her place nearly every night—unless she was sleeping at his.

"Man, that guy of yours has one heck of a body on him."

"Kathy!" Alina said, not necessarily shocked but definitely embarrassed, because she knew Trevor had heard every word her friend said. "You have a boyfriend!"

"Yes, I do." Kathy took one of the bags of chips and opened it. "But it's not like I'm asking Trevor to drive me around in a minivan. I'm just stating the obvious."

Alina simply shook her head, giving up. Her friend was the very definition of the *inappropriate neighbor*.

"So I guess Trevor said he loves you, huh?" Kathy asked out of the blue as she nibbled on a chip.

Alina did a double take. "What?"

"You're glowing," Kathy explained. "I figured you and Trevor are in love."

Alina heard a chuckle from the bedroom and had to ignore the curious look Kathy threw that way. "Yes. Trevor said he loved me…and I said I love him in return."

Kathy smiled broadly. "Finally. So you guys getting married soon?"

Alina gaped at her friend. "Kathy, slow down. We've only know each other for a month."

Kathy nodded thoughtfully as she ate a few more chips. Picking up the bag, she called to Molly. "Come on, girl. Can't keep Katelyn waiting." Opening the door, her friend turned to look at her. "By the way, I'll take that as a yes, since you didn't actually say no."

Alina would have tried to get in a snappy comeback, but the door closed behind her friend before she could come up with anything. Trevor came out of the bedroom with a big grin on his face.

"Marriage, huh?" he said. "That friend of yours might be onto something."

With that, Trevor walked over to hold open the door for her, leaving Alina to wonder what the heck her best friend had just started.

Epilogue

REBECCA BRANNON LOOKED UP FROM HER COMPUTER as William Hamilton walked into her office. It was early, and her secretary wasn't in yet, so there was no one to see him. Which was exactly the way Rebecca preferred it. She might be appointing William the director of the DCO, but she still wanted to maintain the pretense that they weren't close. She wanted to sell it as a management decision, and a chance to take the DCO in a new direction after the debacle that was Thomas Thorn.

William came around her desk and gave her a warm kiss on the cheek that lingered there as he traced his fingers down the arm of her expensive suit jacket. Not that Rebecca necessarily minded. William was a very attractive man, even if he was a few years older than she was. He knew his way around the bedroom even better than he knew his way around the corridors of power in DC. As long as he recognized who was running things, she had no problem with him engaging in a bit of sexual game playing.

"I saw on the news last night that Chadwick-Thorn is going to be broken up and sold for spare parts," he said as he took a seat in the chair in front of her desk. "Well played, Rebecca. Though I have to say, I thought you would have been satisfied to have the man dead. Destroying his legacy seems a bit excessive, don't you think?"

Her mouth tightened. "Thorn was an obnoxious pig.

I didn't have the chance to enjoy seeing him get shot in the head, so grant me the small pleasure of destroying the company he spent much of his life building. I'm also arranging to have his absurd mansion over near Embassy Row torn down and turned into a dog park. I find great pleasure in the thought that there will be dogs shitting on the place where the man used to lay his head."

William arched a brow. "Remind me never to get on your bad side."

Rebecca smiled. "I just did."

He inclined his head. "I thought you'd want to know that I'll be stopping in at the DCO this week and introducing myself to a few of the people there, especially Landon Donovan and his partner, Ivy Halliwell. Once again, I have to commend you on a game well played. I have no idea how you convinced John Loughlin to walk away from the organization."

She stood and walked over to a low credenza that hid her refrigerator. Opening the door, she pulled out a small carton of orange juice. She held it up to William, giving him a questioning look, but he shook his head. She poured a single glass of juice and brought it back to her desk.

"Sorry to interrupt you, but these long hours dealing with Thorn and his schemes have made a mess of my routine. My blood sugar levels are a train wreck."

William nodded, waiting while she sipped her orange juice. Normally, she'd never reveal a weakness like this to anyone, but William already knew about this particular weakness, and many more. Besides, there was a certain power to be gained by letting a man think you trusted him. It made him malleable if handled correctly.

"I simply spoke the right words when John was at his weakest in those fragile hours when he thought his wife might die," she said. "At a time like that, it's not hard to convince a man that his priorities have been askew."

The look of admiration William gave her would have made her blush if not for the fact that he was likely trying to play her. She didn't resent him for that. It was simply what they did with each other.

"And those hidden shifters John worked with?" William asked curiously. "They're out of the picture as well?"

"Most likely." She took another long sip of juice, relaxing as she felt the sugar flood her body. "Everything I've learned so far indicates their involvement was in direct response to Thorn. With him and John out of the picture, they shouldn't be a problem for us."

After that, the conversation quickly turned into a brainstorming session on how William should handle his takeover of the DCO.

"You need to be subtle," she warned. "There are several agents who bear watching, and I don't just mean Donovan and Halliwell. As Thorn discovered, to his unfortunate demise, those people are dangerous if you rile them up. The situation calls for a deft and sure hand."

William smiled. "As I'm sure you remember, I've always had a very soft touch."

She returned his smile, only partially out of a desire to manipulate him. William truly had always been good with his hands. She remembered that quite clearly.

"And Dr. Mahsood?" he prompted. "Have you decided what you're going to do about him? The last time I talked to him, he assured me that with the research and DNA samples he was able to take with him out of the facility in Maine, combined with the genetic material from Thorn's latest hybrid variety, he could have a functional serum very soon."

Rebecca considered that for a moment, knowing what she had to do, but hating it at the same time. "I believe Dr. Mahsood has exceeded his usefulness. He, and all evidence of his research, need to disappear."

William frowned. "Seriously? We've been funding his work for a decade. Now that he's close to finally producing a hybrid that's able to completely blend in with the rest of society, you want to cancel the program and kill him? I thought you two were friends?"

Rebecca sighed. In many ways, William was a brilliant man. But in other ways, he lacked vision. And sometimes, he was too sentimental for his own good. "I want to end the program because we don't need it anymore. Now that we control the DCO, we have access to the very best covert agents in the world. The only thing that can get in our way now is our past. If Landon Donovan discovers proof that we were actively involved in hybrid research, we'd lose everything we've gained. We have to make sure that doesn't happen. That means we have to make Mahsood disappear. I feel terrible doing it to a friend like this, but it simply must be done."

William leaned back in his chair and sighed, fully aware of how the game was played. "So, what do you plan to do about Ashley? Aren't you worried about your daughter being on the loose?"

Rebecca abruptly realized she hadn't given her daughter a single thought since hearing about the events up in Maine. Then she took another sip of juice and reminded herself to check her blood sugar level after William left. "Not really."

William frowned. "Perhaps you should be. According to Mahsood's report, the girl is psychotic and hates you with a passion. She's bound to turn up at some point, probably at the worst possible time."

Rebecca waved away his concern. "The girl is too unstable to come after me. She's probably lost in the forests of Canada, scratching fleas like the animal she is. If she hasn't frozen to death already."

William didn't say anything for a while. But then he shook his head. "Sometimes I think you forget that Ashley is your daughter, and that she carries the same cold-blooded, vindictive DNA that runs through your veins. I think it would be a serious mistake to simply leave her out there on her own."

She considered that for a time, then decided William was right. If she was going to clean up the loose ends, she might as well take care of all of them at once. "Okay, deal with her. The same way you're going to deal with Mahsood."

He raised an eyebrow, but didn't dare say anything. Finally, after regarding her in silence for a while, he glanced down at his watch. "I'll take care of everything, after I stop by the DCO." Getting to his feet, he came around the desk to give her a peck on the cheek again. "I'll let you know what my impressions of the organization are later this evening."

She nodded. "Do that."

Rebecca turned her attention back to her computer, expecting William to leave, but then she realized he was standing by the door looking at her. "You never told Ashley about me, did you?"

Rebecca regarded him for a long moment, then laughed. "Why? Are you worried she'll come hunting for you if she knows you're the father who had her locked away in a psych ward her entire life to protect her mother's political future, simply because she was born out of wedlock?"

William didn't seem to find her question amusing, which only made it even funnier. Scowling, he walked out, closing the door behind him. Suddenly, Rebecca wished Ashley did know who her father was so she could make the man sweat a little bit more. Not that it really mattered, since the girl wouldn't be around much longer.

Acknowledgments

I hope you enjoyed *Her Dark Half*! After all the crazy stuff that happened in the previous book, *Her True Match*, I needed a hero and heroine to make things right in the X-Ops world, and Trevor and Alina did all that and more. With Thomas Thorn finally out of the picture, things seem like they might be getting back to normal at the Department of Covert Operations, but we all know that sometimes things aren't always as they seem. You're excited for the next book now, aren't you?

This whole series would not be possible without some very incredible people, In addition to another big thank-you to my hubby for all his help with the action scenes and military and tactical jargon, thanks to my agent, Bob Mecoy, for believing in me and encouraging me and being there when I need to talk; my editor and go-to person at Sourcebooks, Cat Clyne (who loves this series as much as I do and is always a phone call, text, or email away whenever I need something); and all the other amazing people at Sourcebooks, including my fantastic publicist, Stephany, and their crazy-talented art department. The covers they make for me are seriously drool-worthy!

Because I could never leave out my readers, a huge thank-you to everyone who has read my books and Snoopy Danced right along with me with every new release. That includes the fantastic people on my amazing Street Team, as well as my assistant, Janet. You rock!

A very special shout-out to our awesome real-life friends, Alina and Kathy, for inspiring the characters in this book. Thank you for being part of the X-Ops series!

I also want to give a big thank-you to the men, women, and working dogs serving in our military, as well as their families.

Another special shout-out, this time to our favorite restaurant, P.F. Chang's, where hubby and I bat story-lines back and forth and come up with all of our best ideas, as well as a thank-you to our fantastic waiter, Andrew, who takes our order to the kitchen the moment we walk in the door!

Hope you enjoy the next book in the X-Ops series coming soon from Sourcebooks and look forward to reading the rest of the stories as much as I look forward to sharing it with you.

If you love a man in uniform as much as I do, make sure you check out my other action-packed paranormal/ romantic-suspense series from Sourcebooks called Special Wolf Alpha Team (a.k.a. SWAT)!

Happy reading!

About the Author

Paige Tyler is a *New York Times* and *USA Today* best-selling author of sexy romantic suspense and paranormal romance. She and her very own military hero (also known as her husband and writing partner!) live on the beautiful Florida coast with their adorable fur baby (also known as their dog!). Paige graduated with a degree in education but decided to pursue her passion and write books about hunky alpha males and the kick-butt heroines who fall in love with them.

Visit Paige at her website, paigetylertheauthor.com. She's also on Facebook, Twitter, Pinterest, Instagram, and Tumblr.